POLES APART

To Ruth,

Hope the research
for this book was
up to scratch!

Enjoy.

Polly

POLES APART

Polly Courtney

ISBN: 978 178306 315 4

Published by Matador
9 Priory Business Park
Wistow Road
Kibworth
Leics LE8 0RX
Tel: 0116 2792299
Email: books@troubador.co.uk
Web: www.troubador.co.uk/matador

Thanks to the real Marta, whose story inspired me to write Poles Apart, and to everyone else who helped make it happen.

ABOUT THE AUTHOR

Polly never intended to become a writer. She discovered her passion by accident, turning her experiences as a junior investment banker into a fictional exposé of the Square Mile in her first novel, Golden Handcuffs. She is a fierce champion of the underdog, rallying against sexism, racism and wealth inequality in her writing and her broadcast appearances.

For more information or to get in touch with Polly, please visit www.pollycourtney.com

OTHER TITLES BY THIS AUTHOR

Golden Handcuffs
The Day I Died
The Fame Factor
It's a Man's World
Feral Youth

PROLOGUE

'Hah!' squawked Rosie, her voice filled with vindictive glee. A talon-like fingernail shot out in Holly's direction. 'You're using the wrong hand! It's European Drinking Regulations here, you know. In the first half-hour, you drink with your left. Don't you know anything?'

Obligingly, Holly downed her red wine, aware of the triumphant pout on Rosie's painted lips. She was usually sharper than this, but tonight new rules kept creeping in that everybody else seemed to know except her. *European Drinking Regulations.* Holly rolled her eyes and sank back in her chair, wishing she had never accepted Tash's pleading invitation to come round. She could have foreseen what a housewarming party with the South Kensington toffs would entail.

A ruckus broke out at the other end of the dinner table. They were playing an intellectual version of 21s, which involved turning your number into a roman numeral, then converting I, V and X into "ooh", "yeah" and "not there", respectively. Holly sighed, watching as Plum (real name Victoria; presumably a nickname picked up at private school, although Holly had never bothered to ask) giggled flirtatiously in the direction of Tash's boyfriend, Jack.

'Ooh, not there!' Tom moaned loudly.

Holly quickly tuned in as the wave of noise drew closer, but not quickly enough.

'Hesitation!' chimed Rosie and Plum in unison. 'See it away!' screeched Plum.

Holly knocked back more wine; white this time. Jeremy, sitting opposite, was looking down his long, unattractive nose at her, swilling what looked like port in his glass. *Some housewarming*, thought Holly.

Tash made a lame attempt at restarting the game before realising that the joke was on her; she'd landed on twenty-one. Polishing off her wine, she emerged from the bowl-sized glass, gesticulating wildly.

'I forgot to tell you!' she cried, looking around the table. 'I have some *bad news*.'

All eyes rested expectantly on Tash. Holly remained silent. Having shared a room with Tash during their second year at university, she had become wise to the gratuitous melodrama. Tash had famously reported an intruder to the police when the electrician (whom she had booked) came round to change the light bulbs.

'As of next week, this beautiful house will not be mine any more.'

The guests – with the exception of Holly – reacted with suitable levels of shock and surprise.

'No! I've been told that I am to share it…' Tash left a long pause, her eyes filled with mock dismay. 'With a Polish girl!'

Gasps and looks of incredulity passed between the guests.

'She's from a small village just outside Warsaw,' Tash explained, 'called Loopoopski or something. Mummy is allowing her to stay for as long as she likes! Oh – and get this. They're charging her *fifty pounds a week*. For a place in South Kensington!'

'Who is she?' asked Plum, above the sound of tutting.

'Mummy used to help organise foreign exchange trips, ages ago,' Tash explained, 'and she stayed in touch with one of the teachers. This is the teacher's daughter.'

'Does she have a name, this teacher's daughter?' asked Holly, brightly.

'*Marta*,' Tash replied, as though referring to a contagious disease. 'Oh and don't ask me to pronounce her surname–'

'Polovski?'

'Kozminski?'

'Pochowska?' came the helpful suggestions from round the table.

'Oh – it is a bit like that, actually. Dabrowska... something like that.'

'We've got a Polish bagel shop just opened near us,' Jeremy announced, as though this was terribly interesting.

'They're everywhere, Poles, these days,' declared Jack disdainfully. 'The government's letting them in to do all the jobs we Brits don't want to do.' He snorted. 'Still... she'd better be bloody attractive.' He yelped as Tash presumably pinched him under the table. 'Sorry.' He shot a cheeky, sidelong glance at Plum.

'Actually, I have a photo.' Tash pushed back her chair, stretching a long arm in the direction of the antique dresser. 'She looks... well...' She screwed up her face, squinting at the picture. '*Polish.*'

Holly leaned forward to get a glimpse of the photo, which Jack was eyeing up approvingly. The image was of a tall, leggy girl in tight jeans and a sweatshirt not dissimilar to one Holly had worn as a teenager. It may even have been from that era, she thought, going by the lurid colours. The girl had long brown hair cut in no particular style and a pale complexion. Despite the amateurish photo – snapped outside a drab-looking building – it was impossible not to be drawn by the girl's eyes: icy blue, turning up at the edges in a momentary smile. She was definitely attractive.

'Well, I think it'd be nice to have a housemate,' declared Holly. 'It's a massive place – you'd rattle around in it on your own.'

'I'm sure I'd find things to do,' replied Tash, raising an eyebrow in Jack's direction.

'I can't believe your parents are letting an Eastern European immigrant be their first tenant!' squealed Rosie.

Tash shook her head, rolling her eyes. 'Frankly, neither can I.'

3

1

'It's not as if I'm going into space,' joked Marta, trying to lighten the mood. 'London's only a short flight away.'

Her parents smiled and glanced at one another. The smiles didn't quite reach their eyes. What Marta had neglected to mention, and what they were all thinking, was that short flights cost money. She wouldn't be popping back for a weekend any time soon.

Marta glanced sideways towards where her best friend Anka stood. Marta could tell she was about to cry. On the other side of her parents, Marta's brother and sister looked small and dejected.

'Stop being so morbid, all of you!' cried Marta. 'We all have phones, don't we? And the internet? Well, sort of,' she added, remembering the last time she had tried streaming video in Łomianki library.

Marta glanced up at the departures board, prompting everyone else to do the same. Her flight was boarding. 'I'd better go through,' she said, suddenly feeling uneasy. This was it. She was about to leave her country. This was the last time she would see Mama, Tata, Anka, Tomek and Ewa for at least a year.

They were close – sometimes too close – in their little house. She couldn't imagine them not being around her. Mama running up the stairs to chase her brother out of bed in the mornings, Tata chiding her sister for not taking long enough over her homework, the five of them sitting down to pierogi or gołąbki at night and her brother whinging that he wanted to watch TV... this was her life. It had been her life for the last twenty-two years.

Anka stepped forward and finally dared to look Marta in the eye. Hers were filling up with tears.

'Będę za tobą tęsknić, Marta.' I'll miss you. Anka looked away, dabbing at her eyes and then bending down, rummaging in her bag. She had dressed up for the occasion, Marta noted. Anka always looked stylish, but today she had on long drainpipe jeans and a tight, sparkly black top beneath the old brown coat she always wore. The glittery eye shadow had gone to waste, thought Marta, watching the streaks of brown liquid run down her cheeks.

'Open this when you get there, OK?' Anka passed over a sizeable parcel wrapped in what looked like magazines and brown tape. 'Sorry about the paper.'

Marta hugged her. She could feel Anka's body heaving and jerking against her own, but she was determined not to cry. They had been friends for nearly fifteen years, ever since Marta had inadvertently rescued Anka – then a plump, goofy-toothed eight-year-old – from a bunch of older girls at the back of the playground. These days, Anka was one of the skinniest girls in town and perfectly capable of fending for herself, but looking back, that first encounter had been a strangely accurate reflection of their relationship over time.

They were both vivacious and smart, always competing for the top marks in class, but Marta had always been the brave one. When it came to trying new things, taking risks and letting go, it was always Marta. Upon leaving school, Marta applied to universities and got a place to study marketing at the prestigious Szkoła Główna Handlowa in Warsaw; one of the best in the country. Anka wasn't sure about leaving Łomianki, śo she stayed and got a job at the bakery. She still worked there now.

It was fair to say that Marta was braver than most people in Łomianki. With a population of only nine thousand, it was one of those places where people reacted badly to change. When Poland had joined the EU in 2004, national newspapers had been brimming with stories of young men and women starting new lives in new countries, of couples fleeing the drab, grey streets in search of adventures abroad… but not the local papers. Deserters were frowned upon in Łomianki. Doing anything different was seen as a sin in Łomianki. The old folk – of whom there were many – looked critically upon those whose son or daughter had moved away. It was that, as much as anything else, that had made Marta desperate to leave. She had to get out of this place. There was so much of the world that she hadn't seen, so much that she was finally being *allowed* to see, and she wanted to explore.

To Marta's dismay, she felt her eyes welling up as she disentangled herself from her best friend's arms.

'You'll miss your flight,' Mama warned, with a note of what sounded like hope in her voice.

Marta turned to her parents. The churning in her stomach was getting worse. She couldn't believe she was actually leaving them. It was hard to articulate why exactly she felt so uneasy, but something definitely didn't feel right. What if things changed in her absence? What if Tata lost his job at Polkomtel? Would Mama get more classes at the university? What if they had to move house? The routine would change and she wouldn't be there to see things through. All her life, Marta's parents had been there, strong and reliable, to support her. But seeing their faces so pale with concern and lack of sleep, it was as though… they looked fragile. They looked *old*. Marta shivered. She had never really considered the possibility that her parents weren't immortal.

She braced herself and switched on a smile through the tears. As she did so, something brushed her hand. Tata was holding out a parcel. It was smaller than Anka's and the wrapping was neater; it was almost like a wrapped-up envelope, thought Marta. She took it, just managing to hold the smile.

'And this,' Mama added, producing what looked like a sack of medium-sized potatoes, bound in reams of plastic tape.

'That's not going to fit in my hand luggage!' exclaimed Marta, already guessing the parcel's contents.

'It fits,' mama urged. 'I tried it this morning. You just have to leave half of it sticking out…' Mama demonstrated, stuffing the end of the enormous package into Marta's rucksack. 'There!'

Marta pocketed Tata's package and went to hug her brother and sister. Even Tomek was wearing a forlorn expression on top of his moody, teenager look. Ewa was frowning. Marta felt bad. She was only twelve; she would miss her big sister.

'Right, I'm off to London!' Marta announced purposefully. She balanced the precarious load on her back, hugging Anka's parcel close to her chest, and set off towards security.

'Don't forget the magazines!' yelled Anka. 'Remember – lots of pictures and not too many words! I want to practise my English style!'

Marta grinned through the tears. She had tried so many times to persuade Anka to follow her passion and do a course in fashion or retail at college, but to no avail. She turned, taking one last look at the five people she cared for most in the world.

'I'll send you some for your birthday!'

2

Marta followed the line of passengers across the damp tarmac and up the steps onto the plane. The wind ripped through her flimsy jacket, chilling her flesh instantly. It was cold, even for Warsaw. She paused as she entered the aircraft and breathed her last breath of Polish air.

'Welcome aboard,' chirped the air hostess.

Marta smiled nervously, holding out her passport, which the woman ignored. It was an odd sensation, stepping along the narrow, carpeted gangway between irritable, preoccupied passengers. It felt familiar and alien at the same time. The Hollywood movies had made it all seem so real, but the details – the noisy hum, the smell of bread rolls, the irritable passengers bending and stretching at peculiar angles – brought home to Marta that she was a novice. Her parents had grown up in a time when travelling out of Poland had been all but impossible and, subconsciously, that sense of restriction had been passed onto her. Only ten years ago, flights had been so expensive that the only option for crossing Europe had been a twenty-hour coach trip through Germany and Holland. Now there were dozens of flights from Warsaw to London every day.

The butterflies were getting worse and Marta could feel her hands shaking. She couldn't tell what was making her nervous. Was it the safety instructions that informed her that in the unlikely event of an emergency, oxygen masks would drop from above? Was it the fact that the wings of the plane seemed to be made from flaps of metal that didn't look very securely fastened? Was it the fact that Mama and Tata weren't here? Or was it simply a fear of the unknown?

Marta had prepared herself as well as she could for her new life, reading books and magazines about London that Mama had borrowed from the university, downloading information packs and immersing herself in endless blog posts by Poles who had made the transition. There was a book called *A-Z* that had maps of every street in London, including the one she was going to live on, and websites that listed all the concerts and shows happening in every part of the city. There was so much going on.

It wasn't just the organised fun you got in Warsaw, like opera, theatre and music concerts; it was real, spontaneous entertainment: open-air comedy shows, festivals on the banks of the Thames and things called 'flash mobs' and 'pop-up restaurants'. There was something about the place that Marta couldn't quite describe… a sense of freedom? Opportunity? Whatever it was, she wanted to breathe it in. She wanted to taste it. She wanted to dive into this crazy world and feel it swirl and flow around her.

Excitement ran through Marta's veins alongside the nerves. She was determined not to be daunted. She wasn't the first Pole to move to England and – as she had to keep reminding herself – she had a better chance than many who moved over. Even Mama had assured her of that, despite her misgivings about Marta's plans.

An air stewardess strutted down the plane, clicking a tiny machine with her thumb, once for every passenger. There was a general rustling as people squirmed in the confines of their seats and the crew busied themselves behind a yellow curtain at the front. Marta didn't want to think about the "unlikely event of an emergency". She had once read that the chance of survival in a plane crash was close to zero; they just put in safety procedures to make passengers feel at ease. She didn't feel at ease.

Marta wondered how many of the people on the plane were travelling with a one-way ticket. Unofficial statistics claimed that more than a million Poles had fled to England during the last three years, although the authorities would claim that the figure was lower than that. If the passengers on this plane were a representative sample, thought Marta, then there were a hell of a lot of twenty-something-year-old Poles in London.

It made her angry that the government was trying to stop young people leaving. What did Poland have to offer them? There were no well-paid jobs, that was for sure. Marta thought back to the grey buildings that lined her old town; the old faces with their blank, disparaging eyes. She loved its familiarity, but at the same time she loathed it. The place was depressing. Most people of her age had moved away; either to other parts of Poland or, more commonly, to Europe. The only ones left were those with no fire left inside them.

It was a risk, she knew that. A girl from her class had moved to London with her boyfriend after graduating. They couldn't even afford to pay for a room in a hostel, so she had taken a job as an escort. Falling for the dream of a better life, she had run off with one of her clients: an older man with a violent streak. Word had it he had taken her passport and held her captive, like a slave with no rights and no official identity. Nobody really knew what happened to Beatrycze, she just disappeared.

Marta was determined that she wouldn't fall into any of the traps. She knew it wouldn't be easy in London. She was prepared to work hard for her money and she was hugely grateful for the generosity of Penelope and Henry, Mama's friends, who were letting her stay in their house with their daughter. She was prepared for the worst, but she knew, deep down, that it wouldn't come to that. Marta was enterprising. She would make things work.

The plane wheeled around on the runway and quickly started picking up speed. Marta watched the metal panels on the wing, wondering whether they were supposed to flap up and down like that. There was a tremendous roaring noise and everything started to shake. Just as the noise became disconcertingly loud, Marta felt herself tipping backwards. She twisted round in time to see the ground tilt and then drop away, very quickly. For the first time in her life, Marta was airborne.

She watched the ugly buildings shrink beneath her until they looked like a satellite image on Google Maps. The nerves were just flying nerves, she told herself. Once she landed, she would be fine. The websites had taught her everything she needed to know about London: how to use the buses, where to live, how to ask for a second helping. She didn't know how long she would stay. Maybe a year, maybe more. There was no need to decide yet. Her plan was to make money, send some back to her parents each month and keep a little aside for herself.

Marta sank into her seat and shoved her cold hands into her pockets. Her fingers curled around something soft and papery. She turned it around, poking carefully at the flimsy wrapping. In the end, her curiosity won her over and she whipped it out, scratching away at the paper.

She could hardly believe it. Marta put the notes back in their little pouch, then brought them out again and counted a second time, discreetly. Tata had given her *one hundred English pounds*. That was nearly six hundred złoty! How could he possibly afford that? Marta felt a lump in her throat. There he was, nodding confidently as she proclaimed that she would make a good living over in London, yet all the while he was squirrelling away his wages to give her something to start her off. Marta took a deep breath, determined to stave off the tears.

The little seatbelt light above her head went off and passengers all over the plane immediately sprang into action: standing, stretching, queuing for the toilet and randomly colliding in the aisles. Marta thought about the parcels stowed away above her head. The air hostess had laughed as Marta had stowed her patchwork lump in the overhead locker above her seat. Marta smiled, picturing Anka surrounded by fashion magazines, wrangling over which pages she would least mind turning into wrapping paper. She unfastened her seatbelt and reached up.

It wasn't even necessary to open Mama's present, Marta knew what it was. She peered through the tear she had made in the paper and caught a glimpse of the *drożdżówka* label. It was her favourite cake. This wasn't the first food parcel Mama had ever made her, but it was certainly the largest. Mama had a knack of cramming in more food per cubic inch than any food retailer had ever achieved.

'Anything to drink for you, madam? Anything to drink?' asked the perfectly proportioned air hostess, whose makeup appeared to have been applied with a spatula and a felt-tip pen.

Marta carefully noted the other passengers' reactions. *Was it free?* Someone behind her was noisily rifling through change in his pocket. *No*, she decided, smiling sweetly and declining the offer.

Anka's present sat bulkily in her lap, a picture of catwalk perfection and brown sticky tape. She was supposed to wait until she arrived. Marta hesitated, then tore at the glossy paper.

She nearly screamed. It was a Malina Q jacket! A gorgeous, turquoise puffy jacket with a faux fur hood lining; –the type she and Anka had been drooling over for months! *All* the rich girls in Warsaw had these. Neither Anka nor Marta had ever been serious about owning one. They cost nearly three hundred złoty! Marta hugged it against her face, breathing in the smell of new fabric mixed with Anka's perfume. Exhaling slowly, she lowered the garment onto her lap, aware of the strange looks she was getting from the woman in the next seat along. Marta didn't care. She had a Malina Q jacket. *Oh, Anka*, she thought as a tear rolled down her cheek and soaked into the bright blue fabric. *I miss you already.*

3

'I sit?' said a faltering voice above Marta's head.

She glanced up to find a young man about her own age, nervously eyeing the seat next to her and pointing at her luggage.

Marta smiled at his improvised sign language and moved her bags, feeling faintly relieved. The coach was filling up and there were some very dubious-looking passengers squeezing down the aisle: rowdy, unshaven men with beer guts, many of them already drunk from the flight over. This guy seemed sober, at least.

'Did you just fly in?' she asked, in Polish.

He looked at her, startled, and then his features melted into a smile. 'Yes.' He removed his baseball cap and ran a hand through his hair. 'How did you know I was Polish?'

Marta shrugged. She wasn't going to embarrass the guy by running through the list of telltale signs: the T-shirt, the awkward stance, the poor English accent, the furtive looks he had been trying to hide beneath his frayed cap. Having spent the last hour watching and observing passengers as they trooped through corridors and queued for security checks, Marta reckoned she could spot a Pole from a Brit without hearing them speak. It wasn't any one particular thing, it was just... a look.

'I'm Marta,' she said, smiling.

'Lukasz.' He offered her a limp handshake. The coach pulled away from its bay, manoeuvring through the sluggish airport traffic.

'You here for good?' she asked.

'Who knows.' It was Lukasz's turn to shrug. 'I've never been to England before.'

'Me neither.' Marta shook her head, feeling an immediate affinity for the guy. 'It's weird, isn't it? Finally being here…'

Lukasz nodded, looking past her and out of the window. Marta did the same. They were on a main road now, rolling steadily through the flat English countryside, sliced up by grey motorways. It felt strange to be on this side of the road. Everything felt strange. The roads were too smooth, the lampposts were different and there were neat green hedges between all the fields. *This was it*, she thought. *This was England, at last.*

'Do you speak any English?' asked Lukasz.

'Yes, although not perfectly,' Marta replied, the worms in her stomach suddenly returning. Her teacher at school had been a firm believer in listening and comprehension, but not such an advocate of proactive speech. This meant that Marta could translate almost anything from English to Polish, but less so the other way round. Her mother had helped, of course, but she still didn't feel comfortable holding a proper conversation in English.

'I don't,' Lukasz confessed. 'But it doesn't matter, apparently. I'm staying with a friend who's been here two years. He says that the language is no problem. He's promised to find me a job.'

'You don't know *any* English?' she clarified, assuming she was mistaken. Surely nobody would consider migrating without speaking a word of the language.

He shook his head. 'It's fine. Gabrjel says he got work the first week he arrived. He didn't know any English then – still doesn't.'

Marta frowned. 'What sort of work? Something involving not speaking, presumably?'

'Construction. Odd jobs. Maintenance, gardening… He's good with his hands.'

Marta nodded. She wasn't coming to England to use her hands. She wanted to use her brain. She had a marketing degree from one of the top universities in Poland. Perhaps Lukasz and his friend hadn't been to university, she considered.

'Gabrjel was a qualified doctor,' he told her, as though reading her mind. 'He had a job lined up at the hospital in Wrocław for three thousand złoty a month. Here, he gets nearly two thousand *pounds* a month – that's twelve thousand złoty! For lugging bricks around. Crazy, eh!'

Marta nodded, feeling something sink inside her. She was used to hearing about qualified graduates moving to England to do unskilled work for five times the salary. The problem was, she didn't *want* to do unskilled work. She had skills. She wanted to use them and be rewarded for them.

'What are you planning to do?' Lukasz looked at her.

Marta hesitated. She was dying to tell him her plans. She wanted to tell him and all the other Polish graduates like him that she was coming over to *use her degree*. But she didn't want to aggravate the young man.

'Not sure yet. I'll find something.'

Lukasz nodded. 'You're lucky, being a girl. You can always get au pair work. The money's OK and they give you a place to live.'

'Yeah,' Marta nodded. The chances of her becoming an au pair were no higher than the chances of her getting work on a construction site. There was no *way* she would stoop to becoming an English family's slave.

'Or you could work in a Polish bakery. Apparently they're springing up all over London.'

Marta gritted her teeth and nodded again. She would rather move back to Łomianki than spend her days smearing cream cheese on bagels. Extracting her phone, Marta brought the conversation to a halt by jamming her headphones into her ears and closing her eyes. For some reason, she felt irritable. It wasn't that she had lost faith in herself or her qualifications; she just didn't like to hear people make assumptions about what she – or, in fact, any other graduate like her – would be doing for a career in the UK. Lukasz was a fool, obviously. He was working towards a different goal. There was no point in listening to him. He hadn't even bothered to learn English.

The crisp dialogue of the podcast reverberated around her head, focusing Marta's mind. It was something she had downloaded from the BBC website before she left. It was a debate about a book she had never read, but that didn't matter. She needed to hear the words, to remind herself that she understood, to convince herself that she had the ability to make something of her time in England. Marta sank down in the seat and leant against the juddering window.

The podcast was just coming to an end when the coach finally pulled up. They were inside a massive, fume-filled bus depot the size of a football pitch. Suitcases and screaming children filled the concrete walkways, colliding like atoms under a microscope. Deafening announcements echoed off every surface. Around her, people rose in their seats, hitting others in the face as they hoisted rucksacks onto their backs.

'Well, good luck,' said Lukasz, looking warier than ever. 'Maybe keep in touch?'

Marta smiled politely. 'Maybe.'

'Here's Gabrjel's number – that's where I'll be staying.' He ripped off part of his cigarette packet and scrawled a string of digits on the back.

'Thanks,' said Marta, doubting that she would ever call the number. 'Good luck, Lukasz.'

He smiled and gave a mock salute. 'Enjoy England.'

4

The question was, *which exit?* If you wanted to visit a science museum, or in fact any number of museums, there were signs saying where to go. But Marta wanted to go to Egerton Square. Her phone had died and all she had now was an address. She was beginning to wish she had kept hold of that *A-Z* book.

'Are you OK?' asked a soft female voice that seemed to come straight out of an English listening test. A well-dressed young lady of a similar age to Marta was peering down at her, exuding an expensive-smelling perfume. 'You look *lorst*.'

Marta instinctively straightened up, trying to obscure her giant food parcel with her new jacket. This was her first opportunity to try out her English. She knew how to respond, she had done this a hundred times in school. But to her shame, Marta found herself wordlessly offering up the scrap of paper on which the address was scribbled.

'Ah, OK.' The woman nodded slowly, giving Marta the chance to study her flawless exterior: glossy, chestnut hair, a natural tan, leggings sprayed onto exceedingly skinny thighs with a pair of high-heeled boots over the top. Marta glanced down at her beloved Malina Q jacket. It shone back at her, brilliant and turquoise and, for the first time since she had landed, Marta wondered whether she might have made a mistake in assuming that fashion crossed geographic boundaries.

'You need Exit 1,' the woman explained, brushing a lock of hair away from her face with the utmost elegance. 'With your back to South Ken, head east along Brompton Road until you reach Egerton Terrace. The square should be a stone's throw from there.'

Marta quickly expressed her gratitude and watched as the figure sashayed up the steps of the station. *A stone's throw.* How far was that? Marta reached down for her leather suitcase, still clutching the parcel, and headed for Exit 1.

'Egerton Square,' Marta read, proud of herself for following the instructions correctly and learning a new phrase in the process. Then she stopped dead. She had known that this was a nice part of London and the five-minute journey had taken her past some fairly impressive residences already. But this was another league again; this was incredible.

Every house on the square had its own set of pillared steps leading up to a double front door, like the White House or a place of worship. Each was unique, too: there was one with exposed bricks and covered in ivy, the next was clad in stone, and another... Marta nearly dropped her case as she caught sight of number fourteen.

It had *flames* outside the front door. Two enormous, flickering torches were placed either side of the Grecian columns and lit up the front of the house like something from a film set. *She was going to live in a house with flames outside the door.* Marta nearly laughed out loud. She couldn't wait to tell Anka.

As she approached, the worms suddenly returned to her stomach. *Was it an embassy building or something? Would she be expected to behave like English royalty?* Or worse still... A horrible thought flashed through her mind. Was she being invited to live here on the premise that she would look after the place? Would she be expected to cook and clean for Penelope and Henry's daughter? Marta took a deep breath and headed up the steps.

Within seconds of ringing the chiming bell, Marta found herself inside a vast, marble-floored atrium being smothered in kisses and deafened by a cacophony of shrieks.

'Hi, hiiiiiii!' wailed the blonde who had opened the door, her face contorted with exaggerated smiles. 'You must be Marta! I'm Tash!'

'Here! Let me take your jacket,' offered a smaller girl with a face like a horse. 'My name's Plum.' She drew closer. 'As in, Victoria Plum?' She let out a deafening hoot of laughter and whipped the Malina Q jacket out of Marta's hands.

'Come *in*,' urged a young man, taking Marta by surprise as he slipped a hand round her waist and guided her away from the door. Marta stole a glance at his face. He was gorgeous: lean but toned, with an angular jawline and dark eyes that melted into an easy smile.

Marta stood still, trying to take it all in. It took a lot of restraint not to just stare, open-mouthed, at the tall girl who had introduced herself as Tash: her new housemate. It wouldn't be accurate to say that she was beautiful, but she was striking. Her face was exceedingly pale, like a china doll's, and framed by waves of perfectly curled blonde hair. Little pearl droplets hung from each of her ears and she wore a soft, blue cashmere V-neck and knee-high boots that were not dissimilar to those worn by the woman at the station.

'Let's go through to the kitchen!' suggested the horse-faced girl. Marta made a mental note to look up the word "plum" in her dictionary; she was sure it was a type of fruit.

'I think a drink is in order.' The good-looking guy caught her eye and winked.

'Sorry – how rude of me!' Tash rounded on Marta as they trooped through the echoing hallway. 'This is Jack,' she announced. 'My boyfriend.'

Marta's spirits fell, just a little.

'And this is Jeremy,' she added, motioning towards the back of the group.

Marta nodded politely. Jeremy was a strange-looking young man. It was as though his head was too large for his body and his nose too large for his face. He nodded in her direction, all the time looking down his huge snout as though he found the whole situation rather distasteful. 'Ve'y nice to meet you,' he said.

Marta smiled uncertainly and gave a little wave. They entered an airy room with high ceilings, vast, polished surfaces and many matching sets of kitchen implements in chrome and black.

'So! What will you drink?' asked Jack. 'Vodka?'

There were screams and whoops of laughter. Marta opted for a gin and tonic, like everybody else, and wondered what was so funny. On Tash's suggestion, they moved to yet another room (there were so many to choose from!), this one described as a "drawing room", although it didn't actually have any drawings in it; only a large, dark oil painting at one end of a man who looked constipated. Tentatively, Marta sank into one of the armchairs.

'So, what's it like, being Polish?' asked Plum, excitably.

'What an absurd question!' Jack exclaimed, before Marta could open her mouth.

'Well, I just meant –'

'How is she supposed to answer that?'

For a second, Marta felt a rush of compassion for Tash's boyfriend. Then he went on.

'She's been Polish all her life, for God's sake! It's not as though she suddenly woke up one day liking dumplings and wearing big furry coats, is it?'

'Don't be racist!' cried one of the girls.

'I wasn't,' Jack replied quickly. 'Polish isn't a race; it's a nationality.'

Marta felt like a child. Everyone was talking about her as though she wasn't there.

Tash pulled a nasty face at her boyfriend, then switched on a smile. 'So Marta, whereabouts in Poland are you from?'

Marta opened her mouth, but suddenly her breath was coming too quickly and she couldn't get any words out. They were all staring at her, waiting for an answer, but the more they stared, the more she felt panicked inside, as though someone was crushing her vocal cords.

'Łomianki,' she said finally, knowing she should follow it with something, but she wasn't sure what.

'Is that near Warsaw?' asked Tash after an awkward pause, speaking noticeably louder and more slowly.

'Yes.' She wanted to elaborate, but for some reason she couldn't think of anything to say, even in Polish.

'It's nice,' she added after a long pause, wracking her brain for something – anything – more. Nothing came.

'So - where - are - you - planning - to - work - in - London?' asked Tash.

Marta hesitated. She wanted to explain that she had graduated from one of the top Polish universities and wanted to join the marketing department of a large UK firm, but she couldn't. It wasn't just that her vocabulary seemed to have escaped her; it was that she knew how ridiculous it would sound, declaring such an ambitious plan when she could barely introduce herself.

'I...'

'Will you get an au pair job?' Tash asked brightly.

A surge of anger mingled with Marta's frustration. She resented the assumption that she could only hope to get work as a nanny for English children. And furthermore, she felt insulted by the implication that she should find somewhere else to live after just five minutes in the house.

'No,' replied Marta, looking her host in the eye. 'I have a degree in marketing from Poland and I hope for using that. I will get a job in the office.'

She was surprised by the eloquence with which she delivered her reply, but not as surprised as those around her. There was a good ten seconds of silence before anyone spoke.

'Wow... Marketing!' gushed Plum, clearly feeling the need to say something.

'It's a novel idea, actually *using* your degree in your job,' mused Jeremy, speaking for the first time. He was swilling his gin and tonic around in ever-increasing circles, watching the vortex deepen.

'I don't know,' replied Jack. 'I may not have done any philosophising or economising since I graduated, but I've experienced plenty of office politics.'

'Jack did PPE at Oxford,' explained Tash. 'That's politics, philosophy and economics,' she said, expressing each syllable slowly as though Marta were lip-reading. 'He works at Goldman Sachs now.

He's an investment banker.'

Marta nodded. There was something about these people that made her feel silly. They were the same age as her, but somehow they seemed… superior. It was as though they felt sorry for her, and not just because she was new to this city. Marta found herself thinking of Anka, her trusty, humble best friend. These people were a different species.

'So…' Jack looked over with a handsome smile. 'D'you know anyone here? D'you have any contacts to get you into marketing?' He raised an eyebrow.

'I…' She trailed off. *Contacts?* She had planned to do all the usual things that people did when looking for a job: trawl the newspaper advertisements, call up companies, look at the job sites online. That was how it worked back home. Wasn't that how it worked over here? The truth was, she *did* know some people who had come over to England, it was just that she either hadn't kept in touch with them or they had returned to Poland. None of them worked in marketing, anyway. Marta had nobody to help her over here.

She would manage, though, thought Marta as she sipped her drink. She would have to. A week was what she had set herself as job hunting time, and that was all it would take. That was all she had.

'If you need any help…' Jack fixed her with a look that lasted longer than Marta thought necessary.

'Thank you,' she replied quietly, wondering what he meant.

5

Marta leant against the cold stone wall, listening to the rhythmic slosh of the Thames beneath her. The speedboat zipped off into the distance, heading towards the huge tower with the pointy roof: Canary Wharf. It was the office block where Tash's boyfriend worked. The mirrored sides gave a warped reflection of the wispy clouds that were blowing across the sky.

To her left was the big wheel. If you watched really carefully and aligned one of the bubbles with a fixed spot in the distance, you could just about make out its movement: twenty degrees every minute, she calculated.

Marta was in the shade of Tower Bridge and the stone wall was making her cold, but she didn't care. She was in London, filled with a boisterous optimism she could barely contain. There was something about this city; a vibe that made her feel free. The place had history, but it wasn't oppressive history. People were proud of it, but they didn't cling to it. They got on with life, went about their business and made things happen. Marta smiled. She was ready to make things happen.

She had allowed herself one day to explore London. She had taken ten pounds from Tata's stash, although so far she hadn't spent anything. Tourist exhibits were out of the question and she was avoiding public transport. It wasn't just because of the money; it was because Marta wanted to see London properly. She wanted to go at her own pace, see the streets from ground level, look up, look down and discover the back alleys that not even Londoners knew about.

Marta could only guess how many miles she had walked today. Setting off at eight this morning, she had breathed in the misty morning air of Hyde Park, discovered the eerie, shaded streets of Mayfair and carved a path through the mayhem on Oxford Street. She had slipped through the ghost town of Holborn, shadowed a Japanese tour around St Paul's Cathedral and wandered through a bleak part of town where every shop sold expensive suits or sandwiches. Eventually, she had crossed London Bridge and followed the river to this unexpectedly quiet, cobbled street at the water's edge.

It was good to have a chance to think. The last few days had flown by in a blur of noise and excitement, and it was only when Marta lay in bed at night that the sounds and shapes stopped whirring round her head… but by that point she was so tired she just fell asleep. This was quite literally the first time she had felt calm enough to reflect, and doing so was bringing about an unexpected revelation.

Marta missed her home town. She missed the place itself, not just the people. Her mind kept whipping up images: ugly buildings, fur coats, brusque shopkeepers… Even the memory of things she disliked – sleet and crumbling roads – would send a shiver running through her when she thought about the distance she had put between herself and these things.

Tash had done her best to welcome Marta into her palatial family home and for that, Marta was grateful. She was all too aware of the kindness bestowed upon her by Penelope and Henry for opening their doors to her at such an absurdly low rate. She was grateful, she really was… but that didn't stop her from missing her old life.

Tash was so different from every girl Marta had met. She was rich, of course, but that wasn't the only thing. It was hard to describe how she differed. In some ways she seemed more confident; she was certainly more flamboyant. But at the same time, she seemed *less* confident. She was needy. She had to be the centre of attention all the time; especially Jack's attention, which seemed prone to wandering.

The water was lapping more gently now and, as the sound of the boat receded into the distance, Marta became aware of a presence behind her. She turned quickly. A young man in a fluorescent yellow jacket was parking a dirt cart up against the wall. She watched out of the corner of her eye as he set about sweeping the area and emptying his load into the cart.

A pleasure boat chugged along the river, blasting out unintelligible commentary to its windswept passengers. She smiled. The street cleaner crept into her field of vision, hoisting himself onto the wall further down and bending over something in his lap. Sandwiches. It was lunchtime. Marta half watched as he unwrapped the tin foil and wolfed it down in record time. He screwed the tin foil into a ball and lobbed it into his cart, where it made a satisfying thud against the bottom.

Marta prised herself away from the wall, contemplating getting some food for herself. As she did, something caught her eye. A blur of red and white. She took a proper look in the workman's direction. He was reading a magazine, and across the top of the cover page was the distinctive red and white flag. *Polski Express,* read the title.

'*Cześć!*' she said, impulsively. It was still a novelty meeting fellow Poles, even though there were more than a million of them over here.

The guy met her eye, expressing no surprise at hearing his own language. '*Cześć,*' he replied, checking out Marta's legs.

'Er, are you done with that?' Marta asked, at exactly the moment he hopped off the wall and tossed the magazine into his cart.

He chuckled, taking another look at Marta's legs. 'Looks like it, doesn't it?' He bent down and fished out the supplement, wiping some mayonnaise from the cover with his sleeve. 'Want it?'

Deciding it would be rude to decline, Marta nodded. 'Thanks.'

'You new around here?' asked the man, addressing her breasts this time. Marta was beginning to wish she hadn't started this conversation.

'I arrived yesterday. I'm not... not based here. I'm staying...' Marta hesitated, not wishing to divulge the location of her accommodation for more reasons than one. 'Somewhere else,' she concluded, lamely.

'Huh. Aren't we all?' The guy rolled his eyes. 'Enjoy,' he said, nodding at the soggy magazine in her hands and taking one last look at her legs.

Marta forced her mouth into a smile. 'Bye.'

There was only one reason Marta had asked for the magazine. It was something she had seen on the back cover; an advert. Spreading the supplement out on the wall, Marta carefully extracted the staples and pulled off the cover, reading the text as she did so. She folded it into eight, shoved the page in her pocket, and set off in search of food. Perhaps today wouldn't be entirely unproductive after all.

6

'Marta? Marta, oh thank goodness you're there. Would you be a sweetie and open the fridge? Only I've just done my nails, and I *need* my skinny latte before I do anything! Could you…?'

Tash rushed across the lounge and threw herself in Marta's direction, dramatically revealing her manicured talons. She was wrapped in a blue silk dressing gown, her head engulfed in swathes of white, fluffy towelling.

Marta rose to her feet and put the recruitment section of the local newspaper, which was turning out to be less than inspirational, to one side. The only offers of employment seemed to be for shop workers and bus drivers, and it was depressing how many of these ads were so obviously directed at Eastern Europeans.

'Oh, thank you Marta!' gushed Tash, fanning her pearly nails in front of her face as the giant fridge door swung open. 'I can't survive without my skinny latte in the mornings and I've got *such* a busy day!'

Marta smiled sweetly. She was dubious of the fact that Tash would die if she didn't have her morning coffee, but she wasn't going to say anything.

'We're doing a girlie sesh,' Tash explained, motioning for Marta to grab the milk. 'It was Plum's idea – you remember Plum? We're shopping all morning, then having a boozy lunch at the Rose Tree and then she's booked us for some beauty treatments. I probably shouldn't have done my nails, really, but you know what it's like when they really need doing…'

Marta dutifully reached into the fridge, nodding as Tash prattled on. The truth was, she *didn't* know what it was like, caring so much about trivial things like nails. She couldn't relate to Tash's worries or to her priorities in life.

A cry of anguish escaped from the English girl's mouth as she registered the small amount of milk left in the container.

Marta held the plastic carton, watching Tash's expression and wondering what to do. In fact, she had known they were running low on milk and last night she had sacrificed her evening hot drink for the sake of household harmony.

'How did that… I mean, when…'

'We had little yesterday,' Marta explained. 'When I look for the milk to do my hot chocolate, there not really enough, I think–'

'Oh, of course,' said Tash, eyeing her carefully. 'Your hot chocolate. You use a full mug of milk for that, don't you?'

'Yes, but I –'

'Well, I suppose I'll have to get some more,' Tash sighed. 'I simply *can't* start the day without my skinny latte,' she said, as though Marta might not have heard her the first time.

Marta took the hint. 'I'll get it.'

'Oh, *would* you?' asked Tash, suddenly all smiles again. 'Only I'd have to get dressed, and my nails…'

'No problem.'

Marta grabbed her purse and yanked open the giant front door. In fact, she was quite glad to get out. Tash was exhausting. It was as though she had two personalities: the caring, easygoing, self-confident one she portrayed and the defensive, insecure one she tried to keep hidden. Like a swan, Tash was beautifully serene, but she was always on the cusp of turning nasty. The only way to placate her, Marta had discovered, was to play to her ego: tell her how gorgeous she looked, how sweet and clever she was.

'Morning,' sang the old man in the corner shop. He was always chirpy, presumably because he made so much money from his customers. The prices were extortionate, even by London standards. A small loaf of bread cost the equivalent of ten złoty – and it wasn't even tasty!

Marta lifted the two-pint carton onto the counter. The shop-keeper thanked her. He put it in a bag, slid it back to her and thanked her again.

'Seventy-five pence, please. Thank you.'

Marta waited for her change and, predictably, was thanked for taking it. She grabbed her purchase and walked out, to the sound of a high-pitched "ding-dong" as the door banged shut.

The English, Marta had observed, were either very polite or very rude. In most parts of London, shops were staffed by snarling, gum-chewing twenty-somethings with little interest in your existence, let alone your wellbeing. But there were pockets of the city – and "South Ken", as Tash called it, was one – where it felt as though staff were so attentive they might offer to walk you all the way home. These pockets tended to coincide with the high prices, Marta had noticed.

A traffic cone blocked her way, marking a section of pavement that had been cordoned off due to a cracked paving stone. That was another thing she had noticed about England. Everyone was treated like children. Everywhere you went, there were signs saying "mind the gap", "slippery floor" or "watch your head", as though nobody was capable of looking after themselves. Back home, you did things at your own risk. If you stepped in dog shit, it was your own fault. God, she missed Łomianki.

'Did you get it?' Tash was upon her as soon as she stepped inside, blue hair curlers springing from her head. 'Oh, you are a *sweetie!* Thank you! Oh good – enough for my skinny latte *and* your hot chocolate!' she gave Marta a quick, meaningful look. 'Tell you what, be an absolute star and make the coffee, will you? I've got to get the timing right with these things or my hair will fry!'

Marta nodded wordlessly. She flicked the switch on the kettle and wandered into the lounge, where a copy of her English CV was poking out from under a magazine. *Had Tash looked at it?* Marta tugged at the sheet and studied it for signs of wear. It looked exactly as it had done when she had handed it over.

Returning to the kitchen, Marta poured the coffee into the frothed, steamed milk, the way Tash had taught her, half-wondering whether she should consider au pair work after all. It felt as though she was heading in that direction.

'Oh, you've used the wrong mug,' Tash exclaimed, appearing from nowhere with bouncy blonde curls. 'Never mind.'

She sighed, taking the coffee from Marta. 'I always have my skinny latte in a *tall* mug,' she explained.

Marta nodded again. 'Sorry.'

Tash sat herself down at the kitchen table and embarked on a thorough inspection of her nails.

'Have you read my CV?' asked Marta. The interview was on Monday, just two days away.

'What?' Tash looked up. 'Oh yes, your... Yes I did.'

'You did?' Marta couldn't hide her surprise.

'Yes. It's very good. The English is perfect.'

'Really?'

'Yes, really!' she cried enthusiastically. 'It's impeccable. You should easily get a job with that CV.'

Marta smiled for the first time all day. Maybe Tash was kinder than she thought. She bounded over to the table and picked up her CV again, proudly folding it in two. 'Thank you so much, Tash!'

Tash smiled as she carefully curled her fingers around the mug. 'Any time.'

7

'*Push* the door!' squawked the tinny voice through the intercom.

Marta fumbled some more with the latch and finally found herself falling through the glass doors and into a hallway filled with plants.

She looked around for the reception desk. There was foliage everywhere. Huge, exotic-looking plants stretched up to the ceiling from bath-sized pots and the air felt laden with moisture. Behind the greenery, Marta could just make out several bright orange panels etched with black writing that presumably spelled out company mottos and mission statements. She had seen it before, only smaller, on the Genesis website. Marta felt a hollowness in her belly.

'Over here,' said a stern female voice. Marta changed direction and clattered over to the source of the sound. The high heels – an insistence by her mother, after a fraught call on Sunday – were making her feel gawky, and the suit jacket, which didn't quite match her trousers, was itching around the collar.

'My name is Marta Dabrowska,' she told the receptionist, who sat, perfectly poised, behind a bright orange, kidney-shaped desk, with nothing more than a keyboard and flat-screen monitor in front of her.

'And you're here for an interview?' the woman asked brusquely. Her jet-black hair was secured with what looked like a skewer, which pulled her forehead taut.

Marta nodded. *Was it that obvious?* She tried to relax, releasing some of the strain in her shoulders and neck, but then it felt as though she was stooping, so she straightened up again. She focused on the ten-foot Genesis logo behind the receptionist's head.

'Ah, yes. You're meeting with John Rayne and Elizabeth Pardoe at ten o'clock. Take a seat.' She waved her hand towards the jungle. 'I'll tell them you're here.'

Marta clip-clopped across the reception area towards an orange sofa that was nestled between two trees. She felt like a children's TV presenter.

Marta had woken at six that morning without an alarm. She had known instantly what day it was, even before her eyes had fluttered open. All night she had dreamt about being late for appointments, missing deadlines and desperately trying to get somewhere on time but encountering setback after imaginary setback. It was a relief, in a way, to wake up and realise she still had one interview left to attend.

In fact, it was her first interview. She was applying for a marketing assistant role at Genesis, a small advertising agency specialising in "innovative campaign strategy development". Marta wasn't fazed by the long words; that was just advertising for you. She had done a whole degree in the subject. Of course, it would be harder when the jargon was in another language, but she would cope. She just wished this place wasn't so... *flawless*. If only there was a ceiling tile missing, or a leaf going brown, or a hair out of place on the receptionist's head. Marta wasn't sure she could live up to such perfection.

'Someone's on their way down,' the woman informed her.

Marta rearranged herself on the fluorescent seat. She crossed her legs one way, then the other, then decided that they were simply too long to cross and tried to hide them under the curvy glass table at her feet. If only her trousers matched her suit, she thought, reliving the moment that morning when Tash had passed her in the hallway. Her disdain had been clearly apparent, despite the winning smile. Tash had looked fantastic, of course, her shiny blonde hair tied up in a lively ponytail, a double layer of brown strappy tops showing off her fake tan and a tight pencil skirt clinging to her thighs above some impossibly high stilettos. Marta was still waiting for one of Tash's garments to make a second appearance; the girl seemed to have an infinite supply of clothes. Still, that was one of the prerequisites, presumably, of being a director's PA at Paul Smith.

In fact, Tash's extensive collection held some advantages for Marta, not least because one of the two wardrobes in Marta's room (which, between them, took up approximately as much space as her bedroom back home) was being used as an overspill, giving her free access to a vast selection of fashion accessories she could only dream of owning. Tash had given her consent, explaining that it was "all last year's stuff". Today, Marta had taken full advantage, spraying her wrists with Jean Patou before slipping a Cartier watch on one hand and a selection of gold bracelets on the other.

There was a tapping sound. Striding across the leafy reception was a young woman in her mid-twenties. 'Marta Dabrowska?' she barked, pronouncing it *brow*, like eyebrow.

Marta smiled and rose to her feet, banging her knee on the table with a thud. 'Yes, is me, yes. Elizabeth Pardoe?'

'God, no!' The girl threw her head back and let out a coarse peal of laughter. 'No, Elizabeth Pardoe is a campaign planner. I'm just an ad assistant! They sent me down to get you. I'm Jenny.'

Marta blushed. She suddenly felt desperate to run away. Jenny was laughing at her. This place was intimidating; she wasn't ready. She didn't want to be going to the seventh floor in a lift made entirely of orange mirrors, and she didn't want to see any more slim, fashionable English girls who were good at their jobs. She just wanted to be back in Poland, where everything was simple, where she was the best and where people looked up to her.

The day before, sitting in an internet café just off the King's Road and browsing through case studies on the Genesis website, Marta had felt calm and relaxed about her interview. She had even felt positive about her chances of getting the job. Marta tried to swallow, but her throat was dry. She must have been deluded. She stood no chance of getting a job at this place.

'Here we are,' Jenny announced as the lift doors slid open to reveal another orange-furnished reception area, this one airier and home to fewer plants.

It was clear from her manner that Jenny didn't have time to chaperone interviewees around the seventh floor. She marched boldly down a corridor, halting so abruptly outside a frosted glass door that Marta nearly slammed into her. With an impatient glare, she opened the door and nodded Marta through.

'This is Marta Da*brow*ska.' Two chairs swivelled round simultaneously to face them. 'Elizabeth Pardoe and John Rayne. Good luck.'

The door fell shut and the handshakes began.

John Rayne was in his mid-thirties, Marta guessed, although his bloodshot eyes and creased skin added a few years. A slender man, he wore black-rimmed glasses and a beige corduroy jacket that combined to give a look that said 'smart but cool'.

Elizabeth Pardoe turned out to be nowhere near as intimidating as the image Marta had of her in her head. She was possibly a little eccentric, if the string of ping-pong balls round her neck were anything to go by, but she emanated a kindly appeal. She was a few years older than her colleague and, if the order of Jenny's introductions was significant, more senior.

Marta's eyes quickly scanned the room. A set of colourful swivel chairs had been arranged in an arc around the oval desk, surrounded by flipcharts and marker pens. In the corner were some large rubber balls; presumably alternative seats for the whacky, creative types. It was nothing like the meeting rooms she remembered from her placements in Warsaw.

'Sit down, darling!' Elizabeth waved at the luminous array of swivel chairs.

Marta settled on a bright yellow chair that was far too high, but was apparently impossible to adjust. She half slouched to compensate.

'Now, we've seen your CV.' Elizabeth Pardoe leaned forwards as though looking at something on the oval desk. Then, without warning, she pushed off with her feet and spun round several times in her swivel chair. Marta watched as the woman faced her once, twice, three times, and then came to an instant halt, flinging her feet on the ground and staring goggle-eyed at Marta. Marta nodded, unsure whether the woman was conducting some kind of test or whether she was simply insane.

'The role is for a marketing assistant,' the woman continued, tapping two of her oversized beads together. They even sounded like ping-pong balls. 'I'll be honest with you, darling. It's low-level. The successful applicant will not be contributing to the creative processes of our key accounts at Genesis. He or she may not even contribute to smaller campaigns. The job is to be the office dog's body, you know?' She cocked her head, checking that Marta understood. Marta had no idea what a "dog's body" might be, but she nodded assertively. She would ask Tash later.

'But that is not to say that the applicant should not have a full knowledge of what we do at Genesis and how we go about our business. This role is for people with integrity, insight, experience and, most importantly, *ambition*. We want people who can *go on* to run campaigns, even if they're taping parcels together and fetching sandwiches at first. OK?'

Marta nodded. This was not what she had expected. It seemed beneath her and over her head all at once, and she was increasingly coming round to the opinion that her interviewer was completely mad.

'Now, John has some questions.' Elizabeth swivelled round and nodded at her colleague.

'Yeah. Right. OK.' John pinched the bridge of his nose then stretched the skin around his eyes. 'So, Marta. Your CV.' He slid the sheet towards him on the table and glanced down at it, while Elizabeth sat bolt upright, staring at the wall behind Marta's left shoulder.

'Firstly, your university. Forgive me, but I've never heard of it.'

'Szkoła Główna Handlowa w Warszawie,' Marta told him quickly. 'It is the best place to do studying of marketing in all of Poland.'

'OK. And is it…' John paused, as though struggling to find the right words. 'Is it *good?* I mean, we can only measure against what we know: Cambridge, Oxford, Manchester… how does it compare?'

If Tash's boyfriend was to be believed, SGH didn't come close to any of the UK universities in terms of quality. But Marta was doubtful of Jack's rationale and reluctant to express his opinions in this interview. The problem was, *she didn't know.* There was no direct comparison between English and Polish institutions, and even if there was, she hadn't seen it and couldn't prove it. All she knew was that she had worked bloody hard to get into SGH and competition for places was stiffer there than anywhere else in the country.

'It's the best in Poland. That is all to say,' Marta shrugged. 'Many people very brilliant at marketing come from Szkoła Główna Handlowa.'

'Such as whom?' asked Elizabeth, from behind closed eyes.

Marta thought quickly. She should have anticipated this question. Surely there was somebody famous she could name? The panic rose up in her throat and as it did so, the answer came.

'Benedykt Luczak,' replied Marta, in a confident tone. Benedykt was not a big name in global marketing. He was in fact her first ever boyfriend and, to the best of her knowledge, he had gone on to become a forklift truck driver, but Elizabeth and John didn't need to know that.

'I'm not familiar with his work,' stated Elizabeth, her eyes still shut.

'Me neither,' muttered John, looking down at Marta's CV again. 'But I'm sure in Poland…' He drew a sharp breath. 'Again, I'm afraid I'm not aware of the companies in your list of placements.'

Marta began to offer descriptions for each, trying to explain that they were advertising agencies just like this although, in reality, they weren't at all like this. Not one of her previous workplaces had contained orange walls or tree-lined reception areas or colleagues like Elizabeth Pardoe, who was rather distractingly lifting her arms like a bird in flight, only very, very slowly.

'I work for six weeks at Young & Rubicam,' Marta explained,

keeping track of the woman out of the corner of her eye while addressing John, who seemed oblivious to his colleague's behaviour. 'It form part of the big global company, WPP.'

John's eyes lit up at this. 'Ah! I knew it rang a bell. They're the ones that did the first T-Trans ad, aren't they?'

Marta had no idea. She had never heard of T-Trans and, in truth, she had spent her six-week placement opening and sorting post.

'Yes!' she cried, nodding. Elizabeth was now holding very still, her arms out wide. It wasn't a test, Marta decided. The woman was crazy.

'OK, Marta, talk me through a campaign you've worked on. Preferably a multi-channel campaign,' demanded John.

Marta swallowed. She had never actually worked on a campaign. She had, however, looked on the Genesis website the day before, where there were plenty of examples of multi-channel campaigns. If she could just switch a few of the names to Polish ones, invent a few details and change the client details…

'I was involved in multimedia campaign for Polish sports clothing brand…' Away she went.

John seemed to be buying it and Marta was soon lost in the flow of her own fabrications. It was going brilliantly, she thought, until Elizabeth Pardoe came to.

'Darling!' she screeched, yanking the CV from under John's elbow. 'What on earth is this?'

Marta stared.

'Your English, darling! It's appalling!'

Marta frowned, assuming that this was one of the woman's strange jokes. Her CV had been checked by Tash, who had said it was fine.

'*I like be ambitious and to find new and different ways to doing things,*' read Elizabeth, distastefully. 'Darling, I simply can't have that. I can't. Not even for an office junior.' She shook her head, in case there was any doubt. 'No.'

Marta was flummoxed. "Impeccable" was the word Tash had used.

'Darling, my four-year-old daughter could write a better CV.'

The woman stared at Marta, her face set in an expression that somehow managed to blend pity with distaste.

'Er, do we have your contact details, Marta?' John asked tactfully.

'They're not even on her CV! Only Polish ones. You do *have* a place to stay in England, don't you, darling?'

Marta blinked back at the woman, her whole world crumbling around her. It felt as though the swivel chair was sucking her down, through seven floors of concrete and into the ground, burying her like a piece of rubble.

'Marta?'

'Yes,' she heard herself reply, in a thin, wavering voice. She was vaguely aware that Elizabeth Pardoe was right; she hadn't updated her CV with her UK address. But that wasn't the real issue here.

'Or a mobile number? Or email?' suggested John, quietly. Another omission, she realised.

Slowly, Marta rose from her seat. She mumbled something about sending them her London address, but she already knew she wouldn't bother.

'Thanks for coming in, darling.' Elizabeth gave a cheery wave.

'Do call, won't you?' John added, kindly.

Marta just managed to reach down for her borrowed handbag and flee the technicolour boardroom before the tears had a chance to flow.

8

The man in front of her stamped his feet in the cold, prompting others to do the same. Marta zipped her jacket up to her chin and scrunched her gloved hands into fists. It felt like home – not just because of the overcast skies and the biting wind, but because of the rows of people wrapped up in fur coats and hats, almost all of them Polish.

Marta tried to guess how many were here. The queue snaked all the way back to the road, densely packed and confined by cordons. Between two and five thousand, she estimated, and every one of them was under the age of thirty. No wonder businesses were shutting down back in Poland; the entire workforce was over here.

There was a noise from the front of the queue. Standing on tiptoes, Marta could just make out the scene up ahead. The main doors were opening. Around her, people started jostling for position.

It was with trepidation that Marta stepped forward with everyone else. The *Polski Express* advert had caught her eye with the phrase "Good work in all sectors", but when she had read the rest of the advertisement, her excitement had dwindled. "No skills or experience required!" screamed one line. "Jobs for non-English speakers!" Looking around at her companions only compounded Marta's suspicions that this recruitment "fair" was very unlikely to offer the type of job she was looking for... but then again, maybe she had set her sights too high prior to the Genesis ordeal?

'Excuse me! D'you speak English? D'you have a couple of minutes?'

A blonde woman stood just outside the entrance, trying to poke a microphone into the faces of passing Poles. Behind her lurked a cameraman, patiently waiting for a catch.

Marta dodged the microphone and barged on, head down. She felt like an animal at the zoo. It was as though they were all on parade in some human circus. She could see the headlines now: *Poles Queue for British Jobs. Service Sector Swells as EU Grows.* She knew how the English saw Polish migrants: as hardworking, unskilled labourers. That was it. As far as they were concerned, Poles didn't have careers, they had jobs. They took British jobs. There was no way she was gratifying that woman with a quote.

The hall was vast, like ten school gyms put together under a giant metal roof. Coloured striplights burned holes in her retinas as she stared up at the giant banners suspended from a lattice of rafters. The stalls – literally hundreds of them – were neatly arranged like the geometric blocks in a game of *Tetris*.

'Jobs caring for the elderly!' cried a young woman in Polish. She leaned out from behind her stall and thrust a leaflet into Marta's hand. 'No English required!'

'Bar work! Catering and kitchen support!' screamed another woman. She had an extra-long stall and a whole team of people behind it. 'Are you interested in kitchen support work?' asked the woman, stepping into Marta's path.

Marta eyed her suspiciously. 'What's kitchen support?'

The woman smiled and produced a flyer in Polish. A glance at the pictures answered Marta's question. "Kitchen support" was washing up. She walked on.

'We only employ Eastern Europeans,' Marta heard one guy explain to a meat head covered in tattoos. 'Some Czech, some Lithuanian, but mainly Poles.' The banner brandished a silhouette of a JCB.

Marta came to the end of the aisle and headed for the next one, picking up pace to make it harder for recruiters to engage her in conversation. How interesting it would be, she thought, if everyone had filled out a form with their qualifications on their way in today. The findings would be shocking. There were probably enough degrees and diplomas in here to run a small city, but the catering woman didn't care about that and nor did anyone else. They just wanted a reliable source of "kitchen support".

'Improve your English on the job!' claimed a hospitality company specialising in corporate functions. Yeah, right. No doubt there were endless opportunities to improve one's English doing "kitchen support", with a crew made up entirely of Eastern Europeans, thought Marta, storming to the end of the next section.

The recruitment fair was not doing great things for her mood. As far as she could tell, the whole event was an excuse for British companies to get together and exploit the Polish migrant community. Marta was willing to bet that none of these firms offered more than the UK minimum wage, which, decent as it was over here, didn't do justice to the skills and experience that so many of these workers had. It made her angry.

'The work is challenging, yes,' one recruiter explained to a girl about Marta's age. Marta slowed down and took in the details. *Meat-Pack*, said the banner. Next to it was a picture of a burger. It was the first time today she had heard language she was used to hearing in the context of careers: *challenging*.

'Sometimes you may be on a twelve-hour shift and you'll be working in a food chiller for up to ten hours of that.'

Marta's heart sank. She skipped the last two aisles and headed for the exit. There were only so many insults she could take in one day.

'Leaflet?' asked a young man in Polish. He was loitering by the door, apparently not associated with any particular stall, although he had more flyers than any of the stallholders. His ruffled, sandy hair and hazel eyes made Marta stop and smile. She took a leaflet.

'What's it for?' she asked.

'Here – leaflets,' he said, pointing at the one she had just taken.

Marta looked at him. 'I know, but what's it advertising?'

'Jobs in leaflets,' he replied.

'But what *type* of jobs?' Marta pressed, deciding that the guy might be slightly dim. Then she realised. The leaflets were advertising jobs handing out leaflets. 'Oh, right.' She laughed softly. 'Thanks.'

Marta pretended to read the flyer as she walked off. She wouldn't throw it away yet; she would wait until she was out of sight.

'Goodbye,' he called after her.

She turned, catching his eye and finding herself faltering.

'Bye,' she replied, feeling fourteen again.

After a brief, awkward pause, Marta raised a hand and headed off towards the main road.

9

Marta squeezed through the immovable mass of bodies and jumped off the bus just as the doors were closing. According to the map she had borrowed from Tash, Bayswater was right near Hyde Park. She had twenty minutes to kill.

The sky was a pure, monochrome white and the trees were still dripping from the overnight rain. Of the few people dotted about the park, Marta seemed to be the only one who didn't have either a dog or a Lycra running outfit. A girl sped past wearing pink mini-shorts with a matching strap around her upper arm, from which protruded several gadgets. That was something Marta had noticed about London. Everybody seemed to live their lives plugged into a device. Necks were craned, ears were plugged and eyes faced down at all times, even when crossing roads. It was a wonder there weren't more accidents, thought Marta, watching as the pert, pink-clad backside receded into the distance.

Seeing the joggers reminded Marta of home. Back in Łomianki, running had been the only means of getting properly warm. She could have run the six-mile route around the village with her eyes shut. Marta missed the cold. England got cold, but it wasn't the icy, blasting cold that cut through your jacket and numbed your bones. She missed the unique combination of sweat on her forehead and sleet on her hair. It was almost tempting to break into a jog just thinking about it. But she couldn't. It wasn't only the borrowed high heels that were preventing her, or even the fate that awaited her in

Bayswater at two o'clock. It was her mood. She couldn't run when she felt like this.

Fifteen days had passed since she had arrived in England: fifteen days of trawling jobs boards, writing letters, filling out forms and attending interviews that left her feeling worthless and dumb. She felt like a failure. It wasn't even as though she had been aiming too high, either. After the Genesis fiasco and a couple more morale-crushing encounters, Marta had lowered her expectations and applied for office assistant, secretarial clerk and shelf-stacker jobs... she had even gone for a job in a Polish bagel shop.

Marta had been turned down for being too quiet, too brash, too keen, too Polish. She couldn't win. English companies only wanted to hire people who had lived English lives and attained English qualifications, and Polish agencies preferred to ignore every word on her CV and treat her as a brainless pair of hands. The most infuriating thing, in Marta's opinion, was the fact that a *Western* European would probably have succeeded where she had failed. An École Centrale graduate would have had no problems explaining her qualifications and foreign experience. French was fine. German was fine. Even Spanish was acceptable. Polish wasn't. She made a decision. If she didn't get today's job, that was it. She was heading back to Łomianki.

'You want good Indian curry?'

'Chinese takeaway for you?'

'Cheap hotel?'

The leaflets came from nowhere, popping out from well-worn sleeves and littering the air around her as she barged down Queensway, heading for number eighty-four. Usually she would have fended them off, but not today. Not when she knew that her only hope of staying in the country was to become one of them. She could hardly believe the way things had turned out. She was signing up to be one of these cold, miserable losers who spent their lives getting rejected and abused by strangers. The idea repulsed her and she hadn't even got the job.

The street could have been in another country, were it not for the black cabs hooting their way down the middle of it. Sweet, sickly incense burned from open shop fronts and the air was alive with the sound of bartering in a dozen languages. Faces were black, white and every shade of brown; more diverse than you would ever see in Poland. Marta liked it. For some reason, it made her feel less alone. This was a far cry from the sneering, wealthy Russians who graced the streets of Kensington.

Number eighty-four was sandwiched between a newsagent and a tattoo parlour. The door looked as though it had once been white, but years of rain and London dirt had turned it brown. There were four buzzers, none of them labelled. Marta pressed the top one and waited.

She was staring at the intercom box, waiting to speak, when suddenly a noise broke out above her.

'*WHAYOUWANT?*'

Marta looked up. A large, ruddy face was peering down at her from three floors up, and beside it was a mat of dark underarm hair.

'I'm Marta. Here to do interview,' she explained.

'*WHAT?*'

'I'm Marta—'

'I CARNEARA WORDYASAYIN', LOVE. FOURTH FLOOR.' The window banged shut.

The door made a mechanical wheezing sound. Marta pushed on it. As she started to climb the stairs, it dawned on her that this hallway, with its peeling paint, splintered floors and broken banisters wasn't all that different from another stairwell she had visited a few years before. For her first placement back in Warsaw, Marta had applied through an agency that was based in a building very much like this, only colder. She had had to sit a test in a room at the top where she felt sure the ink would freeze before it left the pen. Sadly, there would be no test today.

Marta finally reached the summit and stood for a few seconds to catch her breath. She was getting unfit. She had been so busy applying for jobs in the previous two weeks that she hadn't granted herself time to exercise. She knew it was wrong, but running felt like a luxury she couldn't afford right now.

'Come in!' yelled the voice that had shouted at her through the window.

As it turned out, when Marta had glimpsed the man's head and armpit from below, she had only seen a fraction of Barry Roffey. His body, a vast, oozing mass, appeared to have been poured into the old office chair; a foam-filled relic that appeared barely able to support his weight.

His office, if that was the right word, consisted of boxes, hundreds of boxes, piled up around an L-shaped scrap of threadbare carpet. In the corner of it sat Barry in his rickety chair, behind a mountain of papers.

'Hello. My name is Marta. I am here to do interview,' she explained.

'To do *interview*?' asked Barry, his face rocking gently with its many chins. 'That's one way of putting it, love.'

Marta stepped forward, her arm outstretched. 'I don't think I sent–'

'Wha's that then?' Barry screwed up his fat face at the sight of the piece of paper being proffered.

'My CV.' Marta had been careful to amend this version, adding her UK contact details, perfecting the sentences and rearranging sections so as to appear more like the examples she had found online. This time, she had not asked Tash for help. She was beginning to realise that her housemate had other priorities besides helping her find a job.

Barry leaned back in his chair. It creaked ominously. 'Did you fill out a form for me?'

Marta nodded.

'Where is it?'

'I sent back straight away to you.'

'Right.' Barry poked ineffectively at the hummocks of paper that formed an undulating surface on his desk. Then he sniffed, loudly. 'Tell ya what, just do another one.' He reached backwards, causing more creaking, and whipped a sheet off the top of one of the piles.

Marta dutifully filled out the required information: name, age, nationality, availability, day or night preferences. There were some tick-boxes at the end that Marta found slightly peculiar, such as criminal record, history of violence, and religion, but she placed her ticks and returned the form to the man.

'Oh good, you're Polish.'

Marta raised her eyebrows.

'I don't get no jip from the Poles – not usually. None of that bloody turban nonsense, or beards.' He snorted. 'Not that you'd 'ave a beard. Hah! But the public don't take leaflets from Pakis and whatnot. Now, when can you start?'

Marta looked at the man in disbelief. She couldn't speak.

'You've put on your form "now", so how 'bout Monday?' He looked at her.

Marta quickly pushed her thoughts aside and switched on a smile. 'Great.'

'You come 'ere at eight, yeah? You take your box of flyers, you go to the zone I tell ya – *no moving out of your zone, alright?* – and you give 'em away. Eight a.m. to eight p.m. with one hour for lunch. You run out, you come back for more. You get rid of your load, OK? No funny business – no binning, no pairing up, no copping off early. You're there to give leaflets out. We've got people checking, OK?'

Marta was dubious as to whether Barry Roffey really had people checking, but she nodded all the same.

'How much–'

'I'm *comin'* to that,' he barked. 'You do Monday to Saturday, same every day, until I say so. If you're planning to bugger off back to Poland, tell me. If you're sick, tell me. I got a phone, so use it. You pull too many sickies, you're out.'

Marta nodded again.

'I pay you fifty quid a day, nothing if you're sick or caught messin' about. End of the week, there'll be an envelope here for you with three hundred quid. OK?'

Some quick mental arithmetic told Marta she would be getting just under five pounds per hour; nearly thirty złoty. That was more than she would earn in marketing back home, but then... things were more expensive here. Marta knew it was a bad deal, but she also knew it was her only option.

It was raining when Marta emerged at street level. Merchants were pulling sheets over their wares and pulling up hoods. The smell of pipe smoke intensified in the saturated air and the pavements became gridlocked by a canopy of umbrellas. Filled with a mix of rage and sadness, Marta made a detour down a side street.

How, after all the effort she had put in at school, at university, on all her placements, had she ended up here? This wasn't her dream: standing on a crowded street trying to shove flyers into the hands of busy Londoners, her knuckles white with cold. It wasn't the dream she had worked for.

Marta wearily made her way back to the main road, not even bothering to dodge puddles any more.

It was a job, at least. It was a way of paying the rent, of keeping herself fed and warm. But it wasn't a proper job. It wasn't a job in an office where she would use all the skills and techniques she had learnt at the Szkoła. She had seen the recruitment websites: slick, glossy and full of promise. They were bursting with exciting jobs in all sectors for all types of people; all types of *English* people. Some even specified which universities applicants had to come from. Oxford and Cambridge were the clear favourites, but Marta already knew that from the conversations she had overheard between Tash and Jack and their posh English friends.

A feeling of gloomy resignation settled on Marta as she pushed her way onto the bus, breathing in the scent of damp clothes and perfume and unwashed hair. She tunnelled through the crowds and found a spot by the back, rubbing a patch in the steamed-up window and trying to deflect her morbid thoughts. Eventually, she recognised the tall, brick buildings that lined Brompton Road. She leaned over to press the button, still lost in shame and indignation from her experience with Barry Roffey. *Please don't let Tash be home yet,* she thought to herself. That was one thing she didn't need.

'Hi! How was your day?! Got a job yet?' sang the familiar voice from the kitchen. Tash was back.

'Hello,' replied Marta, heading straight for her bedroom.

'Want a cup of tea?' asked Tash, peeping out from the kitchen looking exceedingly smug. She had changed into yet another outfit: soft pink trousers and a tight hooded top that revealed a band of perfectly tanned midriff.

It was an uncharacteristically thoughtful offer, Marta noted, feeling bad about her plan to head straight upstairs.

'OK.'

'So, any luck today?' asked Tash.

Marta forced herself to do the one thing she really didn't feel like doing, which was to smile.

'Yes!' She nodded. 'Not a great job, but at least I will earn money. Three hundred pounds a week!'

'Oh, *well done!*' cried Tash, clasping her hands together. Then she paused, frowning. 'A – a week?'

'Yes!'

'Right. Er, good.' Tash smiled brightly. 'What's the job?'

Marta shrugged. 'Oh, paperwork mainly,' she said, trying not to lie.

'Paperwork? Is that all they told you? How very vague!'

Marta shrugged, determined not to let her face fall. Tash was really beginning to annoy her.

'Some sort of transactions,' Marta added, again not entirely lying.

'Is it in a nice office, like you wanted?' Tash probed. Marta began to wonder whether she had been followed out this afternoon. A brief vision of Tash creeping down Queensway to see what her Polish housemate was up to flashed through Marta's mind, but she forced it out.

'It's in a beautiful office,' she lied. 'I have my own desk and a small plant, like this–' she sized up her imaginary pot plant in her hands, 'and the people are very great. Is near Victoria,' she added, for a touch of credibility.

'Well, that's *excellent*, Marta,' Tash exclaimed, handing over a

49

cup of tea and chinking her own against it. 'Here's to your new job in *paperwork!*'

10

Tash was looking at her in the mirror, barely disguising her contempt. 'Are you sure you don't want to borrow a coat?' she asked.

Marta looked down at the turquoise jacket that hugged her upper body, admiring the way Anka's gift was such a perfect fit. 'I'm fine, thank you.'

Tash finished straightening her perfectly straight hair and pouted critically at her reflection. Marta wondered whether she should have made more effort. It was her first night out in London. She was wearing a plain black top and jeans – the ripped ends hiding a pair of grubby trainers – and only a dusting of makeup. How much trouble did English girls go to?

'I think there's some jewellery and stuff in that cupboard in your room,' Tash said pointedly. 'Feel free to use it.' Marta took the hint and went back to improve herself.

She held a string of blue beads up against her neck. The thing about Tash, thought Marta, rifling through the trinkets like a child in a dressing-up box, was that she actually had no idea how fortunate she was. She lived in this beautiful world where everything was new, fashionable, expensive and pristine… and she assumed everyone else lived there too. The other day she had stepped over a homeless man wrapped in a blanket outside the supermarket, ensuring her suede knee-high boots remained immaculate, and exclaimed, 'Why don't they just get a job? I'd rather sit in an office all day than lie on the pavement!' Marta wondered what Tash's parents were like. Mama would know. Maybe she would ask her about Penelope and Henry.

'*Wow*,' uttered Tash, clearly impressed with the transformation. 'Look at you, gorgeous girl.'

Marta smiled bashfully. She had, in her opinion, gone overboard: accentuating her ice-blue eyes with mascara and bringing out her cheekbones with blusher. The trainers had been replaced by dainty high heels – another find from the second wardrobe – making her long legs appear even longer. Evidently Tash approved.

It hadn't been Marta's idea to come along tonight. It hadn't been Tash's either; in fact, Marta suspected that Tash would have preferred not to have her Polish housemate tagging along. Plum, the horse-faced girl with the loud laugh, had decreed that she simply *had* to come to Blushes on Saturday for Jeremy's birthday.

'Ready?' asked Tash, giving herself one last glance in the mirror.

'Ready.' Marta smiled, determined to quell the churning sensation in her stomach. She couldn't pinpoint exactly why, but she didn't feel at ease with Tash and her rich friends.

Their strides synchronised as they clip-clopped down Draycott Avenue, heading in the direction of King's Road. Marta could imagine how they looked to passersby: two friends on their way to a bar or restaurant. That was almost accurate, she thought. Sometimes, when Tash was in a good mood and when they found a subject they could both talk about – usually Tash's hair or outfit or something in a magazine – Marta actually felt as though they *were* friends, but not real friends. Not like Marta and Anka. They couldn't talk about anything real.

Marta couldn't imagine getting close to Tash, or in fact any of the English girls she had met. It was difficult to explain why, but it felt as though they had some kind of buffer around them; a layer of something that stopped anyone from getting too close. Their priorities were different, too. And they were complicated. They kept things from one another; Marta had seen it. They faked their emotions – feigning surprise when they already knew, pretending to care when they didn't – so it was impossible to tell what they really felt.

'Who will be there?' asked Marta, hearing the nerves in her

voice. She didn't really know any of them properly and although Tash was her pseudo friend, Marta was all too aware that her housemate wouldn't bother sticking around when the likes of Jack and Plum started to vie for her attention. And there would probably be lots of people like Jeremy, who, despite Marta's best efforts, just didn't seem to have any time for her. Suddenly, the image of a bar full of young men like Jeremy, sitting in a row looking down their oversized noses popped into her mind and she nearly stopped and turned back the way they had come.

'Jeremy, obviously,' Tash replied. 'And Jack will be along later. Who else…? Plum… Oh!' She looked at Marta. 'Holly! You'll get to meet Holly!'

Marta waited for an explanation.

'You'll get on well with Holly, I can tell. She went to a state school.'

Marta frowned. 'What's–'

'I know her from Cambridge; we shared a room in our second year. She's…' Tash paused for a second. 'She's different from most of my friends.'

Marta allowed Tash to guide her into a sharp left, lost in every sense of the word.

'The second-year room ballot is random and if you come too far down, you end up sharing,' Tash went on, stepping aside for a group of young men in crisp, pink shirts whose aftershave caught the back of Marta's throat. 'I was devastated when I found out, but as it happens, I was lucky.'

Marta nodded, only half listening. It was the best way, when Tash prattled on like this.

The pavement narrowed and it became more difficult to navigate in parallel through the stream of evening revellers. Middle-aged women with well-dyed hair flaunted fur coats, while the men wore starched trousers and polo shirts, some of them even sporting bowties. Marta was suddenly glad of Tash's gaudy jewellery and the shoes that were giving her blisters.

'Here we are!' announced Tash, slowing to a halt outside what looked like an expensive café. Opulent laughter spilled through the open door and an orange glow lit up the pavement. Marta prompted Tash to go first and then stepped inside, into a world of white teeth, sparkling jewellery and swooshing, glossy hair. Twenty-somethings filled the bar, all of them smartly dressed and unbelievably good-looking.

'He's booked out the downstairs,' Tash explained, picking her way down a set of spiralling, wrought iron steps at the back of the room. Marta followed with considerably more difficulty. Every time her heel landed, it got lodged in a gap, requiring her to yank her foot free like a bird trapped in sticky paint. After what seemed like an eternity, she made it to the bottom and braced herself to face the braying crowds.

To Marta's relief, the crowds turned out to be braying in no particular direction; as far as she could tell, her entry had gone unnoticed. The relief was short-lived, however, usurped by the terror of something far worse than falling down the stairs, or having nobody to talk to, or being presented with a hundred Jeremy-like figures looking down their enormous noses at her. The fluttering sensation in the pit of her stomach was due to the fear of *spending money*.

The tables were arranged in a T-shape, each place laid with at least four knives and forks and multiple wine glasses. Napkins were arranged like bouquets in the middle of each setting and every person had been given a little parcel wrapped up in fine silver gauze. *Drinks and nibbles*, Plum had said. This was a five-course meal! Marta couldn't bring herself to think about how much she would end up paying this evening. She had set aside twelve pounds. *Twelve pounds.*

'Tash! Marta!' someone shrieked. 'You're just in time!'

There was a painfully loud hoot of laughter and Plum's grinning face appeared before them. Marta was ushered into the corner, where she hovered awkwardly, making way for a procession of smartly dressed waiters who had just been given the instruction to enter: one carrying a cake in the shape of what looked like a piano, one shielding the candle's flames, one brandishing a gigantic knife and one following behind with no apparent role. Suddenly, the room was filled with the most harmonious, voluminous tones, music erupting around them like something you might hear in a cathedral service on a special occasion.

'Har-py bath-day to yooooou,' they sang, 'Har-py bath-day to yooooou.' Tenors and sopranos began adding their own parts. 'Har-py bath-day dear Jer-a-meeeee...' Everybody paused, as if they knew to expect the elaborate descant cadenza from the young man next to Jeremy... 'Har-py bath-day to yooooou!'

There was a magnanimous roar and a clamour of applause that was probably audible at street-level. 'Hip-hip!' yelled someone, above the din. 'Hooray!' came the response. 'Hip-hip!' 'Hooray!' 'And one for lark, hip-hip!' 'Hooray!'

More roaring, more whooping, more clapping. Marta just stood in the corner, staring. Had they *rehearsed* for this? Was this normal? Did they always put on such an elaborate performance for someone's birthday? Jeremy was beaming like a little boy, peering down at his cake as though deciding where to make the first cut. 'Gosh! It's got pedals and everything! Splendid!'

'*Weird*,' muttered a voice near Marta's ear.

She looked round to see a girl of about the same height, with a freckly face and brown hair tied up in a rough ponytail. Marta looked around, but couldn't see anyone else for whom the comment might have been intended, so she braved a reply.

'What?'

'Weird time to have cake,' said the girl, her eyes narrowing as she surveyed the scene of revelry. 'Who eats *cake* before dinner?'

Marta shrugged, unsure as to whether an answer was expected, but failing to come up with one anyway.

'I guess it's so Jezza's choral chums can stuff their faces before they bugger off to entertain the Queen or whatever.' The girl snorted and reached down for her drink; a pint of beer, Marta noticed, smiling. She hadn't seen anyone drink beer since she had arrived. Tash's friends favoured spirits and fancy cocktails.

'The Queen?' Marta was perplexed now, but also intrigued. The freckle-faced girl reminded Marta strangely of Anka. She was blunt and straightforward, unlike the other girls over here.

'Oh, I dunno what they're off to do, but it's usually some concert in the Royal Albert Hall or whatever. That's why they're all dressed up.' The girl nodded at a tall, lanky man in a bowtie nearby. Crumbs were shooting out from between his teeth as he guffawed at another man's joke.

'Are they... a choir?' asked Marta.

'Oh – I thought you knew them!' The girl looked searchingly at Marta, as though seeing her for the first time. 'They're Jeremy's "muso" mates. He was the organ scholar at our college and now he plays for some London choir or other. Hence the heavenly voices just now. Sorry, I don't think we've met.' The girl offered her hand. 'I'm Holly.'

Marta smiled. So *this* was Holly. 'Hi. I am Marta – living with Tash.'

'Oh! You're the Polish girl, right? Tash told us about you!'

Marta smiled nervously.

'How are you settling in?'

Before Marta could answer, a hush fell on the room, prompted by an insistent fork-on-glass chime.

'Ladies... and gentlemen!' bellowed Jeremy.

'*Please God, not another song,*' Holly muttered under her breath.

'Thank you, everyone, for coming along tonight. It means a great deal to me to have you all here and I'm particularly honoured to have received such a tuneful birthday greeting!'

There was a polite patter of applause, which died out quickly as people realised they were applauding themselves.

'And now we must say farewell to the Philharmonic boys...' There was a collective "*aaaah*". 'But for the rest of you, please sit down!'

Marta looked around for Tash and saw her sliding elegantly into a seat between Jeremy and Jack, who had just arrived. There were no spaces anywhere near her.

'Shall we squeeze in here?' asked Holly.

Marta shrugged and took her seat, inwardly leaping for joy. It was silly, really, but it felt as though she had made a friend. Sort of.

Her joy quickly evaporated when she remembered about the five-course meal.

'Am – am not eating,' she explained hastily, shifting into a gap between laid places. 'Am not very much hungry.'

Holly frowned. 'You serious? You're not taking Jezza up on his offer of a free slap-up dinner?'

Marta hesitated, not sure whether *free slap-up* meant the same as *free.*

'God, I've been starving myself for days!' Holly went on, shaking the napkin out of its floral arrangement and stuffing it onto her lap. 'Free meal on Jez... Get stuck in!'

Marta's mood lifted but she couldn't quite be sure. There were at least twenty people down here; surely Jeremy wasn't paying for everyone?

'Free?'

'Yeah.' Holly nodded, reaching for a breadstick. 'Jezza's minted. He doesn't care.'

'Mint...?'

'*Minted.* Mega-rich.'

'Oh.' Marta felt the relief start to envelope her. Slowly, she shifted back along the table so that she was sitting in front of the laid knives and forks.

Holly smiled. 'Come on. We've got some serious eating to do.'

Grinning, Marta leaned back as an army of waiters appeared with the starters.

Over the course of the next few hours, Marta learned a great deal. Holly gave her a brief synopsis of most of the people around the table, including details about who came from where and who had slept with whom. Plum, it turned out, had been a busy young lady, getting round most of the male members of the group with the exception of Tash's boyfriend, Jack – although Holly suspected that this was only a matter of time. Marta was somewhat shocked to learn that Tash was reigning champion of the "Great Quad Race", a

57

naked run around the old courtyard of their university, but she didn't doubt Holly's word. Despite having known the girl for only a couple of hours, Marta felt she could trust Holly in a way she couldn't trust Tash or Plum or the rest of them.

The coffee cups came out and Marta noticed Holly suddenly look at her watch and grimace.

'*Shit.* I've gotta go. Said I'd be at my mate's do by ten.'

She stood up. Marta felt a flutter of panic inside her. She had enjoyed herself so much that for a moment she had forgotten the stress of being among strangers in a strange, foreign place.

'Hey, here's my card. Give us a shout if you ever get bored of horsy talk and sherry parties. My mobile number's on the back.'

Marta flashed a grateful smile and took the card.

'Oh and good luck,' Holly added quietly, nodding in Tash's direction. 'She's not the easiest to live with.'

Marta watched the tall brunette bound up the stairs, two by two. Then she looked down at the card in her hand. The words were embossed in a bold, elegant font that gave it an aura of utmost importance.

Holly Banks

Associate

ANDERTON CONSULTANTS

Marta ran a finger over the surface one last time and then slipped the card into the back of her wallet.

11

Bayswater felt different at this time of day. The air was crisp, the pavements clear and the stalls shut away behind rusty, graffiti-scrawled shutters. The rustle of money changing hands had been replaced by the humdrum patter of commuters on their way to work.

Marta was not wearing a suit. She was dressed in jeans, several T-shirts and her Malina Q jacket. On her feet were her tatty but comfortable trainers. She had a long day ahead of her.

'S'OPEN!' yelled the distinctive voice as she rang the bell.

Her journey up the stairs was hampered by a large number of people coming the other way, each laden down with boxes. Marta took refuge in the corners of the staircase, letting people pass and then scampering up to the next waiting spot. The load-bearers were mainly men, she noted, most of them her age or a little older. From the grunts of conversation she overheard, there were a number of Poles and a few Czechs. *Just how Barry liked it*, she thought wryly.

'You gonna stand there all day?' yelled Barry from inside his "office". Marta had been waiting for the last person to pass with his box, but he seemed to be struggling just inside the door. She slipped inside as he fumbled.

''Ere you go,' Barry barked, nodding at a box that was slightly smaller than the ones she had seen the others carrying. Marta wondered whether her boss had moved from his chair since she last saw him.

'And if I… If I run out?'

Barry let out a course grunt of laughter. 'Oh, y'won't run out, believe me. You've only got 'alf there!' He motioned to another identical box on the floor.

Marta carefully lowered herself with the first box and stretched her fingers around the second. The combined weight of the two boxes was almost more than she could lift. Surely this was more than the others had been given?

'Eight 'til eight, OK, with an hour for lunch. Your pass is in the box. That's for if anyone asks questions. Now, 'ere's your zone.'

Marta staggered over and perched her load on the edge of his desk. She watched as he highlighted a wobbly circle on a photocopied map of central London.

'That's where you cover, right?'

Marta nodded. The area included Farringdon tube station and a grid of streets that formed a wonky square around it. With horror, Marta realised that her "zone" included the street where Genesis was located.

Marta strained to pick up her load again. She wondered how she was supposed to get the boxes to her allocated zone and how, once she got there, she was going to keep them with her as she wandered around. Barry hadn't mentioned anything about logistics and Marta sensed that he wouldn't be much help if she asked.

Marta turned and found herself slamming straight into the other guy, who had been mending a tear in his box by the door.

She gasped an apology in her native tongue.

The guy took a step back, allowing her through. 'Polka?' he asked, smiling.

Marta grinned back. The guy had messy, sandy hair and his eyes, which were an unusually light hazel, seemed to sparkle as he smiled.

'It's you,' said Marta, waiting until they were safely outside Barry's office.

He nodded, grinning. 'Dominik.'

'Hi. Again, I mean. I'm Marta.' She laughed nervously and gingerly made her way down the stairs, unable to see the steps on account of her load.

'Is this your first day?' Dominik called down to her.

'Yes. You?'

'My third month.'

'*What?*' Marta was shocked. Surely nobody stayed in this job for long? She certainly didn't intend to.

'Is it OK?' she asked, squeezing past another girl on the stairwell.

'It's a job,' he replied carefully. 'What's your zone?'

They were nearly at the bottom of the stairs now. 'Farringdon.'

'Huh,' Dominik nodded. 'Round the corner. I'm Holborn.'

Marta had no idea about London geography, but she was happy to take Dominik's word for it. They eased themselves through the exit and stood hoisting their loads into more comfortable positions. Marta's arms were hurting already.

Suddenly, Dominik's easy smile fell away.

'Don't you have transport?' he asked.

Marta shook her head uncertainly.

The boy shook his head wearily. 'Barry is such a *dick*. He didn't mention it at all?'

'No.' Now Marta was worried. Was she supposed to have a car? She didn't even have a driving licence and couldn't imagine trying to get to grips with London traffic and driving on the left and parking… not to mention the cost of owning a car.

'You gonna go by tube?'

Marta shrugged. 'Was planning to.'

Dominik paused for a second, staring at the ground, balancing his load on a bollard and rubbing his forehead. 'Hmm.'

Marta waited hopefully. It wasn't just the idea of some kind of transport solution that appealed, it was him. The idea of a Polish friend in London suddenly appealed more than anything; particularly a cute, Polish friend like Dominik.

'OK. How about this? I've got my scooter…' Dominik pointed with his foot towards a rusty machine that had been propped against the kerb. 'So I can load it up with all the leaflets, then I'll meet you at

Farringdon. If you get the tube from Bayswater, we'll probably arrive at the same time.'

Marta nodded gratefully. She wondered what the catch was here.

'Oh, and here's my number in case we somehow don't hook up.' Dominik pulled a leaflet from his stash and scribbled on it.

'Thanks.' She looked at the leaflet. It was an advert for some sort of dieting service.

'God, you've got a big wad here,' he noted, heaving her second batch onto the rickety carrier. 'You want me to lose half of these on the way?'

He was smiling, but Marta couldn't tell whether he was joking. Did people bin some of their leaflets? She remembered Barry's words from last week: *I pay you nothing if you're caught messin' about.* 'I'll manage,' she told Dominik.

He laughed. 'I was joking.' Then he lowered his voice. 'Although seriously, you're not gonna get through all these, so I suggest you leave some with me. We can always meet up if you run out.'

Yes please, thought Marta, relishing the idea of meeting up with Dominik. 'OK. See you at Farringdon?'

'See you there.'

Marta headed for the tube station carrying nothing but Dominik's leaflet. Things felt better all of a sudden. She had a job of sorts that paid reasonable money, a place to live, a few English friends, and now she had Dominik. Well, she had Dominik's phone number, at least.

He was waiting for her outside the station, his hair slightly flattened by the helmet, but no less messy. 'Cześć.'

Marta returned his cheeky grin. Excitement bubbled inside her. 'Thanks so much.'

'You know what you're doing?'

Marta pulled a face. 'Er, giving out leaflets?'

He looked at her appraisingly, the smile lingering on his lips. 'Have you done it before?'

She shrugged with fake confidence. 'How hard can it be?'

Dominik raised an eyebrow. 'OK, then. You're on your own.' He handed her one of her boxes. 'Gimme a shout if you get through that lot, I'm just up the road.'

Marta laughed as he kicked his machine into life. It took three attempts to make it work. 'Half an hour, I tell you!' she yelled above the popping noise.

He pulled his visor down and shook his head, then swung the scooter into a sharp U-turn and disappeared up a side street.

12

'Where shall we head first? Austique? Marosa? Oh you would *so* love the accessories in Marosa – they've got Emma Hanbury! Austique is good too, but more for lingerie. Mind you, they always have some gorgeous dresses.'

Tash prattled on about various designer outlets on King's Road, oblivious to Marta's bored silence. Marta had no intention of shopping in any of the places her housemate had mentioned. She had known it was a bad idea for Tash to come along, but Tash had insisted. She was convinced she could help Marta find the perfect gifts.

Unfortunately, Tash didn't quite understand the budget constraints Marta had in mind. When Marta had picked up her first pay packet – a brown envelope containing fifteen £20 notes – it felt as though she had hit jackpot. She had the equivalent of nearly 2,000 złoty in her wallet. But once she had paid Tash for three weeks' rent, put enough by for bus tickets and food, and kept some aside for emergencies, she had found herself clutching just £35. She doubted that would be enough to buy one gift, let alone three. London prices were frightening.

'Oh, *Karen Millen!*' cooed Tash as they turned onto the main high street. Without even a cautionary glance for traffic, she danced across the road, pulling Marta along by the hand. 'Is your friend into fashion? I bet she would adore the dress I saw in here the other day.'

'Er…' Marta hesitated. Anka loved fashion, but not the sort of fashion that would bankrupt her best friend. 'I have not much money to spend,' she explained.

'Well, it's always worth a look, isn't it?' Tash grinned, pulling a small shift dress from the rail and hooking the hanger over her neck. 'What d'you think?'

It very quickly became clear to Marta that this trip wasn't about Anka, or Mama or Tata or anyone else for whom she might have bought presents back in Poland. It was about Tash. Tash viewed spending money as a leisure activity, not a functional exercise. Marta could see from the way Tash's eyes scanned the racks of clothes, the movement of her fingers as they caressed the fabrics, that it was her favourite pastime. The longer it took and the more money she spent, the better.

'I think it is not a good shop,' she told Tash, wondering how to explain the money issue. 'I don't want to spend–'

'Oh, don't think about prices at this stage! You'll never get anything if you do that. Take a look around, pick out anything that you think you might want and try it on, *then* decide whether you can really afford it. That's what I do.' She pulled a face as if to say *naughty me.*

For a while, Marta played along. She tried to be more like Tash, flitting about the shop, grabbing handfuls of garments, flinging them over her arm and dashing into the changing rooms. The problem was, Marta *wasn't* like Tash. She didn't shop for fun, she shopped for a purpose and she didn't enjoy trying on hundreds of beautiful tops she would never be able to buy.

'Tash, I will go to other shops now,' she said, trying to employ some English tact.

'Don't you like Karen Millen?'

Marta sighed. How could she make Tash understand? 'Problem is, I have not much money. I don't–'

'Oh, I've got *just* the thing! You're right – clothes are too expensive. They're probably too bulky to send, anyway. Let's go across the road, there's an Accessorize. That's probably more up your street. None of their stuff lasts more than two months, but at least it looks nice to begin with. It's great for gifts.'

Tash quickly ushered her out of the shop, simultaneously dumping her armful of expensive clothing on a nearby assistant.

'Look at this! It's a treasure trove!' Tash gleefully set about scrutinising the shop's interior. It was true; the place sparkled. Every wall was densely packed with bracelets, necklaces, rings and hairclips arranged in blocks of colour around the shop.

Marta headed for the emerald section, picking out a pair of dangly earrings she knew Anka would love. There was a matching pendant on a silver cord. Marta flipped over the price tag. Her heart sank. Fourteen pounds, just for the pendant. The earrings were twelve pounds fifty. If she bought either one, that would use up her entire allowance. She could imagine the disappointment on her best friend's face, unwrapping the single jewel that looked, frankly, not unlike the ones you could get in a Polish market for 12 złoty. She returned the jewellery to the rack.

'How about this?' Tash asked excitedly.

Marta turned to find her fingering the most garish collection of jewels she had ever seen. It looked like some sort of triangular doily made out of fluorescent, sparkling beads. 'What... is it?' asked Marta.

It's a choker – a necklace,' said Tash. 'Isn't it incredible?'

Marta nodded warily. Incredible seemed to be an appropriate word.

'And it's only twenty-five pounds!'

'Oh,' replied Marta, deadpan. 'I think it is not Anka's style.'

Tash raised her eyebrows. 'Huh.'

Marta had another go at breaking away from her housemate. 'Tash, am very sorry but am not on the good mood for this. I think I might–'

'Oh no! You poor thing. I *hate* not being in the mood for shopping. I know exactly what you want–'

'Tash, I–'

'No, really. I get this too sometimes. What you need is a chai latte and a slice of low-fat lemon cake, and I have *just* the place to go for it! Come to think of it, that's what I fancy. Come on, we're going to the Bluebird!'

The Bluebird, it turned out, was a vast, whitewashed building set back from the road behind a row of pillars. In front of it, sheltered by ornate glass parasols with heated stems, sat a bunch of Kensington locals, all immaculately dressed and sipping exotic-looking drinks.

'Is it warm enough to sit out, d'you think?' asked Tash, not pausing for a response. 'No, let's head inside. It's nicer in there anyway.'

Marta felt awkward as soon as she set foot on the polished floor. She hated it when they rushed up to take your coat, called you *ma'am* and asked repeatedly if everything was alright.

'We'll go into the lounge,' announced Tash, leading the way across the wooden floor into a sun-drenched conservatory. She headed straight for a pair of cream armchairs that were carefully arranged around a marble-like cube.

Chai latte was a strange, sickly drink. Marta couldn't say that she liked it, exactly, but the low-fat lemon cake was tasty enough. Tash extolled the virtues of living in Kensington with its marvellous array of shops and parks and its wonderful mix of people. Marta wasn't sure that "mix" was the best word to describe the well-dressed young mothers pushing deluxe baby-wagons, the beautiful twenty-somethings wearing angora and the endless stream of smartly dressed couples trailing miniature versions of themselves on reigns. Yes, she had heard foreign accents – mainly Russian and French – but these people were all the same type. They were all rich.

'So, how's the new job?' asked Tash, surprising Marta with the selflessness of the question.

'Good,' she nodded.

'Any nice men in your office?' Tash raised a perfectly plucked eyebrow.

'Um…' Marta's thoughts flitted instantly to Dominik and she felt her lips curling into a smile.

'Ooh, there is! How exciting! What's his name? What does he do?' Tash waved her fork in the air, her eyes wide.

'He's called Dominik – he does, er, similar things to me.'

'So… tell me more!'

Marta shrugged. It was obvious that Tash didn't really care about Marta's life; she just wanted gossip, something to tell her friends about.

Tash tutted. 'OK, fine.' She sulked for a moment, but not for long. 'So, let's decide what you're going to buy!'

Marta sighed. She had to put an end to this.

'Tash, you don't understand. I have little money here. I will get more, as I do more work, but I must be careful. I can only spend thirty-five pounds on present today. That is all.'

Tash frowned. 'OK. Well… that's fine. We'll just have to rethink our shops a little. I mean, you can still get a nice box of cosmetics for thirty-five pounds… or a top, or–'

'No, Tash!' Marta said, louder than she had intended.

There was instant silence. Tash glared at her. Clearly nobody ever shouted at Tash.

'Sorry,' muttered Marta. 'But you still don't see.'

To her horror, Marta found that tears were welling up behind her eyes. If she blinked, they would start streaming out. All of a sudden, she felt small and weak. She felt like a failure. It might have been the persistent reminders from Tash that she was poor, or maybe it was the fact that she spent her days being invisible, being looked through and shouted at, or maybe it was the realisation that she was living in a world in which she didn't belong. She didn't know. All she knew was that she wanted to be back in Poland.

'I have thirty-five pounds *all together*,' she explained. The tears flooded her vision and started rolling down her nose. 'That's the problem.'

Tash screwed up her face. 'All together?' she repeated, as though perplexed.

Marta accepted the tissue that Tash was holding out. She felt so ashamed. She was ashamed to be crying, ashamed to feel so out of place, ashamed not to have found a proper job. She had come over here with the intention of making money – enough money for herself *and* for her family back home – and somehow she was struggling even to make ends meet for herself. It was embarrassing. Back in Poland, everyone talked of the salaries being five times higher over here, but they never talked about the expense of living in London. It didn't add up. She couldn't make it work.

Tash looked at her. 'You know, maybe this isn't the time to go shopping.' She glanced up at a passing waiter and motioned for the bill. 'Perhaps you should wait until next week.'

Marta nodded, pressing the tissue into the corners of her eyes. Tash was being surprisingly intuitive.

'D'you know what I'd do? I'd go back to the house, run myself a nice bath and *relax*. Don't get worked up about silly things like shopping! Ooh – here's the bill. There are some lovely new bath salts in the cupboard.' She reached into her handbag. 'I might just stay out a little longer – Julia Farshaw has a new collection and she's got these *adorable* little wraparound tops.'

Marta nodded. She wondered whether Tash really cared, or whether the run-a-bath suggestion was simply a way of relieving herself of her blubbering Polish housemate.

'Oh, d'you know what, I've got no cash! Would you mind?'

For a moment, Marta thought she must have misunderstood. She looked at Tash, studying her face for a sign that this was a joke, or a misunderstanding.

'Only I don't think they take cards here,' Tash explained apologetically.

Marta looked down at the bill. Eleven pounds sixty. That was a third of her gift budget.

'Thanks, hun.' Tash got up quickly and then stooped as she made to leave. '*Don't forget to tip,*' she hissed in Marta's ear, before straightening up again. 'Have a lovely hot bath!'

'See you later,' Marta managed, her voice breaking on the last word.

Five minutes later, she wandered out of the overpriced café feeling as low as she had ever felt. One thing had become apparent: she *had* to get a proper job.

13

The marijuana hit the back of Marta's throat, sending her brain reeling back to the playground in Łomianki where, as teens, she and Anka used to enjoy the feel of the night air on their cheeks as they floated up and down on the seesaw getting stoned.

Marta's thoughts shot back to the present as a figure crept out of the shadows, mumbling drunken, aggressive words in her direction. She walked quickly, hands in pockets, skirting round a bunch of kids on bikes and turning into St Leonards Road. She was beginning to understand why North Acton was a cheap place to live.

The houses were small and terraced, and behind them were large expanses of industrial wasteland and blocks of flats. A streetlamp shone down on a stained, soggy mattress that leant against the peeling paintwork of number twelve.

The door opened before she reached it. Dominik was wearing low-hanging trousers and an old blue T-shirt that hugged his upper body, which was surprisingly toned.

Maybe she should have made less of an effort, thought Marta, suddenly feeling overdressed. After her experiences with Tash's friends, she had taken to borrowing her housemate's heels and applying full makeup for every occasion.

'You look… nice,' Dominik said, his eyes bashfully skirting her body.

Marta smiled, catching her first glimpse of the interior: taking in the peeling floral wallpaper and wonky lampshade.

'There are seven of us here,' Dominik explained, motioning for her to head inside. Sorry... It's a bit of a mess.'

'*Seven?*' Marta edged her way down the narrow hallway. The house couldn't possibly have had more than a couple of bedrooms.

'Yeah. The Croats sleep in the lounge.' Dominik pointed towards the small room at the front of the house. Marta poked her head in as they passed. The dirty brown carpet seemed to pervade throughout, as did the floral wallpaper. Two scruffy-looking men occupied the space in front of the TV, thumbs manically working their games consoles.

'That's Yishai and Uzoma. Think the others are out. Yeah, we've got two Israelis, one Iranian, two Croats, one Nigerian and me. Quite a mixed bunch.'

Marta caught a whiff of damp as Dominik led her through to the kitchen at the back. The surfaces were coated in a grey sheen and the windows looked almost frosted with grease.

'Oh.' Dominik dived to one side, bending over something on the floor. 'This thing...'

Marta watched expectantly as he placed a shoebox on the small kitchen table and started rummaging inside it. He had told her the previous week about a 'thing' he had found, but he hadn't been able to give it to her before now because it needed 'fixing up'. Marta was intrigued.

'Here.'

He placed what looked like a scratched lump of plastic in the palm of her hand. It was heavy, though, and despite the tyre marks across the top, Marta recognised the Apple logo.

'Sorry about the dents.' Dominik grimaced. 'Think it got run over.'

Then Marta saw the headphones. She turned the phone over in her hands, running her thumb along the deep groove that cut across the screen.

'Doesn't it belong to someone?' she asked, not liking the idea of handling stolen goods, or the idea that Dominik was *that* type of guy. It suddenly dawned on her how little she knew of this man who had invited her to his festering home. For a moment, she felt like running straight back down the hallway and through the front door.

'Relax.' Dominik smiled. 'The SIM was damaged so there was no way of tracing the owner. Not that the owner would want it back in that state, anyway. I reckon some city boy dropped it on his way to work. I picked it up in Holborn.'

Marta turned the device around in her hands. The scuffed plastic felt strangely comforting to touch, as though the phone was already a part of her. In a practical sense, it was a significant improvement on the cheap brick of a phone she had brought with her from home. Dominik had laughed out loud when he first saw it.

'Does it work?' she asked.

'Turn it on.'

Marta fumbled for the button and then watched as the screen lit up. The image was sharp and bright.

Dominik plugged the headphones into the socket and gently inserted one into Marta's ear, the other into his own. Suddenly, eighties rock music blasted around her head.

It stopped as quickly as it started. 'Ah, yes. Sorry.' Dominik looked embarrassed. 'I loaded it up from Yishai's computer.'

Marta shrugged. For her, the best part wasn't the music or the screen or the whizzy controls; it was the fact that she had a proper phone, like everybody else. And Dominik had given it to her.

'Don't… *you* want it?' she asked.

'I've got one. A crap version – not Apple – but it's OK. This one's yours, scars and all.'

Marta started scrolled through the colourful icons on the screen, mesmerised.

'You're not stuck with those songs,' Dominik explained. 'We've got tons on here.' He motioned to an upright computer in the corner of the kitchen. 'Yishai cleans offices and they were getting rid of their old computers at the last place he worked. They didn't wipe the hard drive before they handed it over, so there are over six thousand tunes on that thing.'

'Six *thousand?*'

Dominik smiled. 'Yeah, but they're not exactly current. Do you have a computer at your place?'

Marta shook her head. Tash had a laptop that glowed white when she switched it on, but Marta couldn't imagine being allowed to use it.

'Well, you can come round for a refill any time.' He shrugged.

Marta nodded, secretly excited about the open invitation.

Dominik lifted the lid on a huge vat-like container that was simmering on the dirty stove. The smell brought back instant memories of home.

'Smells nice. What is it?'

He reached into the vat with a spoon. 'Only soup. Nothing special.'

'Potato soup?' Marta asked hopefully. She was missing her mother's homemade cooking.

'Exactly.'

Marta perched timidly on one of the wooden chairs, leaning towards the table and then pulling away at the sight of a semi-solidified lump of what looked like curry. The house was a health hazard. Marta didn't mind, though. At least it was cosy. Given the choice between Dominik's dirty hovel with its steamed-up, greasy windows and Tash's spotless mansion, she would opt for this any day. The South Kensington place was vast and luxurious, but somehow it made her feel claustrophobic. She lived in fear of drinking from the wrong glass, upsetting her host or spilling something on the lambswool carpet.

Dominik moved confidently about the kitchen, stirring, tasting, wiping and inspecting thoroughly before use, much to Marta's relief. He seemed even more at home in a T-shirt and apron than he was out and about on his scooter.

'You should try getting work in a kitchen,' she suggested as he set the bowls down on the rickety table. Her mouth was watering; it smelled exactly like Mama's.

Dominik smiled wryly. 'I have done, and failed. D'you want salt?' He offered her a small, grimy pot. 'Believe me, I've tried getting work in just about everything. I got turned down for the chef's job, then turned down for the chef's *assistant* job. Apparently I had the *wrong background in food.* Like English meals are harder to cook than Polish ones. They offered me dishwashing work, but the pay was even worse than this flyering shit.'

Over soup and a bottle of wine, they talked about the various career options Dominik had explored since coming to England. He had studied finance at the Jagiellonian University in Krakow, one of the best in the country. Like Marta, he had moved over with ambitious plans. He had intended to get a job as an investment banker or fund manager over here, but after three months of gradually lowering his expectations, the best he could achieve was Barry's leaflets. After a while, Marta stopped asking. It had been knockback after knockback and it didn't seem fair asking him to relive them all.

'That was *delicious,*' she said, mopping up the last of her soup with a hunk of stale bread.

'Not exactly gourmet,' he said apologetically. 'I've got brownies though, if you want one.'

'Homemade?'

Dominik smiled. 'Yes, but not by me. Yishai's girlfriend. Ah, hello.'

The two housemates she had glimpsed earlier wandered into the kitchen. One of them – Yishai, Marta presumed – headed for the vat of soup on the stove and ran a finger around the inside.

'Mmm,' he nodded appreciatively. 'Not bad, Dominik.' His accent sounded Arabic, she thought.

'Have some. We're done.' Dominik turned to Marta. 'Shall we nab the lounge?'

Marta nodded, trying not to laugh. In Tash's place, the 'lounge' was this enormous front room with heavy drapes, leather sofas and the thick-pile rug. She took pride in entertaining guests in there. This lounge was like a teenager's bedroom.

Dominik quickly swept the room of dirty plates, mugs and wires, pushing aside a tray of what looked like the insides of a computer. They sat on lumpy cushions, the tin of chocolate brownies between them, bottle of wine on the floor.

It felt so good to be speaking Polish again. Marta had been so busy getting to grips with London life that she hadn't had time to think about home. London was so different from Łomianki. Everything here was instant and on tap. People didn't catch your eye or nod "good morning". Everyone queued, even when they didn't need to. Somehow, being here with Dominik, she could feel herself escaping back to her old life, her old personality. She knew it was crazy to say so, but it felt as though Dominik had been a part of her life for years.

'There *must* be a way for us to get proper jobs,' Marta declared, returning to the recurring theme as she bit into a brownie. 'I can't bear the idea of working for Barry for the next year.'

'If you discover it, let me know.' Dominik leaned down and topped up their wine glasses. 'They don't *want* to employ us – except in menial jobs, like sweeping streets and wiping toilets. I'm never going to use my finance over here. I've accepted that. My qualifications mean jack shit to these guys. They can't even pronounce the name of my university.'

Marta was silent. She didn't like to hear Dominik's reasoning. She couldn't bear to hear him denounce them as worthless, as nothing more than hired hands. She was aware that Dominik had been here a while, that he had had more time to try – and fail – to achieve his dream. She sensed that he had become bitter and resentful of British employers and that he had stopped considering the idea of a proper career. But she hadn't. She wouldn't. Marta felt sure there was a way of breaking into the professional world over here. She wasn't going to push it now, though.

Over more wine, they talked about home, friends, family, university, sports… at one point the conversation even turned to politics. It turned out their birthdays were a day apart, although Dominik was a year older. He had also played football at Jagiellonian with someone she knew from school.

'You working tomorrow?' asked Dominik, suddenly lifting the second bottle of wine and finding it empty.

Marta glanced at her watch and realised with a sinking sensation that it was nearly midnight. 'Yes.' She grimaced. 'I'd better go.'

'I'll walk you to the station.'

'You don't—'

'Seriously, Marta. This isn't South Kensington. There's a murder every week around here.'

'OK,' Marta conceded, secretly pleased at the outcome.

'You're lucky to live with such nice people,' Marta commented as they walked down the dimly lit street. Their hands weren't quite touching, but they almost were.

Dominik smiled. 'We get on alright. Probably 'cause none of us speak the same language.'

'But at least you're… in the same world,' said Marta, hoping he knew what she meant.

'Hmm. A world of crap jobs and cheap food. Yeah. We're all there.'

Marta laughed. She would give anything for a housemate who understood.

They stopped just inside the station and stood, quite close, facing each other.

'Well, see you at Barry's, I guess,' he said.

'Thanks for tonight.' Marta looked away. She wasn't just thanking Dominik for the soup and the brownies. Maybe the wine had gone to her head, but she really, really wanted to kiss him.

Dominik leaned forward and pecked her lightly on the cheek. He smelt good.

'Goodnight, Marta.'

She smiled, pulling away. 'Goodnight.'

14

'Watchya back!' yelled the driver of a scratched white van as Marta came to a wobbly halt between his front wheel and the kerb.

She pulled her ancient bicycle off the road and yanked her headphones out. Her heart was racing. The van pulled away in a plume of blue smoke that quickly engulfed her. She had never been very proficient at cycling, even on the quiet roads around Łomianki. Here, it was becoming increasingly evident that she was risking her life with every pedal. Perhaps listening to music as she rode was one risk too many, she considered.

The bike was an old one that a housemate of Dominik's had 'found'. It was probably stolen like the phone, she thought, but frankly Marta preferred not to think about that. Much as she enjoyed her collaboration with Dominik and his rusty scooter each morning, she was grateful for the independence afforded by the clunky old bike. It had been customised for her purposes with a large plastic crate attached to the back.

Today she was stationed in Chancery Lane. She had never been there before, but Dominik had warned her. 'You'll feel like scum,' he had said. 'Everyone wears pinstriped suits and they'll look right through you – if you're lucky. One guy actually batted me away with his umbrella.' Marta wasn't looking forward to it.

Setting her box down on the pavement, Marta chained her wheel to the railing, using a padlock that was probably worth more than the bike. It was just gone eight o'clock and already she was beginning to see what Dominik meant.

Suits, briefcases and smart shoes rushed past in a blur. Everyone was on a mission. They marched alone, staring straight ahead like members of a virtual army. They all looked so *serious*. Maybe this was what happened to people in positions of responsibility. Perhaps if Dominik found his footing in finance and she worked her way into marketing, then this was what they would become.

Marta braced herself. There was a knack to giving out leaflets. She had spent the last week honing the technique. Smiling was key, and it was important not to take rejection personally. People were more likely to take a leaflet from someone who was proactive than someone who looked as though this was their last hope of a job. That was Marta's theory, anyway.

'No thank you,' said a prim lady in a lilac suit; the first to actually catch Marta's eye. A young man shook his head without even looking at her and another barged straight into her shoulder as though she didn't exist.

Marta began to see what Dominik meant. Nobody wanted a leaflet. By eleven o'clock, she had had enough of grinning maniacally at strangers, leaping in and out of their paths and seeing the pavement papered with unwanted leaflets. Marta had got through about a fifth of a box – *one* box – which, by her calculations, meant that she would need eighteen more hours to get rid of her assignment.

It had become standard practice for Marta to take a wad away with her each night and place them in the community recycling bins on the way home. Usually there weren't too many, but today she had a feeling there might be an entire box. If it hadn't been for the threat of Barry's 'people' patrolling the streets, she would have packed up and gone home right now. Nobody wanted a leaflet. Nobody wanted her there.

Marta was considering calling Dominik to suggest an early lunch when something prompted her to look up. It sounded like a donkey braying. Scanning the thin, mid-morning flow of suits, Marta quickly identified the source. A fear crept over her as she spotted the face of the girl in the tight black pencil skirt and silk blouse. It was

Tash's friend, Plum. She was clip-clopping along the street beside a similarly dressed young woman, her arms waving madly, in full flow.

It was too late to move out of the way. Marta stuffed the handful of leaflets into her pocket and froze, looking at the ground in the hope that Plum, like everyone else that morning, would look through her and not at her.

'Marta!'

Marta looked up, feigning surprise.

'What on *earth* are you doing here?' Plum's eyes were wide, darting from Marta to her friend and back again as though the chance encounter was truly the most exciting thing that had happened all week.

'I'm...' Marta frantically tried to think of a reason for being there. She had told Tash her offices were near Victoria. 'Shopping,' she said, finally, resisting the urge to check that the box of leaflets was still balanced on the back of her bike near the road.

Plum frowned. 'In Chancery Lane? Gosh, what a strange choice!' She let out a whoop of laughter.

'Shopping for... gloves,' Marta explained, spotting a shop selling mountaineering and outdoor equipment.

'Hah! I would have thought you had good gloves already, being Polish!' Plum turned to her friend. '*Marta's Polish*,' she explained, in a keen whisper. 'Sorry, I didn't introduce you. Fi, this is Marta. Marta, Fi. Fi's another trainee at Freshfields.'

Marta nodded, wondering what Freshfields might be. It sounded like an organic supermarket chain.

'Well, we'd better let you go and buy your gloves!' Plum cried enthusiastically.

Marta smiled, inexplicably desperate to glance at her box of leaflets. It was like an itch.

'Have a lovely day, won't you? I'll see you at the dinner party!'

Plum and her companion strode off and, for the purposes of her story, Marta made a half-hearted move towards the outdoor equipment store. When she was sure the girls had gone, she returned to her spot, taking in the sight of her overloaded bicycle and feeling the weight of it drag her mood down.

Dinner party. Hideous words. Marta was not looking forward to next Friday. Tash had decided, in her role as chief social butterfly, that it was time everybody got together and 'had a jolly good piss-up'. This, as far as Marta could make out, would mean ten couples plus Marta sitting around the oak dining table drinking sickly liqueurs and talking about people she didn't know.

Marta's heart was still racing from the encounter with Plum. She figured that Tash's friend was probably too self-absorbed to think much about Marta's supposed glove-buying activity and was unlikely to relay the story to Tash, but Marta didn't feel comfortable. Plum was conniving. Marta had seen the way she caught Jack's eye when Tash wasn't looking. That girl was not your average Freshfields checkout girl.

Marta extracted the roll of leaflets from her pocket and tried to flatten them with her palm. *Primera Sport*, screamed the gaudy heading in blue and yellow. *New health & fitness centre. One month's free membership.* She flipped the top one over. There was a map showing the location of the gym. It was a couple of blocks up the road.

From the other pocket, Marta pulled out the photocopied sketch that marked out her zone. It appeared that she wasn't allowed to veer more than two hundred metres from Chancery Lane tube station, which restricted her from going to the actual location of the gym. She thought about this, a seed of frustration growing inside her. It was like being a tethered goat with no access to the most fertile land.

Marta understood marketing. She knew the saying: *Half of all the money you spend on advertising is wasted; you just don't know which half.* She was fairly sure that paying somebody to thrust leaflets at the wrong type of people in the wrong part of town was a waste of money.

It wasn't far to Holborn. Marta unlocked her bike and wheeled it along on the edge of the pavement, the unwieldy box slipping this way and that on the back. Barry ought to be pleased, she thought. She was helping his client to achieve a more targeted marketing campaign.

As she passed the shop selling gloves, something occurred to Marta. She parked her bike and grabbed a handful of leaflets.

'Hi,' Marta beamed at the shop assistant, a gawky young woman with ginger hair and an awkward smile. 'Can you help me?'

The girl gave a little shrug and laughed nervously. 'I'll try!'

'I have these leaflets. They are on subject of new gym nearby and I thought it would be great if you keep these, perhaps on the desk just here—' she placed the stack next to the cash register – 'so that customers get free membership.'

The redhead nodded like a little sparrow. 'Oh, of course! Er... why not?'

'Thanks!' cried Marta, walking purposefully out of the shop before the girl's supervisor appeared. She felt pleased with herself; she had just offloaded a fifth of her day's assignment in one go.

There were other outlets on the way up to Holborn. Marta left leaflets in two more outdoor clothing stores, a cycling shop and even a couple of cafés. It was easy. She couldn't understand why she hadn't thought of it before. There was even a huge gym fairly close to the site of the one she was advertising, so Marta spent a good half-hour catching people on their way to and from fitness classes, rapidly getting through her stack of flyers.

'Hi!' she said, embarking on her now-familiar routine in a small running shop just off the main street. Somehow, she could tell that this one would be trickier than the others. The manager was a short, bespectacled man with an unsmiling face and suspicious eyes. 'Could you help me?'

'Not if you're trying to sell me something,' he snapped.

'Oh, I'm not,' Marta replied truthfully. 'I just was thinking if you'd like to put—'

'Give me one of those.' He wrenched a leaflet from her hand. 'Bloody flyers. You know, I get enough of these things through the door at home. I bin the lot of them, you know, and that's what I'll do with these.'

'Oh, OK. Am sorry.' Marta edged towards the door.

'You got a licence for this, anyway?' he yelled, scrunching the leaflet in his fist. Marta backed out and left the door to slam. She took hold of her bike and pushed it into the road, barely waiting for a gap in the traffic. It was time to head back to Chancery Lane, she decided. She had used enough initiative for one day.

15

'Come along, Marta! Guests are arriving!'

The words were innocuous enough, but Marta knew what they meant. Tash had taken her aside earlier and explained that it would be 'nice if we could both be around for meeting and greeting – you know'. Yes, Marta knew. She knew what her role was tonight: fetching drinks, taking coats, serving food... whatever else the host had in mind.

She abandoned the exercise of trying to read Anka's email through the scratched screen of her phone and reluctantly headed downstairs.

'Marta?' Tash called again, with a veneer of bonhomie. 'Tom and Rosie are here!'

'Coming, yes!' Marta cringed at her reflection as she yanked open the bedroom door. She was dressed, on Tash's insistence, in one of the items hanging in the spare wardrobe: a red cocktail dress made from flimsy material – and very little of it. The low-cut design revealed more of her cleavage than Marta ever dared show and the hem barely reached halfway down her thighs. She crept down the stairs, tugging frantically at the top and bottom of the tiny dress in equal measure.

'Oh, there you are. Could you–'

'Wow!'

'He-*llo*.'

'Marta!' Plum threw her hands up dramatically as Jack turned and let out a low wolf-whistle. Six pairs of eyes stared up at her.

Tash whacked her boyfriend in the stomach. 'Doesn't she just? It's a Justine Westby, you know. Last season's… slightly too tight… but yes, stunning! Now Marta, would you just take Plum's coat? And – oh! Jeremy's here!'

Tash clattered over to the front door, her shrieks echoing off the high ceiling. Marta dutifully dealt with coats, feeling even more self-conscious than before. *Too tight?* Tash had earlier proclaimed the dress a 'perfect fit'.

It was a relief when, ten minutes later, jackets hung, drinks poured and canapés distributed, Marta entered the lounge to find a familiar face in the crowd. Almost devoid of makeup, Holly's face smiled back at hers. She was dressed, rebelliously, in jeans.

'How's things?' Holly mouthed, so that only Marta could see. Before Marta could respond, Tash jumped in.

'You two have met, haven't you? Now Holly, there's one more person on his way, and I think you'd really – ooh! Here he is!' Clapped her hands as the doorbell chimed. 'Marta, would you…?'

Marta turned silently and slipped out of the room, glad to escape the ogling stares of Jeremy and Jack and the sidelong glances of Rosie and Plum. She was beginning to wonder whether the outfit she had been squeezed into was all part of Tash's plan to isolate her.

The man on the doorstep was a stocky young man with a ruddy face and a thick head of ginger hair that rolled in waves down the back of his neck. His eyes were just about level with her chest, which made Marta feel instantly uncomfortable.

'Hi.' She took a step backwards, encouraging him in.

'Good *evening*,' he replied, not moving, his eyes roaming hungrily up and down Marta's body. 'And what a fine way to be welcomed, if I may say so. Are you Holly, by any chance?'

'No,' she replied bluntly. 'Marta. Come in.' She slipped behind the open door, wondering whether there was some kind of plot between Tash and her friends to set Holly up with this man. She shuddered.

'I'm Hugh,' announced the short man, casually tossing his coat on top of Tash's Indian bamboo stick display as he strode through the hallway. Marta made a mental note to remove it when she got a chance.

Hugh clapped his hands together, rubbing them eagerly as he swaggered into the lounge. A polite murmur rippled through the room, but it became evident that nobody knew who he was.

'Ah, Hugh! Hi!' cried Tash, emerging from the kitchen and flinging herself upon him. 'Let me introduce you! Jeremy, Plum, Tom-and-Rosie, Jack...' She steered him in a quarter-circle and gave him a meaningful look. 'And Holly. Everyone, this is Hugh. A family friend from way back.'

'Nice to meet you,' they chimed simultaneously.

'Oh, and Marta,' Tash added, as an afterthought. 'Marta, will you get one more gin and tonic? Let's move through to the dining room.' Tash skipped out, beckoning the guests to follow.

Marta did as she was told. The idea that Tash might have fixed *her* up with one of her old 'family friends' made her feel slightly sick, but on her return to the dining room, a quick glance at the laid table allayed her fears. There was no extra place beside hers; in fact, it turned out that Marta's *was* the extra place. Squeezed like a child's seat on the corner of the mahogany table was a kitchen bar stool, aligned with a miniature set of cutlery. The ludicrously high stool was for her.

'Hugh, you're at the end, opposite Holly,' Tash said pointedly. 'Tom-and-Rosie, you're up this end with me. Plum, you're between Holly and Jack, and Jeremy... Oh, good.'

Jeremy was already seated at the head of the table, pouring red wine into one of the many glasses in front of him. Awkwardly, Marta slipped into the space between Jeremy and Hugh, lifting her left buttock just enough to perch on the black leather stool. She felt like a tennis umpire overseeing a very small game.

'So, what is it you do, Hugh?' asked Holly, loudly, clearly hoping to create a distraction amid Marta's evident distress.

'I'm an equity sales trader,' the man replied smugly. 'I work at Goldmans, same as Jack, actually.'

'How *interesting*,' Holly replied, glancing briefly at Marta.

Marta smiled into her wine, relaxing a little as the alcohol took hold and the conversation began to flow around her. It was easier to eavesdrop than to play an active role, Marta found – and besides, she had duties to perform.

'*Starters!*' mouthed the host, jabbing a finger over her shoulder in the direction of the kitchen. Marta slipped off her stool.

Preparation for the evening had not been arduous. The food had arrived at two o'clock in a van with pictures of fruit on the sides. Inside the plastic bags were plastic containers, and inside the plastic containers were portions of food, all laid out on paper plates and ready to eat. Tash had instructed Marta to transfer the dishes onto proper plates, hide the packaging and read the instructions for reheating... and that was it. The rest of the day – well, Tash's day, at least – had been spent applying face masks and fake tan.

'*You lose!*' roared Hugh, pointing at Marta as she hopped off her stool fifteen minutes later to collect the plates. 'Jack was thumb master and you didn't notice!'

Marta looked at the ruddy-faced man. He seemed to be accusing her of something, but she had no idea what and she couldn't work out why the other guests were all grinning at her the way they were.

Holly leant forward. '*It's a drinking game,*' she said quietly. 'You have to look out for certain things happening throughout the meal. Jack was thumb master, which means that whenever he puts his thumb on the edge of the table, like this–' she nodded at her own and then everybody else's, which, Marta realised, were all gripping the edge of the table as though it was some kind of giant remote control, 'you have to copy. The last person to do it has to down their drink.'

'OK,' Marta replied slowly, wondering what all this meant. What was this crazy game? Whatever it was, they all seemed to be taking it very seriously. They were still looking at her now, as though they were waiting for her to do something.

'Drink!' cried Jack, leaning across the table to top up her already full glass of red wine.

'Show us what Eastern Europeans can do!' added Hugh, leaning unnecessarily close.

Slowly, she realised. They wanted her to drink her glass of wine, all in one go. Marta didn't like red wine. White was OK, but red… She had managed to consume nearly two glasses tonight – more out of necessity than desire – and she already felt quite queasy. Another glass would make her sick.

'She'll see it off really quickly, I bet,' squeaked the excitable Plum, as though she were watching a freak show.

Marta couldn't help thinking of parties back home with Anka and the others from the village. Sure, they had got drunk in their time. Sometimes in winter they would meet up after Anka's shift and go drinking at the bar opposite, singing and laughing until three in the morning, when the smell of cooked bread would fill the night air. On icy nights, Anka would sneak in and grab baking trays, which they would use as sledges to get home. *That* had been fun. Marta gripped the stem of her wine glass, bracing herself.

She tipped her head back and opened her throat. The vile liquid filled every cavity, her mouth was brimming with the stuff and yet there was still more in the glass. Heavy, viscous and intoxicating, it felt like a poisonous blanket was descending upon her.

Marta was vaguely aware of the voices: grunts of encouragement, screams of delight and noisy, meaningless yelling. She was drowning, quite literally, but she knew that giving up was not an option.

'Finally,' jeered Jeremy, as Marta placed the empty glass back on the table. Her stomach was heaving and her head felt like a buoy at sea, bobbing and spinning, unsure which way round it should be. The walls of the room were billowing, the table wobbling beneath her. Marta clung to it, waiting for the world to stabilise and the moment to pass.

Tom-and-Rosie let out a patter of applause and Plum squawked something stupid about Eastern Europeans. Marta reached for a nearby glass of water and took a gulp.

'*You OK?*' mouthed Holly, catching her eye. Marta nodded.

'Let's hope we can trust her with the plates!' squeaked Tash. A ripple of laughter travelled round the table. Feeling steadier, Marta pushed back her stool and started gathering nearby sets of cutlery.

There was a loud, metallic "clang" followed by a shattering sound, and then silence. Marta looked at the source of the noise. Her stool lay horizontal on the polished slate floor, the glass shards around it not quite hiding the jagged crack that ran through the marble-like tile.

'Evidently not,' muttered Hugh, grimacing.

'*Oops*,' added Plum, exchanging sly looks with Jack.

'I'll give you a hand,' Holly said quietly, following Marta out to the kitchen.

The physical damage didn't take long to repair. Marta swept the glass into the bin, while Holly covered the area with a plastic bag – nominally to prevent people cutting themselves, but Marta suspected it was largely to delay Tash's reaction to the broken tile. Marta's pride would take longer to mend.

'Brilliant! Sausages!' announced Hugh as the main courses were delivered with the utmost care. Marta watched Tash flinch at the reference. She too had made the mistake of calling them sausages earlier.

'Mini chorizo fingers,' the host corrected.

'Well, OK then...' Huge had a zealous look on his face, apparently undeterred by the correction. 'That means we can play a whole new game: Pass the Mini Chorizo Finger!'

Marta watched in disgust as Hugh slowly pushed the sausage into his mouth, then brought most of it out again, gripping the very tip with his teeth. Then, to her horror, he leaned towards her, the meat still trapped between his fat lips, and waggled it in front of her mouth.

What was this game? She leaned backwards, shying away from the abhorrent sight. *Why did they have to play games over dinner?* Marta didn't get it. *Why couldn't they just talk?* The laughter was deafening. Plum seemed to be caught up in a fit of hysterics. 'Take it from him!' yelled someone. 'Take the finger!'

Reluctantly, Marta opened her mouth and accepted the greasy sausage, biting only the very end, and avoiding Hugh's salacious gaze.

Marta had never been so close to such an obnoxious man. She was still feeling ill from the wine and on top of that there was a smell of putrid garlic, either from the meat or from the red-head's mouth; she couldn't tell. Slowly, with his eyes still locked onto hers, Hugh pulled away, leaving the sausage dangling from Marta's lips.

It became apparent that Marta was expected to pass it on to the person on her right. Unfortunately, this was Jeremy. Stiffly, she turned in her seat and focused hard on the end of the sausage. She was determined not to look at the giant nose looming on the horizon.

Plum's whooping was getting louder and Hugh was making comments under his breath that Marta didn't fully understand, but took to be dirty. Jeremy's nose eclipsed everything in her field of vision except the small stretch of meat and suddenly, it all just felt too disgusting and Marta jerked backwards, releasing her grip on the sausage.

It turned out that Jeremy hadn't fully engaged and before Marta had even licked the salt off her lips, the sausage came tumbling down between them, bounced off her leg and onto the floor.

'Rubbish! Only three!'

'Drink!'

'More wine!'

Marta's glass was topped up to the brim with wine, and this time it was white. The very sight of it made her feel sick.

'I can't,' she said, shaking her head.

'No such word!'

'I thought Poles could handle their drink!'

'Lightweight!'

The insults were coming thick and fast, but they didn't change her mind. She stood up, felt the world wobble, grabbed onto the table and promptly sat down again. The whole room was fluid. The oil painting opposite was changing shape and the carpet kept rising up to meet her. Slowly, Marta stood up again, picking her way towards the door via various pieces of furniture.

'I lie down. Feel funny,' she mumbled.

In the safety of her bedroom, with a litre of water and a slice of chleb from her mother's food parcel inside her, things felt better again. Marta wandered over to the en suite bathroom and leaned against the sink, staring at her reflection and trying to hold herself perfectly still. The red dress had worked its way up as she had climbed the stairs and now barely covered her buttocks. She looked like a stripper, thought Marta, drunkenly wondering how much strippers got paid in this country and whether they really did have to strip completely and whether...

Her bedroom door was creaking open.

'Hello?' called Marta, knowing who it would be. Holly was the only person in this house who cared – except Tash, but she only cared about her tenant's capacity for serving desserts, which was questionable now. Marta leaned out of the bathroom.

She jumped. It wasn't Holly. And it wasn't Tash either.

Jack was standing in the doorway. He had very muscular arms, Marta noted, distracted from the question of what he was doing in her bedroom.

'Just wanted to check you were OK,' he said, moving towards her. 'They gave you a pretty hard time down there.'

Marta nodded, suddenly remembering the fact that the flimsy dress had ridden up to her waist.

'No, don't do that,' said Jack, as she pulled the fabric down over her thighs. He was smiling. 'Leave it.'

Marta froze. Jack had his arm round her waist and her legs were entirely bare. He was stroking her hair, gently, telling her not to worry about what had happened downstairs. In other circumstances, she might have enjoyed being taken into the arms of such a handsome man. She might have relished breathing in the scent of his aftershave and allowed him to move his hand down, over her shoulder, onto her breast and to her nipple, all the while reassuring her in a deep, authoritative voice.

But the handsome guy was Tash's boyfriend. Marta pulled away, stumbling backwards towards the bed. Jack followed. With one hand still cupping her breast and the other around her waist, he moved with her. She tried to spin free, but her coordination was out and she felt weak in his powerful grasp.

'No!' she hissed, too afraid to speak out. The bedroom door was half open and there was every chance one of the guests – or worse, Tash – would come looking for her.

Marta twisted, but Jack moved with her, pulling her off balance and sending the pair of them tumbling onto the bed.

'Oh, it's like that, is it?' asked Jack, smiling down on her as he pinned her arms to the bed. His body was hot and heavy on top of her and she could feel his erection. 'God, you're beautiful.'

'Jack, please–' Marta writhed, but her struggles were futile. He was crushing her.

'Shhhh,' he coaxed, waiting for her to be still. 'Don't worry.'

His breath smelt of wine. He was drunk. Marta felt instantly sober.

'Marta, I need to stell – I need to tell you something,' he slurred. 'I… I want you,' he whispered, lowering himself upon her again. 'Not Tash. I want you. I wanna fuck you.'

Marta lay still for a second. For the first time, she felt scared: not just scared of what Tash might say if she found out, but scared of what Jack could force her to do.

Suddenly, his lips were touching hers, gently at first and then with more force. His tongue worked its way into her mouth. Marta tried to turn, but he had pinned her hair to the bed and she was trapped in his embrace, forced into silence by the fear of being found. The panic rose up inside her. It was like a nightmare. She wanted to cry out for help, but she couldn't.

It stopped as quickly as it had started. They both heard it at once: the sound of footsteps on the stairs. Marta's heart started pounding. Jack quickly rolled off her and over the side of the bed. The creaking stopped. The floor on the landing had thick-pile carpet, which made no sound. Marta waited. Jack's stifled panting was making her nervous.

Marta rearranged herself on the bed, smoothing down the rumpled duvet and running a hand through her knotted hair. Her dress was twisted and it seemed impossible to find a position that didn't reveal either her pants or part of her bra.

'How are you feeling, Marta?' chirped a voice out of nowhere. In walked Plum, her eyes boring straight into Marta's with a very unconvincing smile.

'Er, not good. Too much wine.' Marta pulled a silly face.

'Mmm. Yes. It's amazing what wine can make people do, isn't it? Anyway, I'm sure you'll be fine. I'll leave you *alone*. See you downstairs in a bit, yeah? Hope you feel better.'

16

'No thanks,'
    'I'm in a rush.'
    'Fuck off!'

Some parts of London, Marta had learned, were better than others for handing out leaflets. Oxford Street was one of the worst. The crowds were so densely packed that oncoming pedestrians had no way of seeing the proffered leaflet until they had walked past, and most of them couldn't read English anyway.

A Japanese man grinned back at her through the lens of a camera and a sea of heads, pausing briefly to frame his shot and then moving on, ignoring her offer of two-for-one at participating opticians. Marta wanted to scream. For nearly three hours she had woven paths in the thick stream of bodies, dodging, chasing, waving and smiling. She had only managed to shift a hundred leaflets.

Her patience boiled dry. *There had to be a better way*, she thought, remembering the small success she had had with the gym flyers the other week. Swimming against the flow of shoppers, Marta headed down a side street, enjoying the relative freedom and personal space. She could hear her mother's words in her ears. *When you come to a problem you can't solve in an hour, spend the next hour doing something else*. Well, she had spent too long on this one already.

CHEAP INTERNET. £2/HOUR, read the sign, held up by a corpse-like man. Marta followed the arrow and slipped through the narrow doorway.

Slinging her leaflet-filled rucksack onto the counter, she fished out two pound coins and followed the man's vague nod towards the terminal in the corner. There was something comforting about internet cafés, she decided, weaving between broken swivel chairs and wooden desks. The gentle tap of fingers on keys, the muted hum of concentration... it was strangely soothing.

Marta stared, unseeing, as the machine flashed up a series of login screens. The day's frustration could not be entirely attributed to the reluctance of tourists to take her leaflets. In fact, the sense of impending doom hat had plagued her for more than forty-eight hours was nothing to do with her job; it was to do with Saturday night. Two-and-a-half days had passed and nobody had said a word. Jack hadn't been round and, to her knowledge, Tash hadn't spoken to Plum since leaving the house in the early hours of Sunday. The memory of that moment with Jack on the bed kept playing through her mind and she was finding it increasingly difficult to keep it inside her.

I have so many unanswered questions, Anka,

she typed, her fingers darting wildly across the keyboard.

Why did he do it? Was it an accident? Does he even remember?
I'm scared of what will happen when he comes round again. And
how much did Plum see? I'm so scared she'll tell Tash!

Marta stopped typing. There was another question she wanted to add, but she didn't know whether she dared. She stared at the smeary, pixelated screen, thinking. Then she hammered out the words.

I know this sounds crazy, Anka, but I keep wondering...
Was it a bad thing, what happened? I mean, apart from
the fact that he's going out with Tash, he's kind of nice.
Sexy. Always in control, if you know what I mean. And I
think he really does like me. Help!

It felt so good to let it all out. It was like coming to the surface and finally breathing after spending too long under water. The response would not be instant, of course, but at least the problem was off her chest. Marta had shared her dirty secret. And although Anka would be hundreds of miles away, confined to the shop floor of the Łomianki bakery, when she got Marta's email, she would understand. She would know what to do.

The sleeves of her beautiful turquoise jacket were getting grubby, she noticed, jiggling the mouse and clicking *send*. There was a lump in her throat as she watched the screen change. *Sent to Anka Kowalczyk*, it said. Suddenly her old life – her friends, her village, her brother, sister, parents and home – seemed infinitely far away, both in distance and in time.

Shaking herself, Marta emptied her inbox of junk, logged off and bent down for her rucksack. As she did so, her mobile phone vibrated in her pocket.

'*Słucham?*' whispered Marta, hurrying out of the café with a brief nod at the dozing man behind the desk.

'Marta? It's me!' Loud, excitable and Polish, Marta recognised the voice in an instant.

'Anka! How strange; I just emailed you.'

'Why d'you think I'm calling? Seriously, Marta, your life is *so exciting!*'

Marta smiled, leaning her rucksack against a wall and perching on it, half focusing on the feet of passersby. The sound of Anka's voice brought back the lump in her throat. Virtually everything in Marta's life, now and in the past, instilled boisterous enthusiasm in her best friend. Perhaps it was because Anka maintained such a narrow, risk-free existence. Maybe Marta was doing all the things Anka wanted to do but wasn't quite brave enough to try – but the truth was, it didn't feel exciting. Not exactly.

'So, more information, please! What exactly happened that night? And I want to hear more about the Polish leaflet man. He sounds cute too. Oh, Marta, your life is like a soap opera! So ridiculous!'

'Ridiculous is the right word,' Marta replied, wryly. 'It's good to hear your voice. How's things? What's going on in your world?'

'Oh, shut up about that! I'm fine, nothing's going on in my world and things in Łomianki are exactly the same as when you left us, except that everyone is two months older and everything happens a little slower, on average, now that you're not here.'

Marta grinned. 'I don't believe you. Has nothing changed at all? What about the mural on the side of the church hall? Is that finished? Weren't they going to put in some traffic bollards on –'

'Marta, shut up! Tell me about your men!'

Feeling herself relax a little, Marta obliged. It was easier to talk about Dominik, so she started with him. She told Anka about the phone and the bike and the soup and the wine, the rusty scooter and messy hair and smiling eyes.

'Enough!' yelled Anka as she started going into too much detail about their night at his place in Acton. 'He sounds lovely.'

'He is,' Marta replied thoughtfully.

'And the other one? The one that nearly *raped* you?'

'Anka! It wasn't–'

'Well, nearly!'

'No,' replied Marta, trying to sound sure. 'He wouldn't have. It was just... I don't know. The thing is, I think he likes me. I mean, *really*. I don't think it was just the wine talking. He gives me these looks when nobody can see, and... well, anyway, I shouldn't even be considering going near him, because of Tash.'

'What? The rich bitch who can't brush her hair without your help? What's she got to do with it? What right does *she* have to dictate–'

'She's going out with Jack. Didn't I mention that?'

'Er... no.' The line went quiet. 'Well, that changes things slightly.'

'Slightly.'

'So, to clarify,' Anka said slowly, after a long pause, 'your house-mate's boyfriend came onto you at your housemate's dinner party and your housemate's mate *may* have caught you two at it on your bed – and you think this might be a good basis for a relationship.'

'We weren't 'at it'! I didn't have any say in the—'

'Ah, so it *was* nearly rape then, was it?'

Marta grunted, defeated. It was true; Jack had held her against her will. Sort of. The memory had blurred in her mind and looking back it didn't seem so unpleasant. In fact, it seemed... well, that was it. She couldn't explain. She was confused.

'So,' Anka went on, 'you're having trouble deciding between option one, Polish Leaflet Man with the cute smile, thoughtful gestures and, from what I can tell, a soft-spot for you, and option two, the English Cheat with the chiselled looks, unpleasant manner, possible alcohol problem – oh, and a girlfriend who happens to be your landlady. Tough decision, Marta. Very tough.'

Marta snorted and remained silent. She wanted to fight back but couldn't think of a point worth making. For all her anxieties, Anka knew how to construct a good case.

'You're right,' she said finally.

'I know. Shit – I'd better go. The bagels are due out. Just promise me this, OK? Promise you'll have nothing more to do with the stupid English boy except to smile politely when he comes round to see his *girlfriend*.'

Marta smiled, pleased to hear such clear advice. 'OK.'

'Promise?'

'Promise. Thanks, Anka.'

'No worries. I like a good drama – but only when it's got a happy ending. I miss you, Marta. We all do.'

Marta's throat clogged up again. 'Miss you too,' she managed, hearing the clatter of the bagel rescue operation in the background. 'Bye.'

She pushed the phone into her pocket, dusting herself down and hauling the rucksack onto her back. As she did so, the phone bleeped. Marta pulled it out again. It was a message from a number she didn't recognise.

Hi Marta, Jack here. I'm sorry. Call if U want. J

Marta stared at the text. She read it four times. Anka's words were still echoing around her head. Nothing more to do with him. Nothing. She reread the SMS one more time, then pressed delete and locked the keypad.

17

'Hello?' Marta said timidly. The display flashed up a London number, but it wasn't one she recognised.

'D'you want the good news or the bad?' asked a gruff male voice.

'Uh, sorry… I…' Marta stammered, wondering whether it was a wrong number.

'I said, *good or bad*,' the man growled down the line, conjuring an image of his face. It was Barry Roffey.

'Um, good,' Marta replied, feeling her hand shake against her ear. Why was Mr Roffey calling her at the end of her shift on a Tuesday?

'Well the good news is that you're getting paid early this week. Like now. In my office. Quick as you can. Get y'skinny little arse over 'ere. By my reckoning, that should be fifteen minutes, if you're where you're supposed to be, which you're probably not. I'll tell y'the bad news when you get 'ere.'

Marta stammered something back, but the line was dead.

It had crossed her mind earlier that she should pop into a couple of the sports stores she had frequented the previous week and try to offload a few more leaflets on them. Surely contact lenses were essential eyewear for serious sportsmen? They would welcome a two-for-one offer from participating opticians. However, the tone of Mr Roffey's voice indicated that the priority for her was to get to his office, rather than distributing the rest of her load. She would find a suitable skip on the way to Queensway and dump them in there, taped up in the plastic bag; the same routine she went through at the end of every day.

It worried her that she had been summoned to her boss' office partway through the week. Pay day was Saturday and she had never before had any communication with Mr Roffey except to pick up her load or her pay packet. She didn't like his tone, either.

There was a litter bin opposite the Hyde Park gates that served her purpose, enabling Marta to climb the dirty stairs with a near-empty rucksack. There were just a few bundles knocking about at the bottom to avoid suspicion.

Barry Roffey was talking to someone in his office. As she raised her hand to knock, she faltered. He was talking on the phone. 'I understand, yes, she shouldn't have done that... Yes, no I know, she's on her way as we speak... Oh, she'll certainly get that, I can assure you... Well, not working for *me*, that's for sure...'

Marta's knuckles drifted away from the door. The snatches of conversation frightened her. Was Barry referring to something she had done? Marta was probably one of his most productive workers; Dominik reckoned so, anyway. Marta's thoughts were beginning to spiral out of control when a loud crash cut them off. It was the phone being slammed into its cradle. Marta seized the moment.

'Come in,' growled her boss.

Barry Roffey's face was a deep purple colour. Reclined in his rickety chair, his rolls of fat hanging out through the gaps and his arms dangling by his sides, Barry's neck and face were visibly pulsating. *Poor heart*, was Marta's first thought on seeing him. *Oh shit*, was her next.

'Marta Da-*brow*-ski,' he snarled, as she inched carefully across the cluttered room. Marta glanced at his face and decided it would be unwise to correct him on his pronunciation of her surname. 'What the FUCK do you think you've been doing?'

'Am sorry?'

'You're sorry?' Barry leant forward, causing the chair to creak ominously. 'You *will* be.'

Marta swallowed nervously.

'I been hearing bad things about you. I been hearing you been dumping leaflets *illegally!*'

Marta could feel the blood pumping ferociously in her ears. This was it. This was the end of her first job in England. And all because someone had found a few leaflets in a skip somewhere – probably not more than twenty – and somehow, God only knew how, they had traced it back to her.

'It was very few–'

'*Very few!*' Barry paused for a second, lowering his voice. 'I've had four complaints about you, Marta Dabraska. *Four!* You've made enemies all over London, as far as I can tell, and that's enemies of the company. *My* company.'

Marta frowned. Four complaints? This didn't make sense. She had been careful about dumping the unused leaflets – never leaving them in the same place twice, always wrapping them, taking care not to be seen...

'Did I tell you to go wanderin' into shops and leisure centres, bullying junior staff into taking your leaflets? Did I? Did I tell you to spend your time millin' round cafés and dropping piles of the things on their counters? NO! I FUCKING WELL DID NOT!'

Marta's frown deepened. So *this* was what it was about. It wasn't the end-of-day dumping; it was her efforts to be innovative. Her attempts at targeted marketing.

'I did not bullying–' Marta couldn't summon her English fast enough.

'Don't fuckin' argue with me.' Barry stared at her, exhaling noisily through fat-blocked nostrils. 'I'm the one who's fendin' off the fuckin' complaints. I've 'ad people threaten to *close me down*, I 'ave. CLOSE ME DOWN.'

'But the workers, they tell me...' Marta's voice petered out.

Barry Roffey was shaking his head, slowly and angrily. 'I've sacked people for being lazy. I've sacked 'em for cheatin', for stealin' – even for rollin' up leaflets an' smokin' 'em. But *never* 'ave I got rid of someone for fuckin' *tresspassin' in shops an' forcin' leaflets on–*'

'I did not force on any people,' she blurted, trying to match her boss for volume. 'I just thought it to be enterprising to–'

'I DON'T PAY YOU TO BE ENTERPRISING!' Barry exploded.

Marta fell quiet. The sound of Barry's laboured breathing filled the room.

'Take this,' he said finally. 'It's y'last two days' pay. More than you deserve, but I'm a decent guy like that. Take it and fuck off out of my office. And *don't come back.*'

Marta snatched the envelope and marched out. She was still shaking, but it was no longer nerves that filled her bloodstream, it was rage. She had been sacked; sacked from one of the most basic jobs in the world. She had been sacked for trying to employ common sense.

The journey through Queensway, across the park and through Kensington passed in a blur, angry thoughts blotting the sounds and sights from her mind. How had this happened? Why had the store managers complained? What was wrong with a bit of cross-selling? She had only tried it in places where the leaflets were appropriate for the shops' target customers and *never* against the will of the shop staff. There were so many rules in this country! In Poland, nobody would lose their job over something like this. Never!

She stormed through Kensington, thoughts crashing round her head. Part of the blame, she acknowledged, lay with her for mis-interpreting the terms of her contract, for being too bold. She had forgotten that things happened differently in London. Everything was regulated. That was why they didn't have roadside snack bars, why there were no flower stalls in Leicester Square, why even the buskers had to stand in silly marked 'zones'. There were rules for everything. Maybe it would take some time to adjust.

By the time she reached the steps of 14 Egerton Square, it was nearly dark. The flames licked up the pillars that flanked the doorway, casting an orange glow on the object that lay by the front door.

It looked like a parcel or a box of some kind, but as she stepped closer, Marta realised what it was. In the orange, flickering light, she could just make out the familiar red stripe along its side. There was no doubt: it was Mama's old suitcase.

Mystified, Marta opened the door to shed light on the case situation, dumping her jacket in the hallway. Her investigation was brought to an abrupt halt by an ear-splitting scream.

'*You little bitch!*' screeched the voice. It came from inside the house and it was getting louder.

Marta leapt backwards, half-tripping down the steps and landing with her foot in a flower pot, dangerously close to one of the flames.

The tall, slender silhouette of Tash, clad in a tight-fitting evening dress and heels, appeared like an apparition in the doorway. 'I can't believe you have the audacity to come *near* this house, you scrawny little *peasant!* Just fuck off back to your country and don't come back. *Ever!*'

The door slammed shut and Marta heard the bolt being drawn across. *Scrawny little peasant?* Marta's English didn't stretch to those words, but she could infer the meaning from the context. She edged away from the door, feeling a mixture of anger and humiliation. Tash's cheeks had appeared swollen and streaked, Marta thought. It was obvious what had happened. Plum had told Tash what she had seen on Saturday night.

Maybe Plum had even embellished what she saw, thought Marta, reaching for the tatty suitcase. That girl had no scruples. It would be just her style to twist things to get into Tash's good books or, more likely, into Jack's pants.

For several seconds Marta stood looking up at the huge front door, coming to terms with what had just happened. Then she hauled the leaden case from the ground and headed back in the direction she had just come. She had been told to fuck off for the second time that day. It seemed that she had no option but to do exactly that.

18

Rain hammered against the café window, almost rivalling Aretha Franklin, who was wailing from the tinny stereo behind the bar. Marta watched the droplets run down the outside of the steamed-up panes, glowing red in the glow of tail lights from a passing car.

She looked up. The waitress was blinking at her with a slightly frightened expression. Marta stopped blowing bubbles in her milk and let the straw slither out of her mouth.

'You want order food?' she asked. Her accent was Polish.

Marta shook her head. She considered responding in their native tongue and striking up a conversation. Maybe the girl could help find her a place to stay? Maybe a job, too.

'No thanks,' she replied in her best English. She would get through this on her own.

She had nowhere to live. It was raining outside and dark. The café closed in twenty minutes. Marta gnawed on the straw. Living with Tash had been difficult, to say the least, but it had been warm and spacious – and cheap, compared with even the most basic of London hotels. She had had an en suite bathroom, for God's sake... and her own TV. She had taken it all for granted. The more she dwelt on what she had lost, the more attractive the option of striking up a conversation with the waitress became.

She had no source of income. It had taken her more than a fortnight to get the job with Barry Roffey and now she was back to square one, with a blank English CV and no chance of a reference from her former employer. The brown envelope in her wallet contained three days' salary, so Marta had just under three hundred English pounds in total. That wouldn't last long.

The priority, she knew, was to find somewhere to go tonight. There was only one place Marta could think of: one place where she would feel welcome, where she might get a home-cooked meal and where there were so many people sleeping on the floor that one more wouldn't make any difference. She pulled out her phone.

'Hi, it's me,' she gabbled the instant he picked up.

The line went dead.

'Hello? Dominik? Hello?'

Marta stared for a second at the dormant handset. She redialled and waited while it rang. *Brrrr, brrrr.* She listened impatiently to the monotonous ring, trying to keep her temper under control. *Brrrr, brrrr.* She lost count of the number of rings. *Brrrr, brrrr.* Eventually, Dominik's voicemail interrupted and then his message: first in Polish, then English.

'Leave me a message and I'll call you back. Keep it short please. Whatever they say, length does matter.'

'Hi Dominik, it's me,' she said quickly. 'Can you call me back? It's urgent. I... I need a place to stay tonight. Maybe for a week. It's... a long story. Can you call me as soon as you get this?'

Marta ended the call and checked her balance. £2.29. The disadvantage of this stolen phone was that you could only get pay-as-you-go packages that seemed to eat through the credit. She slurped up the last of her milk and tried not to think about Tash's outburst. She had been upset. She was a sensitive girl, Marta knew that. It was probably a perfectly reasonable reaction to whatever Plum had told her, Marta decided, before pushing her glass away and accepting that she was lying to herself. She hated them both. She hated them all: Tash, Plum, Jack, Tom-and-Rosie... the whole lot of them. They were enemies to her. Aliens. She didn't belong in their world and never would.

Marta checked her watch and thought about calling Dominik again. Perhaps he was on the tube. Maybe he had gone into a tunnel before. Or maybe he'd had another call waiting and taken that. She picked up the sticky menu and gazed, unseeing, at its text. Down, up. Down, up. She picked up the phone and pressed redial.

The phone rang a couple of times and then the voicemail kicked in prematurely. Marta stopped the call quickly, but not quickly enough to prevent 20p being wiped from her balance. She slumped back against the plastic, foam-filled seat. Marta knew what it meant when a call went to voicemail partway through a ring. It meant that the recipient had pressed *reject*. Dominik had rejected her.

Marta pondered this odd behaviour. The last time she had seen Dominik, he was his usual cheeky self; dodging death on his scooter, carrying leaflets about town, laughing and joking about how much he hated his job. They'd had a coffee before starting work and he had suggested meeting up again for a meal some time. Why would he reject her like that?

Marta jumped as her phone started vibrating in her hand. It was a message. A message from Dominik.

DON'T CALL THIS NUMBER AGAIN.

Marta stared at the capitalised words. *What?* He was cutting her out of his life? Marta wondered whether Dominik was playing some kind of joke, or whether he had swapped phones with someone and not told her. She thought about calling him to find out, but the message was disconcerting. It scared her.

The waitress approached timidly, her body language telling Marta what she already knew.

'We close now,' she whispered apologetically.

Marta nodded. She dropped the semi-masticated straw in the glass and handed it over. Aretha Franklin's backing girls were silenced, mid-chorus, and suddenly the only sound was the pounding rain on the window. The waitress flicked the main lights, casting a guilty glance in Marta's direction. Perhaps she understood, thought Marta. Perhaps she too had been in this situation and recognised the look of despair on Marta's face.

What now? Marta suddenly felt incredibly lonely. She was sitting in a closed, dark café in a strange city with nowhere to go and no one to call. There was literally no one. Her bottom lip began to tremble and she could feel tears start to build up behind her eyes.

'*Everybody out!*' yelled a voice. Through the tears, Marta watched as a fearsome-looking woman with dyed red hair stepped out of the kitchen, waving a broom in Marta's direction. It really was time to go. But where?

Marta hauled her suitcase out from under the table and rose to her feet. Everything she owned was crammed into that old leather box; at least, she hoped it was. She hadn't even checked. Sniffing miserably, she lugged whatever it was through the café door.

The rain lashed down on her face, soaking her skin almost instantly. It was only as she tried to manoeuvre herself under a newsagent's awning and felt a large, cold droplet trickle down the back of her neck that Marta realised something. She had left her jacket at Tash's.

Marta collapsed on the ground, sobbing. Anka had given her that jacket. She had spent half a month's earnings on the beautiful thing and now it was hanging in Tash's hallway, or lying in her dustbin, and there was almost no hope of ever seeing it again.

Where was Dominik? Why had he deserted her? Two days earlier he had asked her to dinner again and now he was gone, cutting her out of his life. Something must have happened. Marta wiped a hand across her wet face, trying to pull herself together. It was impossible. Everything just seemed so bleak. She had nothing to live for in England.

Marta's hand wrapped around her phone again. She needed to pour everything out to her best friend. She started to dial and then stopped. She couldn't spend her last £2.09 on an emotional conversation with Anka. It would upset her friend, which would upset Marta even more, and then they would both be in floods of tears, Marta would have no credit left and she would *still* have no place to stay. Despite everything, she had to think rationally.

Marta's fingers were numb and it took a while to work the stiff latch on the suitcase. Eventually, the lock slid open. Leaving only a small opening for her wrist, she reached inside. To her relief, she found herself touching the familiar fabrics of her belongings. She felt her way through the mess, finally recognising the texture of her old hooded top and pulling it out.

Before closing the suitcase, Marta slipped her hand back inside and felt around in the secret lining. Another wave of relief washed over her as she felt the wiry wool of her old sock and the roll of notes inside. Kneeling on the dirty tarmac, she counted it. Three hundred and twenty pounds, including this week's pay. That was nearly two thousand złoty. In Poland, that would be enough to live on for a month, but here it would barely last a week. Some youth hostels charged £20 per night, according to Dominik, but Marta had no idea where to start looking. A crazy idea was starting to form in her head. It involved a bus trip to Heathrow and a last-minute flight back to Poland.

Marta sucked in a deep breath and wiped a sleeve across her wet forehead. She *couldn't* return to Poland after just two months. That would make her a failure. Two months and she had barely broken even, once you factored in the airfare and the £100 Tata had given her, which Marta was determined to pay back. She had intended to come to England and start a career. She wanted to make her family proud. She couldn't face sloping off home with her tail between her legs, explaining to everyone that England had proved too much for her.

At least she had a good grasp of the language, thought Marta, brightening slightly at the thought of the waitress who could hardly speak English. *She* had a job. *She* was getting by. If she and thousands like her could do it, then Marta could too.

Suddenly, inspiration struck. There *was* someone else she knew over here: someone who spoke no English, but who might be able to help her. He had certainly seemed friendly enough and she knew he had contacts over here...

Marta pulled out her wallet, rummaging among the notes and folded receipts and finally pulling out the torn-off piece of cigarette packet with the phone number of Lukasz's friend.

'*Słucham?*' someone slurred, when the phone was finally picked up. There was a lot of shouting and shrieking in the background, above the sound of garage music.

'Hi!' shouted Marta in Polish. 'I'm a friend of Lu–'

There was a clattering sound as though the receiver had been dropped on a hard tiled floor, then another whooping noise. After some more clattering, the guy's voice came on again. 'What?'

'Is Lukasz there?' Marta asked loudly.

'Who?'

Marta sighed impatiently. This was costing her money. 'Where are you?'

'London!' replied the guy, laughing like a hyena. He was clearly off his head.

'Where exactly?'

There was a sharp 'ding', a bubbling noise, and then silence.

£1.69. That was all she had left and she wasn't any closer to finding a home for the night. In desperation, she scrolled through her messages, wondering whether there was a trace of the one Jack had sent her. Not that she relished the idea of begging anything from Jack, who was the root of all her home-related problems. Despite the cold, Marta was glad she hadn't retained his number.

She stared into the darkness, thinking about Dominik and what might have happened. A hundred possibilities spooled through her mind, none of them plausible. She wanted him more than ever. She wanted an explanation. She wanted a place to stay, and most of all she wanted to feel a pair of arms around her.

Stuffing the soggy piece of card back in her wallet, Marta prepared to make the journey to Acton. It was a bold move and she felt nervous about what might await her, but it was her only option.

Her wallet wouldn't shut properly. There was something inside that didn't quite fit in the notes section with all the other bits of paper and junk. She pulled it out, folded it in two and stuffed it back in, yanking the zip shut. Then she opened it again. Her heart started pounding as she realised what it was that had been sticking out. It was Holly Banks' business card.

With a shaking hand, Marta punched the number into her phone.

19

Marta stepped out of the bath and rubbed herself dry with the thin, green towel she had been given. There was a stain in the corner and it felt rough on her skin, but it smelt clean enough. She thought back to the soft, fluffy white robes that had hung from the heated rails in her private bathroom and smiled. Old towels didn't matter. Nor did brown marks on the bath or blobs of toothpaste all over the sink.

In the steamy fug, Marta could feel herself beginning to relax. In fact, the anxiety had started to ebb almost as soon as she had been shown through the paint-stripped front door and stepped over the mound of junk mail. Even crossing Kilburn High Road and seeing the handmade sign advertising "Cheap phone calls to Eastern Europe" had lifted her mood.

The streets were bustling, even at nine o'clock at night, and not with the type of people that filled the tree-lined Kensington roads. There were no super-slim mothers with pushchairs, no dolled-up rich kids with straight, whitened teeth, no city slickers in pinstripes. These were real people: men spilling out of betting shops, mums smacking rampant toddlers, drunkards singing, babies screaming... And Marta liked it.

'Time for a drink?' asked Holly, as Marta crept into the kitchen wearing a borrowed tracksuit. Her own clothes were tumbling round and round in the dryer, her suitcase having proved about as water-proof as a flannel.

'Yes please.'

Holly peered into a cupboard and then withdrew, looking unconvinced. 'OK. Looks like Rich has drunk most of my stash, so it's beer or beer, I'm afraid. D'you drink beer? I could do tea or—'

'Beer is good,' Marta said gratefully. 'Who is Rich?'

'Oh – housemate. There are two: Rich and Tina. We're all friends from uni – but don't worry, they're not from the same bunch as Tash and that lot. Rich was an engineer with me and Tina I know from hockey.'

Marta nodded. She accepted her beer and looked around the tiny kitchen. The house had a cramped, cosy feel, like Dominik's – only this one seemed mildly more hygienic.

'So,' said Holly, sitting down at the mini kitchen table and kicking out a chair for Marta. 'Not a good day, then?'

Marta smiled. She cracked open her beer and took a swig straight from the can. *This* was how drinks were supposed to be served; not with ice and a twist of organic lime.

'So, you were halfway through telling me about Jack. What happened after Plum caught you two together?'

'Nothing.' She shook her head. 'Nothing. So I think, is OK. I don't need to worry. Nobody know what happened and Plum, she will not say anything.'

'And then what?'

'Well, then I get home today – no, wait. I forget something. He send me a message.'

'Who, Jack?'

'Yes. It says *sorry*.'

Holly screwed up her face. 'Did you reply?'

'No. I throw away as soon as it come. I don't want nothing to do with Jack.'

Holly gulped down her beer, nodding. 'Damn right. What a git.'

'So then I get home today and Tash, she put all my things in the suitcase and leave in the garden and I go inside and she come out from somewhere, nearly push me down the steps. She stare at me and says, "Get out and fuck off back to Poland, you bitch peasant,"

113

or something like this. She was *scary*, Holly. Very scary. I wanted to explain, but couldn't. She shut the door. What is *peasant?*'

Holly shook her head, taking a large sip of beer. Once she had swallowed, she looked at Marta. 'Did you try and explain?'

'I wanted tell her it was him, her boyfriend, but I don't get time. She was upset. I look at her face and it was red, like she was crying, you know?'

Holly nodded. 'I suspect Plum might have employed a little artistic licence when recounting what she saw to Tash. She's like that.'

Marta looked at Holly for a moment. 'But you are friends?'

Holly shook her head, wearing a dry smile. 'Not really. I wasn't friends with that lot. I got to know them when Tash and I shared a room. On her own, Tash is alright. She's insecure, but deep down… Well, I dunno. I may have read her wrong. Anyway, my real friends are people like Tina and Rich.'

'I don't understand them,' Marta admitted. 'They are so *compli-cated*.'

Holly nodded. 'Very true.'

Marta took another sip and thought about the 'Kensington lot', wondering what it was that made them so different; or rather, what made Marta different from them. Maybe it all came down to money, she conceded. All their lives they had had people to do things for them: nannies to change their nappies, parents to drive them around, tutors to school them through exams, friends to get them jobs. Mama always said it was healthy to experience some hardship in life. For Tash's gang, hardship was being told by the waiter that their favourite dish was no longer on the menu and that they would have to pick again.

There was a noise as though someone was trying to break the latch on the front door.

'That's Rich,' Holly explained calmly. 'His key doesn't work very well.'

The scratching noise was followed by a heavy thud, then a grunt, then the sound of the front door slamming. Holly leaned back in her chair and poked her head round the doorway. 'Hi!'

Rich was tall. He had light blond hair, freckly cheeks and blue eyes that crinkled naturally into a smile; a smile directed at Holly.

'Meet Rich. He's a defected engineer, like—'

'Defective?' Rich interrupted. 'I was perfectly good!'

'Defect-*ed*.' Holly rolled her eyes. 'He's doing a teacher training course. I know, poor kids. Rich, this is Marta. We're rescuing her from the evil clutches of Tash Gordon. She'll be staying on our lounge floor for a bit. Hope that's OK.'

'Cool. Nice to meet you.' Rich bounded over and shook Marta's hand. 'Welcome to the cesspit.'

Marta frowned, still smiling. She didn't know what a 'sex pit' was, but it sounded rude.

'He means it's a dump. Which it is,' Holly explained. 'You probably noticed that.'

Marta smiled. 'You never see my place back in Poland.'

'By the way, Rich, I see you've devoured our drinks cupboard with the exception of the dubious liqueur with no label,' Holly commented.

Rich pulled a face. 'Ah. That was the guys this weekend. I'll replenish it right away. Well, soon. At some point. In the meantime, I guess there's no chance of a beer, is there?'

Holly rolled her eyes and reached backwards, yanking the fridge door open.

Rich tore open his can, ruffling Holly's hair and pulling out a seat next to hers. 'So, what d'you do, Marta?' he asked.

Marta faltered. This was the part she hadn't yet told Holly.

'I...'

'You work in marketing, don't you?' prompted Holly.

Marta exhaled uncomfortably. 'Well, I would like to. But today I lost my job.'

'How careless,' joked Rich, swigging into his beer. 'Where did you last see it?'

'Shut up, Rich. What d'you mean?'

'Well, I had this job. And today, the boss he call me into his

115

office and tell me I make too much trouble, so I must leave. So now I have no job.'

Marta was beginning to feel upset, just telling them. Maybe alcohol on an empty stomach was a bad idea. Her bottom lip was beginning to tremble. She knew what the next question would be, and she didn't want to answer it.

'Trouble? What were you doing?' asked Holly.

This was it. This was where Marta had to explain that the last few weeks of her life had been spent standing on street corners handing out pieces of paper.

'I… well…' Marta collected herself. She was going to have to tell them. 'My job was leaflets,' she said. 'It was giving out leaflets. Silly job, I know. But I couldn't get any better. My English is not perfect, so cannot do marketing here, they tell me. So I give out leaflets, you know?'

Holly nodded. Rich was squinting into his beer can as though something unexpected was floating inside it.

'So anyway, these leaflets, they for all kinds of things. Sometimes gyms, sometimes phone calls, sometimes banks… all sorts. So when I give out these things, I start to think, *Why I don't put these leaflets in clever places, where right people will see them?* You know, like leaflets for gym in sports shops, and leaflets for optician in old-people coffee shops… but the places, some of them don't like me putting the leaflets. Some get angry. They call Mr Roffey, my boss, and he contact me, and bang! My job is gone, 'cause I am troublemaker.'

Holly was looking at her with a puzzled expression.

'He fired you because you were putting some thought into his clients' marketing strategies?'

Marta nodded sadly.

'Well the guy's an idiot, then! He doesn't deserve to have you on his payroll.'

Marta managed a smile. It was nice of Holly to be on her side, but it didn't change the situation.

'Tell you what,' said Holly, looking intently into Marta's eyes. 'I've got a few ideas about where you might wanna work. Places that *value* initiative instead of sapping it out of you.'

Marta's head shot up. 'You do?'

Holly nodded vaguely, looking into space.

Rich leaned towards Marta. '*She's having a brainwave,*' he confided.

Before the brainwave could materialise, however, there was another sound at the front door, this time more of a battering noise, as though someone was ramming a large object against it.

'Tina,' both Holly and Rich declared simultaneously.

'She's drunk,' added Rich, leaning sideways to get a view of the small hallway. Then he jerked back to the table. '*And not alone,*' he added in a whisper.

Marta sat quietly, watching Rich watch Holly, who was watching the door. Eventually, after an extra-loud thump, footsteps could be heard from the hallway.

'*Now she's instructing the guy to go into her room,*' whispered Holly, tilting back on her chair at quite an extreme angle. '*Ooh, and now she's heading this way.*' She and Rich swung back to the table and took sips of beer.

'Hi Tina!' cried Holly, with mock surprise that was lost on the striking black girl whose long legs were carrying her in a wobbly fashion across the kitchen towards the tap.

Marta watched as the girl filled her second glass of water. Her eyes shone out against her dark complexion, wandering all over the place but retaining a defiant beauty. She was dressed in a tight-fitting suit with impressively high heels.

'Hello! Ooh, hi. You don't live here.'

'Well observed,' said Rich, shaking the droplets off his shoe as Tina tottered over, water sloshing over the sides of her glass.

'Actually, she does,' replied Holly. 'She's staying for a bit. Marta, meet Tina. Tina's a professional pisshead and part-time trader at JC Morley.'

'Nice t'meet you,' slurred Tina, tripping over her own foot and landing in Rich's lap. 'Ooh. Hello.'

Rich carefully righted his housemate and propelled her towards the door. 'I think you'd better get back to your room, hadn't you?' He gave her a meaningful smile.

'Hmm. Yeah, well goodnight everyone. Goodnight – hic – Martha!'

They all waited until the footsteps had receded into Tina's bedroom and then burst out laughing.

'Well, that's Tina. I think that just about sums her up, don't you?' said Holly.

'I'd say so.'

Marta laughed. 'She seems nice.'

'She's great,' Rich nodded. 'It's just a pity she needs men in pinstriped suits to tell her that.'

'C'mon, Rich.' Holly rolled her eyes. 'She's only having fun.'

'Sorry. It's just that I've got the room next to hers.' He rose to his feet. 'Which is where I'm heading. With earplugs. G'night all. Sleep well.'

Rich disappeared with a final glance in the direction of Holly, who didn't seem to notice. Draining her can, she slowly crushed it in one hand and then turned to Marta.

'You must be knackered. Wanna go to bed?'

Marta nodded. She hadn't had a chance to notice before now, but she was exhausted.

Lying on the sofa bed beneath Holly's sheets and a hairy eiderdown, Marta let her eyes fall shut. Almost immediately, she slipped into a semi-lucid state in which shapes moved and morphed, and sounds ebbed and flowed. Just as she felt herself floating off into another place, there was a creaking noise. A shaft of light fell across her eyes.

'I was thinking, Marta.'

Marta hauled her mind back to reality. Holly was standing in the doorway with a glass of water in her hand. 'I know it's easy for me to say, because I grew up in this country and I went to a uni that everyone recognises and I'll probably never have a problem getting work… but I think you'll do fine here. You don't need to push yourself so hard. I know you've got to earn money and you want a career, but you've got plenty of time. You can stay here as long as you like. Maybe slow down a bit.'

The words slowly infiltrated Marta's brain.

'That's what people tell me, anyway,' Holly added. 'Not that I listen. I'm impatient, like you. Just thought I'd pass it on. Night.'

20

It was strange to hear her mother's voice coming so clearly through the speakers of Holly's computer.

'I'm good! Things are really great,' she lied. There was no other way with Mama; she would be booking herself on the next flight to Stansted if Marta so much as hinted that something might be wrong.

'Are you calling me from inside a tin can?'

Marta laughed. 'I'm using Skype,' she explained, careful not to let slip who the owner of the computer was. As far as her mother knew, she was still living happily in Egerton Square.

'Right,' her mother replied, uncertainly. 'Oh, I meant to say. I popped into the bakery yesterday. Anka has a new phone. It's so small I thought it might get lost in her ear!'

Marta smiled, wondering whether her friend had relayed any of their recent conversations to her mother. 'How is she?'

'She seems well. Said you had a nice chat the other day. Told me all about your new life... You are taking care, aren't you? Eating well and getting enough sleep?'

'I'm fine,' Marta assured her, hoping Anka hadn't mentioned anything specific to her mother. Sweet and exuberant, Anka had been known to put her foot in it more than a few times before.

'...I know you don't cook properly for yourself,' her mother went on, 'but you must make sure you get enough vitamins. English food is so bad – they process all the nutrients out and replace them with salt…' She went on about essential minerals for a bit, allowing Marta to tune in and out at will, making the appropriate noises at regular intervals. Then she dropped the question Marta had been dreading.

'How is Tash?'

Marta swallowed. She had meant to tell her mother about the eviction. Mama was open-minded, sensible and understanding. But she also worried. The idea that Marta was now living with someone she didn't know would frighten her, especially if she knew that her old housemate, the daughter of Mama's friend, was no longer speaking to her except via curt text messages to Holly.

'She's fine!' Marta lied. 'We get on so well.'

'Oh, good! I was going to write to her parents this week, just to thank them for putting you up in their house and lending you their daughter, so to speak. Maybe I should send Tash something, too? D'you think she'd like a little Polish gift? Maybe some Łomianki pottery?'

'Er, maybe,' Marta jumped in, panicking slightly. The answer was *no*, Tash would *not* like a Polish gift of any kind and there was every chance she would come round and clobber Marta with any Łomianki pottery that she received in the post… but she wasn't going to relay this to her mother. 'She has quite fussy taste, Mama. Maybe wait until I next come to visit and I can pick out something I know she'll like?'

'Yes, OK. Good idea. I'll write to Penelope and Henry and leave the gift for now. What's the house like? Is it very big? I think Penelope said there was a grand piano! Do you play it?'

'Everything in the house is grand,' she replied. 'Not just the piano. To tell the truth, I've been too scared to lift the lid on the keys; it must be worth thousands. Everything is worth thousands, Mama. It's crazy. There are *flames* either side of the front door.'

'Oh, how wonderful. You must take some pictures! Will you send me some photos?'

Marta mumbled affirmatively, panicking a little more.

'And some of you and Tash? I'd really like that. *My daughter in London*,' she mused, the pride evident in her voice. Marta hoped she would forget this idea. 'Speaking of pianos… Your sister accompanied Tomek in the school concert two weeks ago. His violin playing hasn't improved much since you left, to be honest – it still sounds like a squeaky door – but the accompaniment was lovely. Oh, and I saw Beatrycze's mother in the interval – d'you remember Beatrycze?'

'Of course.'

'Well she went off to London too, I'm sure you remember. According to her mother, she's happily married to an Englishman – a doctor, I think she said.'

Marta made an appropriate noise, flinching at the thought of what had really happened to Beatrycze. She wondered how much of what was reported about successful Poles in Britain was actually true. It seemed that everyone was spinning their own set of lies.

'I think her mother was rather impressed when I told her about you finding a proper job so quickly. How's that going?'

Marta stared at the screensaver of Holly's computer. The word *WORK!* was bouncing around the screen in a chunky 3D font, compounding her unease. She had to come clean. She couldn't keep lying to her mother.

'The thing is,' she began, 'the work wasn't quite what I'd expected.'

'What d'you mean?' There was tension in her voice. 'And why are you talking in the past tense like that?'

'Um… I left. A few days ago.'

'Oh.'

Marta held her breath. In just one syllable, her mother had managed to convey such deep disappointment.

'Why did you leave?' she asked, quietly. 'Wasn't it challenging enough? What exactly were you doing there, anyway?'

'Um, I was…' Marta couldn't bear it. She *couldn't* tell her mother the truth. 'It was paperwork-based. And no, it wasn't challenging enough. The work was boring and I wasn't using anything I'd learnt on my course.'

'Oh dear,' her mother replied, sounding worried. 'I know how impatient you can be, Marta. You didn't leave too soon, did you?'

Marta nearly laughed. 'Don't worry, Mama. I haven't thrown away an opportunity. It was never going to be a good career move, working there. It was just a job. I'll find something else.'

'I'm sure you will,' said Mama, with a little more confidence. 'You know what's best. You'll get yourself another job in no time.'

There was a pause while Marta considered telling her mother the whole story: about Barry, about getting sacked, about the futility of looking for a career in England. Before she could though, Mama was off again, talking about how well Marta had done in her degree, how there weren't many people who had achieved such high grades from Szkoła Główna Handlowa, how nobody else would come close in terms of qualifications.

Marta tried to let it wash over her. She wasn't going to point out that she had come top of her year at an institution that nobody here had heard of. She wasn't going to explain the stigma that came with being from Eastern Europe, or the underlying assumption that Poles were skilled only in manual trades, valued only by their 'strong work ethic'. She wasn't going to tell her mother that having a marketing degree could actually be a bad thing; that the theories she had learned in her degree had lost her the only job she had found.

'How's Tata?' she asked, when the patter finally dwindled.

'He's good,' her mother replied.

The sudden curtness caught Marta's attention.

'Is he still being screwed at work?'

'N-no. Well, yes – in fact, they're having a bit of a restructure in the cabling department and his job has shifted slightly.'

Marta tensed up. 'What d'you mean, *shifted*?'

'Well, your father has been moved to another department. Temporarily, they say. Polkomtel's under new management, you know that?'

'Mmm.' Marta hadn't known that. She felt bad for not knowing.

'The new bosses seem rather... ruthless.'

'Mama, are you saying Tata might lose his job?'

'No!' she replied quickly. 'No, some of his colleagues might, but he'll keep his – just a different one. You don't need to worry, he's fine. Happy as ever in his new role!'

The sudden lightness in her voice worried Marta. 'You will let me know if anything changes, won't you?'

'Of course! Yes, of course I will. Oh, that reminds me, he's asked me to find some super-strength indigestion tablets. God knows where I'll get them from.'

'What?'

'Oh, he's started getting terrible indigestion. I blame the water. They're fiddling with the supplies and adding all sorts of nasty things… It never tastes the way–'

'Mama, since when has Tata been getting indigestion? Has he been to the doctor about it?'

'Doctor? Why would he go–'

'Because it might not be indigestion! He should see the doctor. I mean, what if it's…' Marta hesitated. Her medical knowledge was limited. 'Something worse?'

'Marta, I think you take after me. Stop worrying! You've got enough going on in your life without getting worked up over Tata's digestive system.'

'OK. But you will make him go to the doctor if it doesn't get better, won't you?'

'Of course,' she replied unconvincingly.

'Good. Give him a big kiss from me. And Tomek and Ewa.'

'I will.'

''Bye, Mama.'

''Bye, darling. I'm so proud of you. It does make me happy to hear about your new life in England. Not many people have done as well as you, you know.'

Marta felt a wave of guilt wash over her as she clicked to end the call.

21

The Bright Sparks interview was not going well. It had been doomed from the start. Ever since she had run over the recruitment specialist's foot with her wheelie chair and knocked a pile of folders onto the floor, Marta had known there was little point in sticking around.

'So tell me about your last placement – if you could call it that. You seem to have worked there for what... four weeks?'

'This wasn't career job,' Marta explained. 'Was just a little job to get me money for paying rent in London.'

'OK,' said the woman slowly. Her red hair was scraped back over her head, pulling the flesh so tight that it was impossible to guess her age. 'And you plan to go into marketing with no UK experience other than this "little job"?'

Marta nodded. 'I have the experience, but in Poland. Have done good work in–'

'I'm sure you have, I'm sure you have,' the woman nodded. 'But you do understand that our clients expect a very high-calibre individual from this agency and so it's our duty to ensure that every one of our 'sparks' – that's what we call them – have the skills, qualifications and *relevant experience* to equip them for a very challenging workload?'

Marta nodded sullenly. She just wanted to leave now. There was no way they were going to hire her as one of their 'sparks', so there was really no point wasting any more time. To be honest, she felt a bit cross with Holly for suggesting she apply. Clearly she wasn't good enough for them. She was too much of an unknown.

'Now you graduated from the Sko – Skol – Shoo –'

'Szkoła Główna Handlowa w Warszawie.'

'Yes, er, there. Could you tell me a little bit about your course? About the university?'

Marta opened her mouth to talk, but was silenced by the sound of the door opening behind her.

'Ah, Laura!' cried the MD, losing interest in Marta momentarily. 'Come in! I was just explaining to Martha here–'

'Marta,' she interjected.

'I beg your pardon?'

'Marta. Is my name.'

'Yes, I know. Sit down, Laura – try to avoid the mess over there. That's our client folders all over the floor. Yes, I was just explaining to Martha how important it is for our 'sparks' to have sufficient experience in their sector before being sent out to clients.'

Laura, a slim, pretty blonde in a tight pencil skirt, pulled up a chair and flashed a business-like smile at Marta. She was probably only a few years out of university herself, but she exuded an air of confident professionalism.

'Imperative,' she agreed. 'Our reputation rests on the excellence of our sparks.'

'Quite,' the redhead nodded meaningfully.

'Good news, though!' chirruped Laura. 'Your tests have been marked and your scores have come through as 'high' in every section!'

A small flame of excitement flickered in Marta's despondent soul. The tests she had sat half an hour ago had been easy. They involved basic mathematics and a bit of commercial awareness, but mainly just common sense. Secretly, Marta had felt pretty good about them.

'You're the first person since I started working here to score full marks in numerical reasoning,' Laura told her, beaming.

Marta beamed back, wondering where this left them.

'Well, that's excellent, Marta,' said the MD encouragingly. Marta took it as a positive sign that the woman had finally learnt her name. 'Well done.'

'Have you done any tests like this before?' asked Laura.

'No. But they quite easy, like problems you get in school,' Marta replied. Perhaps they thought she had cheated.

'Polish school,' said the MD with raised eyebrows, looking meaningfully at her subordinate.

'Oh yes,' said Laura, turning back to Marta. 'When did you come over to England?'

Here we go, thought Marta. Another inquisition about how little experience she had in UK marketing. 'Two months ago.'

Laura nodded. 'Okaaaay,' she said, glancing sideways at her boss. 'And you haven't worked here in any other capacity, have you? Any shop work? Any au pairing?'

Marta sighed. 'No.' She couldn't keep the resentment out of her voice.

'Because you see, the thing is, Marta, you can't really expect to leap straight into a career over here with no demonstrable capabilities.'

'I have them,' said Marta defensively. 'Just not in this country.'

'Mmm, yes,' said Laura, looking again at her boss. 'Relevant experience is very important, and I'm afraid to say, I don't think your placements in Poland will carry much weight with potential employers here.'

'Then how do I get relevant experience?' asked Marta, plain angry now. She didn't care about working for Bright Sparks any more; she just wanted to prove her point.

'Well, that's the difficulty, I agree.' Laura looked a little flustered.

'I cannot get experience anywhere because I do not have experience,' Marta went on. 'Is crazy! I just want experience – not lots of money or anything like this… Just some time in good English company, but nobody give me that chance!'

The woman leaned forward across her desk and looked Marta

127

in the eye. She paused for a second, then spoke, slowly. 'I hear what you're saying, Marta. It's not easy for people like you.' She pursed her lips, still looking right at her. 'Now. We have over a hundred clients on our books – nearly half of them marketing firms or others that would suit your skill set.'

Marta nodded, waiting for the 'but'.

'But we operate on a need-to-hire basis here, which means that we can only assign sparks to projects as and when the requests come in from clients. It sometimes takes months to find work, even for our best sparks – and that might only be a fortnight's placement. Our clients are highly selective and very demanding.'

The woman paused, smiling at Laura, who nodded subserviently.

'You have an added disadvantage,' the woman went on, 'in that you've never really worked over here. We have over five hundred sparks on our books and we assign projects on the basis of track record. Let me advise you, Marta. Sign up to a number of agencies, not just Bright Sparks, and *badger* them. Be persistent.'

Marta nodded again, wondering where badgers came into the plan. This was surely the most irritating woman she had ever met.

'Something will come up, I'm sure. You're a smart girl, Marta, as your test results show. We have your details on file. We'll call you if anything suitable comes up.'

22

Loud, angry bass reverberated beneath a tuneless chant that consisted mainly of the word "fuck". It wasn't ideal running music, but it suited Marta's mood. She pounded down Kilburn High Road, oblivious to the pedestrians who were forced to swerve out of her way.

Back home, Marta had taken up running as a way of getting warm in the winter months, but today it wasn't about getting warm; it was about cooling off. She needed to run off her rage.

Marta turned down a road that looked as though it led to the park, not really caring where she ended up. Her life was a disaster. She had come to England to start a career, to elevate herself and to help her parents. She had ended up with no job, no home and almost no money.

Marta picked up speed, taking advantage of the empty pavement and tail wind. Her chest was starting to ache now. She had heard nothing from Bright Sparks, of course – or from the other four agencies she had joined. She didn't expect to hear from them. Nobody wanted to hire a girl with a Polish degree whose English wasn't quite perfect.

The drums were beating out a deafening finale and, after a short pause, Marta's ears filled with the sound of a gentle crooning about birds falling in love. Marta skipped tracks. She was beginning to wish she had taken the opportunity to change the playlist before Dominik had gone cold on her.

Dominik. Marta tried to shift her thoughts on, but the image of his grinning face from inside the scratched scooter helmet wouldn't leave her head. She had called a couple of times, but each time he had put the phone down on her as soon as she had started to speak. There was clearly something going on that Marta didn't understand, but whatever it was, she thought, she didn't need to be messed about. She had other priorities, anyway. She just had to move on.

The road opened up and Marta found herself nipping between vans and trucks on a fume-filled, six-way junction. Her thoughts returned to her lack of employment. Was it this hard for everyone who came to England, she wondered? Did they all meet the same brick walls trying to fit in?

The answer, she knew, was *no*. Not everybody found it this hard, because not everybody tried to fit in – not properly. Others were content to waste their university degrees laying bricks and fixing leaks and wiping babies' bottoms. There were qualified neurosurgeons driving forklift trucks around warehouses and nuclear physicists cleaning tube station toilets. Marta wasn't prepared to do that. She had pride. She had a degree.

Her footsteps fell in time with the music, the rapper's chant pushing her to run faster than she would usually go. He was talking about being chewed up, spat out and booed off stage. About pain. About a nine-to-five. Her lungs were hurting with every breath, but she powered on, her breath rasping as the music became more urgent and desperate.

Desperate. That was how Marta felt. She was desperate to be part of this city, desperate to reach out and seize the opportunities on offer, to experience the freedom she saw all around her, to taste the excitement… but it was all passing her by. She couldn't get a piece of it because its doors were closed. She couldn't break in.

A pair of workmen in yellow vests looked up from their newspapers and whistled appreciatively as she ran past. Marta rolled her eyes in their direction. Crazy men. Crazy, lazy men. English labourers never did any 'labour'. She could see why the Polish graduates had a reputation for working hard.

Marta let gravity do the work as she pounded down the gentle slope that led to the park. Perhaps it was the music or maybe it was the warm, spring-like air, but something had started to lift inside her. The whole city was full of crazy people, she decided, thinking of the over-polite newsagent, the women queuing outside the post office and the little boys in miniature suits on the King's Road. It was a crazy city with crazy rules and closed doors, but she wanted to stay. She wanted to make her mark. She was *determined* to make her mark. Like Michael Marks.

Michael Marks had come over with nothing. He was a Jewish refugee who came over to escape persecution in Poland. Marta had read his biography. He had set up his store with a five pound loan from someone he didn't even know; someone who had seen his potential and had faith in his idea. A market stall was all it was, to begin with, but it grew. It grew and grew so that soon there wasn't a single person in the country who hadn't heard of Marks and Spencer.

If he could do it, thought Marta, then so could she. It was just a question of finding that person who would see her potential. Of all the recruiters she had met in the last week, surely *one* of them would take that risk?

A Queen song came on and Marta found herself flying down a wide, sun-streaked path, lifted by the music. Holly was right. She didn't need to push herself so hard. Something would come along. It didn't matter that Dominik had gone from her life. Holly and Tina and Rich were her new friends, and thanks to them she had a place to stay. She could make things work over here. Nothing was impossible. It just took patience. Suddenly, her earlier despondency seemed like a distant memory; all that mattered now was the future.

A man on rollerblades came powering towards her. He was built like an athlete, his smooth, brown skin toned to perfection, his teeth bright white. Marta smiled back at him. Perhaps she would meet a new man over here. Perhaps one of the agencies would take her on. Perhaps she would make her mark over here after all. Marta ran on, fuelled by a newfound energy. Suddenly, anything seemed possible.

It was almost by accident that she found her way home. Turning into what she thought was a side street that led to West Hampstead,

Marta realised she was already back on Kilburn High Road, just down from Holly's flat. She walked the last few metres, stretching her overworked muscles and shaking her limbs as she went.

'Cześć,' said a voice as she burst through the front door.

Marta looked up. Walking towards her through the kitchen, with a can of beer in his hand, was Dominik.

'You thought you could hide from me?' he asked in Polish, grinning as though nothing was amiss. Holly was leaning against the kitchen table, watching.

Marta stared, her mind burning with hate and lust all at once. Dominik was here. She didn't know what to ask first.

He laughed softly, watching her expression. 'You made it hard enough to find you. That woman you lived with–'

'You went round?' Marta asked, quickly trying to piece everything together. 'To Tash's?'

Dominik nodded. 'My phone got nicked and you never came round. How else was I supposed to find you?'

Relief flooded Marta's body. 'How…'

'With difficulty. I got your address from the boss. Eventually. Then I went round and–'

'You could've been killed,' Holly put in, a smile dancing on her lips.

'Well, I wasn't. Quite the opposite, in fact.'

'What d'you mean?'

'She's an animal, isn't she? Is she on heat or what?'

Marta cringed. 'She's newly single, I think. My fault, apparently.'

'Ah. That would explain what she called you.'

Marta watched as a smirk crept up Dominik's face.

'What? What did she call me?'

'D'you mean before or after the treble gin-and-tonic?'

'Ugh. You didn't, did you?'

'It was free booze and I was going out after. Besides, she wouldn't have given me your address otherwise. Ugly trollop. That's what she called you. Twice.'

Marta opened her mouth to shriek an obscenity about Tash, but as she did so, her phone rang. She took it, motioning for Dominik to stick around.

'Is that Marta Da-brow-ska?' asked a woman in clipped English.

'Yes,' she replied, sidestepping in front of Dominik, who appeared to be moving towards the front door.

'My name is Caroline and I'm calling from a firm called Bread and Butter; a London-based agency that specialises in sourcing catering and waiting services for corporate events.'

Marta pulled the phone away from her ear just for long enough to hiss, '*Don't go – won't be long!*'

Dominik was already scribbling something on a notepad by the door.

'...where we got your details. Now I know you applied for office work, but we wondered how you might like to try...'

Dominik tore off the sheet and handed it to her. *Call me*, it said, then a number. He slipped backwards through the door with a grin. Marta watched him disappear, wishing she hadn't taken the call.

'...wondered whether you'd be interested in doing some work for us.'

Marta watched Dominik fling himself onto the scooter and kick it into life. It fired up first time. 'When?' she asked, trying to focus.

'Saturday night. It's a corporate function. A dinner in Soho Square. You'd work six 'til two and get seventy-five pounds. Just ordinary table service. Nothing special.'

Marta was still high from her run and from the realisation that Dominik was back in her life. She looked at the scrap of paper. Things were looking better already. She had no idea what the work entailed, but this was clearly an opportunity and she was going to seize it.

'Why not?' she said. 'Sounds good!'

23

Folding napkins. That was Marta's first task. It rivalled her previous job in terms of intellectual stimulation, but at least it didn't involve such public humiliation. At least here she was providing things that people wanted, although that wasn't much consolation. It was still a terrible job.

'Your apron's skew-whiff,' chided the stroppy, middle-aged woman who seemed to be in charge. Marta obediently yanked the waistband round on the monstrous garment. 'And hurry up!' the fat woman added, looking over her shoulder. 'You should be done wi'napkins and onto wine by now!'

Marta upped the pace of her folding. *Skew what?* She felt like a robot on a production line: lift, shake, fold, arrange and fiddle until it looked more or less right relative to the ridiculous number of forks on the table. Not that a robot would be dressed in such a frumpy outfit, she thought. The skirt was designed for someone twice her width and half her height, and the shirt was like a tent.

A cold draught swirled through the marquee, setting tablecloths flapping and flower displays wobbling on their stands. Six men in black T-shirts appeared at the entrance, holding up pieces of marquee fabric and looking perplexed.

Folding her last serviette and nudging it gently into position, Marta picked up her empty box and headed back to the 'hub', as it was known.

The men in T-shirts were wrestling with a large plastic banner right in front of the entrance. Marta watched, unimpressed, waiting for a clear passage. They had to be English, she thought, noting that four out of the six men were standing around watching.

Marta coughed. A couple of them glanced in her direction. Nobody made any effort to move out of her way.

'Wha' was that about getting things laid, Jay?' yelled the guy holding the end of the banner. The others all roared with laughter, their eyes swivelling to meet Marta's cold gaze.

She focused on the text as the guys tried to establish which way up the banner was supposed to go. WELCOME TO THE 200TH ANNUAL CAMBRIDGE ALUMNI DINNER, Marta read as it was hoisted into position. A shudder ran through her. Beneath the words was a man-sized crest in red and yellow that she recognised from Tash's framed photographs.

The clowns finally finished erecting the banner and shuffled sideways. There was another comment that Marta didn't understand and more raucous laughter as she finally slipped through the gap.

'You on wine?' asked a girl, pointing accusingly at the mound of brown boxes in the corner.

Marta nodded timidly.

'You better hurry up. They all need to be done for after the champagne's run out, innit.'

Marta nodded again and reached for the first box.

The 'crew', as they were called, consisted of thirty girls in their late teens or early twenties. A third of them were English and the rest were Poles, Czechs and possibly Romanians; Marta couldn't quite tell from the accents. It was easy to tell who was who, because the English girls were all wearing lots of makeup and had adapted their uniforms by rolling up their skirts and unbuttoning their blouses. They also stood apart, as though they were afraid of catching something from the 'foreign' girls.

As Marta twisted the corkscrew into yet another bottle, she decided to try and break down the divide.

'So the event is for who?' she asked, addressing the blonde who was perched on the champagne rack nearby, composing a text message.

'Uh?'

'Who is it for, this night?'

The girl didn't reply. She just scowled unpleasantly at Marta.

'Whassup?' another blonde sidled up to the first.

Out of the corner of her eye, Marta watched as the girl nodded in her direction then, making no effort to lower her voice, muttered, 'Fucking weirdo, trying to start on me.'

'Fuckin' hell. Hey, look. I've got some fags. Let's go find the toilets.'

The two girls hurried off. Marta tried to focus on pulling out corks, but her mind was lodged on what had just happened and she could feel the familiar glow of shame spread up her cheeks. It wasn't as though the girls had said anything particularly bad; it was more what they *hadn't* said that bothered her. It was the way they ignored her, the way they pulled faces behind her back and made out that she was 'starting', whatever that meant.

Marta knew she shouldn't take it to heart. She knew that after four weeks of being subjected to a constant stream of rejection, she ought to be tougher than this. She ought to be able to handle nasty looks, lies and snide remarks. But it still stung. It wasn't nice to be made to feel like this.

Marta's thoughts were interrupted by a Polish voice.

'Need a hand?'

A dark-haired Polish girl with a pale complexion that was not dissimilar to her own was leaning on the champagne rack where the blonde had been resting.

'I was giving out drinks, but I've been demoted,' she explained. 'The fat boss told me to help out back here.'

Marta smiled conspiratorially. 'I don't think they like us,' she said.

The brunette raised an eyebrow. 'Of course they don't. We bring down their wages, don't we? Pass me that corkscrew.'

'You'll get blisters,' Marta warned, showing the girl her sore, red palm. 'You mean they get paid less?'

'Less than they used to, yeah. The English girls got nearly forty złoty an hour before we came along. We'll work for less, so they have to. It's no wonder they hate us.'

Marta thought about this as they worked their way through the mountain of boxes, working in companionable silence. She hadn't really considered the economics of the situation. She hadn't imagined that the English girls actually suffered directly from the influx of people like her, but looking at it that way, she almost felt sorry for them. Almost.

The gentle hum of people at work was shattered by a loud squeal. Marta looked round to see the fat woman dragging two girls across the hessian matting by their ears, it appeared, causing considerable noise from them both.

'Get offa me! I'll fuckin' sue! Let goa me!' screamed one, while the other just made yelping noises, like a dog.

'I'll get offa you when you've explained what you was doin' back there,' replied the overweight mistress. Finally, she let go of the girls' ears and they both squirmed backwards. Marta recognised them as the blonde girls from earlier.

'Was you smokin' in the portaloos?' demanded the woman.

'No!' said the girls together, equally unconvincingly.

'Are you tryin'a lose your jobs, girls?' asked the red-faced woman, suddenly noticing that all her staff were standing around, staring. 'Get back to work, all of you!'

'No, we ain't,' Marta heard one of the blondes reply, as she turned and sank the corkscrew into another cork.

'Then whose are these?' she asked, waving a packet of cigarettes in their faces. Marta watched out of the corner of her eye as she opened her next bottle.

'Hers,' snapped the girl, pointing boldly at Marta.

Before Marta could defend herself, the other girl leapt to the defence of her friend. 'Yeah, they're hers. We was just flushin' 'em down the loo, innit.'

Marta was shaking her head, horrified. 'They not mine cigarettes, I promise!' she said. 'I don't have no–'

'Shuddup!' yelled the woman. 'I've had enough. You're all lying, far as I can tell, so just get back to work. You two, what was you on before?'

The two English girls faltered for a moment, then the blonde pointed at the stack of unopened bottles. 'Openin' *them*.'

The woman sighed. 'Well get back to it, OK? We ain't got no time to waste. You–' she pointed at Marta. 'Dunno what you're doin' there. Start puttin' garnishes on plates.'

The canvas quarters were quiet for a good thirty seconds while everyone watched the ferocious woman storm out. The only sounds were the sizzle and chatter from the kitchen and the muted hum of a string quartet in the main marquee. Marta crept over to the table of plates, still reeling from her ordeal. Any semblance of pity had been replaced by a bitter resentment of the English girls. They were mean and conniving, just like Tash's friends.

It was with trepidation that Marta set foot on the uneven marquee floor, her arms stacked precariously with plates. It had taken three girls and several minutes to load her up and for Marta to learn how to walk with the things, and she hadn't even practised unloading.

There were hundreds of people in the marquee, all dressed extremely smartly: black bowties for men, long, shimmering dresses for women. Marta scanned the room, counting the ornate table decorations and working out that there were two hundred and forty guests present. She crept slowly towards her designated table.

As she hovered uncertainly between the elbows of two men, feeling the top plate start to slip, one of the guys noticed the lettuce leaf fall onto the table and graciously relieved her of the sliding plate, freeing up her right hand and averting catastrophe. Marta thanked the man, who smiled back, his kindly face pitted and wrinkled with age.

The man motioned for his companion to move his elbow so that Marta could guide the next plate in and, somewhat miraculously, another one was unloaded. She moved round the table, growing in confidence and deciding that this waitressing thing really wasn't so hard after all.

She was stooping between two finely dressed elderly ladies, unloading her final plate, when it happened.

'My goodness! Marta!' cried a voice that sent a shiver running down Marta's spine. Even before she had seen the whole face, she knew who it was.

'Jeremy!' she cried, trying to mask her dismay. She was determined to handle this in a professional manner, showing interest in his attendance at the event. 'You are celebrating the Cambridge aluminium?'

Somehow, Jeremy managed to look down on her, despite the fact that he was seated, and therefore a good few feet lower. He looked slightly confused, eyeing her carefully for several seconds in which Marta could feel the eyes of every guest around the table boring into her baggy, unflattering uniform. Then he started to smile.

'Aluminium!' he said, his eyes full of mirth. 'Ha! Alumni, aluminium. I'd never thought of that! Oh, goodness...' He chuckled to himself, exchanging glances with some of his companions, who started to smile.

Marta managed to hold her expression, not enjoying the situation at all.

'Oh, dear me,' Jeremy muttered, still guffawing. 'Alumni means "of the establishment". It means ex-attendee – of Cambridge in this instance. It's nothing to do with aluminium.'

Marta nodded, seeing her mistake. It really wasn't *that* funny, she thought, trying desperately to hold her passive smile. There were worse mistakes she could have made.

'Marta comes from Poland,' Jeremy announced to the table.

'*Ah,*' chorused everyone around the table. The man next to Jeremy, a stout, middle-aged man with more chins than hair, leaned back in his seat and looked up at Marta. '*Good for you!*' he exclaimed, patting her backside approvingly. 'Need more like you in this country, we do. Hardworking folk who don't mind getting their hands dirty! Splendid! Good for you.'

Marta decided that it was time to leave. There would be no more waitress service for table eighteen – not from her, anyway. She muttered something about bread rolls and hastened back to the hub.

Marta stood, staring at the tessellating plates on the table. Her mind was not on the job. It was on how to escape from the job without forfeiting her seventy-five pound pay. She slipped off to find the portaloos.

Sitting on the flipped-down toilet seat, her head resting in her palms, Marta felt her phone vibrate in the saddlebag of a skirt pocket. With a heavy heart, she pulled it out.

I'm so sorry. I fucked up. Hope you have somewhere to stay. Let me make it up to you? Jack

Marta let out a long sigh. *Jack.* He was the cause of so many of her problems. He came from a world she despised: a world where she was the laughing stock, the foreigner, the hired help. He was no different from Jeremy and the rest of them – only better-looking and smarter with his words. And yet... Yet he wasn't ridiculing her like Jeremy had done. He was checking up on her. He clearly felt bad.

Marta pushed herself to her feet, looking around and reminding herself that she was standing in a plastic toilet cubicle, skiving from a job that involved serving food to rich types in bowties: rich types like Jack. Holly had warned her about this. She had predicted that Jack would spring into her life on the rebound.

Marta unlocked the flimsy, carpeted door and returned to the hub in search of someone who would swap roles with her.

24

'What did you do?' asked Dominik, mopping up the coffee that Marta had spilt on the plastic tablecloth.

'Hid in the kitchens,' she grimaced. 'I had to. All the jobs seemed to involve going into the marquee. I told the chefs I'd been sent to the kitchens to help. They gave me odd jobs to do: pouring gravy, squirting cream, you know... I think they felt sorry for me.'

'You were squirting cream 'til two in the morning?'

'Apart from when I was hiding in the toilets.'

Dominik pulled a face. 'Sounds fun. Will you work for them again?'

Marta hesitated. At two o'clock in the morning on Sunday, she had vowed to herself that she would never again stoop as low as she had done that night. Even without the Jeremy incident it would have been degrading. But now, faced with the choice of Bread and Butter Catering or being out of work again, she felt less sure. Marta shook her head and gave a slow, uncertain shrug.

Dominik stared into his cup. They were sitting in the Polskie Delikatesy in Acton. It was a shop, really, but it had a couple of tiny tables by the window and they served a full range of Polish snacks. Across the road was a Polish newsagent.

Marta shook her head, smiling. 'Like a corner of Warsaw,' she said. 'Is this your little Sunday routine, then?'

Dominik smiled sheepishly. 'I know, it's sad. But I miss home. I come here on a Sunday and I'm greeted in Polish, I get served in

Polish, I read the news in Polish… It makes a break from the other six days. Oh, thanks–' Dominik leaned back as the pretty young waitress slid a plate of jabłecznik onto the table between their cups.

The petite waitress smiled at Dominik and slipped away.

'That's Dominika,' he explained, blushing a little, Marta thought. 'Her parents run the place. They were first-wave immigrants after the war. Sweet girl. Always gives me some sort of freebie, ever since I started coming in.'

'Ever since she started fancying you,' Marta teased.

Dominik rolled his eyes. Marta looked out of the window. Her own words had stirred something inside her. A niggle. She didn't like the idea of Dominik with another girl.

There was an awkward silence. Dominik took a bite of the *ciasto*. Marta did the same.

'I'm jealous,' Marta mused, after several minutes.

'Why, because Dominika fancies me?' Dominik asked quickly, with a grin.

'Oh, no!' Marta's laugh sounded false, even to her. Her thoughts had moved on, but it was interesting that Dominik's hadn't, she thought. 'Because you live in a place like this,' she explained. 'A place where you can get *kabanosy* and *chleb* and *ogórki kiszone* five minutes away from your house.'

Dominik shrugged. 'Acton has its downsides,' he said. 'Like the chances of getting your phone nicked by a bunch of kids on bikes…' He smiled wryly. 'Anyway, isn't Kilburn the same?'

Marta shook her head. 'It has a few Polish shops, but not like this.'

Dominik nodded vaguely, his gaze shifting to the group of young men who were congregating on the pavement opposite. They were Polish; Marta could tell by the week-old stubble and the expressions on their hollow faces.

'It's Mariusz and that.' Dominik leaned over and banged loudly on the window.

Marta watched as a couple of the guys raised their hands in mock salute.

'I met them a few months ago,' he explained. 'They live down the road.'

'What are they doing?' asked Marta. 'They look like they're waiting for a bus, but they're not gonna catch one there.'

'Wrong,' replied Dominik, picking at crumbs and downing the remains of his coffee.

Marta frowned at him. 'You have to stand at a bus stop to get a bus, Dominik.'

Dominik smiled. 'Not this sort of bus,' he said. 'Watch.'

They continued to stare at the bunch of guys, who stood barely moving, with their hands in their pockets. After a couple of minutes, they stirred. A battered old hatchback pulled up alongside two parked cars.

'They're not all gonna fit in that thing.' Marta stared.

Dominik just grinned.

Marta's bemusement grew as the men disappeared into the car one by one. By the time the sixth and final man had levered himself into the back, the vehicle was visibly rocking from side to side. Eventually, the door was hauled shut and the car pulled sluggishly away.

'Where are they going?' she asked.

'To work,' Dominik replied. 'Have you never seen that before?'

Marta shook her head. She had seen groups of young men lurking randomly on street corners, but she had never stopped to wonder why.

'I joined them once,' Dominik told her. 'Never again though – unless I lose the leafleting job.'

'Where did they take you?' asked Marta, feeling naïve.

Dominik laughed. 'It wasn't as though they were holding me hostage – I did *ask* to go. We went to a building site somewhere north of Ealing. Random labour, nothing hard. The money was OK, but not as good as Barry's. The journey was the worst bit. They kept farting; they thought it was funny. Most of them were drunk. I was squeezed in at the end with some guy's arse in my face.'

Marta cringed. 'Stick with the leaflets for now,' she advised. They looked at each other and burst out laughing.

'Have you ever been to the Wailing Wall?' asked Dominik.

'The what?'

Dominik shook his head disapprovingly. 'Don't you know anything about this city? Do you know where Hammersmith is?'

Marta hesitated. 'I've seen it on the tube map...'

Dominik rolled his eyes. 'Honestly, Marta. It's the Polish capital of England!'

'I've spent too much time hanging out with rich Brits,' Marta admitted.

'Well, if you think Acton's like home, then you should see Hammersmith. The Wailing Wall is like a home to half the Poles here; it's the reason most of them came over.'

'What *is* it?'

'Well, it started off as a newsagent's window,' Dominik explained. 'It was a place where you could put cards offering services or asking for work. But then they ran out of room in the window, so they extended it halfway along the street. Now it's mainly online, but it started in Hammersmith. Honestly, you should check it out: requests for plumbers, builders, cleaners and au pairs – and "masseuses and escorts", obviously.'

Marta rolled her eyes, feeling the conversation creep back into its default groove.

Dominik seemed oblivious. 'Worth a trip,' he said. 'That's how I originally found Barry's. Although...' He grimaced. 'I wouldn't hold your breath for a great salary. The employers have got wise to it and they only offer what they can get away with, which is usually shit.'

Marta nodded. That seemed to be what was happening. Poles were earning themselves a reputation as England's low-cost workforce.

The waitress brought over the bill – which seemed surprisingly cheap – and Marta emptied her wallet on the table, leaving enough to cover it while Dominik fished out a sizeable tip for the waitress. 'I'll get the next one,' he said. 'Maybe I'll have a real job by then.'

The way he said this last sentence made Marta stop in her tracks, halfway to the door. 'Have you applied for something?'

'Don't get excited,' Dominik rolled his eyes. 'I won't get it. It's driving tube trains.'

'Oh.' Marta couldn't hide the disappointment in her voice. 'Why?'

Dominik frowned. 'What d'you mean, why? Because driving trains offers a good salary? Because I have to get out of this dead-end leaflet job?'

'But I mean, why another crappy menial job?'

For a fleeting moment, Marta thought she saw a flash of irritation cross Dominik's face. 'It's not menial; it's skilled. They train you up on the job, and if you work nightshifts the pay's really good.'

'But...' Marta didn't want to antagonise him, but she just couldn't keep her opinions to herself. 'Shifts driving underground trains, Dominik? You're a finance graduate! You went to Jagiellonian! I mean, I know we're only young, and I know I sometimes aim too high and set myself up for a fall and our English isn't perfect, but... don't you want a *proper* career?'

Dominik sighed. 'Of course I *want* a career. I'm just realistic about my prospects of getting one. I've been here for nearly a year now, Marta. Believe me, I've tried.'

Marta said nothing. It wasn't the first time she had heard him say this, but the frustration burned inside her nonetheless. There *had* to be a way of getting somewhere in this country, and surely it didn't involve driving trains in dark, smoky tunnels or serving dinners to rude Englishmen?

They walked towards the station in silence.

'Maybe you could work your way up within TFL,' she suggested quietly, after a few minutes. 'Maybe you could get yourself into the finance department when you've been with them for a while?'

'And maybe not!' replied Dominik, mimicking her hopeless enthusiasm.

Marta nodded, as though defeated, but she was still secretly hopeful that there was another way. They had reached the station, but Marta didn't want to leave. 'What's in the bag?' she asked, just to prolong their conversation.

Dominik looked down at the lumpy plastic bag in his hand. 'Oh – my sister's birthday present. She's twenty-one next week. I thought it would fit in a post box, but it didn't.'

'What is it?'

Dominik looked down, guiltily. 'Well, I know it's cheap, but... well, it's playlists. Ripped music. I personalised the inlays, though.'

Marta smiled. 'That's nice.'

'You reckon? Oh good. I was worried I'd come across as tight. Or penniless, which wouldn't please my parents.'

'I know the feeling.' Marta looked at him. His expression had changed. He was studying her, his hazel eyes scrutinising her face with unexpected intensity. Then he moved closer. She held his gaze, feeling his hand brush hers, fingers finding their way between hers.

The bag fell to the ground between them and Marta felt Dominik's other arm slide round her waist. She could barely breathe. His chest was against hers, his face so close she could practically feel the air move as he blinked through long, thick lashes.

Marta felt herself stumbling up against him. Dominik's lips touched hers, just lightly, then more firmly, urgently, his tongue gently exploring her mouth. She didn't want it to end. It was something she had wanted for so long, although she had never admitted it to herself, and now it was happening, just as she had forced herself not to imagine.

It had to end, though, and when they finally pulled apart, Marta could tell that Dominik felt the same.

'Bye,' she said softly when Dominik's hand fell away from her waist.

'Bye.' Dominik slowly untangled his fingers from hers.

Marta looked away, suddenly bashful. 'See you next week some time?'

Dominik nodded. 'I'll call you.'

Marta turned to enter the station, grinning like a little girl.

25

'Pints all round?' asked Holly, looking around at her housemates.

There were nods of agreement from Marta and Rich.

'With chasers!' cried Tina.

Holly pulled a face. 'It's a school night, T.'

Tina rolled her eyes in disgust, but didn't push the point. They were sitting in a corner of their local, which was one of the classier establishments on Kilburn High Road; not that this meant it was classy.

Marta's phone pinged in her lap, sending a shiver of excitement through her. It was Tuesday, two days after the kiss, and she knew who had sent the text.

> Don't tease me, M – I wouldn't object to seeing you in a waitress outfit, although… have you considered a career as a nurse? Mmm. Dinner Fri? Dx

'What are you doing down there?' demanded Tina, testing out the sturdiness of the little stool upon which her tiny buttocks were perched.

'Nothing,' Marta replied quickly. She hadn't told anyone about what had happened.

'Who are you texting with that massive grin on your face?' Tina asked suspiciously.

'No one,' said Marta, wondering how she could account for her smirk. 'I was just…'

Without warning, Tina's slender brown arm reached across the table like a snake's tongue and snatched the phone out of Marta's hand.

'Hah! Let me see!'

Marta watched in horror as Tina's dark, beady eyes scanned the text message on the screen.

'It's in Polish,' Tina declared, disappointed. 'What does it mean?'

Marta shrugged. 'Nothing much.'

'Nothing much!' she cried, exchanging a triumphant look with Rich. 'Nothing much indeed…'

Marta took her phone back. She could feel the blood rushing to her face. 'It's about… stupid stuff. Nothing.'

'What's about nothing?' asked Holly, returning from the bar with her fingers stretched painfully around four pints.

'A message from D-kiss to Marta that made her blush when she read it,' replied Tina. 'Who's D-kiss?'

With Holly's assistance, the housemates quickly worked out that the mystery man was the guy who had come to the house to find her two weeks before. Tina rushed to declare her approval.

'He was *cute!*'

'And he braved Tash's to find you,' added Holly.

'So, have you shagged him?' asked Tina expectantly.

'Tina!'

'What?'

'You can't just–'

'Why not?' Tina frowned. 'So have you, Marta?'

Marta shook her head, overwhelmed. 'No! Stop!'

'Yes, stop,' echoed Rich, speaking for the first time. 'Tina, some people don't start their relationships by sleeping together.'

There was a swift exchange of looks between Holly and Rich that didn't go unnoticed by Marta.

'We are not boyfriends and girlfriends,' said Marta, by way of a final explanation. 'We only friends, but on Saturday we realise we maybe like each other more than that, and… we kissed.' She looked down at her beer.

Both Tina and Holly nodded, slowly. Everyone was grinning, now – even Marta. She hadn't expected to confide in her housemates, but now she had done, it felt good. Over the last week, she had ended up cooking for Tina and Rich a few times when they got back from work. It was a way of paying them back for the rent-free accommodation. Despite their different backgrounds, Marta felt strangely comfortable around them.

'So, when are you next seeing each other?' asked Tina.

'Friday. We go to dinner, I think.'

'Very nice,' Tina replied. 'Has he got his own place?'

Marta shook her head. 'He share with six other.'

'Oh, crap,' Tina grimaced. 'Does that mean we all have to avoid the lounge on Friday night?'

It took a couple of seconds for Marta to realise what Tina was saying. 'No!' she cried, embarrassed. 'Can I have my phone back, please?'

Tina tutted and handed it over. 'By the way, you know you've got a voicemail on there, don't you?'

Marta frowned. She hadn't noticed. Glad of the distraction, she put the phone to her ear.

'*Welcome to the voicemail message centre for oh, seven, nine–*'

'BAW-BAW-BAW-BAW!' A tuneless voice started yelling into the pub's PA system.

'*What the fuck…?!*' screamed Tina.

'Open mike night,' Holly mouthed back, nodding towards the back of the bar where, on a sunken stage, four gothic teens in leathers were throwing their heads around beneath the bright coloured lights.

Marta abandoned her attempts to retrieve the voicemail and looked at her housemates.

'Down our drinks and then leave?' suggested Holly, just as someone had the foresight to turn down the amps.

'Thank the fucking Lord,' said Tina, as the foursome continued to jump about on the stage, seemingly oblivious to the snub.

Marta tried again to retrieve her voicemail, while Tina continued to swear at anyone who would listen.

'*Welcome to the voicemail message centre for–*'

'That's not fucking *music*, is it? No one wants to be subjected to that when they're out for a quiet pint...'

'*You have one new message.*'

'It's open mike, Tina – that's the whole point. It's to give bands a chance to perform live when they can't get proper gigs.'

'Yeah, well there's a *reason* these guys don't get booked for proper gigs, isn't there? They're *shit*.'

'*Hi, this is a message for Marta Da-brow-ska,*' Marta heard, pressing her head against the earpiece to make out the message above Tina's rant. '*It's Laura here, from Bright Sparks.*' Marta's heart started thumping. She thought back to the terrible interview where she had run over the director's foot and embarrassed herself with her lack of experience. '*I wonder if you could call me back about some potential work we have for you. It's an assistant analyst position at a strategic marketing consultancy near Holborn. Two weeks' work, starting next week, so the sooner you can call me back the better. My number is...*'

Marta let out a little yelp, curtailing Tina's argument instantly. 'They find me a job! Is the agency you told me about, Holly... They want me to work in strategic marketing place for two weeks!'

Marta's housemates stared, slowly realising the significance of the news.

'That's awesome!' cried Holly.

'Congratulations!' yelled Tina.

'Great stuff. Well, at least I think it's great stuff. What company is it?'

Marta shrugged uncertainly. 'Place in Holborn. I have to call them back.' She gasped as something occurred to her. 'You think it's too late? You think they might give job to someone else when I didn't call back? Oh no! Am an idiot! I should have seen voicemail...'

Rich shook his head. 'Stop worrying, Marta. They'll give you time to call back. Just make sure it's first thing tomorrow. What's the role? What will you be doing in the way of market-based strategising?'

Holly whacked him. 'Shut up, Rich.'

'No, really, I just wondered what–'

Holly silenced him with a look. This was a recurring argument between Holly and Rich. Holly worked in a big consulting firm and she was miserable: constantly exhausted and irritated with the corporate machine. Rich didn't understand why she stuck with it. Perhaps he thought she should go into teaching, like him. She hadn't dared ask Holly about the history between them.

'Anyway, when does the job start?' asked Tina brightly. 'Assuming they haven't given it to someone else, that is.'

Marta smiled nervously. 'Next week.' Her stomach was already churning with nerves. Rich's words had filled her with fear: not just fear of losing out on the job, but fear of not being able to cope if she got it. The world of marketing strategy was filled with jargon and buzz words – foreign buzz words. Holly often came home late at night, moaning about it. If *she* struggled, how was Marta going to cope?

'A toast!' cried Tina, just as the band started up again. 'From canapé waitress to strategy consultant in one fell swoop – woo hoo! To Marta's new job!'

'To Marta's new job!' repeated Holly and Rich.

Marta watched as her glass was buffeted in all directions by the other three. She didn't feel brave enough to celebrate her new job – not yet.

'I haven't got it yet,' she said modestly. 'And it's only two weeks of work. But I will impress them. I will make them want me for longer. When I put a foot through the door, they will ask me for full-time job!' Marta paused for her housemates to appreciate her use of colloquial English. 'And I will have proper salary and I will pay proper rent! I promise, it will happen very soon.'

Marta took a swig of beer, feeling a spark ignite inside her that she hadn't felt in a while. This was her first real opportunity in England and she wasn't going to let it slip away. There would be no more desperate searches for poorly paid menial jobs. This was it. This was the start of her *career*.

'What?' asked Marta, suspiciously, when she realised that Holly, Tina and Rich were all trying to conceal smirks.

Tina's shoulders were shaking, her head bowed low as she struggled to restrain herself. Holly was trying to confine her giggles to her pint glass. Rich leaned forward.

'I'm not sure putting your foot *through* the door is the sort of entrance they're looking for,' he said.

Marta looked at him. 'I got it wrong? The phrase?'

Rich gave her a quick, surreptitious nod. 'You get a foot *in* the door – you don't put your foot through it.'

'Well, I'm gonna go and put a foot through the bar,' declared Tina. 'And this time I'm getting chasers!'

Marta laughed, she couldn't help it. These English people had such crazy expressions. She tipped back her glass and drained it, slamming it down on the table the way she had seen people over here do. Maybe she didn't have all the phrases quite right yet, but she was getting there. At least she was beginning to feel welcome. Soon she would be getting to grips with the English workplace just as she had got to grips with the social side. She would get there; Marta felt sure she would.

26

'Just tell me, Dominik. I hate secrets.'

Dominik gave a cryptic smile. 'You won't hate this one.'

They were crawling through the Friday night traffic in a taxi. *A taxi.* It had already cost Dominik twelve pounds and they had barely left Kilburn. Marta shot him a sidelong glance. He had had his hair cut for the first time since she first met him and he was wearing a shirt. She couldn't get used to the look. It was like seeing a footballer wearing a suit for the first time. Marta liked it, although she was beginning to wonder whether the evening might warrant something smarter than the short black skirt and knee-high boots she had chosen.

'I've got some news,' Dominik announced, his hazel eyes glinting.

Marta looked at him. She knew instantly what it was. There was only one thing it could have been. He had got the job driving trains underground. She was pleased, in a way, but not surprised. The only surprise was that Dominik hadn't expected it himself.

'Well?' she said. 'You tell me yours and I'll tell you mine.'

'Yours?' Dominik's gaze flicked quickly from her bare thighs to her face. 'What's *your* news?'

Marta coyly raised an eyebrow. In fact, she was dying to tell Dominik her news, but she didn't want to steal the spotlight. She had called the agency first thing on Wednesday, having convinced herself overnight that they had given the job to someone else, but miraculously, they hadn't. They gave her the details of the two-week placement and told her to start the following week.

'I've got a new job,' said Dominik, predictably.

'Brilliant!' replied Marta, trying to sound enthused. He was planning to spend eight hours a day below ground; eight hours in a dark, polluted tunnel, his only contact with other people through a one-way intercom, and then only to instruct passengers to move away from the doors. And then there were the suicide jumpers... The thought of hurtling into a leaping figure at forty kilometres an hour, seeing the blood drip down your windscreen as you pulled into the station... 'The tube driving job?' she asked, as brightly as she could.

Dominik shook his head, smiling. 'No. I took your advice and made a few applications. It's been a busy week.'

'Really...?' Marta was intrigued.

'I'm going to be a finance assistant at a small law firm in Holborn.'

'Holborn!' Marta blurted.

'Yeah. Why?'

'That's where I'll be working,' replied Marta, hurriedly. 'For two weeks, at least. I've got a placement through Holly's agency. A real job, in strategic marketing!'

Dominik slid sideways in the cab and, quite unexpectedly, kissed her hard on the lips. Before Marta knew what was happening, it was over and Dominik was back in his seat. 'Of course you have. I knew you would.'

Their mini celebration was thwarted by the cab driver ramming open his hatch and asking Dominik for directions. They were somewhere near Hyde Park, Marta noted, and they seemed to be heading towards Kensington.

'We're not going to Tash's for dinner, are we?' she asked with an anxious expression that was only partly faked.

'You've ruined the surprise!' Dominik feigned annoyance and then leaned forward to direct the driver. 'Anywhere here on the left is good,' he told the man as they cruised down a residential street lined with expensive parked cars.

Marta hopped out, trying not to look as Dominik handed over what must have been a full day's salary to the cabbie.

'Where are we?' she asked.

Dominik just took her hand, grinning, and led her across the road towards an unobtrusive brick house that looked much like all the others on the row, except that its windows were flanked by neatly trimmed greenery. Above the door was a quaint hanging sign that said *Wodka*.

They were ushered inside by a middle-aged woman in a spotty dress, whom Marta instantly knew to be Polish. It was a Polish restaurant. Young Poles flitted smoothly from table to table and the smell of good, Polish food filled the air.

Marta breathed deeply, marvelling at the setup. The restaurant was small and split into two halves: one with heavy oak panelling and dark velvet drapes and the other, where Marta and Dominik were seated, bright and airy with white floor tiles and colourful oil paintings.

'It used to be the Kensington Palace dairy,' explained Dominik. 'A guy called Jan Woroniecki opened it twenty years ago and it's been in Polish hands ever since.'

'*Amazing*,' exclaimed Marta as a dog trotted under their table.

'*Chodź tutaj!*' screamed the woman in charge, sending the mongrel scampering to the back of the restaurant via a small piece of cheese on the floor.

'Just like at home!' said Marta, remembering the restaurant in Łomianki where the resident dog had got so fat that it no longer fitted between the tables. It just lay on the doormat, opening and shutting its jaws.

The waitress took their drinks order in Polish.

'*How did she know we were Polish?*' hissed Marta, when the girl was gone. '*Is everyone?*'

Dominik just smiled. Marta continued to gaze around her. In the darker half of the restaurant, the tables had been pushed together and were occupied by a group of young Poles; she could tell they were Poles from the regular cries of '*Na zdrowie!*' and the chinking of glasses. They were loud, but not in an English way. There were no cries of 'Drink! Drink!' There was no standing on chairs, no clumsy escapes to the toilets. The rest of the restaurant was filled with couples and small groups, some clearly Polish, others who were not so easy to pinpoint.

The waitress returned with two ice-cold Żywiecs and helped them narrow down the impossibly long list of delicacies from the menu. *Gołąbki, leniwe, kaszanka*… all her favourite dishes were here. Marta could feel herself grinning. It was just like being back home.

'Proper *chleb*,' Dominik remarked, tucking into the bread. 'It's even better than the stuff I get on Sundays.'

Marta took the piece he was holding out, laughing at the reference to his Sunday ritual.

'What?' he said, clearly reading her mind. 'You know Yishai from my house goes over to Israel with an empty suitcase every two months. When he comes back it's full of home-cooked food.'

'Is there no Israeli café in Acton?' asked Marta, tucking into the stuffed cabbage leaves that had appeared in front of her.

'Not yet. There are African takeaways and jerk chicken outlets and there's even the odd English café, but English cooking sucks.'

Marta laughed. 'My housemate Holly has a rule for her cooking: she says any meal must take less time to prepare than it takes to eat.'

'What? That's crazy!'

Marta shrugged. 'She's English. Busy person. No time to cook.'

'What does she live on?'

'Sandwiches, mainly.'

Dominik shook his head, reaching across the table and swiping a mouthful straight off Marta's fork. '*English*,' he said, grinning as he swallowed her food. 'Gotta love the English.'

They fell into a comfortable silence, exchanging smiles and occasional remarks as the noise level around them rose. Marta's stomach started to fill, but the wine was washing everything down nicely. Twilight turned to darkness outside and an old-fashioned street lamp flickered on, casting an intermittent shaft of light across

Dominik's sandy hair. His eyes, Marta noticed, kept making detours when he looked at her face, roaming over her body when he thought she wasn't looking.

Marta pushed her plate aside, finally admitting defeat. As she did so, the hubbub was interrupted by the sound of a shrill English voice at a nearby table.

'*Go, lab, key,*' the woman was articulating to the waitress, a timid girl who could have been the younger sister of the one serving at their table. She was lifting her shoulders apologetically and trying to catch a glimpse of the woman's menu.

'GO, LAB, KEY!' repeated the woman, who was dining with a man of a similar age – mid-forties – and of an equally impatient disposition. They were both staring at the girl as though she were completely stupid.

Marta smiled and leaned over. The room swayed a little, telling Marta that she was drunk, but she didn't care.

'It's ga-wob-ka, not go-lab-key. It is *you* who make the mistake.'

Marta turned back to her meal and chopped up the last few pieces of sausage meat, with no intention of eating it. She could feel Dominik's eyes upon her and she suspected he wasn't the only one staring. A hush had fallen on the restaurant and the sound of her knife on the plate seemed painfully loud. She continued to chop, unabashed.

'What?' said Marta, looking up a moment later when the collective chatter had swelled once more. Dominik was still looking at her. 'Well there's no point in being English about it, is there?' She shrugged. 'The woman was being rude; someone had to tell her.'

Dominik nodded, smiling. Marta looked up again. This time she held his gaze. His smile faded gently and his hazel eyes stared into hers. She watched him, feeling the electricity run between them as the moment went on and on, neither daring to move. Then the waitress swooped over to collect their plates and the moment passed.

'So... new job.' Dominik grinned. 'Does this mean I'll never get to see you in that attractive waitress uniform you told me about?'

Marta glared at him with mock menace. 'Don't even joke,' she said. 'I'm not putting that whale outfit on for anyone – not even you.'

Dominik pretended to sulk, but his act was interrupted by the waitress asking about desserts.

'I can't,' Marta told her, genuinely upset that she hadn't left room for kolache with cream. Dominik apologised and asked for the bill.

'Fancy finding a bar halfway between yours and mine?' he asked as he surreptitiously handed over a wad of notes that must have come straight from his last brown envelope.

Marta stood up – too quickly, it transpired. She grabbed onto the back of her chair and waited for the floor to stop sliding around. The wine had gone to her head.

Re-orientating herself, Marta realised that the piece of furniture propping her up was not actually a piece of furniture after all. It was Dominik's arm.

'Thanks,' she uttered, feeling stable again, but embarrassed. She could feel the heat of his arm around her waist and it was comforting to feel it still there as she moved across the restaurant. The team of waitresses said a friendly goodbye and the proprietor insisted on one of her staff pouring fluorescent *ajerkoniak* into shot glasses for them to drink on the way out.

It was Dominik's idea to get another cab. 'Let's live like Londoners,' was all he said when he saw Marta's bemused expression. 'We'll be earning London salaries soon. Stop worrying.'

Marta might have worried had she not consumed so much wine. They hadn't even started their new jobs yet and hers was only temporary. But tonight she felt rash. Dominik was right. Soon they would be earning proper money. Soon they wouldn't need to worry about the cost of a cab. They were moving up in the world.

The taxi swung into Knightsbridge, sending Marta slithering across the plastic seats and into Dominik's lap. She clambered off, tugging her clothes back into place and wishing for a moment that she had opted for a longer skirt.

'Sorry,' she muttered, pushing the locks of hair off her face as she tried to right herself. Somehow her legs were still entwined in his.

'No worries,' he said, grinning. Marta flailed some more, then realised why she was finding it so hard to right herself. Dominik had her trapped around the waist. She stopped struggling. Dominik loosened his grip, allowing her to wriggle round so that she was nestled against him, her head on his shoulder. She could feel it move as he lowered his arm.

Marta let Dominik slide a hand into her hair and bring her face towards his. She could smell his scent. She breathed it in, running a hand up his shirtsleeve, feeling the contour of his muscles underneath.

'We're not going to a bar, are we?' he murmured, touching her lips gently with his and pulling away just enough to focus on her eyes.

Marta smiled. She could feel her breathing become quicker, more shallow. Dominik's lips pressed against hers once more and then she realised: *they had nowhere to go.* She was sleeping in Holly's lounge and Dominik shared his room with a dozen young men.

'Dom–'

He silenced her with his lips and Marta was lost again. Her skin tingled where his fingers touched her. The kissing was deeper, more urgent. They were locked together and it felt right, as though they could stay like this forever.

'WHERE EXAC'LY IN ACTON?' demanded the driver, suddenly.

Marta sat up, yanking her skirt down from around her waist and trying to compose herself.

'St Leonards Road,' Dominik replied calmly, simultaneously pulling Marta back into his lap. 'Just off Victoria Road.'

Marta said nothing as they pulled up outside number twelve. She allowed Dominik to guide her out of the cab, not wanting to deal with the reality of Croatian housemates or sofa beds.

The house was unexpectedly empty.

'*Where is everyone?*' whispered Marta, half expecting a musical fanfare as a crowd of Nigerians jumped out from behind the door.

'*Away!*' Dominik whispered in response, walking backwards and drawing her close as he kicked the front door shut. 'There's some Czech national holiday this week and the Israelis have decided that now is a good time to visit their hometown near Gaza. Not sure where Uzoma is, but he's out late most nights.'

Dominik had hardly finished his sentence before Marta felt his lips against hers. He took another step back, guiding her towards him, drawing her into a part of the house she had never seen before. They seemed to be under the stairs. Stooping and shielding her head with a hand, Dominik led her into a small room with a sloping ceiling that stretched all the way down to the floor. It was like a cupboard; a cupboard equipped with an airbed, stereo, laptop, dartboard and mini bar.

Collapsing on the bed was inevitable; there wasn't space for them both to stand in the small stretch of floor at the end of the room. Quite how they got from being vertical in the doorway, fully clothed, to being horizontal on the bed, semi-naked and drinking shots of limoncello from miniature tea cups, was a bit of a blur.

'I'm worried about your bra.' Dominik smiled, pouring another shot and placing it on the ledge that served as the bar. 'I don't want it getting sticky.'

'Mmm,' said Marta, rolling so that she was on top of him, her breasts lightly touching his bare chest. 'What should we do about that?'

Dominik ran a finger lightly over her skin, travelling from her hip to her waist, over her ribs and up to her face, veering casually over an erect nipple on the way. Marta caught her breath. His hand slid up to her cheek, his eyes not leaving hers. Then it slithered down once more, stopping again as it reached her breast and teasing her with his light touch through the lace. She rose to her knees, straddling him, and undid her bra as he watched, his eyes feasting on her naked breasts.

'And what about *your* clothes?' she asked, bending down to kiss him and tasting the sweet, syrupy liqueur on his lips as she undid the buckle of his belt.

'Mmm,' he grinned, kissing her again as the jeans came off. 'It would be a shame to see them get dirty.'

27

Marta's eyes fluttered open and then closed again. She was awake, but only just. Her body felt heavy and tired and at the same time... *sticky*. She ran her tongue round the inside of her mouth. It tasted of damp walls with a hint of lemon. Her head was throbbing.

Marta allowed herself a quick squint at the world through half-closed eyes. The wall was made of panelled wood and seemed very close to her face. It was a bit like being in a coffin, in fact.

Marta's eyes opened, suddenly remembering. *She was in Dominik's bedroom.* She had slept with Dominik. She was lying with him, naked, in his bed. Her mind filled with questions. Was this bad? Should she have held back? What would Dominik think? Did it mean anything? Would it happen again? God, she hoped so.

She turned her head, very slowly. A tuft of sandy hair was poking out from under the duvet next to her and Marta could just make out his long, sandy eyelashes in the dim light. Marta watched him, listening to the soft, steady purr of his breathing. Her right leg was between his, so she couldn't move – not that she wanted to.

'Marta,' Dominik uttered, shifting towards her, eyes still shut.

Marta wriggled closer, aligning her body with his under the covers. He reached out and pulled her towards him, his eyes still shut but breaking into a smile. Then he was on top of her, looking straight into her eyes sleepily, but lustfully. She lay back, feeling Dominik's erection digging into her groin. He rearranged the locks of sticky hair around her face as though composing her for a photo. '*Gorgeous,*' he said, lowering himself so that he was almost inside her.

The moment was shattered by the sound of a high-pitched ring-tone. They tried to ignore it, rubbing against one another, kissing.

The ringing didn't stop.

'Is that yours?' Dominik reluctantly raised himself from her body.

Equally reluctantly, Marta nodded.

'Want to answer it?' he asked, propping himself up on one elbow.

'No.'

Finally, there was peace. Dominik rolled towards her again and started tickling Marta's thigh. She was feeling weak. His hand slid masterfully up her leg, but just as she thought she couldn't take any more, it stopped. Dominik looked at her. 'It's ringing again.'

He was right. The phone – wherever it was in the jumble of clothes, tea cups and Dominik's belongings – was bleeping again.

'Hello?' she groaned, once her fingers had finally made contact with the scratched lump of plastic. She couldn't think who might be calling her from a withheld number at nine o'clock on a Saturday.

'Marta, it's me.'

She recognised the voice, but it sounded strained. 'Holly?'

'Yeah. I didn't wake you, did I?'

Marta looked round at Dominik, who was sitting behind her on the bed, his legs wrapped around her waist. 'No! I was up!' She gently removed Dominik's wandering hand.

'Oh good. Only I'm trying to get hold of Tina and she's not picking up. I just wondered whether she was in the house?'

'Um…' Marta shivered as Dominik started nibbling her ear. 'I don't know…'

Holly tutted. 'Might've known. She's not back from wherever she was last night, is she? Dirty stop-out.'

Marta felt a pinch of guilt. 'I guess.'

Holly sighed. She sounded tired.

'Are you OK?' Marta asked softly.

'Well, no, not really.' She sighed again. 'I've been in the office since eight yesterday morning and I've still got fuck loads to do before our deadline at two today – God knows why the deadline is two o'clock on a Saturday – and there's no way I'll be able to make today's hockey match, which I'm supposed to be captaining.'

'You been in the office since twenty-five hours?' Marta asked, incredulously. Surely it wasn't possible to stay awake, *working*, for that long?

'Yeah, and counting.' Holly sounded really miserable. Marta couldn't imagine what Holly was doing at Anderton's, but whatever it was, she seemed to do a lot of it. Too much.

'Look, if Tina makes a reappearance, can you tell her I'm desperate to get hold of her? She'll have to stand in as captain for today and we'll need to find a sub for me… fuck knows who we're gonna get at this short – oh my God. Hang on…'

'What?'

'Marta. You're fit, aren't you?'

Marta had lost the thread of the conversation and was distracted by Dominik's stray hand. 'I fit?' she repeated, feeling very hot all of a sudden.

'Yes – you're fit. You do sport… you could stand in for me!'

'You mean… I play?' Marta was struggling to stay in control. She needed to tell Dominik to stop, but she couldn't.

'Yes! Brilliant! OK, Marta, when Tina comes back, just ask her to sort you out with kit and stuff. She knows where everything is. Oh, and tell her she's captain. Match starts at one. You're meeting in the changing rooms at half twelve. Good luck!'

28

'OK! Pothithions!' yelled Tina, removing the purple thing from her mouth and spitting a mouthful of phlegm onto the fake green turf. 'Defence, sort yourselves out at the back. Chelsea Ladies have got some really good strikers, so you'll need to be on your guard. Vic and Sam on the wings, me up front... who else...?'

Tina looked quite imposing, standing there in her tight purple skirt and Kilburn Ladies top, her long, skinny thighs disappearing into thick padded shins and mean-looking boots. She was one of the only girls on the team who managed to look stunning as well as scary. Most, it had to be said, just looked scary.

'Marta, where d'you wanna play?'

Suddenly, everyone was looking at her. Marta shrugged, feeling somewhat queasy and slightly unnerved that her housemate had turned all bossy and organised.

'OK, you can play up front with me. Guys, for those of you who haven't met Marta, she's our housemate and she's standing in for Holly today. She's fast but her ball skills may be a bit rusty.'

Marta didn't catch everything Tina said, but she got the idea. She did, however, seem to be leaving out one vitally important fact: that Marta had never played hockey before.

'Tina, I want to explain that I–'

'Marta, you'll be great,' Tina said quickly. 'You've got nothing to worry about.'

Marta had everything to worry about. Like the fact that these balls they were whacking around were very, very hard. And the fact that nobody had told her where she should stand on the giant pitch or what she should do when she was there. And the likelihood of her teammates with bandanas and muscular legs passing the ball to her and getting angry when she messed it up. And, of course, the fact that she was still drunk from last night and was frankly in a bit of a daze.

The brief lesson she had received from Tina on the tube would have to suffice, Marta realised, seeing the other girls migrate to the expanse of plastic grass. She shoved the plastic block into her mouth, readjusted the flappy skirt and jogged onto the pitch with everyone else, deciding that this would be an excellent learning experience.

Marta trotted over to the spot where Tina was pointing and waited for the game to begin. Directly opposite her was a frightening looking girl with red hair and big thighs who was grunting like a tribesman. The Chelsea Ladies looked pretty fearsome in their slinky yellow and brown kit. Marta looked over to the middle of the pitch, where Tina and her opponent were bent over the ball, poised for action. A small man in black and white hovered next to them, whistle in mouth.

The most peculiar thing happened next. The girls in the middle started bashing their sticks against one another's, directly above the ball; as if they were performing some sort of ritual. Then all hell broke loose. One of them hit the ball, which went zooming towards the opposition and stopped next to a girl in yellow, who whacked it in the other direction. The ball flew at high speed between yellow and purple players, moving so smoothly it appeared to be hovering above the green surface. Marta, meanwhile, ran randomly up and down her part of the pitch wondering what she should be doing.

Up, down. Up, down. Then it happened. Marta made contact with the ball – only briefly, and only to send it shooting off the pitch towards the perimeter fencing – but it was contact nonetheless. Marta was the closest player, so she took it upon herself to fetch it. This was when she learned how hard it was to push a small, heavy object along the ground with a spindly piece of wood. It was like

166

trying to rescue an insect from the surface of a swimming pool using a broom handle.

'You take it!' yelled Tina, when Marta had finally coaxed the ball back onto the pitch.

Marta shook her head, shrugging. What did that mean? *Take it where?*

Eventually Tina came to the rescue.

'I'll take it!' she yelled, running over wielding her stick and brandishing a row of purple teeth. 'You go down the line!'

Marta gratefully relinquished the ball and from that point onwards she adopted a different approach, loitering in the free space near the goal where the ball rarely travelled.

After what seemed like a very long wait, the whistle blew and Marta's ordeal was over. She dragged her stick towards the little hut, thanking God that her limbs were still in working order and her face intact. She hadn't scored any goals for the opposition, which also seemed like cause for celebration.

Tina was already in full-on celebratory mode when Marta arrived, whacking other girls on the back and punching the air with her fist.

'We should be really proud, girls! Nil-all against a team that's won every game this season… not bad!'

There were nods of agreement, accompanied by a slurping sound as a bag of chopped-up oranges came out of somebody's bag.

'In the second half, we need to be more aggressive,' said Tina.

Marta stared at her. *Second half? They were only halfway?*

Marta's fears were confirmed as the pep talk progressed. They were about to go back out onto the pitch.

'Marta, you need to mark more closely. Your player's good, so stick tight,' Tina instructed.

Marta nodded obediently. Stick tight. Mark closely. This was worse than marketing for jargon.

'Let's go!' yelled Tina, shoving her block into her mouth and tossing the orange peel onto the ground.

For Marta, the second half consisted of an exhausting game of follow-my-leader, with the redhead perpetually in the lead. She was, considering her stocky build, remarkably fit and she didn't seem to like Marta tagging along, but tagging along was the instruction she had been given and Marta knew how important it was to follow instructions in this country.

Something exciting happened just after the referee said, 'Two minutes, ladies'. Tina stopped the ball with her stick and cleverly weaved it past several of the yellow players, almost all the way to the goal. As she lifted her stick to bash it past the goalkeeper, one of the Chelsea girls whipped the ball out from under her and sent it rushing towards the redhead.

Marta tried to intercept the ball but failed, leaving it to bounce off the redhead's stick and off the end of the pitch.

'Corner!' shouted one of Marta's teammates as she trotted off to retrieve the ball. 'Well done Marta!'

Marta had no idea what she had done, or not done, but it seemed that a good number of her teammates were assembling in some sort of semi-circle around the goal, while half of the yellow team was loitering inside the goal looking angry. Marta awaited further instruction, but there was none.

'Tina…?' said Marta, quietly.

Tina glanced sideways, then back to the girl with the ball, who was crouching on the back line like a cat waiting to pounce.

'Just try and get a goal!' she screeched, as the girl made to hit the ball.

It all happened too quickly. Marta was vaguely aware of the sharp pang all the way up her right arm and her ears registered the faint thud, but mostly she just heard screaming: ear-splitting screaming, coming from all around; and underneath it, the sound of a whistle.

'What happen?' she asked, as Tina came running towards her, wielding her stick high above her head and whooping.

'We fucking won! That's what happened! Thanks to *you!*'

Marta frowned. '*Really?*'

'Yes! You're our hero! Well, strictly speaking that girl on the opposition who pushed the ball in is our hero, but you helped it in!'

There was a flurry of handshaking, hair ruffling and backslapping as the girls trampled happily off the pitch. It seemed Marta's earlier clumsiness had been forgiven, and some of the girls, Marta noted as they pushed open the doors to the Chelsea clubhouse bar, were even mistakenly talking about 'Marta's next match'. She smiled, knowing full well that the praise wasn't warranted, but she lapped it up all the same.

'Am not staying for much long,' she explained to the girl with pigtails who was sliding a huge jug of frothy purple drink towards her.

'Why the hell not?' the girl demanded. 'This is the most important part of the match!' She sloshed a pint of cocktail into the plastic glass and moved on to the next.

The truth was, Marta needed to go back to bed. She needed to sober up, sleep, eat, drink water and reflect on the last twenty-four hours. Getting drunk with English girls in a noisy bar was not the right way to straighten out tangled thoughts.

Marta sipped her purple drink. It was disgusting. Sickly and sour at the same time; like blackcurrant mixed with piss. She swallowed it, wiping her mouth and wandering off towards the toilets.

She was making her way back through the sweaty bar, trying to think up a credible excuse for leaving early, when someone tapped her on the shoulder.

'Hey.'

She recognised his voice instantly, but she couldn't place it. Marta turned and felt herself freezing over. There, in the middle of the bar, surrounded by sweaty, brutish lads and dressed in a rugby shirt and jeans, was Jack. Tash's boyfriend. *Ex*-boyfriend.

'So, you're playing for the Kilburn Ladies now?' he asked. His hair was still wet from the shower and he looked like someone from an aftershave ad.

Marta looked at him blankly. 'Just today. Holly couldn't play.'

'Did you win?' He seemed oblivious to her cold stare, his eyes dancing flirtatiously.

She nodded, deadpan. It was hard to believe she had been the least bit tempted by Jack before. Of course, his chiselled features and rugby build were a draw for any girl, but he was obnoxious. Marta could see that now. He was obnoxious and *boring*.

'Well done.' Jack smiled, moving closer so that only she could hear above the din. 'Listen Marta, about that text I sent.' He looked down at the floor as though finding it difficult to find the words, although Marta suspected it was all an act. 'I meant what I said. I'm sorry. About everything – including going out with Tash in the first place, but that's another story. I just...' He ran a hand through his wet hair. 'I just want to make it up to you. To apologise.'

Marta's expression didn't change. She knew that his words were designed to soften her, to melt her frosty exterior, but they left her cold. She watched as Jack went through what was no doubt a practised set of moves: looking away, eyes roaming the blank space between them, hand awkwardly scratching his head... and all she could think about was Dominik.

'You must've gone through hell when Tash kicked you out and it was my fault, Marta. I just wish I'd been there for you. You should've called me. I would've helped.'

There were so many things she could have said to this. A set of angry stock phrases bubbled to the surface of Marta's conscience and she was vaguely aware of the venom with which they ought to be delivered, but she couldn't be bothered. It would be a waste of breath.

'I'm fine,' she said.

'Well,' said Jack, looking genuinely stumped by her lack of interest. 'Just call me if you fancy that dinner. The offer's open. You've got my number.'

'No I haven't,' replied Marta.

'Oh right,' said Jack, with only a hint of shame. Then, to Marta's astonishment, he reached into his back pocket and handed over a business card. 'Like I said, the offer's open.'

Marta took the card, flashed him a false smile and headed off to join the others, planning to lose the card on the way.

29

'You can go on up,' the receptionist informed Marta primly. 'First floor. Just ask for David Lyle.'

Marta stepped into the lift, checking her suited reflection in the mirrored walls. In the short ride up, she tried to compose herself, testing out different facial expressions and postures. None of these made her look any more relaxed.

'Ah, hello!' cried a squeaky male voice almost as soon as the lift doors opened. Marta stepped into the lobby – a strange experience due to the large number of yellow and green shapes suspended from the ceiling – towards a short, grinning man. He was wearing a flowery shirt and jeans. Marta instantly felt overdressed.

'Marta Daba-daba-duda, or some such unpronounceable name, I presume?' He offered her a firm handshake.

'Da-brov-ska,' she said, clearly but politely.

'Excellent. Well, come on through. I'm David Lyle. Like the sugar – ahahahaha! I'm managing director here. Welcome to Strat-isvision.'

Marta followed the man through a swipe card door and into a huge, open plan office. The yellow and green theme from the lobby extended throughout the office.

'Bet you can't guess our corporate colours!' he joked as he led her through a green foam archway erected between desks, which seemed to serve no other purpose than to take up space. Marta tried not to look too alarmed as she glanced round the room. It was buzzing with activity: phones ringing, printers whirring, people rushing from desk to desk. It looked so intense – but so *silly*, with all these coloured shapes. And she was definitely overdressed, she decided, judging by the glimpses of leather boots, skinny jeans and big, tasselled belts she caught as she followed the MD through the room.

'My office,' he announced, holding open the door of an all-glass room in the middle. There was a band of opaqueness at shoulder height (head-height for David Lyle) that Marta supposed was to prevent people from looking in, although it didn't seem particularly effective. She felt as though she were in a goldfish bowl.

'Sit!' he commanded, motioning to the colourful chairs that were strewn around the oval table. 'So! You're here with us for what... two weeks?'

Marta nodded.

'And very nice it is to have you, too. So, d'you know what we do here at Stratisvision?'

Marta nodded again. She had studied the website very carefully on Holly's computer. 'Help clients solve marketing problems in strategic and pragmatic ways.'

David drew back his head in mock surprise. '*Very* good. So, you've done your homework. But d'you know *what we do,* I mean what we *stand* for? What we're *like,* as a company?'

As the MD leaned forward, Marta noticed a string of beads around his neck. It was the sort of jewellery a beach bum in Australia might wear, she thought.

'We *make love to our clients!*' cried the man, banging the table with his palm and looking at Marta. 'Ha. Not literally, of course. Well... unless you want to. And let me tell you, sex is positively encouraged in this firm. *Positively encouraged.*' The director gave her a lingering look. Marta wished she had opted for the trousers rather than the skirt.

'No, we make love to our clients *metaphorically,*' he said. 'We are passionate about our clients. We get close to them. We understand their problems. We know what keeps them awake at night. And that's the important thing. Whatever you end up working on here,

172

remember that: make love to the client.'

Marta gave a nervous laugh, although she suspected this wasn't the appropriate response. Mr Lyle seemed deadly serious.

'Moving on!' cried David, leaping out of his seat and wandering over to a bookshelf that exhibited, in front of the colourful book spines, a set of origami animals in yellow and green. 'Take this,' he said, plucking out a slim booklet and tossing it onto the table. 'That tells you everything you need to know about us.'

Marta flicked through it politely. It was full of swirly patterns and colourful pictures, with occasional words written in huge, chunky fonts. 'Thanks,' she said uncertainly.

'Now you're probably wondering what on earth you'll be doing here for two weeks, hmm?'

Marta was actually wondering what on earth David Lyle had on his feet; his shoes looked like leather flippers. She nodded.

'Well, the fact is, I don't know. But I do know that we're bloody busy right now and there's no shortage of work! I expect someone will grab you the minute you sit down, so be prepared for that.'

'OK.'

'Not that you're likely to be workshy... being Polish!'

Marta gritted her teeth. She felt like a zoo animal that was being taunted.

Finally, David yanked open the door, sticking his head into the open plan office.

'Kim! Kat! Nik!' he called. 'Would one of you show our lovely Polish temp around the office?' He turned back to Marta and lowered his voice. 'Never can tell the difference between them,' he said, smiling.

A doll-like figure approached David's office. Kat had white-blonde hair, dark, tanned skin and a natural beauty that was marred only by her sour expression.

'OK, let's go,' she said brusquely, marching off towards one end of the office. 'This is Patricia Catermol's office? But she's not around? She's the CEO?'

Marta trotted to keep up with the girl, whose voice seemed to lift at the end of each statement, as though she were asking a question.

'You'll hardly ever see Patricia, she's so busy? You've met David, and this is Joan, Peter, Charlotte, Dean...' the list went on. Marta nodded and smiled, forgetting every name as soon as she heard it.

'...this is me? And that's Nik and Kim?' finished Kat, strutting back to where they had started.

'Thanks,' replied Marta, feeling a bit overwhelmed as Kat returned to her seat and got back to whatever she had been doing.

Eventually, one of the other slim, pretty girls – Kim or Nik – looked up and said, 'You can sit anywhere; we hot desk.'

Marta nodded, none the wiser. *Hot desk?* She wandered to the next block of kidney-shaped desks and stopped at an empty one, faltering as she waited for the young guy – the only one who had smiled at her when she had been paraded around – to look up.

'I can sit here?' she asked.

His head shot up and he smiled again.

'You seat anywhere – ee's hot desking.'

Hot desk-*ing*, noted Marta. His speech sounded funny. Maybe he was foreign, she thought hopefully. He looked foreign: dark eyes, dark eyebrows and hairy chin, all slightly askew as though his features had been fitted together in a rush.

'Thanks.'

Marta sat down and rattled the mouse. Everything in this office was shiny and new; most of it yellow or green.

Ten minutes later, she was still sitting there. She had read – or at least, studied the pictures in – the colourful Stratisvision booklet four times and followed every link on the Stratisvision website. Now she was bored.

There were two other people on the curvy desk besides Marta and the guy with the wonky features. One was a middle-aged woman with short mousy hair and a scowl, the other was a good-looking man in his thirties with black-rimmed glasses and a serious expression as he stared at his screen. *Everyone* was staring at their screens. Marta seemed to have picked the one desk that was exempt from frenzied activity.

A full thirty minutes later, just as Marta was considering heading back into David Lyle's office and reminding him of her existence, the wonky-faced guy popped his head up.

'You smoke?' he asked.

Marta nodded. She didn't smoke, but today she would. If inhaling a bit of nicotine was what it would take to penetrate this mysterious consultancy and lift her chances of a proper job offer, then she would take the health risk.

'Come. I show you smokers' corner,' he said, revealing another crooked smile.

The first drag was a surprisingly pleasant experience, considering she hadn't smoked a cigarette for nearly eight years. Marta breathed deeply, letting the fumes fill her lungs. Doing nothing was, it transpired, remarkably stressful.

The guy's name was Carl and he was Italian. As it happened – much to Marta's delight – he had started at Stratisvision in the same way as her: as a temporary assistant analyst. He spoke softly, but was open and frank.

'I'm guessing you don't know anyone?'

Marta shook her head. 'Apart from David Lyle, who tell me about having sex with clients, and Kat, who ignore me,' she explained.

Carl nearly choked on his cigarette. 'Oh dear.' He coughed. 'Not a good start, then. You want a summary?'

Marta exhaled. 'Yes please.'

'Kat and Nik and Kim. They are all di same: fashionable girls who spend most days on Facebook. They do di 'fun' projects,' he explained, carving out quotations in the air. 'Like the clothing rebrands and sports drink campaigns.'

Marta nodded.

'Neil is the same level, but he only does spreadsheets, I think.' He took one last drag on his cigarette and stubbed it out on the metal grate. 'On our desk, there is Joan and Dean. Joan I hope you will never work for. She is... how do you say... manic depressive? Dean, he is very senior, even though only thirty-one. Do not joke

175

around with heem!'

She nodded. 'So, I choose a good place to sit, then?'

Carl raised an eyebrow. 'Then there is Charlotte, the one who does the marching around the office. She is an *angry woman*. Look out for her. She is the one with the beeg, fuzzy hair.'

Marta nodded, trying to store all the details for future reference.

Carl tucked the cigarettes away in his pocket, squinting in thought. 'These are the main ones. Oh – I forgot the most important! Patricia. The CEO. She is also scary, but crazy. She is not here much. But the reason that Kat is here? She is Patricia's niece.'

Marta took a deep breath as they headed back to the office, feeling the jitters return. She was grateful to Carl for sharing his knowledge with her, but there was one more thing she needed to ask.

'Carl,' she hissed, just as he raised his card to the swipe card door. Then she paused, suddenly unsure of herself.

He looked at her quizzically.

'I have no work,' she whispered, eventually. 'Should I ask someone?'

Carl laughed, shaking his head as he proceeded to swipe them through. 'Marta, if you have no work, this is a good thing. You do not say anything. They are paying for you to do nothing. Wait a bit, and the work will come – too much, for sure. But until then, just enjoy the quiet!'

They re-entered the office, ignoring the scowls from the staunch non-smokers.

Enjoying the quiet was harder than it sounded for someone like Marta. Even as she sat down at her desk she could feel the irritation beginning to burn. She picked up the booklet and flicked through it again, despite already knowing every page off by heart. Her foot started to jiggle under the table. She moved the mouse. The website was still there: bold, colourful and full of meaningless words. She hated having nothing to do.

Suddenly, the noise level picked up behind her. It sounded as though an elephant were charging through it with someone very noisy on board. The floor was actually shaking.

'Not the brand egg! No, yes… the segmentation. We need to rethink. I'm going to get someone on it today…'

Careering towards Marta was a woman with a large amount of frizzy brown hair and a very loud voice.

'That's what I said!' the woman barked into her phone as she drew level with Marta's desk. Marta swivelled back to her screen and pretended to read something on the website.

The conversation ended abruptly, and Marta became aware of a sound right next to her ear. She turned, uncertainly, and found the woman leaning over the desk, staring at the side of Marta's face.

'I'm Charlotte,' she said brusquely. 'I believe you're here to help. I'm working on a project for PopsCo and we need an extra pair of hands. Now, write this down. Natural. Fresh. Authentic – are you writing this? Good. Rustic, real, healthy. That'll do. Got that? Right. I need a moo ball in A1 for each. Have them on my desk, end of play today. Good girl.'

The woman paused briefly to check there was something scribbled on Marta's notepad, then rushed off. Marta let out the breath she had been holding, staring for a long while at the words on the page. *What was her task? What was a moo ball?*

Eventually, she conceded defeat. She needed help.

'*Carl!*' she whispered.

'Oh dear,' he replied, quietly. 'You are working for Charlotte…'

Marta pulled a face. 'Had no choice! What is a moo ball?'

Carl stared at her, then suddenly burst out laughing.

'What?' She looked around, afraid that she had said something stupid.

He looked up and laughed again. Finally he replied. 'Ees not a moo ball; ees a mood board!'

'Oh, right,' said Marta, none the wiser.

Slowly, Carl explained. A mood board was a collection of images that represented a mood or state, stuck onto a piece of cardboard. It sounded pretty basic, actually.

'And where I get the pictures from?' asked Marta, not quite believing that her task was so simple.

Carl looked at her with a glint in his eye. 'Have you ever used a site called Google?'

Marta smiled, embarrassed, and turned back to her screen. She popped her head up a few seconds later.

'*Thanks,*' she whispered.

He smiled. 'No problemo.'

30

'OK, so what do I cook tonight? And where is Holly?' Marta looked around the kitchen. 'She never come home any more.'

Rich took a swig of beer, smiling absent-mindedly. 'Working late,' he said. 'She texted earlier.'

Marta screwed up her nose. 'She spend all her life in that office,' she said, peering into the fridge. 'Just you and me, then? You like the meat pie thing I did?'

Rich blinked, as though only just registering the question.

'Yeah. Loved it. Best thing I've had in ages. But hey, Marta, don't feel obliged to cook, will you? I can do some pasta or something. I really don't mind.'

Marta shrugged. 'If I not paying the rent, I should pay in some way. And anyway, I don't like your English cooking style. It is…' Marta struggled for the word. 'Blank.'

Rich frowned. 'Do you mean bland?'

Marta thought for a second. 'Yes, I mean bland.'

'OK then.' Rich pulled a face as though mildly offended. 'Suit yourself. I'm more than happy to eat whatever you cook.'

Marta set about preparing the dinner, thinking back to meal-times with her little brother and sister. Tomek had loved this dish. Rich sat slumped at the kitchen table, flicking over the pages of one of Tina's magazines. He wasn't even pretending to read it.

'What is your problem?' she asked as she started chopping the meat.

Rich looked up, smiling a little. 'Marta, in this country if you ask that question it generally means you want to pick a fight with someone.'

Marta absorbed this nugget of information, perplexed yet again by the English way of doing things. Why couldn't they be direct about anything?

'It's not so much *my* problem, anyway. It's Holly's,' explained Rich. 'I'm worried about her.'

Marta nodded, feeling around in the fridge for vegetables, with mild trepidation at what she might find. It was true that Holly had problems. She worked all day and all night and she seemed to be getting more and more miserable.

Rich lurched forward as the fridge door swung shut, catching it just in time to grab another beer from the door. 'Ta. I don't think it's just work that's the problem,' he said, cracking open the can. 'Holly's always worked hard. That's the way she is. That's why she got a first when the rest of us all got two-ones.'

'What did you get?' asked Marta, intrigued about this part of their lives. It was amazing to think that while she had been living at home in Łomianki, travelling in to the Szkoła every day and coming home to her family, Holly, Tina and Rich had been living in one of those ancient stone college buildings in Cambridge with courtyards and fountains and butlers. It sounded like another world when they described it: like something you might read about in a fairy tale.

'Two-one,' Rich replied, shrugging. 'I wasn't prepared to put in the hours during our final year. Holly was.'

Marta started stripping the old, yellow strands from the outside of a leek, hoping to find something less rotten inside.

'So, what is Holly's problem, if it not the hard working?' Marta was as curious about Rich's interest in Holly's problems as she was in the problems themselves.

Rich took a swig of beer, squinting into space. 'I dunno exactly. She just hasn't been herself for the last few months – ever since she really got into her job. She's uptight.'

'Up tights?'

'Up *tight*. Tense. Stressed.'

Marta nodded. That was certainly true. Holly used to be the life and soul of every event. Even when she had first arrived, Holly would tell funny stories, play practical jokes and make her housemates laugh. Now she just went to bed.

'I don't think consulting is right for her,' declared Rich.

Marta eyed him carefully as she scraped the dissected leek into the bin, having peeled off every rotten layer and finding herself holding a soggy stump. Rich was very perceptive, she thought – when it came to Holly, at least.

'She always wanted to be the best,' mused Rich, swilling the remains of his beer around in the can. 'At hockey, music, dancing, even *drinking*... That's why she went into consultancy, I reckon. It wasn't because she wanted to do it; it was because that's what all the best people were doing.'

Marta chopped up the remaining vegetables and dropped them into the pot. She was feeling a little uncomfortable hearing Rich delve so deeply into Holly's psyche, but at the same time she was fascinated. He clearly knew a lot more about their housemate than he had let on. He was right, too, Marta thought. Holly *was* driven by success. That was why she had landed a place at one of the most prestigious firms in the world, and that was why she spent so many days and nights in the office. She just wanted to succeed, to do well. Marta knew how that felt.

'That's why she's wearing herself out in this job,' Rich went on, 'because she can't bear to do anything badly.'

Marta left the food to simmer and joined Rich at the kitchen table, grabbing a beer for herself on the way. There was one question she had been dying to ask him since the day she moved in and it finally felt like the right time to ask.

'Rich,' she said, waiting for him to meet her eye. 'Are you in love with Holly?'

The can froze midway to Rich's lips. He stared at Marta, his brow crumpling into a frown. 'What...?' he said, not very convincingly.

Marta continued to look at him. 'You care for her so much,' she said simply. 'I think you love her.'

Richard's eyes flitted away to the floor. A darkness was creeping up his neck. 'We're... we're mates. We're just friends. I mean... yeah, we're close, but... No, we're just mates.'

Marta nodded, smiling a little as Rich continued to evade her eye.

'OK,' she said, reaching back into the fridge and grabbing him another beer. 'I only wondered.'

'Yeah well, now you know.' Rich glanced at her briefly, yanking his beer open with unnecessary force. *Like a frustrated teenager*, thought Marta. He couldn't talk about his feelings. English people were like that: up tights.

'Now I know,' said Marta, nodding. 'You want sauce with your meat pie?'

31

Marta didn't so much hear the woman's approach as *feel* it. Desks wobbled, pens rolled onto the floor and screensavers dissolved in her wake.

'Something else for you,' she said, leaning on Marta's desk and giving Marta a surprisingly full view of her swinging breasts. 'I need a deck of presidents in above-the-line media campaigns for the beverage project I mentioned. Probably fifty to sixty presidents will do, one per slide. Each slide should contain – write this down – the brand, the campaign, dates, outcome and stats where you can get hold of them. OK?'

Marta nodded confidently. 'Fine.' She had no idea what the woman was on about, but she was beginning to realise that Charlotte wasn't the sort of person to spare time for explanations.

'Email them to me by lunchtime tomorrow,' she instructed. Then she was gone, whirling through the office like a tornado.

A deck of presidents. Like, the President of the United States, she wondered? Marta stared at the notes she had made, wondering where she was going to find sixty presidents and wondering how this all fitted in with beverages.

A full minute later, Marta was still staring at the notes, frowning. The instructions were no clearer now than when Charlotte had barked them at her.

'You OK?' said a voice. It was Carl, espresso in hand.

'No,' she admitted, sounding more despondent than she had

intended.

'No panic. What's up?'

Marta sighed. 'This,' she said, pointing at her own scribbles. 'It make no sense and Charlotte need it by tomorrow lunch.'

Carl squinted at the page, which contained a messy combination of English and Polish. 'I can't read it. What does it say?'

'I have to find fifty to sixty presidents. Then I put each president on a page and write about all these things.' She indicated the scribbled list.

Carl was looking at her as though she were mad. 'Presidents?' he asked. 'Are you sure she said that?'

Marta nodded miserably. 'Fifty to sixty presidents.'

'You are sure she didn't say *precedents*?'

Marta looked at him blankly.

'I think it's more likely she said precedents,' Carl explained, with a faint grin. 'You know? Examples of things that have happened before?'

Marta began to smile. *Right.* Yes, that made more sense.

'You know what, Marta, you may be "in luck", as they say.'

Marta watched as he sat down and started clicking his mouse.

'Excellent,' he said, finally. 'You are *in luck!*'

Marta got up from her chair and skipped round to his side of the desk. He was opening up a presentation.

'I did thees for David two months ago, but he never looked at it,' said Carl. 'It's a set of brand and campaign precedents in the soft drinks market. Take a look.'

Marta scrolled through the presentation with growing excitement. 'Carl, this is exactly the thing I have to do! Can I use this? Are you sure?'

Carl shrugged. 'Why not?'

Marta was beside herself with gratitude. 'You can send me this?' she asked. 'And of course, I will tell Charlotte that you did it,' she added.

Carl smiled, crookedly. 'Perhaps say that I *helped* with it. That way we both get some credit.'

'OK,' she nodded enthusiastically. 'Thanks!'

Marta set about tweaking her colleague's work to suit her purposes. Less than an hour later, she was heading through Holborn with a feeling of lightness inside her, having completed her second major task for Charlotte – with a bit of help from Carl.

Dominik's hand slipped round her waist, jolting Marta out of her euphoric daze.

'Hungry?' he asked, planting a kiss on her lips.

Marta smiled, allowing Dominik to pull her close. He was wearing a suit again. He looked almost like a proper businessman, thought Marta, finally pulling away and noticing that his crisp, white shirt was still creased from the packaging.

She grabbed his hand and turned them both in a quarter-circle, then led the way down a side street.

'Where are you taking me?' he asked.

Marta shrugged. 'No idea. Let's explore.'

They found a small café on Red Lion Street that was filled with professional-looking types carrying briefcases and holding important-looking meetings over laptops.

'So, how is it?' asked Marta.

'You first.'

Marta pulled a face. 'Variable,' she replied. 'There are nice people, boring people, nasty people and crazy people. The work is fine, but only after the guy opposite has explained everything.'

'Guy opposite?' said Dominik, raising an eyebrow. 'You haven't met a new one already, have you?'

Marta smiled, squeezing Dominik's thigh under the table. 'Not like that,' she replied. 'Carl is nice. He's Italian. And he looks funny, like this.' She pulled her face into a peculiar shape.

'Good.' Dominik leaned back as the young waitress who had been hovering nearby leaned in with a basket of cutlery.

'Have you chosen?' she asked in Polish. Marta grinned. It happened so often now: in shops, in bars, in stations… She no longer got excited. They gave their orders and thanked the girl in Polish.

'She's probably got a degree in nuclear physics,' said Marta, cynically.

Dominik shook his head, smiling. 'You can't change how things are. Anyway, she might enjoy working here.'

Marta looked over at the girl, who was crouching beneath the counter to mop up a spillage. Marta looked back at Dominik, her point made.

'How about you?' she asked, resolving not to think about the bigger issue any more.

Dominik extracted a toothpick from a grubby plastic container on the table and started idly picking dirt from his nails. 'It's harder than I'd imagined,' he confessed.

'What d'you mean?'

'Well, I've only ever done placements before. The accounts I saw then were in perfect shape and everything pretty much ran itself.'

'So what's the difference here?'

Dominik winced as he poked the splint straight into his flesh. 'The accounts are a mess,' he explained. 'The previous guy was incompetent and… I don't know. I guess it'll just take time to put things in order.'

'But that's a challenge,' Marta pointed out, with a glint in her eye. 'That's a good thing, isn't it? You wouldn't get that driving tube trains down tunnels.'

Dominik reluctantly smiled. 'I guess you're right.' The smile faded into a pensive expression.

'Aren't you supposed to be a financial assistant?' asked Marta as the food appeared. She hungrily bit into her sandwich, continuing to speak through a mouthful of tuna. 'That sort of implies that you're assisting someone, not doing it on your own.'

Dominik nodded, waiting for the strands of stringy cheese to break off between his mouth and the panini. 'That's the theory, but there doesn't seem to be a financial director. One guy told me he'd been recruited, but he was serving his notice elsewhere; another said he was on holiday, and one guy just looked at me blankly. It's weird.'

They chewed on their sandwiches and drank their tea the Polish way: with lemon, not milk. Reluctantly, Marta checked the time. Their half-hour was nearly up. Her legs were wrapped around Dominik's under the table and his hand was lightly tickling the inside of her thigh. She didn't want to move.

'Back to it?' asked Dominik, finally.

With a sigh, Marta nodded and they rose to their feet, leaving a generous tip. What she really wanted to leave on the little silver dish was a note with the contact details for Bright Sparks, but she knew this was a stupid idea. Dominik was right; she couldn't change how things were.

'Same again later in the week?' asked Dominik.

Marta allowed herself to be pulled close, her hands feeling their way into the small of his back. She could feel Dominik's breath on her hair and, for a second, she wished she didn't have to head back to the office.

'Depends on work,' she replied. 'But I hope so.'

32

Marta followed her colleagues through the crooked doorway, ducking low to avoid hitting her head on the wooden beam. The place looked funny enough from the outside with its black walls, little windows and colourful plants on the roof, but it was even stranger inside.

It took a few seconds for her eyes to adjust to the darkness. Ye Olde Pub was like something from two hundred years ago – only without the straw on the floor or the donkeys in the corner. Weak rays of light trickled through the grimy windows on the street side and an orange glow emanated from the bar.

'Follow me!' instructed David Lyle, the only person who was so short he didn't need to bend down. He was clearly proud of this 'monthly drinks' initiative, thought Marta, following him down a set of wooden stairs that reminded her of the ladder she had had on her bunk bed as a kid. Some of her colleagues actually had to hang off the banisters for the last few steps to avoid knocking themselves out on the ceiling.

'Here we are,' announced David, clapping his hands gleefully at the sight of the reserved signs on the tables. 'Let's get the tab going!'

Marta looked around in awe. The room was no bigger than Holly's bedroom, yet crammed into it were a dozen small cast-iron tables with miniature seats and even smaller stools, as though the bar staff were used to catering for groups of school children. How on earth were all of Stratisvision's employees going to fit in here?

'What's everyone drinking? Beer? Wine? I'll get a mix,' said David. 'In separate glasses, don't you worry,' he added, looking at the nearest person, who happened to be Marta. She gave an obliging smile.

The director disappeared down some more steps and while he was gone the room started to fill up with sweaty bodies. Marta looked around for someone to talk to.

'They *need* our help,' declared Charlotte to a group of senior-looking consultants Marta didn't recognise. 'They just don't have the skillset internally.' She moved further into the throng.

'She has *so* had surgery,' said Kim to a group of similarly dressed girls. Marta jostled her way to the edge of the group, hoping to make eye contact with one of them. 'Apparently she's had her legs lengthened,' said one girl. Marta joined in with the looks of disbelief. None of them noticed her. 'They break your bones and put bits of plastic in before they heal,' the girl went on. The circle remained firmly closed. Marta sidled into a corner.

'*Never* pay their bills on time,' moaned Joan, who rarely did anything but moan, as far as Marta could tell.

Just as she was debating going over to talk to Neil, the office geek, Marta heard the familiar jovial tones of the boss.

'Coming through!' he cried, brandishing above his head a large tray of drinks. He had managed to spill a good deal of the contents over the floor and other customers on his way over, but this didn't seem to bother him.

'Ciao,' said a voice right next to her ear. 'Looks like I made perfect time!'

Marta smiled. Carl was beside her, watching the procession of bar staff follow in David's wake with more drinks and a cloth.

It occurred to Marta that Carl was standing very close. It was definitely closer than was necessary, even given the cramped conditions. He had become quite familiar with her over the last few weeks and Marta was grateful for all the insights, jokes and cigarettes he was willing to share. But it was beginning to dawn on her that there was a distinct possibility that the young Italian fancied Marta.

'My round,' he offered, winking. 'What would you like?'

Marta opted for beer, feeling a mixture of dread and guilt descend upon her. She had to tell Carl about Dominik quickly, before he made a move.

'Na zdrowie,' said Carl, returning with two pints. 'I learned that today.'

Marta smiled awkwardly, holding up her drink. 'Na zdrowie. And who taught you that? Google, perhaps?'

Carl grinned. 'My best friend.'

There was an awkward pause. Marta was desperately trying to work out a way to weave Dominik's name into the conversation.

'Bad idea, these drinks,' said Carl eventually.

'Why?'

Carl shrugged. 'Look. It just gives the cliques a chance to grow stronger and makes the loners feel even lonelier.'

Marta followed his gaze. It was true. The cool gang – Nik, Kat, Kim and a couple of others – were clustered in the middle sipping wine and looking beautiful, their heads close together as though they were sharing stories about people nearby. Neil was sitting alone on one of the miniature stools, making patterns in the condensation on his glass.

Marta nodded slowly. *My boyfriend thinks… My boyfriend always says…*

'David's idea, of course. He thinks it's good for team morale. He is wrong. He would do better to give everyone money for drinks and let them go spend it anywhere they like. Then they would thank him. We could go to a bar far away from this crowd and actually enjoy the drinks.'

Marta agreed, nervously. She couldn't tell whether Carl was speaking hypothetically. She hoped so.

'Any minute now,' he said, in a warning tone, 'he will jump up onto one of those seats and start waving his arms about.'

As they watched, a clearing began to form at the back of the group and there was a collective movement away from it.

'Ladies and gents! Good evening!' cried the director from his elevated position on one of the rickety stools. 'Shuddup!' he added when everybody ignored him. Slowly, the hubbub dropped to a murmur.

'It's good to see so many of you down here this evening... good to see that the free drinks bribe still works.' He paused to wait for the laughter, which sounded weak and forced when it finally came. 'Anyway, yes, so it's been a good month for Stratisvision. A *very* good month. We've won lots of new business and I know we've been working our socks off as a result.'

'*Some* people have,' whispered Carl quietly. 'Others have been playing golf.'

Marta nodded, wishing he didn't have his mouth quite so close to her ear.

'And to that end, we've been pretty damned profitable,' announced David, reaching down with his right arm and clicking his fingers. Someone perceptively passed him his pint. 'We put over five hundred grand in the bank this month – wham, bam, thank you mam – and it's looking like June will be another big month.'

The man took a large gulp of beer and held the glass down at his side, waiting impatiently for someone to take it.

'Now, for those of you thinking, *bloody hell, when's the work gonna end?* then the answer is *soon*. And by that, I don't mean we're gonna lose all our contracts – God forbid – I mean we're gonna make some new hires.'

Marta felt Carl nudge her in the ribs. Was David Lyle talking about hiring her?

'We're advertising for analysts and assistants as we speak, and for those of you who don't know, we've already got a temp in to support the consultants. Marta? Where's Marta, our lovely Pole?'

Marta could feel the spotlight swivel onto her as she reluctantly lifted her hand.

'Hi,' she said, smiling nervously.

'Whether or not there'll be pole *dancing* later remains to be seen,' David went on, chuckling at his own joke. A few sharp breaths were drawn around the room – the most notable by Charlotte, who stood in the corner with her eyes fixed coldly on the boss.

'Well, that's all I'm going to say,' finished David, not showing any sign of embarrassment. 'It's been a bumper month, so let's get bumper pissed!'

He hopped off the stool, landing almost on top of Neil.

'So,' said Carl, raising an eyebrow. 'You got the moment of fame.'

Marta took a small step back.

'There's always someone he picks on,' explained Carl, edging forward to close the gap. He was definitely flirting, she decided.

'Usually a girl,' he added.

Marta lifted her glass and drained it. Carl noticed and rushed to catch up.

'Another?'

Marta nodded, watching as he weaved through the crowds to fetch the pints. She *had* to tell him about Dominik.

He returned with two fresh beers and an overzealous expression. 'They're talking about you over there. I didn't know you lived in Kensington. That's not for from me!'

Marta frowned. 'I used to. Who is talking?'

'The girls.' He nodded to where Kat and her cronies were huddled, heads close, voices muted. 'So, you don't live there any more?'

Marta shook her head, concerned by the fact that Kat's gang were talking about where she used to live. How did they know? What were they saying?

Before Marta could probe, a stocky figure crashed into her field of vision.

'Marta!' cried David. 'There you are! I hope I didn't embarrass you just now.'

Only yourself, thought Marta, smiling sweetly at the director as Carl slipped away into the darkness.

'I've been hearing great things about you!' He peered into her face. '*Great* things.'

Marta wondered whether he really had heard anything at all, or whether he said this to all the girls. 'It is very interesting work,' she replied.

David beamed at her. 'That's what I like to hear! An interested Pole. An interested, hardworking Pole!'

Marta managed to maintain her smile, despite the fact that the director had started gyrating in front of her and revealed a white band of flab around his waist every time he lifted his arms. 'Bit of dancing later...?'

Thankfully, it was at this point that David Lyle realised his glass was empty and bounded off to get another drink.

Marta turned to find a taller, leaner figure towering above her. It was Dean, the high-flying thirty-one-year-old with dark-rimmed glasses and square jaw.

'So, how are you finding Stratisvision?'

He would be devastatingly handsome, thought Marta, if he just allowed himself to smile every now and then. He was *up tights*.

'Good, thank you. Interesting work,' she parroted, remembering what Carl had told her on her first day. Dean was young, but senior.

'That's good to hear,' he said, deadpan.

Marta couldn't think of what to say next. All she really wanted to do was ask Dean whether she was on the list as a potential 'new hire'. She couldn't help thinking that someone other than David Lyle would have a say in the recruitment process and possibly, *hopefully*, that someone might be Dean.

Just as Marta was contemplating opening up a conversation about her latest project, Dean switched on an apologetic expression and shifted away.

'Will you excuse me? I must catch Charlotte before she leaves.'

With a twitch of his lips that was probably Dean's idea of a smile, he swung up the stairs in pursuit of the disappearing fireball.

Marta took a swig of beer, scanning the room. She wasn't sure whether she really wanted to find Carl. A waitress was weaving between bodies with a tray of what looked like fried worms. Marta watched as David Lyle took a handful and tipped his head back, throwing the things down his throat. She ventured towards the waitress.

A tentative bite indicated that the worms were, in fact, batter. *Battered batter?* Marta subtly scattered her handful on the floor and washed out her mouth with beer, stopping by a group of consultants and finding her mind wander back to the perplexing question of how Kat and her girls knew where she used to live.

Nobody noticed her at the edge of the group. Marta shifted sideways and noticed Carl perched next to Neil in the corner, desperately trying to catch her attention with a "rescue me" look. Marta deliberately misread the signal and waved back, moving out of sight. She raised the glass to her lips and then stopped herself. She was drinking too fast. This was not the time to get drunk, no matter what David might say.

The toilets were tucked away under the stairs behind a lattice of low-hanging beams. There was a queue, of course. There was always a queue. English girls seemed to take twice as long to pee as Polish girls. Marta pulled out her phone on the off chance that Dominik had replied. She had two unread messages: one Polish, one English.

Of course I do. Can't do 2moro but Sun? Dxx
We still haven't gone for that dinner. Let me know when –
I'll take u anywhere. J

Marta stared at the handset. She couldn't quite believe what she was reading. Jack was still going on about that dinner they were never going to have. Didn't he understand? Marta read it one last time and pressed *delete*. Maybe he had never experienced rejection, she thought. That was possible. He was very attractive and he could be quite charming, but that was all.

Marta reopened the message from Dominik. Her heart still lurched every time she saw Dxx. She wanted to be with him now. She wanted to see his smile, to watch his lovely hazel eyes dance as he talked… if only she didn't have to stay in this strange English pub with these strange English people. If only this wasn't her biggest chance yet to secure herself a proper career in England.

'You gonna go?' asked a girl, poking her in the back. Marta practically fell into the cubicle.

When she re-emerged, a familiar figure was leaning into the mirror. Marta recognised the suede knee-high boots and tight jeans.

'Sorry, hon.' Kat flicked her white-blonde mane in a giant swoosh and smiled falsely at Marta.

Hon. Short for honey. Marta wasn't naïve enough to think that the term was one of endearment. The girls used it all the time; she had heard them. Marta smiled back. Maybe it was the alcohol, but she felt more determined than ever to hold a conversation with this girl. Besides, she wanted to know what they had been saying about her.

'How are you?' she asked, washing her hands.

'*Great?*' Kat leaned in again and started perfecting her lashes with a finger. 'A bit drunk?'

Marta nodded, shaking the water off her hands and deliberately timing her exit to coincide with Kat's. *A bit drunk.* Three words, that was a start.

'Me too! I think it is David's plan,' said Marta, following her closely through the toilets and back into the hubbub.

'That'd be right,' muttered Kat, dipping her head as they re-entered the reserved area. Marta darted round to her side.

'I have never… shagged in a taxi,' said one girl, looking around at the faces and lingering pointedly on Kat's as she rejoined the circle.

Kat's mouth turned up on one side in a half smile. 'Oh, *very* good,' she said, rolling her eyes as though in a mock sulk. 'Hand me my wine?'

Marta watched as the yellow liquid disappeared down Kat's throat. There was a murmur of appreciation as the skinny blonde drained the last drop and held out her empty glass to the group. Someone took it and headed off for a refill.

'We're playing *I have never?*' Kat explained to Marta.

Marta nodded, grateful that a space had been made for her in the group, but apprehensive about what this game might entail. She remembered Tash and the others sitting round that polished oak table, cackling as they caught each other out and forced one another to drink.

'Girls, you all know Marta, don't you?' Kat pouted at the other girls.

There were nods and fake smiles all round.

'OK, your go,' said Kat. Everyone looked at Marta.

Marta took a deep breath. She was fairly sure she knew how the game worked, but she wasn't convinced she wanted to play it.

'I have never...' *understood why you rich English types can't just talk, like everyone else.* 'Kissed a girl on lips,' she said finally, quite pleased with her response.

A surprising number of girls in the group raised their glasses.

'I'm bored with this game?' said Kat, glancing at Marta as though she alone was responsible for dampening the excitement. Those in mid-chug lowered their glasses, clearly relieved.

None of the girls had been enjoying the game, observed Marta; except the vindictive Kat, perhaps, who was clearly the leader. Marta wondered what the gang would do if Kat were to leave the company. Would they find their way into the office each morning? *Stratisvision without Kat,* mused Marta. It would certainly make life more enjoyable.

It came as something of a surprise when the girl on Marta's right suddenly turned to her with a smile.

'So, how's your first week been?' she asked. Marta vaguely recognised her as one of the graphics girls from the far side of the office. She was pretty in a feline way, with upward-slanting eyes and jet-black hair that flowed like liquid down her back.

'OK,' replied Marta, wary of the fact that the CEO's niece was standing beside her.

'You're working for Charlotte, aren't you?' asked the girl.

Marta nodded, pulling a face that could have meant anything. She guessed Charlotte probably wasn't a big hit with the gang.

'Bad luck.'

Marta shrugged. 'She is a demanding woman,' she said, not

quite ready to open up.

'That's one way of putting it. *Workaholic loony* is another. Seriously, if she hasn't bitten your ear off in a violent rage yet, you must be doing something right.'

Marta smiled, encouraged by the girl's frankness and wondering whether the girl might turn out to be another office ally.

'I think she liked the work I did,' Marta told her. 'But I had some help,' she confessed, suddenly wanting to tell someone.

'Who from?'

'Carl.'

'Oh yeah?' asked the girl, raising an eyebrow. 'The Italian stallion's been helping you out, has he?'

Marta rushed to explain, feeling slightly horrified that rumours might be flying round the office about her relationship with Carl. 'He just give me a presentation he did,' she said. 'Then I give it to Charlotte and try to say it's Carl's work, but she never listen. She just take it and think that I did it.'

'Huh.' The girl looked at Marta, her cat-like eyes squinting hard. Marta suddenly regretted confiding in her. 'So you took credit for Carl's work, did you?' she asked.

Marta opened her mouth to explain, but the girl's face said it all.

'Looks like you *have* learnt something in your first week,' she said, smiling coldly – or conspiringly – Marta couldn't tell. 'Nice one.'

Marta had one last go at explaining, but she found herself talking to the girl's slick, black hair. The circle had closed. She was on her own again.

33

Dominik wasn't at home. Marta peeled back the soggy mattress and squinted into the front room, but she already knew he wasn't there. A dark-skinned limb stuck out from beneath a pile of bedding; its sole pink, like a baby's. Dominik's housemates generally spent Sunday mornings in a semi-comatose state on their living room floor, but Dominik didn't. She must have just missed him.

Marta let the mattress spring back to the window and let herself out through the rusty gate. She headed up the road, hoping she could remember the shortcut he had shown her a couple of weeks before.

The air was almost warm on her skin. They were experiencing one of England's random warm spells, or perhaps the start of spring; it was hard to tell which. Marta slowed down, enjoying the heat of the sun on her back and the sound of birds cheeping from the telegraph wires overhead. Even North Acton – crumbling, derelict and graffitied – looked nice this morning. If you looked past the cheap neon shop signs and tatty, weathered awnings that lined the shops, there was some beautiful brickwork underneath. Marta stepped around a puddle of dried vomit on the pavement. Nothing could dampen her mood today.

It was as though all the parts of her life were finally slotting into place. She had a job; admittedly only a short-term one, but that would change in the next few days, she felt sure. She had friends and a place to stay – again, only temporary, but she would soon be able to pay her way – and she had Dominik. That alone was enough to keep the smile on her face.

Marta thought back to that miserable recruitment fair back in January. Even then, as he had handed her that misspelt leaflet and grinned that sheepish grin beneath his tousled, unkempt hair, she had felt the spark between them. Weeks later, standing at junctions trying to thrust flyers into reluctant hands, there was only one thing that brought some excitement to her day: the prospect of lunch or coffee with Dominik.

It was madness, really; not Marta's style at all. She didn't go 'soft' like some of her friends did when it came to men. She had had plenty of relationships back in Poland: most of them lighthearted flings, but a couple were more serious. She and Piotr had lasted nearly three years. Tall, sporty and extremely good-looking, Piotr had also been sensitive. He was always second guessing Marta's needs and providing support before she even knew she needed it. He was a qualified doctor, too, with a good job in Wrocław. To everybody in Marta's life – Marta's mother's included – Piotr could do no wrong. He was 'the one'.

The problem was, Marta didn't need a 'one'. She didn't like to rely on others. She was strong and independent. She had split up with Piotr as soon as she made up her mind to come to England and, although she had never told anyone this – not even Anka – the break-up hadn't really hurt her. The only pain was a phantom pain she felt for Piotr, who was beside himself over the split. That was all.

She didn't need anyone else. Marta had come to this conclusion before she left Poland. She was strong enough on her own. But now she had met Dominik... Well, it felt different. It felt as though she *did* need him, although she couldn't articulate why. It wasn't that she *needed* him, exactly; she just... wanted him. She wanted him the whole bloody time.

The red and white bunting above the *delikatesy* fluttered into view as she rounded the corner and Marta found her step quickening. She could just about make out the movement of people inside, although it was difficult to see anything clearly because of the sun's reflection on the glass.

Marta's attention was diverted for a moment by a stunning young blonde strutting along the pavement up ahead. Marta wasn't the only one watching the girl's boobs bounce up and down in the flimsy top that revealed a glimpse of flesh above the microscopic skirt. A couple of lads on bikes were wheeling their way towards her and an old man was pretending to adjust his cap across the road. Marta smiled; it was warm today, but not *that* warm.

The girl hesitated outside the delikatesy, looking up at its name and then down at something in her hand. Marta wondered whether she might be a prostitute, meeting a client on a very low-grade job. Maybe she was Polish, thought Marta sadly, thinking of the cards Dominik told her about on the 'Wailing Wall'. After one last glance at the name, the girl pushed open the café door. Marta watched as she slipped inside, her silver high heels catching the light as she mounted the small step. She wasn't a prostitute, thought Marta. She looked too self-conscious in that tiny outfit. She was clearly just trying to impress.

It was only as Marta skipped across the road that she looked up again at the delikatesy. What she saw made her stop right there in the middle of Victoria Road. A horrible, sickly feeling engulfed her and she could feel something hot rising up in her throat. She didn't want to believe what her eyes were seeing. *Dominik was kissing the girl.*

Marta moved, zombie-like, to the line of parked cars that ran parallel with the shops and the delikatesy. She couldn't take her eyes off the scene in the café. Dominik had risen from his seat by the window – the seat *she* had occupied two weeks previously when they had shared ciasto before their first kiss – and was standing, embracing the girl.

Marta stared, horrified but transfixed as her world fell apart before her. Their faces were so close and they were kissing, not on the lips, but tenderly, cheeks touching, exchanging words and smiles and then kissing some more. Their arms were all over each other. Marta moved into a doorway, her breath coming quickly, her brain unable to settle. She wanted to come up with a rational explanation, or a plan of action, at least. But all she could think about was the fact that Dominik was kissing another girl.

She spied on the pair from the doorway, feeling her heart race with fury as they sat down and the girl ran a hand through Dominik's hair. Dominik leaned forward, grinning, and touched her face in some way – Marta couldn't see how, as his body was obscuring her view. *His body.* That body that had been naked on top of hers. Inside hers.

The same waitress who had served them before approached the table and flirted with Dominik, exchanging words and saying hi to the girl as though she was someone Dominik wanted her to meet. *His next conquest*, thought Marta. Was this where he took all his ladies? Did he run through exactly the same routine with them all? Would they be off to the Kensington restaurant for dinner in the next few weeks, heading back to his cupboard of a room at the end of the night?

Marta felt sick. The questions were tumbling around in her head, but there were no answers; only a huge, hideous realisation screaming out at her: *Dominik was a cheat.*

With a final glance at the giggling couple, Marta turned her back. Unseeing, she picked a route back to the tube that circumvented the café window. She hadn't noticed before, but her eyes had been filling up. Now her cheeks were wet and she could barely see through the tears. Marta didn't care. She didn't want to see. Right now, she didn't care if she walked in front of a London bus. Any physical pain would be better than this.

How could he? She wanted to know. *Who was she? Were there others? Was Marta just one of many in Dominik's string of 'special' girls? Did she mean anything to him at all? Were they all just conquests? Was he really like that? How long did he think this could last? How could she have made such a huge, huge mistake?*

The questions kept coming. Horrific scenes kept running through her imagination: Dominik saying goodbye to Marta after their first kiss and heading off to meet the blonde. Dominik washing his sheets between girls to make sure no long, blonde hairs or short, dark ones gave his game away. Dominik meeting Marta for coffee then whizzing off on his scooter to meet the next girl. Dominik putting crumbs of ciasto into the blonde's beautiful mouth, then kissing her… It was like torture, but Marta couldn't make the images stop.

By the time she reached the tube station, the shock had begun to wear off and Marta's distress had morphed into rage: rage against Dominik, but mainly rage against herself. Her biggest mistake was to let Dominik into her life. She had spent time with him, opened up to him, opened her fucking *legs* to him. It was her fault. She had broken her own rules and gone soft on a guy.

This was why she never got too involved, thought Marta, wiping a bare arm across one eye and then the other. Her vision cleared a little and a watery impression of the eastbound platform came into view. *The deeper you got, the further you had to swim to the surface when it all fell apart.* Marta took a deep, shaky breath and slowly exhaled, feeling the emotions churn relentlessly inside her.

The train rattled to a halt on the platform and Marta stepped inside. She was strong and independent. She didn't need a man. She didn't need Dominik. She would get by just fine without him. In fact, she was already doing fine on her own.

34

'Does that sound OK, hun?' asked Kat, smiling down at her through perfectly curled lashes.

Marta nodded, although it sounded anything but OK. It sounded very confusing. 'Just a question,' she said, choosing her words carefully so as not to appear stupid. 'Where are these informations, exactly? Do I find them on the internet?'

Kat pouted at herself in the reflective office window. She no longer appeared to be listening. 'Yeah, and the places I told you about? Datamonitor, Keynote, Mintel, Forrester... you know?'

Marta nodded and ducked as the blonde ponytail flicked round in her face. The doll-like figure strutted off towards the cluster of desks that the 'gang' had chosen to occupy on this particular day. Marta sighed and leaned back in her chair, lifting her notepad with little enthusiasm. *Datamonitor, Keynote, Mintel, Forrester... no, she didn't know. What were these things? How could she find out without exposing her ignorance, and without asking Carl? And frankly... Could she be bothered?*

She stayed there, slumped in her seat, staring at the jumble of words in front of her. She wasn't thinking about the words. She wasn't thinking about the task Kat had set her, or the difficulties of working for a stuck-up bitch who had a chip on her shoulder and who seemed determined to see people fail, despite calling everyone 'hun'. She wasn't even thinking about the fact that Charlotte had set her a deadline of three p.m. today for something else; an equally demanding and mystifying task. She was thinking about Dominik. She had been trying to put him out of her head all morning. Despite the lack of sleep and the freshness of yesterday's revelation, she had made a concerted effort, to focus on the presentation. She was doing her best to think about brand synergies and partnerships in the carbonated soft drinks market, but her brain kept making the wrong connections. PopsCo... retailers who sold cold drinks... cafés... that café in Acton... that blonde... Every time, she had to erect buffers in her mind and set her brain back on track. Every time, her brain would find a way back to that horrible scene.

She didn't have time to daydream. With Charlotte's presentation and Kat's cryptic demands, Marta had a near-impossible task ahead of her. She should have felt pleased that so many people were loading her up with work and been eager to get it all done. She was becoming a valued member of the team: an asset. It was exactly what she had been striving for. But somehow, she didn't feel valued. She just felt miserable.

It was irrational, she knew that. They had only been together for a couple of weeks. Nothing changed in that amount of time, did it? She was still the same independent girl she had always been. Dominik was still just a guy she had met, someone she could just as easily forget. She had a job and that was still her priority. She had a career to carve out, a life to lead. It was just a question of putting that episode behind her and getting on with building a future.

Except it wasn't that easy. Oh, God, if *only* things hadn't changed in the last few weeks. If only she could get on with her life as it had been before Dominik stepped into it. If only she could clear him and all his memories from her mind, erasing every moment they had spent together: the time he had handed her that leaflet; the time they had collided in Barry's office; the time he had cooked her soup; the time he had kissed her; and the time he had stroked her hair in the back of the cab... They were etched into her mind. She couldn't erase them – not least because he was still texting her. Marta pulled her phone towards her again, tears building up behind her eyes.

Fancy lunch 2day? I have something to tell U. Dxx

Damn right he had something to tell her, thought Marta, sending the phone skidding across the desk. She wouldn't be meeting him for lunch today – or ever again.

An hour later, the presentation had barely evolved. Marta stared at the words in front of her. Teen Preferences for CSD Brands. Apart from the title, the slide was blank. Marta snapped out of her daydream, realising that she had been trying to picture Dominik as a teenager: scruffy, cute, energetic and always smiling. Marta shuddered and forced herself to consider the slide's content.

'What's that?' asked Kat, appearing from nowhere and frowning at Marta's screen.

'Oh, is something for Charlotte,' Marta explained, expecting an outburst regarding her prioritisation.

'Oh, right,' Kat said simply. She leaned closer, pushing her pert bottom into the gangway just as Dean walked past.

'It's for PopsCo,' Marta explained needlessly. There was a PopsCo logo on every page.

'Right,' Kat nodded, straightening up and checking her reflection again in the window. 'You know, you don't need to write proper sentences when you do presentations like that? Note form will do. I've worked for Charlotte a lot. That's what she likes. It's the content she wants, not the sentences. When d'you think you'll be able to start on my work, by the way?'

Marta stared for a second, gobsmacked. Kat was *being nice*. 'Er, after three o'clock. I will finish Charlotte's before then.'

Kat nodded, straightened her silky top and flounced off.

By some miracle – or maybe as a consequence of the hint that Kat had given her – Marta *did* finish Charlotte's work before three o'clock. At two forty-five, she flicked through the slides one last time, closed the file and pressed send. The presentation was rough, but it was bursting with content. Marta felt rather pleased with herself. She hadn't thought about Dominik for at least five minutes.

Even though her office was at least four blocks from Dominik's and there was no way he would be in town at three o'clock, Marta couldn't bear the risk of running into him. She dashed into the nearest shop and grabbed the cheapest bread roll she could find, almost knocking over a guy in a flowery shirt who was joking with someone just inside the door. Looking back, she realised with dismay that the holidaymaker was in fact her boss. Luckily, David Lyle was too busy high-fiving the café owner to notice her.

Kat's task proved harder than Marta had imagined. After nearly an hour, she had just about managed to ascertain that the strange names in her notebook – Mintel, Keynote and so on – were research agencies and, according to Google, they charged up to $5,000 per report. In some cases, parts of the reports were available to view online, but these were always the boring parts, or the parts with no data. Surely Kat hadn't intended for Marta to buy any reports like this? And if she had, why hadn't she mentioned it?

Marta stared at the screen, quietly drumming her nails on the desk. She had two options and neither appealed. One: ask Carl. Two: ask Kat. Option one was the easiest, but Marta was desperately trying to avoid the onset of more rumours about her and the Italian Stallion. Besides, he had already done her one huge favour and she didn't want to be any more indebted to him. Option two was unappealing as it involved entering the cool zone of the office and exposing her ignorance to everyone in the 'gang'. After a few seconds' deliberation, Marta rose from her seat.

They were laughing at something as Marta approached. Kim and Nik were making comments and provoking the others to turn round in their seats, at which point they would collapse in fits of giggles. Kat was trying to keep a straight face but failed every time her eyes met anyone else's. As Marta got closer, she realised they were laughing at her.

She continued towards them, determined not to let it show that she knew or cared. One of the girls leaned sideways and whispered something to Nik, who looked down at Marta's shoes and expelled a snort of laughter. There were more suppressed giggles and fleeting glances in her direction.

Marta continued towards them, eyes straight ahead. She should have anticipated it, really. She knew that she didn't dress well enough for this place. She hadn't bought any clothes since she arrived in England, apart from a belt to replace the one that had broken around her suitcase, and that had been a cheap, thin belt, not the fashionable type these girls wore around their hip-slung jeans. And her old brown shoes were pretty unfashionable, even by Polish standards.

'Hi,' she said, trying to sound confident despite the eruptions of giggles around the table.

'How are you getting on, hun?' asked Kat, patronisingly. There were more snorts of laughter.

'I need some help,' Marta said quietly.

'You need some help?' repeated Kat, loud enough for most of the office to hear. 'What on?'

Marta explained her predicament regarding the reports and Kat nodded understandingly.

'OK,' said Kat, glancing quickly at the other girls and catching a raised eyebrow from Kim as though they were sharing a private joke. 'Here's what you need to do.' She exchanged looks with another girl across the table. 'You need to ask our research person for help. She's that woman in the spare office at the end?' Kat pointed towards the glass-walled office next to David Lyle's, which Marta vaguely remembered from her two-minute tour on day one. Inside was the woman with the orange tan whom Marta had seen flitting about the office from time to time. She was wearing a bizarre green cardigan that reached all the way down to the ground and a hair clip like a tiara.

'Research person?' she repeated, confused as to why Kat hadn't mentioned this before.

'Yup, that's her. Just go in and tell her what you want.'

Marta nodded. It all seemed too easy. 'So I just... go ask her for all the informations?'

Kim looked up. 'Make sure you're clear about what you want?' she advised. 'You've got to be firm or she'll get it wrong.'

Marta frowned. They were suddenly being all nice again. The

earlier joke appeared to have been forgotten and the girls were all studiously staring at their screens again.

'OK,' said Marta. 'Thanks.' She consulted her notes quickly to remind herself of exactly what she required and headed off to meet the research woman.

Her gentle knock was ignored. Marta knocked again and walked in.

'Excuse me, but I need you to get some informations,' she said. The woman barely moved. She must be slightly hard of hearing, Marta supposed.

Suddenly, an overly tanned face was staring at Marta, blinking. 'I'm sorry? What?'

'I need some information,' corrected Marta, hoping her grammatical mistake had gone unnoticed. 'Some research, please.'

The woman was staring at her as though she were asking for a frogspawn cocktail. 'Have we met?'

Marta took an apologetic step towards her, holding out her hand. 'No, sorry. Marta.'

'Patricia,' said the woman, still frowning. 'And what exactly did you say you wanted?'

Marta froze. Something had just clicked in her mind. *Patricia*. She recognised that name. Then she realised. This was not a research person who spent her time fetching reports from Keynote and Datamonitor. This was Patricia Catermol, Stratisvision's CEO.

'I just... um, I think... I just wanted to introduce myself,' Marta mumbled unconvincingly. Then, with more confidence, 'and to say that I am very much enjoying working here. Nice to meet you.'

Patricia was still frowning, but it was now a frown of curiosity rather than incredulity. 'OK! Well, nice to meet you, Martha.'

'Marta,' she corrected, switching on a smile and leaving the room.

Her heart was still pumping like a steam engine as she sat on the flipped-down toilet seat and stared at the ends of her scuffed brown shoes. She had pulled it off, thanks to some quick thinking and a bit of luck, but only just. It was unbelievable that anyone would be vindictive enough to play a trick like that to someone who had done them no harm. What was up with those girls? They really had it in for Marta and she had no idea why.

She went the long way back to her desk, avoiding the inevitable ridicule from Kat's clique. There was only one way of getting this work done – and she *was* going to get it done, especially now. She would have to ask Carl.

'Have you looked on the V-drive?' he asked, looking at her as if this was the most obvious thing in the world. 'She did… tell you about the V-drive, didn't she?'

Marta frowned. *V-drive?*

Carl rolled his eyes and indicated for her to look over his shoulder. 'See? All the reports are filed by agency name, alphabetically. We subscribe to most of them: Datamonitor, Euromonitor, Findnote, Geobrand…'

Marta stared, nodding grimly at the evidence before her as the realisation slowly hit home: they were determined to make a failure of her.

'Thanks Carl,' she said, regretting her earlier coldness when he had wished her good morning.

'No problemo,' he said. 'The V-drive,' he added, looking up at her and making a gesture with his fingers and tongue that she hoped wasn't an attempt at seduction. 'Always remember the V-drive.'

Marta nodded awkwardly and hastened away. He was going all creepy on her. She had to get him to back off – but carefully, because she needed him. Marta cringed. Why was everything so complicated?

Her phone was ringing when she approached her desk.

'Hello?' she gabbled, just in time.

'Cześć!'

No. She had finally managed to banish him from her mind and now he was here, in her ear, cool and chirpy as ever. A weird mixture of emotions ran through Marta's mind. Was it possible to hate someone and desperately want them at the same time?

'Listen, Dominik–'

'Can you talk? I've got news!'

Marta started to rise from her seat. She didn't want her colleagues to hear her end the relationship. As she bent down to lock her computer, she sensed a presence behind her. She turned. The phone fell away from her ear, and as Charlotte's eyes bored into hers, she fumbled and ended the call.

'I got your presentation,' the woman said, coldly.

Marta just nodded. Several people on neighbouring desks were pricking up their ears, alert to Charlotte's tone.

'Now Marta, I know English isn't your first language, but I'm afraid this just *won't do.*' She slammed a print-off of Marta's work on the desk. 'It's like an analyst's subconscious ramblings. It's... thoughts! Notes! The slides are barely intelligible – let alone sufficient for us to show to the head of marketing at PopsCo. How are we supposed to convince them with this?' She rifled through the pages and stopped at one of the later ones. '*Underground/niche brands popular when not deliberate, e.g. teens.* What on earth is that supposed to mean? It's just... gobbledegook!'

'I was told–'

'I'm afraid you need to buck up your ideas, Marta,' said Charlotte sternly. Marta noticed David pop his head out of his fishbowl office to see what the noise was about. 'We don't make exceptions for nationality here.'

Marta sank back into her chair. She felt despondent and a little embarrassed, but most of all she felt incensed. Clearly Kat had tricked her, *again*, and this time she hadn't got away with it. Angrily, Marta opened up a browser and logged onto her personal email. She was in no mood to complete the assignment for the heartless blonde bitch – not now. Later, for sure. She wasn't going to fall into yet another trap by failing to do her work, but right now she just needed to calm down. She needed to pour everything out in an email to her best friend.

There was one unread message in her inbox. Marta skimmed it as she prepared to let rip, then quickly found herself taking in the words.

Hi Marta!

We have wifi! Finally! I'm rather slow at typing so I won't write much but your sister is very quick so she'll be in touch soon I'm sure.

We are all well here. I hope you're still enjoying your job and eating enough vegetables.

All our love,
Mama x

PS What did you buy Anka for her birthday? We are dying to know!

Marta closed her eyes and buried her head in her hands, feeling the blood drain from her body. She couldn't believe she had forgotten. She had missed her best friend's birthday.

35

'And then I forget Anka's birthday!' finished Marta, slumping onto the kitchen table.

Tina leaned over and extracted two cans from the fridge. 'Who's Anka again?'

Marta shook her head at the beer that was sliding towards her. 'My best friend, in Łomianki. I never miss it, *ever*, in my life since I was five!'

Tina pulled a face as though she couldn't see what all the fuss was about, pushing the can back towards Marta's head.

Marta sighed, ignoring it. 'I messed everything up.'

Tina frowned. 'No you didn't. From what you've told me, it's other people who've messed things up for you.' She cracked open both cans and took a huge swig of hers. 'Apart from the birthday thing,' she added, 'which was your fuck-up.'

Marta rolled her head sideways to face Tina. 'Thanks.'

She could feel Tina's eyes on the side of her face. Marta didn't care what she thought. Too many shitty things had happened today for Marta to care about anything. At some point, she knew, she would have to try to rectify it all: call Anka, send a parcel by express mail, make a last-ditch attempt to impress her colleagues, speak to Dominik for the very last time... but for now she just felt like wallowing in self-pity.

'Why do they hate me?'

'Who? The girls in your office?'

'Yes! I did nothing to them – nothing! But they hate me.'

Tina sighed and met her eye. 'D'you know the word "prejudice"?'

Marta nodded. At school she had watched a film called *Pride and Prejudice* in English lessons. She remembered the puffy skirts and men in cravats. Elizabeth had been *prejudiced* against Mr Darcy because he was too proud.

'They don't like you because you're different.'

Marta shrugged, her arms still spread across the table. 'Everybody is different.'

'Well, some people don't like that.' Tina kicked her gently. 'You should count yourself lucky; at least people only start discriminating once you've opened your mouth. They judge me as soon as I walk through the door.'

Marta looked up, briefly emerging from her sulk to consider what her housemate was saying. To her, Tina was a bossy, smart, fun-loving girl. Marta had never imagined that anyone would see her differently. But of course they did. For the first time, Marta wondered what it would be like to be Tina. In some people's eyes, she was 'the black girl', just as Marta was 'the Polish girl'. Maybe Tina was right about Kat and that lot. Maybe they were *prejudiced*.

'Y'know what?' said Tina, eventually. 'You need a night out. You need to forget about what's-his-face and those bitches from work. Come on, let's–'

'I don't want a night out,' Marta protested, pushing the beer away from her once and for all and hiding her face in her arms. 'Am not in the mood.'

A night out with Tina was the last thing she wanted. Marta's world was gloomy and dark and claustrophobic, and for now that was how she liked it. The idea of sharing her evening with people who saw the world as rosy and full of promise… it didn't appeal. She didn't want to don a false smile and drink pints with rich English boys. She wanted to dwell on the misery of now.

'Shut up and stop feeling sorry for yourself,' said Tina, pushing the beer so quickly across the table that Marta was forced to sit up to avoid being covered in froth. 'Now *drink!*'

Marta looked at her housemate. She was back in hockey captain mode. Marta obediently took a small slurp.

'Now, you can stop worrying about your friend. I'll get something couriered to her from work tomorrow morning – it'll reach her by noon. What's she like? Does she like clothes? Sport? Fashion? Films? Bestiality–'

'Fashion,' Marta interrupted, reluctantly engaging in the conversation. 'She loves English fashion: magazines, clothes… these sort of things.'

'Well that's easy then. My desk secretary has shitloads of girly magazines and I can use up some of the Accessorize vouchers I've had for yonks and never planned to spend. Sorted. Now, let's go and get changed.'

'Tina…' Marta moaned, pleading with tired eyes.

'Stop whinging. I've felt like this too, you know. I know the cure.' She smiled. 'It's a good shag.'

Marta looked at her, horrified.

'Or at least a good night out,' Tina added. 'Oh, in fact…' Her eyes lit up. '*Brilliant*. Some of the lads are out tonight celebrating a massive trade that went our way. I nearly joined them, but then I realised that Shanksy, the guy who – oh never mind. It'll be a good laugh. Oh my God, I just realised. Bufty! You are *so* gonna love Bufty – I can just tell!'

'What is Bufty?' asked Marta, not the least bit convinced.

'*Who* is Bufty. He's the most incredibly fit, sweet, intelligent, good-looking guy on the planet. He trades derivatives on the desk next to me. You'll adore him. Now come on!'

Marta found herself being hoisted upwards by a firm grip on her arm. Against her will, she knocked back the rest of the lager as Tina held her hostage in her walk-in wardrobe, picking out ridiculous outfits for her to try on.

'Nothing *too* sexy,' she muttered, holding a black cocktail dress up to Marta's shoulders. 'Most people will've come straight from work. Hmm. How about these? Ooh, *perfect*.'

Half an hour later, the girls were stepping out of a taxi beneath a vast building made of concrete and glass, both dressed in tight, pinstriped trousers and tops that would surely never be worn to the office. Marta was doubtful about this *city chic* look Tina had cultivated, particularly when it came to the red push-up bodice that pressed against her breasts beneath the suit jacket, but her housemate had insisted.

'We'll have to walk from here,' Tina explained. 'Cabs are only free to and from the office.'

Marta nodded, wondering how Tina would justify a journey to the office at half past eight at night. The walk was not a long one. Jamie's was a slick-looking bar and its exterior was surrounded by clusters of dark-suited bodies. It was clearly the JC Morley local. There must have been a hundred people standing outside; most of them in their twenties or thirties, and nearly all of them men. *No wonder Tina loved her job*, thought Marta.

'They'll be inside,' announced Tina, walking quickly but saucily towards the entrance. Heads were turning. Marta found it difficult to avoid locking eyes with the young men in their well-cut suits, ties loosened around their necks, jackets casually slung over one shoulder.

'There they are!'

Elbows out, they made their way through the bar. There was something uncanny about the level of attractiveness of the clientele, thought Marta, scanning the men as they cut through the crowd. Every one of the after-work revellers was incredibly good-looking. The men, who outnumbered the women by about ten to one, were chiselled, tanned and well-built; if sometimes a little stocky. The women were slim, elegant and perfectly proportioned. It felt as though they were on a movie set.

'Hey, look who's here!' cried a large, bearlike man, emerging from a group of young men and hauling Tina towards him. 'Thought you were gone for the night?'

Tina didn't seem to mind or even notice the quick grope of her backside as the man guided her into the thick of the crowd. She simply grabbed Marta's arm, keeping her close, and yelled, 'Guys, this is Marta! She's my housemate!'

There was a roar of general approval, followed by an abrupt stampede towards them.

'Champagne?'

'Cocktail?'

'What're you drinkin'?'

'That's Dish,' explained the bearlike man as a blond, shiny-faced youngster went off to fetch the drinks. 'He's the one who did the trade today. Drinks're on him.'

Marta nodded, trying to relax while taking everything in. She was losing Tina in the crowd.

In another situation, it might have felt good to be plied with expensive drinks by a selection of suave young men. They were lovely to look at, for a start, and they seemed very keen to engage in conversation. But as she had told Tina before, she just wasn't in the mood.

'*Champagne*,' Dish announced, returning with two oversized flutes and a new bottle. He expertly popped the cork and filled the glasses above everybody's heads without spilling a drop.

'I'm Ben, by the way,' he said. 'But they call me Dish.'

'Nice to meet you,' she said, opting not to ask him about his nickname, which she felt sure he was waiting for her to do. He was probably her age – early twenties – but he had a cockiness about him that seemed both youthful and mature at once. He reminded Marta of a door-to-door salesman: the type that won't take no for an answer.

She glanced round to look for Tina, who had disappeared in a frenzy of roaring and jeering. It was already apparent to Marta that she was on her own for the night. Or rather, she was with the boys for the night.

'This is James,' added Dish, making room for another man who was cutting his way through from the bar. Marta tried not to stare as she shook the man's hand. She couldn't take her eyes off his face. The man was *beautiful*. His skin was dusky and his eyes, though ice blue

216

like hers, were slanted in a way that suggested he might have a streak of Asian ancestry. He, more than anyone else in the bar, looked as though he belonged on a film set.

'Or Bufty,' he added, as though slightly embarrassed. 'That's what they call me.'

Marta nearly said something, then forced the champagne to her lips. So *this* was Bufty.

Flattering though it was to be eyed up, chatted up and entertained with such intensity, it felt awkward being the centre of attention in a crowd of strangers. After her first glass – which was the equivalent of three normal-sized champagne flutes – she slipped off to the ladies'.

Her reflection stared back at her: tired, confused and barely recognisable beneath Tina's makeup. She could slip away. It was probably the best thing to do. Tina wouldn't mind. Let's face it, she hadn't brought Marta here for purely selfless reasons. In fact, Tina probably wouldn't even notice her go.

One more drink, she decided. That would be all. Leaving now would be rude, but only one. A hangover was the last thing she needed in the office tomorrow.

Waiting to be noticed on the fringes of the group, Marta started to have second thoughts. Maybe she should leave now. She had nothing in common with these champagne-drinking traders apart from their colleague, whose house she happened to be living in. She didn't want them to feel obliged to talk to her. She didn't want to be force-fed alcohol. She didn't even know what they would talk about if they got into conversation.

'So, Tina mentioned you're Polish,' said someone, emerging at her side with a fresh glass of champagne. It was Bufty. She nodded, her eyes fluttering to the ground as she caught his mesmerising smile.

'Me too. Well – a quarter,' he added sheepishly.

'Oh! Mowisz po polsku?' asked Marta, excited about the prospect of common ground and the chance to speak Polish.

Bufty pulled a face. 'Sorry – no idea. My grandmother wanted her kids to grow up English, so it never got passed on. Bit of a waste really, as Polish is becoming the second language over here...' He smiled.

Marta laughed. 'We're everywhere.'

Bufty tilted his head. 'Not so many on the trading floor.'

'*Yet*,' added Marta, with mock severity. 'We won't be working in bagel shops and building sites for ever.'

'Maybe,' he replied vaguely. Marta waited for him to expand, but he didn't. She wondered whether Tina was right about the prejudice thing. Surely Bufty wasn't prejudiced?

'So where do you work?' he asked.

Marta told him, missing out the bit about her contract running out at the end of the week. He nodded. There was no sign of prejudice. For a while, they stood sipping their drinks in what seemed like companionable silence as the noise level around them continued to rise. Then, for some reason, Marta found herself telling Bufty everything: about her search for work, the recruitment fair, her leaflet job, the agency interviews and then her current, precarious role at Stratisvision. Bufty sipped his champagne, looking at her through half-closed eyes and nodding, gently.

'What a shocker,' he said when she told him about Kat and her dirty tricks. 'Tell you what. You should quit. You should walk in there tomorrow, slap them round the face and walk out. That's what I'd do. You shouldn't have to put up with that crap.'

Marta hesitated. Was he joking? Had he not listened to anything else she had told him? Had he not grasped the fact that Stratisvision the only part of her CV that gave her any chance of getting future work in this country; that without it, she would almost certainly fail to build up a career?

'I quit my first trading job when they didn't give me the bonus they'd given the analysts the previous year,' Bufty went on, with a hint of pride in his voice. 'They were offering us seventy grand when it was a well-known fact that they had paid six figures the year before. I mean, granted, the markets were in a better state then, but I demanded they match it and they didn't, so I quit.'

Marta nodded silently. They were speaking on different levels. Marta was talking about stepping onto the employment ladder and trying to cling on; this guy was talking about leaping off the ladder at the other end. Six figures? In his first year of work? That was just *crazy*.

She let Bufty talk. It was enlightening to hear his views on the world, even though it seemed like a different one. Salaries, promotions, bonuses, appraisals, trades, assessments and after-work drinks: these were his areas of speciality. Marta was more and more intrigued by this place they called 'the city'. She could see its appeal, and not just the financial appeal. From what Bufty was saying, it was a special place where alpha males (and occasionally, females) got together and used their incredible intellect to do groundbreaking deals under a huge amount of pressure. It sounded exciting as well as lucrative.

The more Bufty talked, the more Marta could see why girls back in Poland aspired to come to England and marry a rich banker; not that this approach appealed to her. Relying on somebody else for an income – especially someone as flirtatious and shallow as Bufty – made Marta feel cold inside, but she knew of plenty of girls back home who would jump at the chance to be with a guy like Bufty.

'…That's what we do to the new guys,' he told her, finishing the tale about poor little Dish, who had been taped to his swivel chair, given a glass of vodka, spun round and then wheeled into the boss' office to vomit.

'So mean!' cried Marta, half amused but all too aware of the parallels with her own situation at work. 'Did he got told off by the boss?'

'Told off?' Bufty laughed. 'God no. The boss thought it was hilarious and ordered him to clean it up – with his bare hands.'

Marta screwed up her face and listened while he started telling her about his own 'induction'.

Several glasses of champagne later, the bear-like man moved clumsily into their conversation.

'What's this, then? Bufty monopolising the pretty Pole, eh?'

Marta and Bufty simultaneously stepped backwards to allow

the man more space. He was swaying quite violently.

'Have you heardtheplan?' he slurred, looking at Marta and hanging off Bufty's right shoulder. 'Going to Abacus! Gonna get rat-arsed!'

'*Get* rat-arsed?' muttered Bufty, when the big man had lurched off.

Just as Marta was about to make her excuses and catch the last tube, her phone rang. She pulled it out of the tight back pocket of Tina's trousers and tried to focus on the display. She was drunk. She peered closer. As she did so, she suddenly found the phone being wrenched from her hands.

'Hello!' bawled the large man, who had reappeared at her side and was frowning as he tried to make out the voice at the other end. 'What? Marta?' He winked stupidly at Marta. 'Oh, she's here alright. But she's… abitbusy!' Another wink, this time at the small crowd of men who were gathering round. 'I don't think she'll be freeforabit! Sorry young man. Goodbye!'

Marta retrieved her phone to the sound of guffaws and applause from the traders. She could guess who had called. Squinting at the handset confirmed her theory.

Well, she thought, letting her eyes wander back to Bufty's and smiling. *Perhaps the trader had done her a favour.* Dominik wouldn't be calling her back for a bit – or perhaps for ever. That was what she wanted, wasn't it? Yes. No. Yes. It felt as though she were playing poker with herself. She was bluffing, or double-bluffing, or maybe even triple-bluffing. It was very confusing. Maybe the guy had done her a favour.

Somehow, Marta found herself heading down the metal steps of a small underground nightclub. The smell of stale dance floor smoke, aftershave and sweat brought back instant memories of nights out in Warszawa with Anka. There were blue neon lights around the bar and the place was heaving with young, suited men and a few women who had hoisted up their skirts and undone some buttons on their blouses to try and compete with the dolled-up hookers who stood around the edges.

Marta wondered what time it was. Perhaps she would still make the last tube if she left after the next drink? It was strange, but she was no longer sure she wanted to leave.

'Come on!' yelled Tina, above the din. Marta just had time to drain her shot and slam the empty glass down before her arm was nearly yanked out of its socket on the way to the dance floor.

The song came to a triumphant end and suddenly Tina was dragging Marta off the floor as quickly as she had pulled her onto it.

'Let's call Holly!' she shouted. 'She works near here – she might be around!'

Marta nodded enthusiastically. because at this particular point in the evening it seemed like a spectacularly good idea. If anyone needed a night out, it was Holly. She spent her whole life in that office of hers and if it was round the corner…

They tottered towards the exit until Tina cried jubilantly that she had reception on her phone.

'Hey babe, is that you? Hol? It's Tina. I can't hear you!' Tina scowled madly at her handset. '*Can you hear me?*'

Marta nearly fell backwards as her housemate lost her footing and fell on top of her, clinging to the banister for support. A bouncer was heading down the steps towards them, Marta noticed, as she grabbed Tina's phone.

'Holly? It's Marta! Are you there?'

'Of course I'm fucking here!' replied Holly, sounding quite cross. 'Is Tina drunk?'

'Yes!' Marta watched as Tina saw off the bouncer with a series of hand gestures and loud explanations. 'But is so good here, Holly, we want you to come!'

'God, you're drunk too, aren't you? Where are you?'

'Place called Alpha… I forgot name. Hang on. Tina, Tina, where are–'

'No, don't bother,' said Holly sternly. 'I won't make it out before it closes anyway. Have fun, though. See you later.'

Marta started to persuade her housemate to change her mind,

but she realised after a while that she was speaking into a dead line. Tina grabbed her phone back. 'Is she coming out?' she asked excitedly.

Marta shook her head, suddenly feeling guilty. Holly sounded so unhappy. Maybe a call from her drunken housemates was not what she needed when she was trying to get her difficult, important assignments done. What was she *doing* there, anyway? Why couldn't she come out, just this once?

The dance floor was filling up. On it, numerous traders were embarking on a flamboyant version of the Englishman's disco dance: shuffling from foot to foot, wiggling their shoulders and occasionally making wild stabs at the air with their fingers. Marta found herself mouthing the words of the song as she and Tina moved back onto the floor.

When the music slowed, Marta found herself in the arms of a tall young man with a spiky quiff. It was strange, really. She couldn't quite work out how it had happened, but here she was rocking gently with him to the sound of some crazy disco tune. It felt, well... quite nice, actually.

Tina had also paired off and, from the corner of her eye, Marta could see their entwined silhouette shifting sideways off the dance floor and towards the darkest corner of the club. Then they disappeared altogether behind the speakers. Marta began to wonder whether the same would be expected of her. She was thinking about this when suddenly her man's arms weakened around her. She looked up.

The spiky-haired man suddenly let go and took a step backwards. Standing over her, smiling, was Bufty. He looked even more handsome now, the coloured lights reflecting off his smooth, exotic skin. Marta found herself pressed up against him, looking up at his eyes. It was lovely. But it was also weird. One minute earlier, she had been in the same position with another man. She felt a bit like a toy that was being shared around.

'Kiss me,' he said softly in her ear.

Right there, in the middle of the dance floor, like teenagers at a school disco, they kissed. Marta almost laughed as she felt his tongue enter her mouth: his wet lips nibbling on hers. It was ridiculous. This man was kissing her in front of all his colleagues in a nightclub full of people. But then, everything seemed ridiculous tonight. Maybe it was the champagne.

'Follow me,' he said afterwards, leading her by the hand towards the exit. He stopped at the cloakroom. 'D'you have a jacket?'

Marta giggled and let out a hiccup. 'Don't know!'

They established that Tina had retrieved her suit jacket and that the flimsy red top was all Marta had had on. Bufty wrapped his suit jacket around her shoulders and, keeping his hand around her waist underneath, led her out.

It was only when her flesh made contact with the night air that Marta realised what was happening. She barely knew him. She didn't even like him much, really. He didn't understand her world and she didn't get his. She definitely didn't want to go back and have sex with him, which was clearly what he had in mind. He probably couldn't even remember her name; he just wanted a fuck.

'We'll get a cab. It's only money,' he laughed, sticking his hand out into the road.

Marta stepped sideways, wriggling free of his grip. She didn't know what to do, but she knew that she had to escape. Despite the fuzzy feeling in her brain, and despite Tina's words, she knew that 'a good shag' was not what she needed at all. She didn't want to be with this handsome stranger. There was only one man in the world she wanted right now, and even though she knew she shouldn't be thinking about him, he was there in her mind, naked and gorgeous on top of her.

A taxi pulled up. Bufty held the door open. For a moment, Marta just stood there. Then she threw his jacket into the back, muttered something about an early start, pulled off her shoes and ran.

36

Marta clicked *accept* and watched the appointment drop into her calendar. *Catch-up.* That was all it said. What was that supposed to mean? Why had David Lyle summoned her to his office at two o'clock with no other explanation than that?

All sorts of possibilities ran through Marta's tired, paranoid mind. Maybe he was going to ask her to leave. Perhaps he was going to question her over the poor-quality work she had done for Charlotte. Or perhaps Kat's clan had played another trick on her and she was about to find out what it was. They had been suspiciously quiet these last few days. Marta closed the mysterious appointment invitation and looked at the document on her screen.

The brief wasn't difficult. It basically involved rearranging numbers in boxes and changing the colours to make them look pretty. Any other week, Marta would have been screaming with boredom at the monotony of the task. Right now, though, it was just about right. She had the attention span of a minnow.

Marta wasn't even sure why she felt so unsettled. She didn't think it was just the fact that she was likely to be out of work in a little over twenty-four hours' time. The agency had hinted at the prospect of more work when she had called them the day before, so assuming Stratisvision didn't give her too harsh a reference, she wouldn't be unemployed for long.

Bufty had apparently asked for Marta's number on Tuesday night, which was flattering, but he hadn't called anyway. Even the fact that her best friend had forgiven her for forgetting her birthday and was saving up to come to London hadn't made an impact on her state of mind.

Mindlessly, Marta dragged, dropped and formatted. It was only when she came to the end of the fifty-page pack that she looked up at the clock. With horror, she realised it was five past two. She grabbed her notebook and launched herself into the gangway.

As she peered through the glass between the frosted panels, Marta could feel her heart pounding against the inside of her chest. Suddenly, she was nervous. Her mouth had dried up and she could feel her legs shaking inside her trousers. She was fully aware that Stratisvision was the only real company to have offered her work in England and that this could be the end of it all. If she got sacked from this firm the agency wouldn't place her anywhere else and she would be back to square one, handing out leaflets – or worse.

'Entrez!' called the director from within.

Marta wiped her clammy palms on her shirt and stepped inside.

'Bon journo,' he said proudly. Marta relaxed a little. It was difficult to feel on edge when the person in charge was David Lyle. He swivelled a full 360 degrees before wheeling his way towards the oval table in the middle of the room.

'Good morning,' said Marta, noticing that her voice sounded higher than usual. Nerves did strange things to the body.

'Yep, just testing out me old linguistics,' he explained, moving a wad of papers to one side. 'Ooh – hang on, you're Polish. Let me see now...' He squinted up to the ceiling, where, Marta noticed, there was a sticker saying "Upside-down thinking" in swirly letters. 'No, don't know it. Bonovska Journovski?'

'Dzien dobry,' Marta replied, smiling as she perched on the seat opposite him.

'Ah, of course! Jen debris!'

Marta forced a laugh, waiting for the 'catch-up' to begin. The longer David Lyle larked about, the shorter her nerves became. She was clamping her knees together under the table in case the trembling affected the furniture.

'So!' David turned to her and grinned, exposing a small piece of what looked like broccoli between his front teeth. 'You're probably wondering why I called you in here on this fine Thursday afternoon,' he said.

Marta nodded politely, her hands balled into rigid fists in her lap.

'Well... Where to begin?!' He fiddled with the leather bracelet around his wrist. 'OK. Appraisals. Now, you may or may not be aware that everyone working at Stratisvision undergoes an appraisal at the end of every piece of work: temporary or permanent, full- or part-time.'

Marta shook her head, wondering what he was talking about. Suddenly, the joker had gone all serious.

'Ah, OK. Well that's probably my fault for not telling you, but anyway.' He leaned back and extracted a folder from a mass of paper-work on his desk. 'This is you, this is.'

Marta watched as he opened the dark green cover with her name on it. Inside were various identical pieces of paper that looked like application forms.

'I've had a quick squiz at these,' he said. 'And, well... it seems as though you're a bit of a schizophrenic!'

Marta frowned. She didn't know what one of those was, but it didn't sound good.

'Some excellent reviews, and some er, less than excellent ones, shall we say.'

Marta waited for him to explain. He clearly wasn't going to show her the pieces of paper.

'So, here's the deal. Everyone in the firm who has got to know you, at work or otherwise, is asked to fill out an appraisal form. Charlotte, Kat, Dean... Carl, Kim, Nik... Ooh. Patricia!' He looked at her, eyebrows raised. '*I say.*'

Marta nodded patiently, wondering where this was all leading. Her hands were getting sweaty again. She was dying to read what these people had written about her.

'Excellent work ethic, helpful, enthusiastic, open…' He flicked through the documents, then stopped on one. 'Uncommunicative, sullen and evasive. See what I mean?'

It was all Marta could do to stop herself from scowling and wrenching the papers from his hands. She could guess who had written those words.

'Project skills, where applicable,' he muttered. 'You've got an "excellent" from Charlotte. That's unheard of. What was this brand precedents work you did for her?'

Marta felt a pang of guilt as she described Carl's presentation. Now was probably not the time to own up.

'Yet you got a "poor" from her on this PopsCo thing.'

'That was Kat!' Marta blurted out before she could stop herself.

The director was looking at her. 'I'm sorry?'

'Er, that was Kat who tell me to do it wrong,' explained Marta, instantly wishing she hadn't said anything. She was coming across as churlish.

He sifted through the papers. 'I don't think so,' he said. 'The "poor" was due to your failure to grasp the English language.'

'But—' Marta started, regretting it. 'Kat advise me wrong. Doesn't matter.'

Lyle nodded as though he wasn't really listening anyway. 'OK, managing your time seems good… Apart from one "very poor". How strange.'

Marta nodded. It wasn't strange at all. Kat had it in for her. She had probably done the same for all the questions.

'And similarly for quality of deliverables,' noted Lyle, confirming her suspicions. 'Very interesting comments on your personality,' he said, lightening up for a moment. '*Bold and assertive* is one person's comment – one rather senior person, too,' he said.

Marta smiled. Kat's trick had backfired.

'…and yet, someone else claims you are "moody, unpredictable and at times downright miserable"!'

Gosh, thought Marta. *This was a horrible process.* She had had no idea she was being so closely scrutinised by those around her. If she had known, perhaps she would have pretended to be a bit happier these last few days.

'Right,' said David, suddenly slamming the folder shut and looking at her, goggle-eyed. 'So what does this all mean?'

Marta looked at him, wondering whether he expected an answer. She certainly didn't have one for him.

'It means that you're a complicated person, Ms Darawavsky!'

'Dabrowska,' Marta corrected quietly. She disagreed with him, but she decided to keep quiet this time.

'But that's not always a bad thing,' he said. Marta tried to work out from his tone whether this was all building up to positive or negative news. It was impossible to say.

'Your work has been variable, just like your personality,' he summarised. 'That seems to be the feedback from your colleagues. But on the basis of the excellent work you did for Charlotte during your first week – and some of the other bits and bobs – I'm pleased to offer you an extension of your contract for the next six weeks, should you want it.' He stared at her, his brow high.

A smile quickly spread across Marta's face. *Of course she wanted it.* She was so shocked that David's speech had culminated in good news, she probably didn't show quite how pleased she was.

'Thank you! Yes, I would like it.'

'Well, we take on all sorts here; we don't mind the odd schizophrenic.' He smiled.

Marta laughed, even though his description of her was wholly unfair. She felt guilty that the offer had been based so heavily on a piece of work that she hadn't actually done, but then she had taken the blame for a lot of things that were someone else's fault, so maybe it all balanced out in the end. It wasn't as though Carl needed any extra credit, after all.

'Just remember what I told you at the start: *make love to the client,*' he said. 'That's what we do here at Stratisvision.'

Marta nodded, even though she had never even met a client, let alone made love to one.

'And you're on three hundred pounds a week, aren't you?' asked

Lyle, scribbling something on the corner of the folder.

'Yes,' replied Marta, hoping that this wasn't an honesty test. She was on two hundred pounds a week.

David Lyle looked up. 'Excellent!' he said. 'Well, glad to have you with us for longer!'

They shook hands.

'Jen debris!' he cried, so passionately that the piece of broccoli shot out from between his teeth and landed on Marta's right breast.

Marta managed to ignore it for long enough to return David's smile and walk serenely out of his office, feeling elated but guilty too. It was time to go and thank Carl.

37

MD: Anka!

AK: Marta! How's Londynia?

MD: Complicated. How's Lom?

AK: Same as… just a few more people gone

MD: Got your text – you're coming over?

AK: Just need to see if the bakery can survive without me
:-)

MD: That's a big if

AK: I'm manager now – did I tell you?

MD: What? No! Congrats!

AK: :-) Don't get excited, it's only a bakery. Will let you
know when I can take some days off. What about your
job? Any news on extending it?

MD: 6 more weeks! Management seems to like me even
though half the company doesn't

AK: Why don't they like you?

MD: Long story. I'll save it for when you come over. More
English girls with something against me :-(

AK: Their loss. Glad you haven't found yourself a new

best friend

MD: No chance

AK: Am wearing those beads u sent me – everyone wants to know where I got them ;-)

MD: Glad you like – do you have a webcam?

AK: !?%*&!? In Łomianki library? You're joking, right?

MD: Right...

AK: I have a pic – one mama took on my birthday. Hold on

MD: Come on! Where is pic?

AK: Patience... Polish connection, remember :-)

MD: Where is it??

AK: Chill out! Here...

MD: *Wolf-whistle* You look like a model!

AK: Yeah right – wearing 7-yr-old jeans

MD: Seriously... gorgeous. You're wasted in that bakery

AK: Thanks – but I'm not following you to Londynia!

MD: Just wait til you come over...

AK: Enough. You getting over the two-timer?

MD: Truthfully, no

AK: You must

MD: I think about him ALL THE TIME

AK: Trick is to find someone else, take your mind off him.

MD: That doesn't work.

AK: Speaking from experience?

MD: *Cringe* Went out this week with mad housemate

AK: And?

MD: Nearly went back with a rich trader

AK: Details??

MD: Quarter polish, actually. Cute. Nice eyes.

AK: You said that about the last one! Stop judging them by their eyes

MD: Sweet too, but way too rich

AK: TOO rich??

MD: Arrogant, patronising...

AK: He should know better

MD: Italian stallion fancies me too

AK: Is that a prob?

AK: Where've u gone?

AK: ??

MD: Sorry – just getting my phone. Got a text... guess who?

AK: Dominik?

MD: Y

AK: Saying?

MD: Hang on...

AK: Tell me!

MD: Marta, what's up? You won't pick up. I don't know if I've done something wrong, but if I have, please tell me. I wanna talk! Call me. Love Dxx

AK: He must think you're dumb

MD: Wish he'd just leave me alone

AK: U gonna call him?

MD: Don't know. Worried I'll fall for his lies & he'll win me back

AK: So don't. He won't call again so it's over. Good riddance!

MD: Hmm

AK: You've got men queuing!

MD: Should concentrate on work anyway.

AK: By the way, you know your mum thinks you've been doing some amazing marketing job since you arrived?

MD: *Flinch* I meant to warn you not to talk about that – did you?

AK: Didn't chat. She just went on about how proud she was :-)

MD: Hate lying to her but she just won't understand how hard it is

AK: Don't worry M. At least u have a great job now

MD: For 6 weeks...

AK: Stop beating yourself up... You've made it. Be proud!

MD: Like mama

AK: Not that proud maybe

MD: Hold on – another text

AK: Popular girl

MD: AAAAAAAAAGH

AK: What?

MD: It's from Jack – Tash's boyfriend

AK: Again?

MD: He says: Hey babe, do U play tennis? I have a court at my club this weekend – mixed doubs. I'll lend u racket etc. Looking forward 2seeing u in short white skirt

AK: Babe? Since when?

MD: He calls me that.

AK: Idiot! Another idiot!

MD: Yeah

AK: Marta............?

MD: Well I like tennis

AK: He's not asking you to play tennis!

MD: I could just play & then leave

AK: Marta, I have a BAD FEELING about this guy

MD: OK you're right. No games.

AK: Exactly. Shit, gotta run – library shutting!

MD: OK kochana – thanks for advice!

AK: Don't be silly – u need it :-)

MD: Shut up

AK: Bye xx

MD: xxxxxx

38

'Great shot, Marta! Where did that come from?'

Marta shrugged as though she barely cared. Actually, she was rather proud. The ball had gone pelting down the tramlines with more precision than any other shot played that afternoon.

'Fifteen all.'

Marta skipped into the service box and waited while her partner prepared for his serve. She was tempted to look back and watch his muscular body stretch up and blast the ball over the net, but she knew you had to try and look professional when you were playing on courts like these.

Disappointingly, Jack's first serve hit the net. Marta darted down to retrieve the ball and waited, praying for the second one to go over.

It did, and with incredible force. Marta watched as the girl made a valiant effort to connect with it, only to find that the serve had been loaded with spin.

'Good serve!' cried the girl's partner, clapping his hand against his racket in recognition. 'You're starting to warm up, aren't you?'

'Thinking about it,' replied Jack, smirking as he neatly caught the ball that was hurtling towards him. He lifted his sunglasses and wiped a hand across his forehead.

Charles was a school friend of Jack's. His girlfriend Tiff had only started playing tennis a year ago, but she was playing a reasonable game. She had had coaching from someone called Mark Peachy or Patchy, who was clearly a big name in tennis, although Marta had never heard of him.

The first fifteen minutes had been a disaster for Marta. Her shots had been wild – so wild, in fact, that one had gone sailing over the fence and into the duck pond – and as a result she had found herself focusing on what Jack and the others were thinking of her instead of on the game itself. The more she dwelt on this, the worse she played. Eventually she pulled herself together, but not before they had lost four consecutive games. She and Jack had ended up losing the first set 3–6, but this set was a different matter.

'Forty-fifteen,' uttered Jack as he moved back to the baseline. He still had a smile on his face, as did Marta. The score in this set was 5–1. They were about to win.

There was a whoosh of air as the ball shot past Marta's left ear. Miraculously, Charles popped it back over, just within Marta's reach. She returned the ball to Tiff, who hit it straight back, and then Marta's impatience got the better of her. She raised her racket behind her head, guided the ball in and then *swiped*, right across the court, in line with the net. Tiff made a half-hearted attempt to move for it, but she was too late.

'*Awesome.*' Jack smiled handsomely, jogging to slap hands with Marta. She felt something leap inside her.

'Yah, well played,' Charles agreed. 'You really got your eye in by the end, didn't you?'

'End?' asked Jack, raising an eyebrow as they congregated at the net. 'You mean you're not up for the deciding set?'

Charles and Tiff looked at one another. 'Gotta scoot I'm afraid,' said Charles. 'Seeing the in-laws at three for afternoon tea.' He pulled a face.

Tiff whacked him in the chest.

'Running scared.' Jack shook his head in mock disappointment. 'Pathetic.'

'Next time,' replied Charles, holding his hand out across the net.

Marta found herself leaning forward to kiss Charles, then Tiff, which was rather bizarre. She hadn't kissed girls like that since she lived with Tash. It was a posh people thing, she decided.

They collected the balls and waited while Jack pulled off his T-shirt and started rummaging around in his kit bag, bare-chested.

Charles let out a low whistle, slapping Jack's sweaty, muscular back.

'Jealous,' Jack muttered, extracting a top and pulling it on. Marta giggled and caught Jack's eye. He was probably right. Charles' body was nothing like Jack's to look at.

'Did you drive?' Jack heaved the bag over his shoulder.

Charles nodded. Tiff pointed towards the car park, where an open-top silver Porsche Boxter was visible through a gap in the trees.

'New car?

'Bonus day,' replied Charles with a wink.

The men admired the machine for a few seconds and then looked at one another.

'Well, thanks for the game.' Charles nodded. 'Looking forward to the rematch. Nice to meet you, Kat! See you soon!' He waved and led his girlfriend away.

As soon as the pair were out of earshot, Marta turned to Jack. 'Why did he call me Kat?'

Jack looked as baffled as Marta. 'I have absolutely *no* idea.' He stared after the couple as they headed off over the perfectly manicured lawn. 'Very odd. I did introduce you at the beginning, didn't I?'

Marta nodded. Charles' slip might have passed unnoticed were it not for the strange coincidence that Kat was the name of her arch enemy in the office.

'He's always been terrible with names. Marta, Kat… they're all the same to Charlie. Anyway, what're you up to now?' he asked. 'You don't have to shoot off, do you?'

Marta hesitated, deciding to put the whole Kat incident down to a spooky coincidence. The fact was, she *did* have to shoot off because she had promised herself that she would play tennis and *only* tennis with Jack today. But the situation wasn't as she had imagined it. Jack wasn't trying it on at all. He hadn't made a single pass at her, and somehow it didn't seem likely that he would. Besides, she couldn't think of an excuse not to stay. Marta smiled and shook her head.

'Great.' Jack looked pleased. 'I'll show you around.'

The place was incredible. Marta had guessed it might be, from the stone entranceway with its uniformed guards, the well-kept lawns and the pond behind the tennis courts.

'This is the lake, obviously,' stated Jack as they walked over a quaint wooden footbridge. 'Now home to one more tennis ball,' he added, teasingly. 'And over there, that's the outdoor pool. It's heaving in summer.'

They followed the winding path up the hill towards a huge Georgian house. It looked a bit like Tash's mansion, only in larger proportions. Marta looked around at the luscious lawns and the colourful flowers that bordered the shrubberies. 'It's like from a film,' she remarked, thinking of the costume dramas she had watched back home.

'They do use it for filming occasionally,' said Jack, looking at Marta and noticing Holly's racket bag on her back. 'I'm so sorry – let me take that.' He reached round and lifted it from her shoulders.

Usually Marta would have objected to such pointless chivalry, but here, in the grounds of such historic splendour, it seemed reasonable to allow the odd gallant act. And besides, her limbs felt weary after running around in such strong sunshine.

'What's that?' Marta pointed at a flat patch of grass to their right, which was separated from the undulating lawn by a hedge. It was so perfectly horizontal it almost looked like a lake, with statues dotted about in the middle.

'That's the croquet lawn.'

'Croaky?'

'Croquet. D'you know what croquet is?'

Marta shook her head. 'Sounds like a disease.'

Jack laughed. 'I'll show you.'

They veered off the path and cut a straight line across the springy lawn. It was only as they got closer that Marta realised the statues were actually people. They were moving about, but very, very slowly. She followed Jack to a gap in the hedge.

'See? There's a series of hoops stuck in the ground, and you have to hit a ball through them using a rubber mallet thing. Look – watch that one.' Jack put an arm gently around Marta's shoulders and pointed.

Marta watched as the white-haired man slowly swung the long-handled mallet between his legs, sending a ball rolling towards one of the hoops.

'Like golf,' she remarked, feeling a slight sense of disappointment as Jack's arm slipped away. 'Fun,' she added, not wanting to offend him in case it was the national sport or something.

He looked at her sceptically. 'It's a load of bollocks.'

They laughed and turned their backs on the slow-motion scene. It was strange, but Marta felt as though she was beginning to feel quite intrigued by the quirky English customs. Maybe croaky was a load of bollocks, as Jack put it, but it had a certain appeal.

'Pimms o'clock?' he asked as they approached the side of the huge white house, where a number of parasols were pitched like oversized daisies on the patio.

Marta frowned.

'Sorry – it's a phrase. D'you fancy a drink?'

Marta smiled. *Another silly English phrase.* A drink was exactly what she felt like, even though it was exactly what she had vowed to avoid. She nodded, despite herself.

'Thanks for coming,' said Jack, once the primly dressed lady had taken their order.

'Thanks for inviting me,' she replied. 'It was a good game.'

Jack squinted down at his feet and then up again. He just couldn't help being sexy, thought Marta, wishing she hadn't noticed.

'I didn't mean just the tennis,' he said. 'I meant thanks for agreeing to see me.'

Marta shrugged as though it were no big deal, which was ridiculous, because they both knew she had been ignoring his messages for months.

'I know I fucked things up for you, Marta. I've been feeling shitty about it ever since I found out what Tash did.'

Marta nodded, not sure what to say.

'There's no excuse for the way I behaved that night.' He paused as the waitress approached with a tray of drinks. The jug was filled with brown liquid in which a rather strange selection of salad items were floating. Jack waited for the lady to head off, then went on. 'Except to say that… well…' He squinted into the sunshine. 'The truth comes out when you're drunk.'

Marta looked him in the eye and managed to hold his gaze. What was he saying? That his drunken fumblings that night were a representation of how he really felt? Marta looked at the ground, unable to maintain eye contact any longer. She remembered how she had felt at the time, when he had pinned her to the bed in that tiny dress… but the more she thought about it now, the more she wondered whether she really *had* struggled, or whether she had secretly wanted something to happen.

'Anyway, I felt bloody awful when I found out Tash blamed you for the whole thing and kicked you out. *Awful*. I tried to tell her, you know. I tried to explain it was me, but the stuck-up cow wouldn't listen. Never does. She just hears what she wants to hear.'

Marta couldn't help smiling at the unpleasant reference to Tash. 'So you're not friends now?'

Jack laughed sharply. 'You could say that.'

They fell silent. Looking at him, Marta couldn't help feeling that Jack's motives for meeting up today weren't as suspicious as she had first assumed. He genuinely wanted to apologise and to clear the air between them. She wasn't sure about the other thing he seemed to be saying… the other feelings he was trying to express. It felt as though the best course of action was to play dumb on that front and pretend not to understand. Life was complicated enough already.

'Nice outfit, by the way.' Jack glanced approvingly at Marta's legs, which she had tried to tuck under the table.

'Thanks,' she said bashfully. It had been a team effort finding white clothes that Holly, Tina and Marta all agreed upon. Her housemates had been all too happy to help dress her for the game on the understanding that she was meeting her 'new mystery man'. They almost certainly wouldn't have obliged had she told them the name of the mystery man, Marta thought guiltily.

Jack reached forward and poured the drinks. Marta accepted her glass, mildly perplexed to find a chunk of apple, a slice of cucumber and a clump of green leaves floating on top.

'Cheers,' 'Na zdrowie,' they said, raising their glasses. Marta threw back her head and swallowed, blocking all thoughts of what Holly might say from her mind. It actually tasted nice: sweet and fruity, but with an alcoholic twist that made Marta feel instantly dizzy.

'It's so pretty here,' she said, looking out at the green, rolling grass and the tennis courts beyond. It was difficult to believe they were in London. 'How do you join this club?'

Jack smiled wryly. 'Don't hold your breath,' he said. 'The waiting list is thirty years long.'

'Thirty years?' Marta spluttered, wondering whether she had got her numbers mixed up.

Jack nodded. 'They give priority to the children of members,' he told her. 'That's how I got in. My parents put my name down before I was even born.'

'Nice place for kids to learn tennis,' remarked Marta, thinking of the crumbling concrete playground where she and Anka had first played. They had had to prop up the net with pieces of wood in the middle, and when it came to calling shots out they had just used their judgement as the lines had all worn away.

'Yeah,' Jack nodded, extracting a strawberry from his drink and eating it. 'So you don't have clubs like this back home?'

Marta rolled her eyes, wondering which world Jack inhabited. 'Most beautiful places got bombed in the war,' she explained, even though there were plenty of exclusive clubs for the super-wealthy – just not for people like her.

They talked for a while about Poland, about the differences between Łomianki and London, and the way things were going.

241

Marta was putting a lot down to the cultural identities of each nation, but she suspected that in truth, most of the differences were down to the different level of wealth she had experienced growing up compared with Jack.

It was interesting to hear things from Jack's point of view. He seemed to have the view that most rich people were rich because they had worked 'bloody hard' and that poverty mainly came down to stupidity or laziness. Marta was curious to find out where the hard-working poor people fitted in and, over the course of their first two drinks, she tried to probe.

'What *is* the minimum wage over here?' he asked, when she suggested that some people might not be able to *afford* a good education. 'I'm afraid I have no idea.'

Marta smiled. 'Here, is nearly one thousand pounds per month if you work full hours. In Poland, is only like two hundred pounds.'

Jack pulled a face. '*Blimey*. How does anyone survive on two hundred pounds? I spend that much on alcohol every *week*.'

His expression suggested a hint of shock and guilt for being so out of touch. Perhaps it was the brown drink with the floating fruit, but Marta could feel herself warming to Jack. He was rich and he lived in another world, but he was intrigued by the lives of others. He was witty and charming, too – and only a little flirtatious.

'I could stay here all day,' he commented, draining his glass. 'Shame I've got to work.'

Marta frowned. 'Work?' It was the last thing she had expected him to say. For a start, he had just consumed a pint of this sickly brown drink.

Jack nodded unhappily. 'And I know what you're thinking. I've had too much to drink. You're right. But there's an acquisition that goes public on Tuesday and I'm on the deal team. I've gotta show face.'

Marta nodded. She had no idea what he did for a living, or what 'going public' or 'showing face' meant, but it was sad that he had to do these things on a Sunday, whatever they were.

'That's the thing about being a banker. You've gotta put in the hours.' He shrugged. 'It sucks, but it'll pay off in the end. Gotta play the long game.'

Marta smiled. She knew all about that. Perhaps Jack's 'in the end' would coincide with her 'in the end' and they could live a rich, happy life together.

Jack paid the bill and Marta let him. Usually she would insist on going halves, but she had a feeling that Jack might take offence. Besides, he clearly wasn't short on cash.

'You work hard, too. I know you do,' Jack said, hoisting both racket bags onto his back. 'I saw that the first time I met you. You've got drive. You're ambitious.'

Marta nodded, slightly surprised at the insightfulness of Jack's comment. To be honest, she had been under the impression that her legs and tits had been the only things Jack had noticed about her during the times they had met at Tash's house. Clearly she had been wrong.

'That was the problem with Tash,' Jack went on, as they wandered towards the duck pond. 'All she wanted to do was buy handbags and get her nails done. It was so tedious. She didn't have a single ambition except to get married and quit work. She didn't even care about her stupid job in fashion – except when it came to the freebies.'

Marta wasn't sure what to say. She wasn't sure she liked the way Jack seemed to be comparing her with Tash, but at least she was coming out favourably.

'Anyway, that's all water under the bridge,' said Jack, appearing to snap out of his reverie.

'I can see,' said Marta.

'Oh – no, sorry.' Jack smiled. 'I wasn't referring to the pond. It's a saying. *Water under the bridge.* It means "all in the past".'

'Oh.' Marta took this in, storing it away in her mental compendium of strange English phrases. Then she laughed. Jack laughed too. They walked under the stone archway and onto the quiet residential road, smiling in comfortable silence as they headed for the tube.

When they reached the station, Jack swung the smaller bag off his shoulder and handed it to her.

'Thanks again for coming.'

'Thanks again for inviting me.' Marta felt her heart lurch.

There was a brief moment of uncertainty, and then Jack leaned forward, kissing her first on one cheek, then the other – the English way.

'Would you... Would you consider meeting up again sometime?' he asked.

Marta smiled, tilting her head and deliberately taking a long time to reply.

'I would consider it,' she said eventually, turning towards the barriers before the grin spread across her face.

39

'Everything OK, girls?' asked David Lyle, grinning stupidly.

Marta nodded silently. Kat was busily sifting through papers on the meeting room table next to her.

In fact, everything was not OK. It was Marta's first client meeting and she had only found out about it that morning when Kat had swanned past her desk saying, 'Don't forget about the Unilight kick-off at ten!'

Helping Kat was never going to be easy, Marta decided. She had clearly neglected to tell Marta about the meeting on purpose to make her look flustered in front of their senior colleagues – and these ones really were senior. A quick glance at the attendee list on the agenda told Marta that even Patricia Catermol would be present. The CEO *never* came to project meetings.

David Lyle started clicking his biro against the table, seemingly oblivious to the irritating noise. They were waiting for Dean to arrive with the clients – and presumably for Patricia to make an appearance, too.

'Oh good. Nice biscuits,' exclaimed David as the small, pretty catering assistant crept in with a trolley of refreshments. He reached sideways and plucked a chocolate wafer from the plate.

Marta looked down at her blank notebook. This was clearly a very important meeting; they never usually had biscuits and coffee wheeled in.

'Want one?' asked David, sending a shower of wafer crumbs

across the table.

The girls shook their heads. Kat was still leafing through her papers: papers that were a mystery to Marta. Marta's phone vibrated silently in her lap. She looked down, grateful for something to fiddle with.

Fancy a mystery excursion next Sat? No need for short white skirt this time – unless you want. I'll pick you up @ 11 your place. J

Marta started to smile, then buried her phone in her lap as she realised Kat was leaning sideways, watching.

'Hello!' cried David, looking up and brushing the crumbs from his shirt, which was a brightly coloured Hawaiian affair with daisies for buttons.

Dean stepped into the glass-walled meeting room, upright and professional as ever. A large man sporting chinos and a red shirt arrived in his wake, followed by a small Chinese girl.

'Stefan! Good to see you!' cried David, rising to his feet and extending both hands as though greeting a long-lost brother. Clearly David owned the Unilight "client relationship". 'You've met Dean, then? And this is Kim, er, Nik, er, Kat... and Marta. They'll be working on the innovation programme with Dean. Patricia's just on her way. And this is...?'

David stooped down and peered at the petite Chinese girl in Stefan's shadow.

'B,' she said, softly.

'B?'

'Nobody is able to pronounce my name,' she explained. 'Just call me B.'

Marta smiled sympathetically as she shook the girl's hand.

Stefan and B sat along one side of the table opposite Dean, Marta and Kat. David poured coffees and spouted nonsense from the foot of the table as they continued to wait for Patricia.

'Well,' said Dean after quite some time. 'We may as well get started without–'

246

'Good *morning!*' sang a warbling voice that filled the room. Patricia was draped in something that resembled an orange sari with gold jewellery to match. 'Sorry I'm late!' She rushed over to Stefan and planted a kiss on each of his cheeks, ignoring B. 'Too much to do and not enough time…'

Dean waited for the CEO to swoop into the empty chair at the head of the table and then had another go at starting the meeting.

'So, thanks for coming, everyone. I presume everybody's seen the briefing pack I sent out yesterday?'

There were nods from all round the table. Marta frowned.

Smoothly, and so slowly that nobody else noticed, Kat slid a wad of papers along the table towards Marta. Marta started surreptitiously flicking through the pages. She felt like thumping Kat under the table. Why had she waited until now to share this?

'So I think we can get things wrapped up pretty quickly.'

Wrapped up? Marta looked at Dean.

'I suggest we whiz through the pack, ironing out any issues as we go along. Kat will be doing a lot of the groundwork,' he said.

Marta glanced sideways at Kat, who was smiling up at Dean. It was good in a way that Marta wasn't being given too much responsibility at this stage, but it was also frustrating. She was just as good as Kat and likely to contribute an equal amount on this project, although she knew she would receive little or no recognition.

There was a rustling noise as everyone in the room turned over the title page of the briefing pack. *Strategic marketing innovation at Unilight,* read Marta, mystified.

'I think we're all in agreement on the project objectives,' said Dean, 'but just to confirm: the purpose of this programme is to develop a consolidated view of our desired B2C market position in light of the changes to Unilight's core business roadmap for the current phase of innovation.'

Marta stared, trying to force her brain to catch up with the words.

'Yes?' asked Dean, looking around the table for agreement.

There were nods from all around the room.

'All singing from the same hymn sheet,' said Stefan, grinning.

Marta was lost. The words were dancing around in front of her – long, confusing and meaningless, and now the client was talking about *hymn sheets*. She wished she had had a chance to see this pack before the meeting.

'And this will be accomplished by the exploration of key strategic themes in the sector,' Dean went on.

Marta hid her frustration. This was *hard*. She was used to marketing jargon; she had studied it for three years. But this was something else. It wasn't just the language barrier. These people seemed to enjoy making simple things complex.

Simultaneously, they turned the page and were confronted with a diagram that looked like a mushroom on its side with lots of green boxes and yellow arrows.

'This is our preferred approach,' said Dean, clearly considering the diagram self-explanatory. 'We call it the innovation capture funnel.'

Marta glanced at Stefan, who was ogling the page and nodding fervently. Next to him, B scribbled frantically on her copy.

'It's the sort of thing that can be tailored to suit our needs,' noted Stefan, still staring avidly at the bizarre diagram.

'Abso-*lutely*!' cried Patricia, nodding excitedly at the client. She was clearly "making love" to him, thought Marta, wondering whether she realised that her sari-like garment was slipping off her left boob.

The page-turning continued. Marta tried to keep up, nodding when others nodded and laughing at the client's jokes. Inside she was drowning; the document meant nothing to her. Her head had gone under when Dean had talked about active feedback loops and KPIs, and now she knew she wasn't coming up again.

'Always worth raising something up the flagpole,' said Stefan in response to an enthusiastic suggestion by Patricia. 'That's the great thing about distributed innovation networks.'

Everybody nodded.

'Speaking of flagpoles,' replied David, his eyes dancing with mirth. He was clearly about to make a joke and Marta suddenly knew what it was. She looked down at her pack. 'We've got our very own Pole!'

The client looked at him, nonplussed. 'Your own pole?'

'Yes! Sitting over there!' David pointed. 'Marta's Polish!'

Stefan gave an unconvincing smile and nodded politely. David Lyle went on, unabashed. 'Yup! Shouldn't have any problems getting the work done with Marta on the team!'

'Great,' said Dean, calmly reclaiming control. 'Well, we probably don't need to go through the last few pages as it's all about the team and you've met us now.'

Marta looked at the chart that listed everyone's roles on the project. On the Stratisvision side, there were only two names: Dean and Kat. She tried not to take it personally.

'Well, thanks everyone. I guess it's just a question of getting *stuck in*.' Dean slammed his presentation pack shut, indicating that the meeting was over. Others around the room did the same.

Marta caught B's eye across the table. It was a question of getting *stuck in*, but not for everyone. Stefan, Patricia, David and even Dean probably wouldn't even attend another meeting after this one. Their presence here was purely cosmetic: to show the other side that they were taking things seriously. It would be Kat, Marta and B getting *stuck in*. That was how things happened in this world, Marta was beginning to realise. The higher you got, the easier your life became.

'Lovely to meet you,' said Stefan, squeezing everybody's hands, one after another. 'See you again.'

The room quickly emptied, leaving Dean, Kat and Marta alone with the uneaten biscuits.

'So. Four workstreams,' Dean summarised. 'Research, framework development, idea generation and third-party involvement. The last one can pretty much be handed to B, as she'll know who the stakeholders are.'

The girls nodded. Marta felt a surge of hope. Miraculously, she had jotted down the four workstreams correctly during the meeting, although she didn't know what any of them meant.

'You OK to divvy them up between you?' asked Dean.

They looked at each other and nodded again. Kat was wearing a beautiful fake smile.

'Great. Well, shout if you have any problems. I'll leave you to it.'

'No worries, Dean.' Kat looked up at him, batting her eyelashes.

Dean looked at her for a second, then nodded curtly and marched out.

Marta stared at the four bullet points. She was rather hoping Kat would suggest they work together on all four elements, but she knew this wouldn't be the case.

'I have a feeling the fourth workstream may take longer than anticipated,' said Kat. 'I'll take on that part.'

Marta frowned. 'But B will do–'

Kat was shaking her head. 'No, B won't do it. They often say things like that in meetings to make it seem as though it's a joint team working together, blah blah blah, but really it'll be us doing the work. That's why they're paying us, right? We're the consultants?'

Marta nodded slowly. She wasn't convinced. Dean had just told them that this piece of work would be handled by B. Kat was glaring at her. 'So that leaves one, two and three for you to do.'

'Me?' Marta looked at Kat, eyes wide with astonishment. She was giving the rest of the work to Marta?

'What's the problem? I thought you were supposed to be good. I'm giving you the easy parts of the project. Can't you even cope with that?'

Marta stared at Kat, saying nothing. *The easy parts.* Yeah right. Marta could see what Kat was doing. She was getting Marta to do most of the work so that she could spend all day on Facebook.

'You are not doing–'

Kat sighed loudly, cutting her off. 'Marta. You're an assistant analyst. I'm an analyst. That means you assist me. OK? I'm asking you to do parts one, two and three, because part four will be time-consuming and difficult. It's not much to ask. But if you think you're not up to the job, I can always tell–'

'No!' cried Marta. She knew that Kat's threat wasn't an empty one. She would take pleasure in telling David Lyle that Marta couldn't manage.

Kat smiled. 'Good. So you're happy with what you're doing?'

Marta nodded. She wasn't the least bit happy, but she knew that prolonging the conversation with Kat wouldn't make her any happier.

'You've got everything you need in that pack,' Kat told her. 'The deadline is a week on Thursday, so be ready to email it to me by the Wednesday before.'

'OK,' said Marta. She felt like crying.

Kat held the meeting room door closed for a second, preventing Marta from leaving. 'You got some glowing reports, apparently. They obviously like you.'

Marta said nothing.

'Just so you know, though, glowing reports don't get you everything.' She yanked open the door and marched out.

40

'Conniving little bitch,' said Tina, shaking her head. 'And she's the CEO's niece, you say?'

Marta nodded. They were propped up on the sofa bed in the lounge with all the windows open, enjoying the night breeze on their faces. Tina was nursing an all-day hangover.

'Thing is,' explained Marta, 'I think she doesn't like me being there. She really, really want me to fail. I don't know why.'

Tina reached into the bowl of popcorn that lay between them. ''Cause she's a jealous cow, that's why. So, d'you think you can do it, all this work she's set you?'

Marta thought for a second. As it happened, one good thing had come out of the day's events. She had returned to her desk after the meeting and stared at the jargon-filled presentation that was supposed to be her guide. During the meeting it had made no sense at all; it was just a wad of fifty pages filled with stupid phrases and diagrams. But after two hours of staring followed by extensive use of the online thesaurus, a few nuggets of sense had started to creep in. She had begun to understand the task.

'Maybe,' Marta shrugged, then with sudden, newfound resolve, 'yes. I can do it. I just need… steering. Is that the word?'

Tina smiled. 'Guidance?'

'Yes, guidance. But I can't ask Kat; she will trick me.'

Tina nodded. 'What about the guy you mentioned… Dean?'

Marta shook her head. 'Too senior. No way.' Dean was far too busy and important.

'Your little Italian helper?'

Marta screwed up her nose. 'Carl. He is so nice, but not involved in this project. I need help on the details. It would take too long to explain him everything. And anyway,' she added, 'I think he like me.'

'Hmm,' grunted Tina through a mouthful of popcorn. 'Tricky.'

Marta nodded. She was becoming quite concerned about the affections of her Italian colleague. He was sweet and kind and always keen to help, but Marta suspected there was an ulterior motive. She couldn't justifiably drop Dominik into conversation any more, but there was another name she thought she could use: *Jack.*

There was a scratching noise at the front door, followed by an eventual 'thud' that reverberated through the wall from the hallway.

'We're in here,' called Tina.

'Fucking lock,' muttered Holly, sighing heavily and collapsing into the tatty armchair.

'Nice to see you, too.'

Holly said nothing. She shut her eyes and let her head roll back. Marta watched her. She looked pale, even in this dim light.

'Holly might have an answer for you,' suggested Tina, letting her arm swing out and hit Marta in the chest. 'She must've seen this a hundred times at Anderton's.'

'Seen what?' asked Holly, lifting her head and opening one eye.

'Marta's got to do some sort of strategic bullshit programme all by herself.'

Holly sighed again.

Tina frowned. 'Well, that's not very helpful.'

Holly clearly wasn't in the mood for jokes. She sat up, dropped forward onto her knees and looked at them.

'I don't have all the answers, you know.'

'Sorry Hol, I didn't mean—'

'I know you didn't, but that's what everyone thinks.' Holly was staring at the carpet, not at Tina. 'They think because I'm a management consultant at a Big Five firm, I must know everything. I must be sorted. I must have everything I want: a fat salary, a work-life balance, a nice bloke… Well, it's not fucking true, is it? I'm earning the fat salary, but that's all.'

Marta and Tina exchanged a quick glance. Marta had never seen Holly like this, and from the look on Tina's face, neither had she.

'I spend my whole life pretending to be a success, making everyone go '*ooh*' when they hear the name of my firm, but I'm living a lie! I'm not a success; I'm just a fucking slave in a big firm where nobody knows my name.'

'You're tired, Hol–'

'Yes, I *know* I'm tired!' She was almost shouting. 'I've been working eighteen-hour days… of course I'm tired!'

Tina nodded silently.

'I can't even begin to explain how much I hate that place,' she said, her eyes randomly roaming the room. 'I hate that place with its fancy glass doors and tinted windows. I hate the work. And I hate the people. I *hate* the people.'

Marta watched in anxious silence. This was not the same person she had met at Jeremy's birthday dinner.

'People at Anderton's only want one thing: to climb the fucking ladder. They're all so busy stabbing each other in the back as they climb they can't even remember why they're there. They're like hamsters, running around in their silly little wheels looking smart and trying to impress, but they don't realise the joke's on them! They all think they've won when they retire aged forty with wives and kids they barely know… but they haven't *won*, because they haven't fucking lived!'

Nobody spoke for a long time. Eventually, Tina looked over at Holly and asked softly: 'Do I take it you're not enjoying work at the moment?'

Holly didn't even laugh. 'I do a project, hand it over, get no thanks and then find the next one lined up on my desk. Then it's the same all over again. It would just be nice to see a bit of reward, just occasionally.'

'Well you do, sort of,' said Tina. 'In your pay cheque.'

Holly groaned. 'I don't care about the pay cheque! I want more than that! I want to know what it was all *for*. I want some respect. I want to feel part of the business. I want–'

'You want your *own* business,' Tina finished.

'No...' Holly faltered. 'Well, maybe.' She looked up and briefly met Tina's eye, then stared hard at a spot on the floor. 'Why did I go into consultancy? What was I thinking?'

Tina smiled. 'Same thing everyone was thinking: that all the best graduates go into the best-paid jobs.'

Holly rolled her eyes, but her posture looked more relaxed, Marta thought. Perhaps her outburst had been therapeutic.

'Maybe you should quit,' Tina suggested, several minutes later.

Holly glared at her. 'Would *you*?'

Marta thought about this for a moment, remembering what the good-looking trader had said about walking out when his bonus hadn't met his expectations. The idea of voluntarily leaving a job seemed so crazy that Marta couldn't imagine it. Then again, she couldn't really imagine this world that Holly and Tina inhabited, either.

'If your parents called you every Sunday to see how your wonderful career was going; if you lied to them each week because you knew they'd be disappointed to hear the truth; if you'd spent your whole life hearing people tell you you'd be a 'high flyer'... would you quit?'

Marta caught Holly's eye. Suddenly, she understood. She was in the same situation herself, having come to London. Everybody back home had such high hopes for her. They expected her to do well. It was exactly the same. Whenever mama called, her voice was filled with so much hope and pride it was impossible to let her down. Marta lied to her, just as Holly lied to her mum.

'You can't quit,' she found herself saying.

Tina was less certain. 'But if you're really unhappy...'

Holly looked at each of them in turn, as though weighing up the arguments. Marta held her gaze. *She* understood, Tina didn't. Maybe Tina had never been in this situation. Maybe she had never *needed* to stick at something to save face.

'Marta's right,' declared Holly. 'I've got to stay.'

Tina wasn't convinced. 'Jobs aren't for life any more. There's no stigma in leaving–'

'Except when you leave after six months,' Holly interrupted. 'No. I've got to stick it out and accept that I'll be miserable and tired and lonely for the next few years.'

'You've got us,' Tina objected.

'Yeah. I've got you, who's off bonking traders every night while Marta's out with her mystery man… I guess I've got to accept I'm not going to meet Mr Right in this–'

'But Holly!' Marta cried. She couldn't help herself. She *had* to get Holly to realise that Mr Right was here, living under the same roof, waiting for her. 'You already–'

There was a scratching noise at the front door.

'Hello! Ooh, *hello*.' Rich stopped halfway into the lounge and froze, staring at Holly. 'Sorry, do I know you?'

Holly smiled for the first time that evening. 'I got transferred here,' she said. 'From a cell block at Anderton's.'

He nodded, taking a closer look at Holly's face. 'You look terrible.'

'Thanks,' she said, laughing softly.

'Only joking.' He leaned forward and messed up her hair.

Holly whacked him on the backside as he bent down to grab a handful of popcorn. He lost his balance and landed between Tina and Marta, his hand in the empty bowl. There was popcorn all over the sofa bed.

'Hey!' cried Marta, grabbing a handful and stuffing it into Rich's mouth. Tina did the same, leaving him grunting and unable to speak. Holly rearranged her hair and stood up, kicking Rich back onto the sofa bed just as he managed to haul himself up.

'Silly boy,' she said, still smiling. 'Right. I'm off to bed. Thanks for stopping me slitting my wrists. G'night, all.'

41

A strip of sunlight pierced through the gap in the living room curtains, glowing red through Marta's eyelids. She turned over and buried her face in the pillow. It was the weekend, she deduced. The sun didn't get that high in the sky until ten or eleven o'clock. She found herself smiling as she worked out what this meant. Today was going to be fun.

She took longer than usual to decide what to wear. It didn't help that she had no idea what she would be doing. In the end, she opted for jeans and a hooded top. It wouldn't do to try too hard.

'You off out?' asked Holly, propping open the fridge door and slurping from a carton of orange juice. She too was wearing jeans, but Marta suspected she was dressed for a day in the office.

'Seeing a friend,' Marta replied.

Holly looked at her, one eyebrow raised. 'A friend…?'

Marta smiled sheepishly. 'A man.'

Holly rolled her eyes. 'You and your mystery man. When do we get to meet him?'

'Maybe soon,' she replied. *Or maybe you already have.*

Holly swung her bag onto her shoulder and headed for the door. 'Well, have fun. I certainly won't.'

Marta pulled a sympathetic face and watched Holly trample forlornly to the front door. She wished there was something she could do to help, but she knew there wasn't. Grabbing a banana from the sideboard, Marta waited a few seconds then followed her housemate out, checking that Holly was a good distance down the road before stepping onto the street.

She wasn't trying to mislead her housemates. She didn't like lying. It was just that she suspected they wouldn't approve if they knew she was seeing the man who had made her homeless in the first place. She wasn't exactly seeing him, anyway. It was hard to explain. She was just letting things happen; seeing where it went. There was no commitment.

Jack needn't have told her what he drove. She made a beeline for the shiny black Audi, instantly wishing she had opted for something smarter.

'Hi,' said Jack, lifting his sunglasses as Marta slid into the passenger seat. He was wearing an open-necked pink polo shirt and chinos that blended into the cream upholstery.

He kissed her once on each cheek, simultaneously reaching across to turn down the music, which sounded like jazz. Marta wasn't sufficiently familiar with English greetings to know what this double kiss meant, but she suspected it indicated formality, not familiarity. In truth, she wasn't sure where she stood with Jack – or where she wanted to stand. She was still working things out. Scenes from their day at the posh country club kept replaying in her mind and she couldn't help thinking that Jack might not be the obnoxious womaniser she had first taken him for. He seemed... sweet. *Gentlemanly.* He wasn't like any man she had ever met. More than anything, though, he was a challenge.

Marta liked a challenge. That was why she had come to England. Jack was one of the trickier challenges she had encountered since arriving because he gave so little away. He played his cards close to his chest and it was virtually impossible to gauge what he was thinking. That intrigued Marta.

'You look gorgeous,' he said, eyeing up her denim-clad legs and expertly manoeuvring out of the space.

So do you, Marta wanted to say, but she held back. Men didn't like to be handed compliments - and besides, she had a feeling Jack already knew how attractive he looked.

They headed for Kilburn High Road. Marta watched as Jack moved slickly through the gears, in total control. A faint voice could be heard above the low-volume jazz, telling him to continue straight ahead.

'Where we going?' she asked, as they crawled between traffic lights. Pedestrians weaved between vehicles, peering into the tinted windows like tourists on safari.

Jack smiled. 'You'll see.'

Marta said nothing. She hated surprises.

'You'll enjoy it, I promise,' he said, turning right down a side street.

Marta remained silent. She hated being told how she would react to things even more than she hated surprises.

They cruised effortlessly along residential streets, the eerie voice on Jack's satnav directing him this way and that. At one point, Marta leaned over to see if the end destination was displayed on the built-in screen, but Jack shook his head, smiling. 'That won't tell you anything – unless you've done the Knowledge.'

'I have knowledge,' she replied sharply.

He laughed. 'Not knowledge. "The Knowledge",' he replied, calmly lifting his hands from the wheel to draw quotation marks in the air. 'It's the test cab drivers have to do to show they know every road in the city.'

'Oh.' Marta screwed up her nose, none the wiser. She decided to pretend not to care where they were going. They were weaving through grey streets that were bordered with crumbling terraces and blocks of flats. Jack pressed a button without moving his hands from the wheel, and suddenly Fatboy Slim was blaring from the stereo.

Minutes later, the drabness gave way to leafy suburbia. The pavements widened and instead of high-rise flats there were Victorian houses, set back from the road behind well-trimmed hedges.

'What dress size are you?' asked Jack suddenly.

Marta frowned. 'What?'

He pulled up to a T-junction and indicated left, waiting for the road to clear.

'You know – size. Like ten? Twelve?'

Marta was trying to work out what possible reason Jack might have for asking this question, but she was drawing a blank.

'Ten most places, but long legs.'

Jack nodded, smiling. He pulled out with unnecessary speed, sending her reeling towards him.

'Why?' she asked, once she was back in her seat.

Jack continued to smile. 'You'll see.'

Marta crossed her arms and stared into the oncoming traffic. What was Jack plotting? Could it be something that involved changing their clothes? Something that involved putting on boiler suits or protective clothing? She shuddered. *Paintballing?*

'OK, I'll tell you,' he said, clearly clocking her irritation. 'We're going to Ealing.'

Marta knew of the place. It was near Acton, where Dominik lived. Its location gave her no hint as to what they would be doing, however.

'Have you heard of Julie Norman?'

Marta thought for a second. It rang a vague bell, but she couldn't put a face to the name.

'The fashion designer?' Jack prompted.

Marta swallowed. *That* was how she knew the name: from Tash.

'She's a family friend of ours and her daughter Emily has just set up her own label.'

'So, we go to see your friend, Emily?'

Jack nodded, slowly, as though brimming with pride. 'She called me the other day and asked if I knew of a lovely lady who might like to try some of her samples.'

'We are going to try on clothes?' Marta still didn't understand. It was flattering that Jack considered her to be a 'lovely lady', but she couldn't work out what was required. Was she to act as a mannequin?

'To keep,' Jack replied, glancing sideways. 'You get to keep anything that fits.'

'Oh.' Marta nodded, trying to appear enthusiastic. Questions were filling her mind. Would it be expensive? Would Jack pay? What if she didn't like the style? Would she have to pretend to find everything 'adorable', the way Tash did in the shops?

'Don't look so worried,' said Jack. 'It's free fashion.'

Marta nodded again, more assertively. *Free.* That was one question answered.

Jack parked the car alongside a small, grassy common. They crossed the road and followed the tree-lined pavement to a small parade of shops. A few had old-fashioned signs hanging over the doors, bearing names such as 'Crop' and 'A Stitch in Time'.

Everything about Emily Norman's store was minimalist and chic. The white fascia was adorned with a small black logo and the name, and there was just a single outfit in the window: a white mini-dress with no price tag. Marta watched as Jack rang the bell. *A bell for a shop?* she thought, her mind racing.

'Jack! Darling!' The door flew open to reveal a tall, elegant woman in her early thirties with flowing auburn hair and heavy makeup. 'God, it's been ages, hasn't it?' Emily flung her arms around Jack, holding onto him for a good few seconds. Marta found herself willing Jack to let go. It wasn't that the woman was attractive; not in the conventional sense of the word, anyway. She was just… well, she seemed very sure of herself. She was wearing high-heeled boots that came all the way up to her knees and a wrap-around woollen dress. Despite the age gap, she clearly fancied Jack.

'You must be…?'

'Sorry,' said Jack, stepping away from the woman at last. 'Emily, Marta. Marta, Emily.'

Emily smiled down from her stilt-like boots, stepping aside to let them through. Inside, the minimalist theme continued. There were mirrors on every surface – including the ceiling – and the transparent clothing racks were hung sparsely with the type of garment only ever seen on the catwalk. Marta instantly thought of Anka.

'Lovely to meet you, Marta. I've been so looking forward to you coming. I *so* want someone to start wearing these things and – oh, look at your legs! They're model legs! You'd look incredible in one of my summer skorts-and-waistcoat outfits!'

Marta smiled back, wondering what skorts might be. She glanced at the nearest rack of clothes. They certainly were high fashion. Most of the garments were so stylish they didn't appear to fall into conventional categories. What would Anka say?

Emily was still beaming. 'Who's for coffee? There's a Starbucks a few doors down – I'll get. I fancy a nice chai latte. What about you?'

Marta flinched, remembering her outing with Tash. 'Cup of tea, please.'

'Just like a Brit!' exclaimed Emily. 'You are fitting in well. Jack tells me you're Polish?'

Marta nodded, wishing he hadn't. It would be nice if, just occasionally, people treated her as a person; not as a *Polish* person. She could already see what was going through Emily's mind: the questions about what Marta was doing over here, where she was working. Was she an au pair? Did she clean toilets?

'What about you, Jack? What d'you fancy?'

Jack shook his head quickly. 'No, I'll get it. You girls get on with the dressing up.'

Without another word, Jack disappeared, leaving Marta alone with the assertive woman in the high-heeled boots. She was excited about the prospect of walking away with an armful of new designer fashion, but she was apprehensive at the same time. She wasn't sure why this woman wanted her to take away her stock. And what were *samples*, anyway?

'Here, let's move that,' Emily grabbed Marta's scruffy handbag and flung it into the corner of the shop. 'OK, so where shall we start? Trousers? I bet you have awful trouble getting them long enough, don't you? Let's see…'

Emily started pulling garments out from a rack at the back, her fingers picking quickly through the hangers. Marta's concerns about choosing suitable clothes were soon dispelled as the designer got to work.

'Let's try that lot for starters,' she said, depositing a mound of clothing in Marta's arms. 'There's a changing room here.'

Marta felt like a contestant on one of those awful image make-over programmes on TV. She obediently took off her clothes.

By the time Jack returned from Starbucks, Marta had already tried on more pairs of trousers than she had ever owned in her life.

'Next!' yelled Emily. Marta dutifully emerged from behind the curtain, assessing the stretch in the fabric around her hips. The trousers were low-slung and tight. They were surprisingly comfortable to wear.

'Bloody hell,' said Jack, looking as though he might drop the three drinks he was holding. 'Incredible.'

Emily rolled her eyes. 'Well, I can't take all the credit!'

Jack just nodded, staring. Marta ducked back into the changing room with a faint smile on her lips.

Half an hour later they had moved on to more daring outfits. The dress that looked like a shawl was rejected on the grounds that it had to be worn without a bra and couldn't be trusted not to slip off one shoulder, as was the chiffon skirt that turned into shorts at the bottom, which looked like something a duke or king might wear in a period drama.

'Done?' asked Jack, addressing Marta's body rather than her eyes. She was dressed in her favourite combination, if not the most adventurous: a silk top with a cutaway neckline and a pair of pale, tight jeans.

Emily folded the last garment and crammed it into the bulging cardboard bag. 'Enjoy!' she beamed, handing the bag to Marta.

Marta smiled awkwardly. She still didn't understand why the designer was happy for her to walk out with all these clothes, but she wasn't complaining. 'Thank you so much,' she said. 'Am so happy for you letting me model these for free.'

Emily looked at her blankly. She opened her mouth as if to say something, then shut it again. Then she switched on a smile. 'Any time, darling!'

'Let's go!' cried Jack, jumping on Emily and smothering her

with a giant hug.

They left Emily on her shop doorstep, blowing kisses as the Audi roared off.

Marta waved back through the darkened window, clutching the bulging bag in her lap. Jack changed up a gear and then slid a hand onto Marta's leg.

'You look amazing,' he said.

Marta smiled. 'Thanks.'

As they hit the main road, she realised something. For the first time in weeks she hadn't thought about Dominik all day. She was finally moving on.

42

'It still hasn't arrived. How big is the file?'

Marta looked up, determined not to be flustered by Kat's tone. 'Is four megabytes,' she said, pressing *send* and hoping Kat wasn't looking at her screen. It was Thursday morning, the day of the final run-through for the presentation that had occupied most of Marta's waking hours over the previous two weeks. She was supposed to have sent it to Kat the night before, but by midnight it still wasn't finished, so she had come in at six that morning to get it done.

'I'll check one more time. If it hasn't reached me you'll have to save it to the drive. She hesitated, eyeing Marta suspiciously. 'Where d'you get that?'

Marta smiled innocently. 'What?'

'That skirt. I've seen it before, in a magazine. Where d'you get it?'

Marta maintained her smile, relishing the prospect of telling the fashion queen something about fashion. 'Is designer. Emily Norman.'

Kat frowned, clearly unable to work out how a Polish girl could afford Emily Norman, but too proud to ask.

'Fuck, it's nearly eight-thirty.' Kat sighed dramatically and strutted back to her desk with a swoosh of her white-blonde hair. Marta grinned. The score was two-nil to her. Not only had she accomplished the impossible on the presentation (it was 'just right', according to Carl) but she had trumped Kat in the fashion stakes.

The office was still relatively empty, but Dean and a few others were in, quietly listening to Kat's performance and no doubt picking up on the fact that Marta had supposedly let her down. Marta turned to her Outlook calendar to check the time of the run-through.

'Got it,' Kat announced from across the office. '*Finally.*'

Marta's diary was empty. She opened up Dean's. His was crammed full of meetings, including one at nine-thirty called 'Unilight run-thru'. Kat's also contained the nine-thirty meeting. Marta frowned and pushed back her chair.

Kat was composing an email. She raised an eyebrow in vague acknowledgement of Marta's presence, but she didn't look up.

'Am I coming to Unilight run-through at nine-thirty?'

After some time, Kat stopped typing. 'No.'

'Why not?'

Kat shrugged casually. 'No need. It's a run-through for David and Dean.'

'But you are going, yes?'

'Yes. They need someone as support, in case they need to make any changes in the presentation.'

'But I *did* the presentation,' Marta argued, quietly but firmly. One of Kat's disciples glanced up, clearly sensing the tension.

'Don't flatter yourself,' Kat told her. 'You did part of the presentation, and I've slotted that into my main presentation. There's no need for you to attend at nine-thirty, OK? I'm sure you've got plenty of other stuff to be getting on with.'

Marta nodded, wondering whether it was worth arguing. The truth was, she had written a fifty-page slide pack, which formed the bulk of the presentation. Kat had added six slides at the back: the six slides B had sent over from Unilight.

'Fine. Good luck with run-through,' she said, storming back to her desk.

It took a couple of minutes for Marta to calm down and then a few more for her to start thinking rationally about what to do. The problem was, Kat would go into that meeting and take credit for all her work – except, of course, the mistakes. Those would be Marta's fault.

Perhaps she would email Dean and show him what she had done. She needed to let the business know how much she had contributed; how hard she had worked. But there wasn't really any way of doing that. This was the real world, not school. Nobody wanted to hear her petty squabbles.

Marta was still pondering her dilemma when her chair was set wobbling by an unknown force.

'Good morneeng,' said Carl, releasing the chair and settling down opposite. 'How ees the presentation?'

Marta shrugged. 'Is done.'

Carl nodded slowly, glancing across the office as Kat was just heading into the meeting room with a stack of papers under her arm. 'Oh. I see. Presentation is in the meeting room and you are not. Oh dear.'

Marta nodded, watching angrily as David Lyle and Dean followed Kat through the frosted glass doors.

Carl shrugged. 'No problemo. If it is good, they will remember you were involved with a good project. If it is bad, Kat will look stupid in the meeting. You have nothing to worry about.'

Marta nodded reluctantly. Perhaps Carl was right. Everyone did work that went unacknowledged from time to time. She just had to try to avoid being put on projects with Kat in future.

It made a nice change having nothing to do. The past two weeks had flown by so quickly she had barely had time to chat or even eat – only occasionally surfacing from PowerPoint to thank Carl for coffee or advice. He had been a hero these last few days.

'Your life gonna be a beat calmer, now?' he asked, popping up from behind his monitor. Marta hesitated, distracted by an email that had arrived in her inbox.

Subject: Last night…
…You looked amazing. I still feel horny now, thinking about you.

Marta frowned, quickly closing the window in case anyone with very good eyesight happened to be walking past.

'I hope so,' she said, returning Carl's smile and clicking on *reply*.

> I didn't see you last night! You are getting confused with another girl... :-)

'Maybe you wheel have time for lunch away from your desk?' Carl suggested hopefully.

Marta took the hint. 'Maybe. And if I do, I will pay for your lunch also.'

It was the least she could do, Marta knew that. And frankly she was keen to repay him in as many ways as possible that weren't sexual.

'That would be nice,' said Carl, smiling.

Jack's reply came almost instantly.

> You didn't see me, but I saw you. You were wearing an incredible dress.

Marta hit *reply*, then wondered what to write. It was strangely exciting to know that Jack Templeton-Cooper had been dreaming about her, but she wasn't sure she wanted to engage in dirty talk over email – especially on her Stratisvision email account.

> What was dress like?

The tremors in the office indicated that Charlotte was approaching. Marta flicked to the PowerPoint presentation and pretended to edit a slide. The stomping came to an abrupt halt by Carl's desk.

'What's your capacity?' she barked.

Marta stared at the slide, waiting for the message alert in the corner of the screen. It didn't take long.

> Transparent.

Charlotte quickly briefed Carl and then charged off, leaving the Italian to breathe a long, slow sigh. 'Looks like lunch ees off,' he said.

'Another day,' replied Marta, feeling sorry for her neighbour, but also a little envious. He was often tasked with big, high-priority projects.

Transparent dresses aside, what are you doing 2 weeks from now? Does a masked banquet in the natural history museum appeal? You'd have to put up with my colleagues for company but it should be a tolerable night.

Marta nearly squeaked with excitement. She pressed *reply* and tried to think of a suitably witty response. That was the thing. Jack was so clever with his words. Something about masks, or natural history…?

'Marta, are you busy?'

Marta whirled round. She had no idea how long Dean had been standing over her.

'A little,' she replied, desperately wishing she had minimised the email before she turned round.

'Could you pop into the meeting room for a sec?'

Marta nodded quickly. Dean seemed angry, she thought. Or maybe Dean always seemed angry. He was a very serious man. Clutching a notebook and pen, she followed him through the office.

Kat was just leaving the room as they approached, followed by David, who was clapping her on the shoulder and muttering '*Great work*,' over and over again.

'How did it go, the run-through?' asked Marta, once they had settled in the empty meeting room with the door shut.

'It went OK,' Dean replied coldly.

'Any changes I need to make to my parts of the presentation?' she asked, wondering whether now would be an opportunity to explain how much she had contributed to this assignment.

Dean screwed up his face, as though he couldn't decide how to respond.

'See, this is what I wanted to talk to you about,' he said, finally.

Marta looked at him, feeling nervous.

'Kat forwarded me the email you sent her this morning.'

Marta nodded again. This was good, in a way. I meant that Dean would know exactly what she had done. 'So you saw my parts of the presentation?'

'Mmm.' Dean nodded awkwardly.

Marta frowned. Didn't he think her work was good enough? That was impossible. Carl had checked it and Kat had accepted it.

'A question for you, Marta.' Dean looked at her sternly. 'Do you really believe you gave a hundred percent to this project?'

Marta hesitated. Was this a trick? Of course she had given a hundred percent. She had been in the office until midnight the night before and had been back in at six that morning.

'Yes, I did.'

Dean closed his eyes, pinching the bridge of his nose between finger and thumb.

'Is my work not good enough?' asked Marta, perplexed.

'That's not for me to say,' replied Dean, pushing up from the table.

Marta mirrored his actions, barely registering her own movement towards the door, or Dean's polite dismissal. She was totally preoccupied. Were her standards too low? Were Carl's, too? She didn't know. All she knew was that Dean was holding open the door in a way that suggested he wanted her to disappear through it – fast.

Maybe Dean was just a perfectionist, thought Marta, plodding gloomily through the office. Maybe he gave everyone that speech. Maybe Dean was one of those people who could never be truly happy. She sat down at her desk. Her phone told her that she had missed a call from Dominik. She pressed delete. At least he had stopped leaving messages. With the thoughts tumbling around in her head, Marta jiggled her mouse and started to redraft her email to Jack.

43

'It is called "May ball", but it happen in June?'

Holly smiled. 'It's stupid, I know. It's just a Cambridge thing.'

Rich nodded, adjusting his bowtie. 'Tradition.'

Marta glanced sideways. She had only just noticed, but Rich was actually quite handsome. It wasn't that he had ever seemed unattractive; it was just that he always looked… messy. Now his old trainers and low-hanging jeans had been replaced with a sharp black suit, he was like a different man.

Marta picked up her pace and turned back to take a photo. She waited as Rich darted between Tina and Holly, reaching out and gently squeezing their bare shoulders. It was the perfect shot: the mottled pink sky bringing out the colour of Tina's fuchsia ball gown and Holly's inky silk dress contrasting with the cobbled streets. Marta looked at the screen, smiling. 'Is beautiful.'

Rich stepped forwards. 'Beauty is in the eye of the beholder,' he said, grabbing the camera.

'Eye of…?'

Rich was already behind the lens, composing his shot. Marta smiled obligingly, feeling self-conscious. It wasn't that she didn't like the shimmery outfit. The dress was divine: light blue to match her eyes. It was just that she felt out of place. This was the stuff of celebrities on red carpets that appeared in magazines. It was the kind of thing Anka used to dream of. It wasn't real. It wasn't for people like Marta.

271

'*Lovely.*' Rich passed the camera back to Holly.

They approached a large, stone archway that looked like something from a Harry Potter film. Etched into the stone was a statue of some king or other and cut into the enormous wooden door was a smaller door that kept swinging open like a serving hatch.

'Got the tickets?' asked Holly. Rich reached into his back pocket and waved two black envelopes in the air. Not for the first time, Marta felt a pang of guilt. Her housemates had bought two 'double tickets', which entitled four people to attend the ball. They had insisted Marta didn't pay on the grounds that the tickets had already been purchased and the forth would only have gone to waste. She felt like a charity case.

'Welcome to our college,' said Tina as they stepped through the cutaway door and entered a huge, grass courtyard bordered by ancient white buildings and flowerbeds. Snaking around the outside of the courtyard, on a path of pale flagstones, was the most incredible array of ball gowns Marta had ever seen, even in Anka's magazines.

Marta shook her head, smiling. It still seemed absurd that while she had been cycling between temporary wooden huts for her lectures, Tina, Holly and Rich had been spending their time in places like this.

'Let's go!' cried Tina, as they exchanged their tickets for small plastic wristbands that looked like cattle tags.

They found themselves in another courtyard, this one decorated ornately with flowers and bathed in coloured lights. It was like walking onto a film set.

'Champagne?' offered a young man in an apron.

Marta took it, remembering what the others had said. *Everything's free once you're in.* The place had a magical feel about it, as though the laws of physics might not apply; as though anything could happen. They drifted along one side of the courtyard, where someone was giving out what looked like seashells. Rich reached out and grabbed enough for each of them.

Marta wasn't convinced. Apparently oysters were a delicacy, but they had the consistency of gritty slugs.

'More champagne?' said a voice.

Marta looked at her barely-touched glass, overwhelmed. In the corner of the courtyard was a small boat – literally, a *boat* – its hull filled with ice and bottles of champagne.

'I'm starving,' announced Tina, who had apparently not eaten since lunchtime the day before in anticipation of a 'massive gorge fest'.

They wandered through more stone archways, over flower-lined bridges and into new courtyards, all lit up in different colours. Chinese stir-fried noodles sizzled, burgers fried and in the middle of a patch of springy lawn, a massive pig was being roasted on a spit.

They opted for the pork and sat down to eat in front of a fair-ground ride, washing it down with champagne. Marta sipped hers carefully. She wanted to remember every single detail of the night.

A photographer leapt out of the darkness and snapped Holly and Rich, obviously mistaking them for a couple. *Easily done*, thought Marta, smiling as the man showed them his handiwork. He had caught them mid-conversation and they were looking intently into one another's eyes.

'Time for dodgems,' Holly said quickly, abandoning the photographer's card and quickly hitching up her dress, ready to go. Marta caught Tina's eye and grinned.

After the exhilaration of the dodgems, they wandered over to a grassy bank that was slowly filling up in anticipation of fireworks. Marta wasn't a big fan, but she had a feeling this might be in a different league from the annual Łomianki display.

Her assumption was right. The sky was ripped apart with a deafening eruption of reds, greens and yellows, accompanied by the pop-pop-pop of explosives. They kept coming, one after another, overlapping in mid-air and shining down as brightly as the midday sun.

'Jazz tent? Casino?' asked Rich when the applause finally died down.

They drifted happily from marquee to marquee, stopping to admire the performances of jugglers, hypnotists and magicians, while nibbling on caviar and chocolate fountains. Marta preferred the outdoor entertainment; the tents reminded her too much of working for Bread and Butter Catering.

After a while, Tina made an excuse and sloped off.

'She's pulled,' explained Holly, nodding towards the good-looking pianist who had just finished his set. Marta smiled, shaking her head in wonder at the way her housemate behaved.

They returned to the main tent, where a bunch of musicians leapt about on a stage, banging drums and scraping at violins as the man at the front shouted 'Skip to the right!' and 'Now change partners!' into a microphone.

Marta found herself following Holly and Rich onto the rumpled matting dance floor. Following orders from the man at the front was harder than it looked. After ten minutes she ducked out, welcoming the blast of cold air on her skin and taking the opportunity to wander freely, taking everything in. She wasn't worried about losing the others; Holly's dress would be easy to spot.

Someone had constructed a small room by partitioning off a stone corridor with swathes of fabric. Inside was a full gambling set-up: everything you would expect to see in a real casino, only perhaps more colourful. Marta weaved between roulette wheels and poker tables, enjoying the carelessness with which the chips were thrown down. It was just a game; nobody was playing for real money.

Marta was considering trying her hand at Black Jack when she saw something that made her mouth go dry. Standing only a couple of metres away, her blonde hair hanging in beautiful, soft curls down her back, was Tash. She was standing side-on, clasping the arm of a suave young man who was placing a bet. He even looked a bit like Jack, thought Marta, turning quickly and slipping away on shaky knees.

Marta was still trembling as she walked up the white steps that linked the courtyards. It shouldn't have come as a surprise. Of *course* Tash was here. Of course she would come back to her old college for the 'May ball'. But that didn't stop Marta from wishing she hadn't.

A disco was blaring from one of the larger halls. Marta hovered in the doorway, perching on a bench at the back of the room. Her feet were hurting and one of the straps was rubbing on her little toe. She smiled as a track that she recognised came on. It was a song from *Grease*. She had watched that film more times than any other.

It took a few minutes for Marta to notice the person sitting next to her on the bench. The only reason she did notice, in fact, was that the bench started wobbling. It wasn't moving much, but small vibrations were being transmitted through the wood, as though… as though the person was sobbing. Marta could just about hear the sniffing between sobs. She looked sideways.

'*Holly?*'

Holly turned, dropping her hands from her face. Her eyes were red.

'What's wrong?' Marta shifted sideways along the bench so she didn't have to compete with the music, wrapping an arm gently around her housemate's shoulder.

Holly shrugged, biting her lower lip to stop it shaking. Another tear rolled down her cheek. 'I just saw an ex-boyfriend with another girl.'

Marta squeezed her arm, holding her a little more tightly. 'Oh, Holly. I'm sorry. You still like the guy?'

Holly shrugged again. 'No, not really.'

Marta frowned. 'Oh. So what is problem?'

Holly shook her head, looking up at the high ceiling as though trying to blink back the tears. 'It just made me realise…' She broke down and started sobbing again.

'Shh,' Marta held her close.'

'It made me think…' Holly seemed determined to explain through the sobs. 'About my old life… I used to love it, Marta. I used to have loads of friends…' She ran a finger under each of her eyes in turn. 'Everything's changed… Everything's awful.'

Holly leaned forward on her knees, letting the tears drip down her face and onto the floor. Her makeup was ruined.

'Let me get you tissue,' suggested Marta.

Holly nodded gratefully as Marta hurried off, remembering a sign she had seen for the ladies' nearby. It was hard seeing Holly like this. She was usually so strong, so resilient. What could Marta possibly say to make things better? It wasn't a simple problem and there was no simple answer. Marta knew that, because she faced a similar problem herself. Everyone said life was easy after university. A degree was a passport to good jobs, good careers… And it was, especially in Holly's case. Holly could do whatever she liked. The problem was, what *did* she want? Nobody talked about the issue of having too many options. Marta wrapped her fist in a bundle of toilet roll and raced back to the disco.

Someone had taken her place on the bench. Marta stopped in the doorway, slowly recognising the stooping physique of the suited young man next to Holly. Rich was talking to her with one hand gently rubbing her arm. He was making her laugh. Holly was looking at Rich through red-rimmed eyes, sniffing and nodding and accepting his offer of a handkerchief. (*What foresight!* thought Marta, crushing the redundant toilet tissue in her hand. *Where on earth had he got one of those?*)

Holly wiped away the tears and slid closer to Rich on the bench. Then she reached out and slowly cupped the side of his face in her hand. Their lips were so close… Marta didn't trust herself not to squeal. She slipped out of the doorway and headed back to the dancing tent, a giant grin spreading up her face.

44

Marta frowned at her handset. *Withheld number* flashed at her as it rang. Eventually, with Tina and Rich both glaring at her, she picked up.

'Hey gorgeous, how's things?'

'*Good!*' whispered Marta, recognising the voice instantly and hurrying into the hallway. Her heart was thumping. She had secretly hoped Jack might call.

'Why are you whispering?'

'I'm not!' she replied, softly. She wasn't actually sure why she was keeping her voice down; she just felt furtive about taking a call from Jack with her housemates in earshot.

'Yes you are.'

'Am not.'

'OK, then.' There was a smile in his voice now. 'Why don't you yell, "*Hi Jack! How are you, babe?*"?'

'No.'

'You haven't told them, have you?' he asked, with mirth.

She sighed, perching on the stairs and wishing – not for the first time – that she had her own bedroom. The living room had all the material things she could wish for, but it lacked privacy.

'It's OK. I know I'm not exactly flavour of the month there. Hey listen, I can't chat as I'm in the office, but–'

'Still?' Marta interjected. It was ten o'clock on a Monday.

Jack sighed. 'Don't ask. You're gonna regret choosing to go out with a banker, believe me.'

Marta smiled. *Choosing to go out with a banker.* Was that what she had done? Were they going out?

'It's about the banquet on Wednesday.'

Marta forced herself not to react like an excitable teenager. 'What about it?' she asked calmly.

'I just wanted to warn you.'

'Warn me what?'

Jack hesitated. 'About my colleagues.'

'Are they as bad as you?' asked Marta, pleased with her little joke.

Jack laughed. 'Worse, I'm afraid.'

'And you think I won't manage?' she asked, smiling. She wasn't quite sure what Jack was warning her of, exactly, but she felt confident that she would cope well. She had come across most types since moving to England.

'N-no,' Jack replied, uncharacteristically hesitant. 'I just mean... well, they're animals, to be frank. Predators. You're an attractive girl, Marta–'

'Thank you,' she interrupted, quite enjoying the conversation.

'They'll try it on, you know? Be prepared for some harassment, OK?'

'Sure,' said Marta, wondering what sort of harassment she should expect and why Jack was feeling so protective all of a sudden. It was nice to know he cared, of course, but really, she could fend for herself.

'And they'll say all sorts of crap about me,' he added.

'What sort of crap?'

'Oh, they'll make up a load of stories about me and other women.'

A brief wave of anxiety flooded Marta's mind. *Was* Jack a womaniser? She was determined to remain cool. 'And why would they do that, Jack?'

'Oh, because it's funny. Because in banking it's supposed to be cool to have eight girls on the go at any one time. I've built up this reputation as a bit of a player – on purpose. You know, just to have a laugh with the boys.'

'How?' asked Marta, wondering how someone 'built up a reputation' as a womaniser without actually being one.

Jack let out a blast of air through his lips. She could picture his muscular shoulders lifting as he shrugged. 'By making stuff up, mainly.'

Marta laughed sharply. 'Like in school?'

'Yeah, I guess. Goldman's *is* a bit like school.'

Marta felt slightly uneasy, but she wasn't going to let it show.

'Well as long as I can make up some stuff too,' she said with false confidence.

'Of course,' Jack replied warmly. 'It'll be fun.'

'Yes, it will.'

'Cool. I just didn't want you to be shocked by their bullshitting.'

Marta was grinning now. 'It is them who will be shocked.'

'Oh really?' Jack suddenly sounded intrigued. 'I can't wait. Are you going to wear a transparent dress?'

'Maybe.'

'You could,' he said, 'as it's a masked banquet, so no one would recognise you.'

'I'll think about it,' Marta replied, coyly. In fact, she already had a perfectly opaque outfit planned.

'See you Wednesday, then. The Rutland Arms at six.'

Marta was tempted to say something about how excited she was, but she restrained herself. 'See you then,' she said coolly.

45

'Brilliant, Marta. I really appreciate your help.' Carl finished skimming through the print-offs and looked up at her, grinning.

'At least someone does,' she said, shrugging.

Carl frowned. "ow do you mean?'

Marta shook her head. She wasn't in the mood to share her problems. 'Doesn't matter.'

Anka seemed to have disappeared. She had been online all morning, keeping Marta amused with stories of comings and goings in Łomianki, but now she wasn't responding. She must've gone back to the bakery. Jack wasn't around either; he was flying to France for some hugely important business meeting. He had his Blackberry, but it didn't feel right sending naughty messages when he was in the middle of a major global transaction.

She didn't have anything to do. Other than the titbits Carl had passed on, she had had no assignments for a whole week now; ever since the day of the Unilight run-through. She couldn't help wondering whether the two things were connected.

Her computer bleeped. She brought up her email, anticipating a reply from Anka. It wasn't from Anka. It was from David Lyles. The title read 'Re: Marta's performance on Unlight'.

Marta,

Sorry not to do this in person but I am out of the office until next week.

The purpose of this email is to give you an official warning about the quality of your work at Stratisvision. Whilst your deliverables in the trial two-week period were of sufficient quality to guarantee you further employment for the duration of June and July, it has been noted that your output since the extension of your contract has been of considerably lower standard – with reference to the Unilight project in particular. It has also been noted that your attitude has been nonchalant when probed on this matter.

Just so you know: under UK law, employers are obliged to give three official warnings before an employee may be asked to leave.

Kind regards,
David

PS – A word of advice, Marta: please don't let me issue you with any more warnings. Your initial appraisal showed real promise and I feel sure that with more consistent diligence on your part, you could go far at Stratisvision. (You are a Pole, after all!)

Marta stared at the email. She reread the main paragraph, wondering for a moment whether David was joking. He was a clown, after all. But the language was the giveaway. It was formal, as though he had copied and pasted it from some official handbook. And there was nothing funny about the 'PS'. He clearly wasn't fooling around.

Marta thought about forwarding it to Carl and seeking his advice. But what could he say? Of everyone she knew, Carl was the one person who almost certainly would never have received anything like this in his life. She played with the scroll button on her mouse. Down, up. Down, up. How could they be warning her about the quality of her work? She wasn't perfect, sure. But she was good. Good enough. She felt certain about that.

As she scrolled, Marta noticed something. There was more text in the email, below David's signature. It looked like... It looked like correspondence between David and Dean. Marta sat up and stared.

David,

See below. I have mounting concerns over this assistant analyst. She had two weeks to complete the task, and output (attached) is brief & shoddy to say the least. Late, too. My impression is that Kat had to pull out all the stops to get it into shape on time.

Spoke with the assistant analyst after the mtg – she was nonchalant, as though proud of her efforts(?)... Official warning?

I'll leave it with you.

Dean

Marta stared, horrified. She felt certain that David hadn't meant to include this exchange in the email to her, but she was glad that he had. 'Mounting concerns?' 'Nonchalant'? But Carl had checked her presentation and said it was 'just right'. He wouldn't have lied. And how could Dean give Kat so much credit when she had done almost nothing in the whole two weeks? She read on.

Hi Dean,

Meeting went well, didn't it? I think we impressed the Unilight team :-)

Sorry to do this, but I feel I ought to share something with you. As you know, the Polish intern has been helping me on the presentation. Below is the email she sent me this morning – a day late and frankly inadequate. Luckily we pulled together a half-decent pack in the end, but no thanks to her.

Let me know next steps following mtg. Happy to make changes etc.

K

Marta was shaking now. She couldn't work out what was going on, but she sensed that she was about to find out... and she knew it wasn't good.

Attachments: <Unilight_presentation_MD_v3>

Hi Kat,

Not finished, but here you go. Is OK but I still need lots of work on it.

Marta

Marta nearly choked. She stared at the screen, looking at the file name of the attachment and slowly working out what Kat had done. *She had forwarded an old email to Dean.* She had made out that Marta had only taken the project so far, and that Kat had stepped in and taken on the rest. She had even removed the timestamp from the email Marta had sent so that Dean would think this was her final effort.

Marta just sat for a moment, staring at the screen, thinking about the various people involved and realising how things looked from their perspective. No wonder the boss was unimpressed. No wonder Dean felt she had been 'nonchalant' during his questioning.

A surge of bile rose up in Marta's throat as she thought about the late nights and early mornings she had spent in the office, perfecting the pack Kat had claimed as her own. Did Kat have no scruples? Did her hatred run so deep that she was willing to see Marta lose her job over this? Thank goodness David Lyle was careless with his emails, thought Marta; otherwise she might never have worked things out.

Action was required. She needed to work out a way of proving to David and Dean that she *was* good after all, and she knew exactly how she would do it. Marta delved into her sent items.

The email was missing. Marta's breath shortened as she stared at the string of messages, looking for the email she knew she had sent and slowly realising that she wasn't going to find it. There was no way of telling David or Dean that she had sent the final pack to Kat on the morning of the meeting. Robotically, Marta rose from her seat and headed for the exit. She needed to breathe.

Both toilets were occupied. Marta was about to head off in search of another option when there was a flushing sound.

'Oh, hi Marta. Nice belt,' sang Kat, emerging from the cubicle and strutting towards the sinks. 'Designer, is it?'

Marta swallowed.

Kat reached for a paper towel. 'They must be paying you too much… You seem to have Emily Norman's entire collection?'

Marta stared at the girl. She had two options: confront Kat now, while she had her at arm's length on neutral ground, or wait for another opportunity that might never come up.

'Kat, I have question for you.'

A look of guilt briefly flickered across Kat's immaculate face. 'Yeah?'

'Why did you send old email to Dean so he thinks I am useless?'

Kat frowned. She looked so perplexed, in fact, that Marta found herself doubting herself. 'What're you on about?' she asked breezily.

'I did all the work for the Unilight presentation and you sent Dean an old email so he thinks you did the rest.'

Kat suddenly lunged towards Marta, getting so close that Marta was forced to bend backwards against the washbasin.

'*Listen,*' she hissed through gritted teeth. '*As I said before, I'm the analyst, you're the assistant analyst. You assist me? If I want to take credit for the work, I will. OK?*'

'But you lied to—'

'And how exactly is that different to what you did, taking credit for the Italian stallion's work?' She raised an eyebrow.

Marta was lost for words. It was *completely* different.

'Look,' said Kat, stepping back from the sinks and heading for the door, her voice suddenly breezy again. 'I suggest you just stay quiet and keep working hard?' she said. 'There's nothing they hate more than a cry-baby here.'

With a toss of her fine blonde hair, she flung open the door and waltzed out.

46

'I think I'm already pissed,' slurred one of the bankers' girlfriends, tripping as she tottered down the steps of the pub.

'It's the masks,' said another, whose face was covered by an elaborate 'Red Indian' feathered affair. 'I can't see a bloody thing.'

The girls turned to look at her and burst out laughing.

'Where did you *get* it, Suze? It's got fully integrated wig plaits and everything!'

Suzie looked at the girl who had asked the question. 'That's my hair,' she said pointedly.

'Oh.'

They followed the suave, suited men up the steps and into the stone building. Jack's colleagues reminded Marta of Tina's workmates: young, good-looking, witty – and very rude. They had already assigned her the name 'Jack's Pole'; apparently to distinguish her from his other girlfriends. At least Jack had warned her of what to expect.

Jack looked adorable. His mask was subtle, like hers, covering only his eyes and doing nothing to disguise his handsome face.

'Shall we?' he said, guiding Marta by the arm as they swept across the pillared atrium towards the red carpet.

It was so exciting to be going out with Jack. He was... *different.* Different in a good way. Being with Jack was like being in another world: a crazy, affluent world where everything was easy and fun. It felt as though he was opening the door into this world and letting her in. She squeezed his arm as they headed down the red carpet.

The banquet hall was like nothing she could have imagined; mainly because, in the middle of it, casting a dark, imposing shadow over the candlelit tables, was an enormous skeleton of a Tyrannosaurus rex.

'Fuck me!' yelled Suze from behind her Hiawatha mask, before tripping over the matting and struggling to right herself.

Jack moved closer to Marta, so that their masks were touching. 'He probably will, later on. That's why JD comes to these events.'

Marta frowned. 'What?'

Jack nodded. 'Brings a different girl every time. They get drunk and then end up shagging in the toilets.'

Marta cringed. Surely that wasn't the point of an evening like this? She looked around, marvelling at the impressive surroundings. The hall was like a cathedral: large and ornate, with gold candlesticks on each of the tables. The whole room was bathed in a warm, red glow.

They moved towards the throng of people at one end, behind which was the table plan. Jack dived through the masses and emerged looking somewhat unimpressed.

'Shit.' Jack looked at his mate, JD.

'What?'

'Roy Butcher.'

Marta exchanged a blank look with JD's girlfriend.

'Bloody marvellous.' JD rolled his eyes inside his mask. 'Who else?'

Jack waved a hand. 'Mainly analysts. Amit, Porker and that Chinese girl in Research.'

JD pulled a face. '*Butcher*. Fucking great.'

Jack noisily cleared his throat, glaring at his colleague as a large, middle-aged man rolled past wearing a Batman mask.

It turned out Roy Butcher was seated next to Marta. He had come with his wife; an equally sizeable lady with an equally loud American laugh.

'So!' bellowed Roy Butcher as soon as the table was full. 'I'm sure you all know me. I'm Roy Butcher, Head of EMEA.'

'Head of *what?*' whispered Marta, in Jack's ear.

'*Europe, the Middle East and Africa,*' Jack replied curtly. '*Don't ask questions like that out loud.*'

Marta nodded, thinking perhaps tonight wouldn't be as much fun as she had hoped.

'Lily,' said the Chinese girl, so quietly that Marta had to lip read. 'Telecoms and IT research analyst.'

JD responded with a giant yawn. He had already poured himself and Suzie a glass of red wine and was almost through his.

'Suzie Ripley,' giggled JD's girlfriend when it was her turn. 'I'm… between jobs.'

Marta noticed a sharp intake of breath from the large man on her left.

'JD, M&A analyst and all-round Goldman slave,' he announced through his mask, which has slipped down over his face to cover his lips. Suze giggled and topped up his glass.

Thankfully, Jack raised the tone with a flawless introduction involving the phrases 'leveraged buyout' and 'corporate restructuring'.

'Marta Dabrowska,' she announced. 'Strategic marketing consultant.'

There were a few uninterested nods before Rod's wife leaned forward and asked, loudly: 'Where are you from, Marta?' At this point, Marta was forced to engage in the usual discussion about how many Poles there were in London now and how they were very hardworking – more so than English people – which meant that they were taking all the unskilled jobs away, although luckily not in finance! Ha!

The masks came off throughout the first course and Marta was relieved to note that the American woman's attention had shifted. Jack was engrossed in a cryptic conversation with JD about 'principle debt', while Suze poured wine down her throat and Lily ate neatly in silence.

Marta ate, feeling suddenly lonely and out of place. She was used to conversations about things she didn't understand. Holly and Tina constantly talked in a business language that was entirely foreign to her, but at least they *tried* to include her. Here, it was as though she had come to the wrong party. They were speaking in tongues. She wondered whether this was how Lukasz had felt when he had got off that bus at Victoria.

The plates were whisked away and replaced by ever-larger ones, accompanied by huge spinning dishes and silver bowls.

'Will you get us another spoon?' demanded Butcher of the waitress – a slender girl of about Marta's age. ''Scuse me! I said, can you get us a spoon?'

The waitress jumped, then nodded politely and hurried off. Marta slid down in her chair, feeling bad for the girl. She knew exactly how she would be feeling right now as she rushed around the kitchens looking for a clean spoon.

Roy Butcher monopolised Jack for most of the main course, even though Marta was sitting between them, caught in the crossfire of spit and noise as they engaged in a mysterious yet animated debate about something she didn't understand. Fingers jabbed at the air, voices rose and occasionally a hand would slam down on the table. Marta's head flicked from side to side like a metronome. She had no idea what it meant. After Jack's earlier warning, she didn't dare ask.

Marta was about to suggest that she swap seats with Jack when suddenly she felt his hand on her knee under the table.

'Mmm, quite,' he said. 'But the European markets have been so quiet...' He located the slit in her dress and started feeling his way up her leg.

'Which is exactly why we need to shake 'em up a bit!' cried Roy, as Jack's hand slid all the way up the inside of her thigh. Marta stopped chewing, letting her cutlery fall to the table. She felt instantly hot.

'Easier said than done,' Jack replied, making contact with Marta's underwear.

'Not when you're Goldman Sachs,' said Roy, leaning across Marta to stare meaningfully at Jack. 'I've seen plenty in my twelve years here...' Marta could feel Jack's fingers touching her. She leant back in her chair, suddenly weak. 'Goldman's can move markets!'

'Move markets,' Jack repeated, eyebrows raised. 'Is that so?'

'Yes it is,' finished Butcher, obviously feeling his point was well made. Marta sat there feeling breathless, wishing they were somewhere else.

Suddenly, Roy's wife started screeching. 'Where is it? I had it just a moment ago!'

Jack's hand quickly slipped away as the tablecloth started moving beneath them. A frenzied search was underway for the American woman's six hundred-pound handbag.

'It was here...' Roy's wife was beside herself. 'That waitress!'

Within seconds, the bag was located on the back of Marianne's chair. Marta managed to slip the waitress a sympathetic smile as she provided Roy with yet another item of spare cutlery after his knife had fallen on the floor in the mayhem.

Marta drank her way through the speeches, as did JD and Suze, both of whom insisted on braying like donkeys whenever the CEO made a comment that was supposed to be funny. Jack had timed his trip to the gents' impeccably and clearly didn't intend to come back before the droning was over.

'The legislative hurdles have been overcome... ...banking reform... ...on track for a record fourth quarter... ...our shareholders... ...our fantastic employees!'

A rapturous applause may have been anticipated by the speaker at this point. All he got was a vague patter from around the room, before JD asked loudly, 'Is he still talking?'

Jack slipped into his seat just as the desserts arrived.

'The rest of the room's having fun,' he muttered resentfully, motioning to the tables around them, which were filled with drunk people falling off chairs, singing, yelling and throwing mini trifles around.

'You missed a great speech,' she said, her eyes telling him otherwise.

Jack smiled. 'I'm devastated. But you know, when a man's gotta pee...'

'Where are toilets?' she asked.

Jack smiled mischievously. 'Is that an invitation?'

Marta looked at him, hoping he wasn't serious.

'We'd only be missing a discussion about global reporting standards–' he nodded towards Roy Butcher, who was bellowing at anyone who would listen.

Marta rose to her feet, disgusted and disappointed. She didn't want to be ravaged in the disabled toilet like some cheap, shameless whore. 'I'll be back in a minute.'

On her return, the area around the dinosaur skeleton had been transformed into some sort of dance floor. A band was playing cheesy nineties tunes and some of the more inebriated guests were lurching around the stone floor, masks wrapped round various body parts.

Jack was waiting for her at the edge of the ring, his bowtie loose around his neck, a glass of wine in each hand. Marta's annoyance receded a little. He looked divine. As she approached, he suddenly tipped back his head and downed his drink in one.

'Why did you do that?' asked Marta, watching as Jack grimaced.

'So we can dance,' he replied, gently placing her glass on a nearby table and slipping a hand round her waist.

It was during the first lap of the dance floor – and it did feel like a lap – that Marta realised why Jack had polished off his wine. It was surprising, she thought, given how good he looked when stationary, but there was no doubt about it: he didn't have a rhythmic bone in his body.

Marta tolerated five minutes of being towed, pushed and bent into position, feeling like a puppet with a deranged handler, after which she feigned tiredness.

'You look so sexy when you dance,' he told her as they retired to the bar.

You don't, Marta wanted to say, but then looked at his glowing, handsome face. 'Thanks.'

They discovered some armchairs and sofas at the end of the room, away from the spying eyes of Jack's colleagues.

'You did well,' Jack said, as they sank into the folds of soft, brown velvet.

'What?' Marta looked at him, hoping he wasn't still talking about the dancing. That would have been a bit much.

'Dealing with Roy Butcher and his wife.'

'No silly questions,' she said proudly.

'Not one. And I'm sorry I left you. JD needed saving – from himself.'

Marta smiled. 'I do fine on my own, you leveraged credit finance expert.'

'Leveraged buyout credit analyst,' Jack corrected, leaning forward and kissing her.

Marta hooked one leg over his, leaving her glass on the table as they embraced. It felt good. Jack was hers.

One o'clock came around too quickly and soon they were being ushered onto the streets of Kensington with a hundred swaying, semi-masked banquet-goers. Jack held out his hand for a cab, keeping the other around Marta's waist.

'Mine's just round the corner. We could walk,' he said, questioningly.

Marta hesitated. She wasn't sure whether she wanted to go back to Jack's. She had had a wonderful night and she could see why he assumed they would go back together. She could understand why he was expecting sex. But it seemed wrong, somehow, to end it like that. Tonight was their first real date. There would be plenty of other opportunities for sex. She was firmly of the opinion that many people – like Tina, for instance – ruined relationships by moving too quickly. She didn't want to ruin this one.

'I think I will go home,' she told him.

He looked shocked. His jaw actually fell open as though he couldn't believe what was happening. 'Was it something I–'

'No! No. I just…' Marta moved closer and gently kissed Jack on the lips. 'Just… Not too soon.'

Jack nodded, kissing her back and holding her tight. 'I understand,' he said, although there was a look in his eye that told Marta

291

he didn't – not really.

They stepped onto the road as a taxi approached.

'Here,' Jack said to the driver, handing two twenty-pound notes through the passenger window.

'Jack, no!' she objected from the back seat.

'No choice,' he said, smiling as he pushed the door shut and patted the roof of the cab.

Twisting round in her seat, Marta watched the broad-shouldered silhouette turn and disappear, wondering whether she had made a mistake tonight. Then she thought about next Thursday's date and the prospect of the one after that, and the one after that. *No*, she thought. *She had plenty to look forward to.*

47

'I can't believe I used to do ten miles without even thinking. I'm so unfit!'

'Don't stress yourself,' advised Marta, wishing Holly would ease up a little. The pace was quick, even by her standards. They were planning to run a seven-mile route around Hyde Park and Green Park, but at this rate they would be lucky to make it halfway without passing out.

'Listen to me! I'm panting like a dog,' Holly gasped.

'You pant like any person running so quickly,' Marta commented, reducing her stride and deliberately falling behind. 'No need for splinting!' she yelled at Holly's back.

'Sprinting,' Holly said, finally letting up and dropping to Marta's pace. 'Not splinting.'

Marta noted the correction, grinning back at her housemate. They ran in amicable silence, listening to the sound of their pounding feet above the background hum of Hyde Park in summer. Marta never bothered with music any more; not just because she was bored with Dominik's donated collection, but because she preferring to hear the sounds of real life: children shrieking, parents scolding, picnics and games in full flow.

'It's nice to feel the sun on your back,' said Holly as they overtook a group of young power walkers in flannel tracksuits. 'I feel like a battery hen, cooped up in that office.'

'Battery?'

'Oh. Intensively reared.'

Marta nodded. *Intensively reared.* That said it all. Marta glanced sideways at her housemate as they ran. She was dying to know what had happened between Holly and Rich that night in Cambridge – or any time since. Everyone was behaving as though nothing had happened; clearly they didn't know Marta had seen them. Tina definitely didn't know anything and Marta wondered whether to let it lie.

'I should run more often,' declared Holly, upping the pace again. 'Makes me feel free.'

Marta smiled, hearing the spark in Holly's voice and deciding that now was the time to ask the question – but not *that* question.

'What does it mean when you get official warning from your company? Will they do a sacking?'

Holly suddenly stopped running. She stared at Marta. 'You've had an official warning from Stratisvision?'

Marta drew a deep breath and nodded, motioning for them to keep running. 'Is complicated.'

They weaved through a flock of children who were crowding around an ice cream van, then Marta told her. She explained about the exchange of emails, the reprimand from Dean and the scary message from David Lyle.

When all was told, Holly shook her head, looking at Marta with a mix of pity and outrage. 'What a nightmare!'

Marta nodded, feeling her legs starting to ache. They had completed the lap of Hyde Park and Holly was leading them towards an underpass that presumably led to Green Park.

'I knew a Kat once,' mused Holly. 'Hold your breath; it stinks under here.'

'Perhaps is same girl?' joked Marta.

'She was definitely nasty…' Holly grimaced as the stench of old urine blew up in their faces.

'Was she Kat Sneider?'

'Dunno, I'm afraid.' Holly took some deliberately deep breaths as they hit fresh air. 'I only knew her through Tash's bloke, Jack. I doubt this Kat would've ended up in consulting, though. She studied art history and was only really interested in hair and nails, from what I remember.'

'Oh.' Marta feigned nonchalance, but her brain was whirring. *Hair and nails. Tash's bloke, Jack.* It *could* be the same Kat.

Holly took them through a gate that led into Green Park.

'This girl...' Marta quickly caught up with her friend. 'Did she have long, white hair and little nose turning up like this?' Marta pressed the end of hers so it vaguely resembled that of the doll-like blonde.

Holly skirted a jogger coming the other way. 'She was definitely blonde. Can't remember her face. She was pretty, I know that. *Every-one* knew that.'

'Is the same girl, I think!'

Holly laughed. 'Why, 'cause they've both got blonde hair and pretty faces?'

'She knows Jack!'

Holly turned to Marta, looking confused. 'What's Jack got to do with anything?'

'He–' Marta stopped herself. She couldn't tell Holly. 'Maybe Kat is friend of Tash, and Tash *think* I am doing the business with Jack! So Kat hate me for that.'

'Hmm.' Clearly Holly didn't think much of Marta's reasoning, but Marta didn't care. She felt sure this was it. This explained everything. Kat knew Jack and Tash. And now, somehow, she knew that Marta was seeing him. Perhaps that explained the reference to Marta living in Kensington that Carl had overheard at the company event!

'Whoever she is, you need to expose her,' remarked Holly. 'That's five miles, by the way.'

Marta instinctively picked up speed. *Only two miles to go.* 'Do I tell someone about the email thing, with no proof?'

'Well, in my experience of conniving little bitches – of which there are many at Anderton's – they're not as hardy as they like to think. She'll crack under pressure, I reckon, if you get her in front of the boss. Drop her in it.'

295

Marta nodded. She knew this was sound advice; it was just a question of putting it into practice. That wouldn't be easy now she had this black mark against her name. Who would David Lyle believe: the slick, blonde analyst whose aunt was chief executive or the Polish assistant who had been at the firm for less than five weeks? It was a risky strategy without any evidence.

'I have a question for you,' Holly said. They had finally settled into a rhythm, their long legs striding in time as they veered off the path, running along the grass beside it.

'You want to know when I move out of your living room?'

'No!' Holly looked quite hurt. 'No – we love you being there! You're the only one who cooks proper food.'

'Oh, good. But I will pay rent–'

'Don't be silly. We work in the City, for God's sake – well, except Rich.'

Marta glanced sideways. It was hard to tell whether Holly was blushing because her face was already red, but there was definitely a hint of awkwardness as Holly said her housemate's name.

'It's… a weird question.'

Marta waited, intrigued.

'Where do you get Polish food from if you want, say, bread or cheese like the stuff you're used to?'

'Why do you want to know this?!'

Holly shrugged as she ran. 'No reason.'

'Well, you can get most things from the Polskie Delikatesy. Everywhere in London has them, but lots in Acton, Hammersmith… places like this.'

'And what are they like, these Pole Skidela… what are they called?'

Marta smiled. 'Polskie, Del-i-ka-te-sy. Polish delicatessen. They just like normal shop in Poland, only very expensive in comparison.'

'Ah.' Holly sounded interested, all of a sudden. 'And is there… a cheaper alternative? A chain? Like a Polish supermarket?'

Marta frowned. 'I don't think so.'

'But you can get Polish food in Tesco now, can't you?'

'Holly, why you asking me this?' Marta scrutinised her friend's face, amused and infuriated at once. It was as though Holly were planning something – something involving Polish food.

'It's for... a project. A project at work. Do you buy your Polish food in Tesco?'

Marta shrugged. 'Sometimes, but only long-living stuff. Not fresh.'

'Long life,' corrected Holly. 'So there's no single place that everybody goes to. Are you in touch with anyone in Warsaw?'

Marta gave up trying to understand Holly's motives. 'Łomianki, yes. Not so many in Warsaw. Some university friends.'

'Right,' said Holly, trying to sound nonchalant. They were nearing a gate that led directly to Green Park tube station. 'Well, here we are. Thanks, running buddy.'

They slowed to a stop, stretching their burning muscles in the sun.

'Same next week?' asked Marta.

Holly started to grimace as though work would dictate the answer, then her expression brightened. 'Yeah, sure. If I'm working, I'll slip out for an hour.'

Marta smiled. 'You're not a battery bird.'

48

Marta's heart started hammering against her ribcage. She had been summoned for another 'catch-up' with David Lyle. The outcome of the last one had been an extension of her contract and a small pay rise. She had a feeling this one would not be so promising.

Marta opened the spreadsheet she was supposed to be working on and scrolled idly down one of the columns. She couldn't concentrate. What if David was calling her in for a second official warning? That meant she had only one chance left: one chance to redeem her career.

She instinctively looked up towards Carl's desk. He wasn't there. Of course he wasn't. Today Carl was locked away in a series of Project Compass meetings with, among others, the cause of all Marta's troubles: Kat Sneider. Marta had set him a challenge. He was to find out whether Kat had studied art history at university.

What would David say at nine forty-five? Marta breathed deeply, trying to prepare herself. Perhaps Kat had played another trick without her even noticing. Would this be the time to try and defend herself? It would seem pathetic, surely, piping up with accusations only when she was confronted with a second warning? Marta got up and headed for the kitchen.

Her secret stash of fruit tea bags behind the microwave was diminishing at a suspiciously high rate; clearly it wasn't as secret as she had hoped. Marta flicked on the kettle and inspected the mugs as she waited for the water to boil. David's catch-up would *not* be disastrous. If anything, it might bring about an opportunity to 'spill beans', as they said over here. She would make sure he came out knowing what was going on between Marta and Kat.

The boiling water quickly turned pink as the berry juices escaped from the teabag. Marta was considering adding half a teaspoon of sugar when suddenly her contemplation was shattered. The screech was like that of a cat in pain.

Marta turned just in time to see Kat's slender figure storm, full pelt, towards the kitchen. Yanking open the fridge, Marta pretended to peer inside it. It was a tall fridge, so the door almost completely shielded her.

'I can't be-*lieve* they're doing this to me,' hissed Kat, clearly addressing the person whose footsteps were struggling to keep up. The pair stopped at the edge of the kitchen, presumably unaware of Marta's presence.

'Isn't there anything Patr – your aunt can do?' asked the other girl, whose voice Marta recognised as Kim's.

'Yeah – and she's already doing it! She's the reason I've only been made *redundant* and not outright sacked, isn't she?'

The girl mumbled something sympathetic. Marta stared at the out-of-date yoghurts and half-eaten sandwiches. It was all a blur. *Kat was being made redundant.* What did that mean? Was it like being sacked, only more polite?

'They say I've been dishonest and that I've not been pulling my weight... well *try opening your eyes*, that's what I say. Take a look at that Polish *bitch* who spends all day asking Carl what to do... *Fuck*, what's daddy gonna say?'

There was no reply from Kim. For a moment, there was nothing from either girl. Marta froze. She felt sure they had noticed her feet sticking out from under the fridge door, or noticed that the fridge was making a whining noise as a result of being left open for too long. Then, much to Marta's surprise, there was a muted sniffle, then a whimper, as though Kat was crying into Kim's shoulder.

Polish bitch? Did they really think that? And did she really spend all her time asking Carl what to do? Marta thought about this as she listened to the muffled sobs. It wasn't true, was it? She didn't ask him much – only the basics to help her get going. Besides, Carl didn't mind; he liked it. Didn't he?

Eventually, the sound of Kat's sniffing and Kim's soothing murmur receded as Kat was led away. Marta tentatively stepped out just in time to see Kat's high-heeled boot disappearing through the exit.

On autopilot, Marta squeezed the last drops of colour from the teabag and tossed it into the bin. She could hardly believe what had happened. Kat had been made redundant. *Redundant.* That meant 'no longer useful', so presumably she wouldn't be coming back. If that was the case, then this was excellent news. But the question was, *why?*

The office was in turmoil. Groups of girls hovered in corners, whispering and pointing; senior managers were rushing around pretending that everything was fine; and David Lyle was shut inside his office with a woman from HR. Carl was in a meeting room with a project team that no longer included Kat.

'Er, Marta? Shall we do our catch-up now?' asked David, leaning out of his office. He was wearing electric blue corduroy trousers that momentarily distracted Marta from the intensity of his expression. She followed him in.

'So…' He leaned back in his leather chair, motioning for Marta to sit down. The door had been shut very deliberately behind them.

'I assume you're aware that we had to let go of one of our analysts this morning,' he said.

Let go of. It sounded as though Kat were a bird who wanted to be set free. Marta nodded.

'I wanted to hear your story first, to be honest, but it all… kicked off.'

Marta watched him carefully, waiting for a question before she spoke. David Lyle seemed uncharacteristically tense.

'I understand you've had a tough few weeks, Marta. I sent you an official warning about the quality of your work, which we now understand was unwarranted and unfair. Apologies. It'll be retracted in due course.'

Marta was jubilant; this was the best news she could have hoped for. She had no idea how David had found out about Kat's campaign, but clearly the news was out. She didn't even have to tell them!

'In case you're wondering,' he said, 'you were overheard talking with Kat about the Unilight project. We pulled off the emails from the server. You worked hard on that presentation, didn't you?'

'Yes.' Marta found herself smiling; she couldn't help it. *Overheard.* Of course. The other cubicle had been occupied when she had confronted Kat in the ladies'. Marta felt her anxieties melting away; she wondered who had been listening.

'In future, Marta, I'd advise you not to keep these things to yourself. You should feel free to air problems.'

She nodded.

'I also wanted to ask whether you'd be happy to take on Kat's role on Project Compass. You'd be working alongside Carl Rossi, under the guidance of Charlotte and Dean.'

Marta's smile widened. To be chosen to work on Project Compass was an honour. And working with Carl… It would be a party compared with recent experiences. 'I would be very happy,' she said.

'Good! Well, that's everything. And obviously, it'd be appreciated if you could be a bit discreet about the details of Kat's dismissal…'

Marta nodded reassuringly. She would be happy never to mention Kat's name again. The whole episode was over – forgotten already.

'Oh, and Marta?' said David as she reached the door. 'Good girl. I mean, well done. I always knew you were a hard worker – not just because you're Polish! I'm glad we've got you on board.' He winked.

Marta turned and fled the room.

It was too early for lunch, but the office felt stifling. Marta needed to get out. Members of Kat's entourage were loitering near her desk, clearly lost without their leader and hoping to glean something from Marta about the circumstances surrounding their ringleader's fall from grace.

'You getting a coffee?' 'Want some company?' they called as she walked past.

'Am meeting a friend,' Marta lied, swiping her card and heading out.

She found herself wandering up High Holborn, meandering left and right, trying to lose herself so she could think. The memory of lunch with Dominik popped into her head. She tried to eliminate it, but the image was vivid. She could feel the embrace, hear the chatter, see his adoring looks as their knees touched under the table. Marta banished the thoughts. He had probably been thinking about that blonde the whole time.

'Excuse me,' said a voice from inside a motorbike helmet. For a fleeting moment, Marta thought it might be Dominik and was irritated to find her pulse quicken. As the helmet came off, though, it transpired that the rider was a woman.

'I'm doing a shoot for *Metro* on high street fashion,' she said, holding up a camera with a long, chunky lens. 'Would you mind featuring? We're doing a piece called "Londoners Looking Hot".'

Marta glanced down at the pencil skirt and tight-fitting blouse that, like most of her clothes, came from Emily Norman. 'Sure,' she said, breaking into a smile.

She was still smiling when the woman kick-started her machine and motored off towards the main road, a dozen photos later. Marta may have had her hopes raised prematurely in the past, but it finally seemed as though things were going her way. Her new life in England was beginning to resemble the life she had spent so many years dreaming about in her cramped bedroom back home. She was fitting in.

49

It was a pleasant walk from Holborn to Bank. The air was warm and the pubs along the way were teeming with young city workers guzzling beer in celebration of it being Thursday. Marta had left work at seven, slightly later than planned, but Jack had seemed fine with the half-hour delay. In fact, he had seemed more than fine, yelling something about 'one more with the lads' above an incredible background din.

It was difficult to know whether to talk to Jack about the matter of Kat Sneider. Of course, it would be interesting to find out how well Jack had known her at Cambridge and whether she and Tash had been friends… any information would be helpful in piecing it all together. Maybe Jack could explain why Kat had been so determined to bring Marta down at work. It would be nice to have someone other than her housemate to talk to about the situation. Poor Holly had enough office problems of her own. But Marta wasn't sure she wanted to delve into Kat Sneider's world. What if she discovered things she didn't want to discover? What if she learned that Jack and Kat had been an item at university? It was quite possible, given the way Kat behaved. How had Holly put it? 'Three years shagging rich boys with too many middle names.' Marta shuddered. If Jack had been one of them, she would rather not know.

Marta took a shortcut around St Paul's, marvelling at the size and beauty of the three-hundred-year-old cathedral. She had read about it in one of Mama's university books. Apparently, the bell inside was bigger than Big Ben. Emerging from the shadow of the building into the sunlight, Marta felt a rush of happiness. She loved London. She loved her routine. She loved living the life that most of her school friends could only dream of back in Łomianki.

She wouldn't ask Jack about Kat, she decided. Who cared what had happened two years ago? Jack was her man now. Her initial doubts about Jack Templeton-Cooper had been so misplaced it was almost funny, looking back. She had assumed him to be an arrogant playboy who couldn't keep his hands to himself, but she had been wrong. Jack was different when you got him alone. He was kind and generous and funny. His wit was sharp; a little cruel sometimes, but brilliant. It felt like a privilege to be around him.

Marta didn't mind that Jack was a bit of a snob. It was a consequence of his upbringing. Most of the time he was humble enough to hear her point of view, but generally Jack was right about everything anyway. He was strong-minded but he was a gentleman, too. He was Marta's gentleman. She smiled as she trotted up the steps.

The bar was surprisingly empty. A few after-work drinkers hovered outside in twos and threes, but evidently the establishment was second choice to the more interesting looking one next door – a mock Gothic tavern called the London Stone, outside which swarmed around a hundred suits. Marta checked her watch. Twenty-five past seven. Jack was nowhere to be seen.

She wandered to the far corner of the empty bar, listening to the hypnotic ringtone and waiting for Jack to pick up. She couldn't help wondering how much thought he had put into the choice of venue; this place had the atmosphere of a dentist's waiting room.

'Hello, this is Marta,' she said in response to his anonymous voicemail. 'I am in the bar and it is half to eight – no, half past seven. I wait outside, OK? See you soon.'

Marta sighed, assuming her position beside the fake greenery that spilled from the window ledges. She felt foolish and awkward.

It was nearly quarter to eight by the time Marta heard her name, in a slurred, loud form, from across the road.

Jack's shirt was hanging out. His tie dangled loosely around his neck and a couple of shirt buttons were undone, exposing a tanned, sweaty chest. He looked… wrecked.

'I'msorry!' he mumbled, lunging at her. Marta accepted the embrace, finding herself locked in a kiss that was somewhat more passionate than she had expected. His mouth tasted of beer and cigarettes. When he finally pulled away, Marta noticed several people pointing and nudging one another outside the London Stone.

'God, you're beautiful,' said Jack, holding Marta at arm's length and trying to focus on her eyes.

'And you are drunk,' added Marta. 'Where were you?'

Jack shook his head and slipped an arm around her waist. He was surprisingly steady on his feet, considering. 'Out with the boys,' he said. 'Completed a deal today so we did lunch with the client.' He hiccupped. 'Not drunk, though. Just tipsy.'

Marta nodded, allowing Jack to guide her away from the empty bar. She didn't know what tipsy meant, but she could only imagine it was several stages after drunk. She was coming to terms with the fact that the evening was unlikely to be the romantic one she had envisaged.

'Shithole, that place. Sorry - I couldn't think of the name of…' Jack squinted up at the name of the bar next door, hiccupping again. 'Mmm. Much better,' he mumbled.

Jack took her hand and led the way through the crowded bar. 'Glass of wine? Something harder?'

Marta looked at him. 'I'd like a beer.'

'Oh yes, of course. Sorry – can't get used to that. Never been out with a bird who drinks pints.' He winked.

Marta rolled her eyes and went off to find some seats, mildly annoyed that yet again she was being judged according to preconceptions: this time for not behaving like a lady and drinking 'ladies' drinks'. She found a seat and pushed away her irritation, determined to keep the mood light.

'I have something for you,' she said, as Jack approached the table with the drinks.

'Really? Does it involve you getting naked?' Jack grinned as he took a large swig of beer.

Marta placed the newspapers on the table between them. 'No.' She opened Jack's copy on page fourteen and waited for him to notice.

Jack squinted at the page. '*High waists are out and the classic tomboy look is making a comeback,*' he read. 'Well that's good news, isn't it? For tomboys, I mean.'

'Look at the pictures,' urged Marta. '*London Looking Hot.*' She pointed.

Jack suddenly slammed his pint down, sloshing beer on the page. 'Fuck – it's you!'

Marta smiled. She could hardly believe it was her either. The image took up most of the right-hand page.

'How did that happen?'

Marta shrugged as though this sort of thing was an everyday event. 'A woman just came and took a photo of me in the street. It's because of Emily Norman's clothes. Everybody commenting on them. My friend Anka – she knows everything about fashion and she is so jealous!'

Marta felt a stab of guilt as she thought back to Anka's last email. She had been wild with envy over Marta's latest acquisitions and Marta had vowed to send her something in the post. *Shit.* That had been a week ago and she still hadn't sent anything.

'God, you're so fit, Marta. Look at that–'

He tried to wipe off the beer he had spilt and ended up spreading the puddle over Marta's face. 'People wonder why I'm going out with a Polish girl and *that... that* is my answer.' He shook his head, smiling.

Marta stared at him. *People wonder why I'm going out with a Polish girl.* He had never said that before. Perhaps he had never been this drunk before. Marta bit back her response. He wasn't just seeing her because of her looks, was he? Jack wasn't that shallow. Surely she meant more to him than that? Jack was still gazing at her from behind heavy eyelids. He couldn't help it, she told herself; he had been drinking since lunchtime. It was the beer talking.

'So, what was the deal you did?' Marta asked brightly.

Jack frowned. 'Deal?'

'The deal you finished today – at work.'

'Oh yes. Newstran. Newstran got bought by Media International. Big acquisition.'

'Oh.' Marta wasn't sure what to ask. 'What do they do, Newstran?'

Jack frowned. 'News. Media.'

Marta glared at him. 'I mean, what sort? Do they write newspapers? Magazines? Websites?'

Jack shrugged. 'Dunno.'

Marta nodded. She wanted to take more of an interest in what Jack did every day to earn his thousands of pounds, but somehow she couldn't muster the enthusiasm – perhaps because he couldn't either. It was as though he didn't actually *care* about what he spent every day doing. He barely talked about it, and when he did he seemed completely uninterested.

The conversation continued in a similar vein. Marta's questions were abundant and Jack's responses vague and random, lacking their usual sharpness and wit. It was only when the subject of strip clubs came up that Jack's face became animated.

'End of the night, standard. That's where the boys'll go later. Have you ever... danced? You know...?'

Marta sighed. She was about to suggest another pint – of water, in Jack's case – when something caught her eye. Walking past them with a tray of drinks was a guy with a very large nose. 'Hey, isn't that–'

Marta didn't get to finish her sentence. Jack's hand, which had been resting gently on top of hers, suddenly tightened like a vice.

'Let's go,' said Jack. 'I've just remembered we should check out this other bar... come on. Let's go.'

Marta frowned, trying to escape his grip as Jeremy headed for a large table full of suited men. 'Jack, why–'

'Let's go!' Jack stood up, releasing her hand just long enough for Marta to grab her bag and then whisking her out of the bar. Marta followed, bemused and slightly angry.

'Where we going? Why, Jack? Why?'

He led her round the corner from the pub and up the street towards Bank.

'I wanna show you this other bar... in fact, no, even better. Let's go back to mine.'

Marta wriggled free of Jack's grip and stopped dead on the pavement. She could only think of one plausible explanation for Jack's behaviour and she didn't like it: Jack hadn't wanted to be seen with her in that bar.

'Tell me why you ran off like that. You didn't want Jeremy to see us? Yes?'

Jack looked utterly confused and for a moment Marta felt guilty for making the accusation, but the longer she waited, the more Jack just mumbled about going back to his place.

He was drunk, she reasoned. Maybe he had a reason for whisking them away like that and maybe he couldn't tell her at that moment. Maybe the reason was quite innocent. Marta looked at his face. His eyes were wide now, darting all over the place. For a moment he seemed almost vulnerable, with his shirt dishevelled and hair tousled.

'Marta, come back to mine,' he pleaded.

Marta felt herself being drawn closer, Jack's arm in the small of her back. He was looking at her, blinking, as though he couldn't bear for them to be apart. Marta felt herself relenting. It wasn't his fault they had made him start drinking at lunchtime. He was *trying* to sober up, she could tell. His fingers were reaching under her shirt at the back, tickling her bare skin. She let him kiss her. It was gentle, much gentler than before. Marta allowed herself to be drawn in.

In the cab, Jack was the perfect gentleman: holding her hand, leaning over with the occasional kiss and doing his best to direct the driver as they wove their way through the back streets of Notting Hill. Marta's imagination ran wild with visions of Jack Templeton-Cooper's house. Would there be pillars and flames, like the ones in Egerton Square? Would he have long, winding staircases for them to climb, entwined, as one? Her questions were answered abruptly as the taxi lurched to a halt outside a row of tall townhouses, most of which had multiple doorbells. Marta hid her disappointment. Jack lived in a flat.

As soon as she stepped inside, Marta realised that her imagination hadn't been so overly optimistic after all. Jack did not live in a flat. He owned the whole building. She gazed up at the high, ornate ceiling and peered through the half-open doors to the sides as Jack led her through the echoing hall across a stone floor that looked like an ice rink.

Jack grabbed her round the waist, pressing himself against her as soon as they entered the lounge. His body smelt of a mix of aftershave and sweat and his grip on her was firm, but Marta didn't mind. She only began to mind when he clumsily fell on top of her on the brown leather sofa, breathing hot kisses on her neck and chest, pinning her wrists against the fabric with his hands. Marta tried to swing her legs to the floor; it was too early for this.

'Going somewhere?' asked Jack, pressing himself harder against her and kissing her more, grazing her chin with his stubble.

Marta wriggled and realised she was trapped. Jack's legs were wrapped around hers, his hands were still gripping her wrists. She tried again. It was no good. It didn't feel right. 'Jack–'

'What?' he asked, looking down at her. His eyes were full of drunken passion.

'I want a drink,' she lied. She just wanted some space; a break from the intensity.

'Good idea,' he replied, sliding off her and reaching for a couple of shot glasses that were barely out of arm's reach. 'Whisky? Brandy? Something else? I've got everything.'

I'm sure you have, thought Marta. 'Whisky, please.'

Jack poured two large splashes and looked at Marta. 'What is it you say?'

'Na zdrowie,' she said, reluctantly taking hers. More alcohol was the last thing Jack needed and, frankly, she wasn't sure she wanted any herself.

'Naz-*drovia*,' he declared, chinking her glass and downing his in one.

Marta obligingly did the same and was surprised by the ease with which it slid down her throat. It was clearly expensive stuff.

Marta was propped up on the sofa now, but Jack was climbing on top of her again, stroking her hair and pawing gently at the buttons on her top. Marta could smell the whisky fumes on his breath. His eyes flicked down to her cleavage as he fumbled one-handed with the top button, then his face was close again and he was suffocating her with his kiss.

It was only later, when Marta surfaced for air, that she realised his left hand had been making progress on her shirt buttons. Jack's hand was clamped around her left breast, her lacy bra rubbing her where he had pushed it aside.

'Jack, please—' Marta pushed on his shoulder, which yielded a little, lifting Jack's face from her body.

'What?' He looked at her. The whisky had been a bad idea.

'No,' Marta begged, trying the other shoulder and hoping that Jack might ease off.

Her efforts were futile. Jack continued to press down on her, expertly reaching round and unclasping her bra. Marta tried again to twist free, but Jack was too strong. Tears pricked at the back of her eyes as Marta began to panic. She felt them leak out and roll down her cheeks, but Jack didn't notice.

'Please, no,' she wept as he pushed her skirt up around her waist, one hand still fumbling with her breasts. Her legs were pinned to the sofa beneath his and he ignored her sobs as he pulled the fabric of her knickers aside with his other hand. In desperation, Marta screamed. The shrill noise pierced through the silence, shocking Jack just long enough for Marta to push herself up on the sofa, away from his clutches. But she wasn't free. To her horror, she felt Jack's hand on her mouth, clamping her head against the cushion. He was on top of her again, his other hand still in her pants.

'Shuddup!' he growled.

She did, but only to bite Jack's hand. He yelped like a boy and

310

let go, but his weight was still pressing down on her. She was in no position to escape.

Then, miraculously, her phone rang. Jack heard it too, and for a moment seemed distracted. Using all her strength, Marta wrenched herself free and dragged herself across the carpet like a slug. *Perhaps it was Holly or Tina*, she thought hopefully. Maybe they would come and rescue her.

'Hello?' she gasped, her voice shaky. Jack was staggering towards her, one hand on his trouser zip. She shuffled backwards towards the door.

'You little peasant bitch!' screamed a voice that Marta recognised instantly. It was her former housemate. Jack's ex-girlfriend. 'First you try to steal my boyfriend from right under my nose, in *my own house,* then you go and monopolise my friends, and now you have another fucking go at my boyfriend! Have you *no* shame? Why don't you just take my advice and fuck off back to your Polish farmyard?'

Marta tried to react, but by the time she had caught her breath, Tash had hung up. *Another go at my boyfriend?* Did she think she was still seeing Jack? Marta looked at Jack, who had frozen, mid-crawl, halfway between her and the sofa. The lust had gone from his eyes and in its place was an expression that looked like fear. Suddenly, Marta realised why Jack hadn't wanted Jeremy to see them together.

'You are still going out with Tash?'

It was a statement, not a question. Marta understood now. She finally knew what type of guy Jack Templeton-Cooper was. He was the sort who actually thought he could have it all.

'Don't go, Marta. It's not like–'

Marta's expression killed off his sentence mid-flow. She hurriedly did up her buttons and headed for the door. Never in her life had she felt this angry, this hurt… this *stupid*. It hurt more than the sight of Dominik with that blonde. In fact, maybe that was what really hurt: the fact that this wasn't the first time she had been used. What kind of idiot was she, falling for cheats like this?

She had her hand on the front door when her phone rang again. She whipped it out, still glaring hatefully at Jack. This time, she was

311

ready with an explanation for Tash.

'Look, I want you to know that–'

'Kto to jest? Marta?'

Marta pulled the handset from her ear and looked at the number. It was Mama.

'Sorry, Mama. I thought–'

'Listen, Marta, I'm sorry. Bad news,' she sniffed. 'It's Tata. He's had a heart attack.'

50

It was getting dark. Marta's eyes were streaming as she ran, so she was only able to see as far as the next pool of light on the road. Her high heels were slowing her down. Which way had the taxi come? She didn't even know where she was heading; she was just trying to escape. She needed a shop, a tube station, a bus stop… anything that got her closer to finding a flight to Warsaw.

She came to a junction and stopped to wipe her eyes. Up ahead there were lights: headlights in traffic jams. She reached down and pulled off her shoes, setting off at a fast jog and taking advantage of the sudden clarity of vision.

The tears didn't stop for long. As she ran, images kept flashing through her mind: Tata in the passenger seat of their rusty old Volkswagen, teaching her to drive; Tata singing tunelessly on car journeys to keep Ewa amused; Tata getting everyone lost during his infamous walks in Kampinoski. He *had* to be OK. He was too young to have a heart attack. It was impossible to imagine him lying in hospital, frail and helpless like an old man. Marta wiped a sleeve across her face. She was approaching the main road.

The bus stop was deserted. Marta could see the taillights of the 209 disappearing into the darkness. She checked the map. It was covered in graffiti, but she could just about make out the details she needed. All the buses went towards Hammersmith. How ironic, she thought. She had always wanted to go to Hammersmith.

It was only as the bus pulled up that Marta remembered she

had run out of money on her travel card. She swiped it on the sensor, knowing that it would turn red and give a telltale double bleep. The driver sighed and looked at her. He opened his mouth to ask for the money and then stopped and just waved her on. Marta mustered a grateful smile. He must have seen her red eyes. Maybe he was Polish, thought Marta, perching on the edge of a seat and watching impatiently as the streets slid past.

They seemed to be passing through residential roads. Marta squinted through the greasy glass, looking for a shop or a cashpoint and seeing neither. She was desperate to top up her phone. It was ten o'clock now. She would never get a flight out that night but if she topped up her phone then at least she could try. Or at least she could speak to Mama again.

A man sat down next to her, filling his seat and a large part of hers with his ample backside. Marta wiped her eyes.

'Excuse me,' she said. 'Can I please use your phone?'

The man glanced down at her bare feet and the dirty shoes dangling from her fingers. 'Sorry – don't have it on me,' he said, shifting sideways and turning away.

Marta pressed her head against the window. She was too distraught to be ashamed. She didn't even care that he had mistaken her for a homeless vagrant. She just cared about making the phone call. Marta bit her lip, trying to stop her mind wandering to visions of Tata. Maybe she should get a taxi straight to Kilburn? She had no money on her, but maybe she would find a cashpoint. Would there be cabs in this area? Where the hell was she, anyway?

Finally, the bus pulled up at a stop where lots of people wanted to get off. There were shops and bars on both sides of the road and the streets were heaving with weeknight revellers. Marta joined the throng and pushed her way off the bus.

The newsagent was pulling the blinds down over his magazines as Marta approached. He shook his head at her. 'Closed,' he said, shaking his head firmly.

Marta yelped in protest. 'Please! I only need phone top-up! I will pay double – please!' She fumbled for her bank card and held it up. 'I need it so bad.'

The man rolled his eyes and reached behind the counter.

'Thank you!' cried Marta, watching as the transaction slowly went through. She was dialling Holly's number before she had even left the shop.

Holly's phone was off. Either that or she was underground. She was most likely at work and didn't want to be disturbed. Marta tried again, knowing it was futile. Infuriatingly, Holly was probably sitting in front of a computer right now, with all the flight-booking websites at her fingertips. But her phone was off. Maybe Marta could find the switchboard number for Anderton's. What was the directory number in this country? She didn't even know.

Predictably, Tina's phone rang and rang, the ringtone no doubt drowned out by the sound of drunken traders in a city bar. Marta needed an internet café. Or maybe she just needed to go home and use Holly's computer. She had to go back for her passport anyway. Her head was such a mess she couldn't concentrate. The flashbacks kept reappearing: Tata playing with Tomek behind the sofa; Tata making clever contraptions out of string when Mama moaned about the lack of drying space in their flat... how was he doing? *How was he doing?* Marta couldn't bear it. She pulled out her phone again and dialled Ewa's number. It didn't ring. Of course it didn't – they would be in the hospital. Marta upped her pace and started running towards the station.

Her phone rang just as she swiped through the ticket barriers. She snatched it out of her pocket, skirting to one side to avoid the flow of people as she headed towards the escalators.

Dominik-home, the display flashed at her. Marta hesitated, almost tempted to pick up just so she could tell Dominik about Tata. She had a feeling he might understand. But she couldn't bring herself to pick up the call. She couldn't even think about Dominik without seeing the blonde girl in that café window and feeling a fresh stab of pain.

Her phone bleeped with a voicemail as she rejoined the flow and headed underground. The line became crackly and distorted, but

Dominik's warm, gentle voice was easily recognisable. She could still picture the smile on his animated face.

'Hey. I haven't heard from you for … assuming you met someone else … to call and say goodbye. I'm sorry it didn't work out … we were great together, but … went wrong. Anyway, I'm moving back to Poland, so I guess … didn't exactly turn … in England … company went bust and then … sister came over and I realised how much I missed home … Good luck with everything.'

Marta's face was so wet with tears she could barely see her way to the platform. *God* she missed Dominik. She missed his cheeky grin, his cynical wit, his voice, his messy hair. And now he was moving back to…

Marta froze, then she headed back up the escalator, fighting against the flow and pressing buttons on her phone as she went.

'Dominik!' she panted as soon as he picked up. 'My dad's had a heart attack. He's in hospital. I need to fly home as soon as I can. Are you near a computer? Can you help? Can you get me a flight? I need your help!'

'Calm down,' he said, bringing a fresh wave of tears to her eyes. 'I'll check for you. I'm flying out first thing tomorrow and I might be able to change my booking to your name, although I think they need twenty-four hours' notice and it's to Krakow, so you'd have to get the train to Warsaw.'

'Is there anything before then?' yelped Marta, aware that they were leaving a lot of things unsaid, but feeling too desperate to care.

'Are you ready to leave now?'

'I need to get my passport.'

'How long will that take?'

Marta looked at the tube map behind her and did some quick sums. 'An hour? Two?'

'Tomorrow it is then. I'll look into changing my flight and failing that I'll book you another one. Get yourself home and call me from there.'

Marta didn't know what to say. She wished he was with her now so that she could fling her arms around him and not let go. 'Thank you.'

'No worries – but you will call me, won't you?'

'Of course.' Marta suddenly realised what he meant. 'I just... I didn't call because...'

Marta was standing at the top of the escalator, ready to head back underground and rush back to Kilburn, but something had just occurred to her. She thought she might have just worked something out.

'Dominik, what does your sister look like?'

'What?'

'Your sister. What does she look like?'

'Well... she's tall, about your height. Blonde hair. Wears too much makeup and dresses like she's some kind of movie star...'

A wave of joy briefly washed over Marta before the reality of her situation came crashing back down on her.

'Why?'

Marta sighed, shakily. She felt so guilty. 'Um... long story. I'll call you when I get home.'

'Make sure you do.'

51

'Have some more tea,' Mama urged, reaching for the pot.

'I won't sleep,' said Marta, shaking her head.

'You won't sleep anyway.'

Marta smiled wryly, passing her cup.

They were sitting on the tatty armchairs that had been there for as long as Marta could remember. The television was on, but neither was watching it. Tata was in a stable condition in hospital, but the doctors didn't know whether he would make a full recovery. It was too late for visitors – even despite Marta's pleading.

'You looked tired, *kochana*.'

Marta nodded. She was exhausted. The flight to Krakow – Dominik's flight – had been delayed by four hours. She had missed her connection at Krakow and used up nearly all her energy fretting about the state of Tata and the possible implications of the delay. Then the rude men in the station had told her that express trains weren't running to Warsaw, so she had got on some sort of pre-war minibus that had rattled its way round most of the villages in eastern Poland before it finally arrived in Łomianki. Without her sister's hourly updates, she might have worried herself to death.

'You do too,' Marta replied. 'Did you sleep at all last night?'

Mama shook her head. 'I tried to read. Then I tried watching television. I even tried to do housework, but I couldn't concentrate on anything. In the end, Ewa came down and kept me company. We watched the sun come up over the hills.'

Marta nodded again. 'Is she OK?'

Mama smiled a little. 'She's a brave girl. She's doing alright.' Tears were welling up in Mama's eyes as she spoke. 'You know she wants to be a doctor when she grows up?'

Marta shook her head. She hadn't known that, but she wasn't surprised. Ewa had always wanted to help people. She was tough, too. If anyone could get over seeing her father collapse in front of her on her bed, it was Ewa.

'And Tomek?'

Mama lifted her shoulders. 'He hasn't said much.'

'Teenagers don't. He'll be fine, as long as Tata's fine.'

Mama nodded tightly, as though she didn't dare speak for fear of bursting into tears. Marta looked away and tried to think of something else to talk about.

'I thought I said to clear out all my old stuff?' She tugged at the fabric of her old towelling dressing gown. It was actually rather nice to be wearing it again. It was comforting, as though nothing had changed since she left, although of course they both knew the opposite was true.

'You know me,' Mama smiled. 'Can't throw anything away. Anyway, you need it in this place.'

It was true. The flat was always cold, even on a balmy evening like this one.

'How is your job, *kochana*?'

Marta looked up. 'Good! I think they will ask me to stay after my contract ends.'

'Of course they will.'

'I can't assume that, Mama. It's not that easy to get good jobs in England.'

'For most people, I'm sure. But you came top of your year at SGH! That sets you apart.'

Marta nodded. Tonight was not the time to try and explain, yet again, the truth about working in England. This was not the time to make her point with tales of doctors packing boxes in warehouses and airline pilots picking strawberries, or the ignorance of English

319

employers when it came to foreign qualifications. She would not tell Mama about the latest government report on how many Eastern Europeans were filling manual labour roles across the UK. Tonight, she would tell Mama what she wanted to hear. 'Yes, I'm doing well.'

'And are there any nice men in your office?'

Marta rolled her eyes. It was a question Mama asked every time they spoke. 'I told you – only Carl, and he's a bit odd.'

'Oh. But what about the young man who gave you his flight?'

'Dominik.' Marta felt a rush of guilt just saying his name. She had, of course, explained the misunderstanding about his sister in the café, but the explanation didn't make up for the months of refusing to talk or answer his calls. 'He's Polish.'

'Oh! Oh right.' Mama sounded disappointed. She had clearly been hoping her daughter would meet a nice Englishman, like most other mothers in Łomianki. Marta wouldn't tell her about Jack.

'He's moving back to Poland.'

'Oh?' There was a brief flicker of interest.

'Well, things didn't work out for him over there and... well, I sort of messed things up between us.'

Mama raised an eyebrow as she took a sip of tea.

'A misunderstanding,' Marta explained, grimacing at the thought of her own stupidity. 'I thought he was seeing someone else, but it turned out to be his sister.'

Mama closed her eyes. 'Oh, *kochana*.'

There was a moment of silence. Marta cursed herself again for being so pig-headed; a trait she had inherited from Tata.

'But you're friends again now?'

Marta shrugged, leaning back in the chair. 'I guess.'

'And you've talked?'

Marta hesitated. They had talked, yes. They had talked about flights and trains and Tata, and briefly they had talked about the misunderstanding about Dominik's sister. But Marta knew that wasn't what Mama meant.

Mama groaned quietly. 'Marta, when will you learn?'

'What? Learn what?'

'To open up! If you'd talked to this boy – what's his name?'

'Dominik.'

'If you'd talked to Dominik before now, you might have saved yourself weeks of pain, *kochana!*'

Marta looked at her. 'What about you? Did *you* share your worries about Tata when you knew he was getting chest pains?'

Mama's face fell. Marta instantly regretted her words. 'I'm sorry, Mama. I didn't mean that.'

Mama looked down at the threadbare rug on the floor.

'No, it's OK. It's true.' Tears were welling up in her eyes. 'I did worry, you're right. And I didn't share it – not even with Tata.' The tears started to flow. 'I should have talked to him. If I'd said something, maybe he would've seen the doctor and not...' She choked on her tears.

Marta felt awful. She crept out of her chair and moved over to her mother's. 'I didn't mean that, Mama. You couldn't have prevented–'

'Maybe I could,' she muttered into the fabric of Marta's old dressing gown.

Marta hugged her more tightly. 'Shh, Mama. You couldn't have done anything. You couldn't. And he'll be fine, anyway.'

In that moment, as Marta crouched beside the old armchair, stroking her mother's hair and squeezing her heaving body against her own, she had a sudden, terrible realisation. Since moving to England, she had lost track of the things that really mattered. She had become self-obsessed, getting excited about seeing herself in a newspaper and wearing the latest season's clothes and going out with rich Englishmen. She hadn't really thought about anyone else for a very long time.

Stroking her mother's back, Marta tormented herself with flashbacks from the past six months. She had really hurt Dominik. She had forgotten her best friend's birthday. She had failed to notice how unhappy Holly had become; Holly, who had stayed up and listened to all her trivial dilemmas. She had used Carl to advance her career without giving anything back – not even friendship. And worst of all, she had gone out with Jack, against everyone's advice, just so that she could live a life of country clubs and expensive wine bars. *Why?* Why did it matter whether her clothes were from Emily Norman or a Warsaw market stall? Why had she opted for fancy restaurants when she could have gone to the polskie delikatesy with Dominik? Marta felt awful. She wanted to wipe out everything she had done during the last six months and start again.

Eventually, Mama stopped sniffing and looked up. Marta stayed crouched by her side, holding her hand.

'Promise me something,' said Mama.

'What?'

'Promise me you'll call this boy tomorrow and *talk*.'

Marta looked into her mother's eyes and nodded, trying to make Mama understand that her days of childish selfishness were over.

'I will,' she said. 'As soon as I've been to see Tata.'

52

'Anyway, I'm going to call him. I owe him an apology, at least. I feel so... stupid. I can't believe I thought he'd do something like that. And from his point of view, I just suddenly *disappeared*. For no reason. Poor Dominik. I'm an idiot, aren't I?'

Tata didn't respond, of course. He had an oxygen mask covering his mouth and plastic tubes coming out of his nose. His eyes were shut. Marta looked down, unable to watch his inert face any longer. There were needles coming out of his hands with more tubes attached, and the bedding had been pulled down over his chest to expose a flimsy cotton gown.

'Anyway, he's moving back to Poland, so that's that. I've got to move on too. I'm lucky to have such great housemates. Tata, you'd love Holly. She's the best. I don't know what I would've done if I hadn't met Holly...'

Marta prattled on. She preferred to talk than stay silent. It helped to take her mind off the sound of her father's soft wheezing and his grey, papery complexion.

Walking in this morning and seeing him like this had been a shock. Mama had warned her, but Marta hadn't believed the situation could really be that bad. How much could he change in just a few days? The nurse had updated them on Tata's condition, which hadn't changed since the day before, and had run them through the procedure for emergencies. Then she had whipped back the curtain. Marta hadn't managed to suppress her gasp.

They had arrived at seven: Mama, Marta, Ewa and Tomek. Marta had stayed while Mama took the others to Saturday school. They didn't want to go, but Mama had insisted. She was adamant that their education shouldn't suffer. Marta was secretly unconvinced. She doubted that her siblings would be able to focus on long multiplication or German grammar after starting the day in the hospital, but she said nothing. Perhaps Mama was right after all – at least when it came to Ewa, who was clearly taking her medical aspirations seriously.

Marta had found herself watching her little sister that morning as she listened intently to the nurse's update and then picked up the clipboard at the foot of Tata's bed and pored over his medical notes. When Marta expressed concern about the number of wires sticking out of his chest, Ewa had relayed an explanation she had heard from the doctor the previous day. Of course, she was anxious, too; Marta noticed her little body shaking as she leant forward to kiss him goodbye. But she emanated an aura of confidence and resolve that defied her years. She would make a great doctor.

'…but Holly and Rich are *made* for each other. Rich has known it for ages, but Holly has been burying herself in her work. Everyone buries themselves in their work over there. At least, everyone with *proper* jobs…'

Marta brought her hand up to Tata's side and softly stroked his motionless palm, avoiding the needle on the other side. His skin was cool and dry, like an old person's. It was impossible to believe that this was the hand that only months ago had pressed banknotes into her hand, gripping her shoulder as Tata bid her an authoritative farewell. This was the hand that had grasped Ewa round the waist and flung her in the air; the hand that built clever contraptions for Mama around the flat and lobbed the old, deflated football across the park for Tomek.

'Tata, you have to help me,' she said, looking again at his lifeless face. 'You have to explain to Mama about my job. My career. She thinks it's easy to get work in England. She thinks it makes a difference that I came top of my year at university. But it's not, and it doesn't. No one over there has heard of SGH. They can't even pronounce the name. I'm just a Polish girl to them – just like all the other Polish girls who come over to change nappies and clean toilets. That's all they think we can do. *I* know I can do it, Tata. I know I can do well in marketing, like I said I would. I'm quite sure once I've proved myself in this job and worked my way up and got a few big projects under my belt–'

Marta stopped. She wasn't sure, but she thought she heard something: his wheezing was louder, more pronounced. She listened in silence, watching his chest and its dressing move up and down. It happened again: another interruption. It was like a short, dry cough from inside the oxygen mask. Marta leaned forward to within reach of the red emergency cord, remembering what the nurse had told them that morning.

'Tata? Are you OK? Can you hear me?'

The wheezing softened again, returning to its gentle routine. Marta's eyes travelled from his face to his chest and back again, filled with a mix of disappointment and anxiety. Was the interruption a good thing? Was he coming round, or was it a sign of more problems? Ought she to pull the cord?

'Tata?' she croaked, suddenly unable to speak for the lump that had risen up and blocked her throat. She could feel her chin wobbling, tears welling up behind her eyes.

She squeezed her father's hand, determined to keep talking, as though somehow her monologue might convey some kind of momentum, or give Tata a reason to carry on.

'Tata, are you OK?' Marta was sobbing now, her voice uncontrollably wobbly. 'Just… wake up, will you? Open your eyes and look at me! Please. I need you. We all need you.' Marta let out a shaky sigh and wiped a sleeve across her cheek.

Through watery eyes, Marta saw a movement. It wasn't a real movement, it couldn't have been.

'Tata?' She stared at his eyes, where the movement had been. Tata remained still, like a corpse. 'Can you hear me?'

Still nothing.

Marta pulled her chair right up to the bed and leaned towards Tata's head. 'Mama needs you,' she said, softly but firmly. She's a wreck. We all are – except Ewa. She's the only one managing to hold herself together. You *have* to get better. And then you have to stop worrying. Mama told me about the redundancies. I know you think it'd be the end of the world if you lost your job, but it… wouldn't. All that matters is you don't lose your…' Marta sniffed away a fresh batch of tears. 'Just get yourself better, OK?'

This time Marta knew she wasn't mistaken. His eyelids flickered.

'Tata?' She reached out, her hand hovering by the red cord.

There was a short groan from inside the mask. Marta yanked on the cord. A low-pitched wailing noise filled the room.

'Can you hear me?' asked Marta, frantic with worry.

There was another groan above the din of the alarm that sounded like a grunt of pain. At the same time, Tata's eyes flickered open and his drowsy gaze slowly turned to Marta.

'He's awake!' cried Marta as three medics quickly piled in and started pressing buttons, checking figures and peering into Tata's eyes.

'Is he OK?'

'Can you step away–'

'Is he–'

'Please.' A fourth woman appeared and led Marta away by the arm as one of the others lifted the gown from Tata's chest and another started pressing buttons on the machines. Someone said something about his heartbeat, but Marta was being pushed through the door, so she was unable to see or hear any more.

'Tata!' Marta tried to stand firm, to catch another glimpse of his face as the team continued to work around him, but the woman was blocking her view.

53

The queue snaked its way out of the shop and into the market square, where it curled to avoid the main dog-walking route across town. Marta assumed her place and waited, inhaling a whiff of freshly baked bread.

The town was quieter than she remembered it being. The square had always been bustling on a Sunday, full of children playing and young parents running after them. That's how Marta remembered it. Now the scene was more sedate: elderly folks bent over sticks, poking at the crumbling pavement and looking up only to moan about the bored-looking youngsters. Mama was right; it was like a different town now.

Nobody seemed to be in a hurry to buy their bread. Old women chatted and grumbled about the heat, couples argued over how much they had spent and several loners just stared, unseeing, through their thick-lensed glasses. Marta found herself becoming agitated at the lack of progress and then immediately cross with herself for feeling that way. She never used to be so impatient. Maybe that was something London had done to her. Everything happened so quickly there. There were fast food outlets on every corner and if you wanted a loaf of bread, you just headed to the nearest supermarket and used a self-service checkout, which took less than a couple of minutes. What would Holly say if she could see Marta now, standing in line all morning? It would be worth it, though.

Marta hadn't seen Anka for more than six months. She had so

much to tell her – not least the good news about Tata. A sense of elation overrode the feeling of irritation as she reminded herself for the hundredth time that morning that she had everything anybody needed in life: she had her family and friends. Tata was going to be fine.

Marta could barely suppress her excitement as her best friend's pretty face, hidden beneath a shapeless blue hair net, tilted to greet her.

Anka yelped – much to the disdain of the clientele in line behind Marta. 'You're here! Oh my God! I tried to call you before, but... is he OK? Hang on. Paulina, could you cover for me? Thanks. Come through here.' She lifted a portion of the counter so Marta could crawl through.

'They think he's gonna be OK.'

'Oh, thank God!'

'When I left him today he was conscious, speaking a little – the doctor said he should make a full recovery if he's careful.'

Anka was beaming. 'I *knew* it!' she cried. 'I prayed for him last night, but I knew I didn't need to. You Dabrowskas are tough as leather, you are. Nothing gets in your way.'

Marta leaned over and hugged her friend tightly. 'I think the heart attack had a pretty good go.'

Anka continued to squeeze her. 'I'm *so* pleased, Marta. I worried all night for you – and you didn't call!'

Marta pulled away gently. 'Sorry, Anka. I've been all over the place. I didn't even know you knew.'

Anka smiled. 'Nothing stays secret in this town for long – you should know that. Mama found out from someone at church whose son is in Tomek's class.'

Marta nodded. She should have called Anka, but she had felt as though talking about Tata before she had seen him might somehow alter his prognosis.

Anka was looking at her. 'You OK?'

Marta nodded vaguely. She wasn't actually sure. They had said that Tata *should* make a full recovery, but what did that mean?

What if he had another attack? What if he *was* made redundant by Polkomtel?

'How's your mama?'

Marta shrugged. 'She seems...' Marta couldn't think of the word. Then it came to her and she voiced it reluctantly. 'Old. They both seem old.'

Anka nodded slowly. 'That's the thing about parents. They do that.'

Marta stood there, feeling her eyes fill with tears. She wasn't even sure whether they were tears of sadness or joy; she just felt suddenly, hopelessly emotional. Tata was fine. He was fine... *for now*. That was it. That was the unsettling truth. It felt as though nothing was guaranteed any more. When she was younger, it had been simple: whatever she chose to do, whatever happened to her, Mama and Tata were there, like rocks, when she needed them. They were always there. They would always be there. But the last few days had jolted her out of that supposition. They wouldn't always be there. At some point, they wouldn't be there.

'Come here.' Anka moved closer and hugged her again. The tears rolled down her cheeks and sank into the fabric of Anka's bakery apron.

Marta tried to explain. 'I thought I was being so grown-up, going to England and starting my own life. Being so independent...'

'You were. You are.' Anka looked at her. 'You're one of the bravest people I know.'

Marta shook her head. 'No, I'm not. I'm not brave. I only do things because I know I've got... I've got Mama and Tata. And now...'

Anka abruptly pulled away.

'Sorry to disagree with you, Marta, but that's bullshit. You're allowed to get upset if something happens to a person you care about. It doesn't make you needy. It just makes you a normal, kind, caring human being.'

Marta shook her head, suddenly desperate to tell Anka the truth. 'But I'm not kind. I'm not caring,' she protested. 'Ever since

I left for England I've become more and more self-centred. I never think about anyone else now – only me, me, me. My job, my man, my life…'

Anka looked puzzled. 'Seriously, you've got to stop beating yourself up or you'll have a breakdown. It's hardly surprising you don't have much time to think about anyone else. You've had a lot on. That's what you're like. You take things on. You're ambitious. That's why you go off and do exciting things while I'm left stuffing dumplings!'

Marta tried to muster a smile. Anka was exaggerating, as always, but maybe it was excusable, given how much she had taken on. Maybe that was why she had forgotten–

'Oh my God! I nearly forgot again!'

'What?'

'Your birthday present!'

'Yes, you sent me–'

'No, no, that was just a little something,' said Marta, remembering guiltily that she had never actually paid Tina anything for the package she had sent over. 'This is your proper gift.' She reached into her bag.

'But I don't want–'

'Open it,' instructed Marta. 'It's not much, but…'

'Oh my God!' Anka extracted the beads from the folds of the Emily Norman collection – Marta's entire collection – inside the package. 'Loads of stuff! Gorgeous stuff!' She trailed the necklace over her skin and tried on the belt. 'Thank you!'

Marta smiled, rising to her feet and admiring her friend's effortless style once again. 'It's not Gucci, but it should last longer than the stuff you get here.'

Anka shook her head, beaming and letting the belt fall down between them. 'I don't want Gucci, silly. I just want my friend back! My lovely, ambitious friend.'

54

Marta was too tired to do anything about the broken wheels of her suitcase, or the fact that her left shoe was rubbing the top layer of skin off her ankle. She was too tired to reply to Holly's text message asking when she would be back and she couldn't even muster the energy to stop off at the corner shop to buy a tin of soup. All she could think about was reaching her makeshift bed and falling asleep.

It wasn't physical activity that had drained her of energy; it was the nerves and worry of the last forty-eight hours – the feeling of being plunged into darkness, not knowing what direction the future might take. Marta had never understood the phrase 'sick with worry', but now she did.

He was going to be fine. That's what they had told her as she left the hospital eight hours earlier. She believed them; she had to, to keep sane. But at the same time it felt as though there was a looming black cloud hanging over her: the possibility that it might happen again. They couldn't rule it out. Tata couldn't guarantee that he would stop getting stressed at work.

Marta plodded on, the wheels of her suitcase stubbornly refusing to turn on the uneven flagstones. Everything would seem fine in the morning, she told herself. She was just tired; problems always seemed worse at night.

Marta stopped a few doors down from her flat and listened. She hesitated, squinting at the window of the lounge – her bedroom. There were silhouettes of bodies moving behind the curtains in time with the beat that was pounding and rattling through the glass. Marta breathed deeply and continued gingerly towards the front door. It seemed increasingly evident that a party was underway.

Before she had even located her keys, the door was flung open and her name was screeched loudly from the hallway. There was a chorus of whooping above the din of the music and even as Marta stooped to retrieve her suitcase, she found herself being tugged down the hallway towards the kitchen, which was brimming with laughter and light.

'My bag–'

'I've got it!'

'Who is–?'

'It's a homecoming party for you!' replied Holly, who looked… well, radiant. She was wearing a bright red dress and her thick, glossy hair had been scooped up on top of her head.

'That's not strictly true,' Tina interjected, appearing from the lounge. As ever, she was wearing small slivers of fabric strategically placed around her slender body. 'It's a double celebration. Holly, have you told her?'

Marta looked at Holly, reluctantly accepting the drink that was thrust into her hand as she waited.

A smile broke out on Holly's face. 'I've quit my job!'

Marta lunged to hug her friend. Relief and excitement flooded her veins her as she squeezed with all the strength she had left.

'Finally!' she said as they drew apart.

'Yeah, well, I think I've done my time. Come on – let's go through.'

They migrated to the lounge, where more faces Marta didn't recognise turned to greet them.

'That lot are traders, in case you hadn't guessed,' Holly explained, pointing to a group of well-groomed young men, who were setting light to a line of shots on the coffee table. Tina slipped in and retrieved her spot among them.

'And these are our uni mates…' She moved towards a group who were trying to breakdance in front of the speaker.

'Tim, Sara, Kieran...'

Marta smiled at the faces as the strangers flowed past. She was beginning to tire of the nodding and smiling when recognition suddenly shook her out of her exhausted daze. She nearly gasped.

'Carl!' she cried, trying not to stare too blatantly at the fact that he was holding hands with another young man. 'Hi!'

Holly looked at her, waiting for an introduction.

'Sorry...' Marta was still in shock. 'This is Carl, from work. And...'

'Davey,' said the other guy, offering his hand and a beautiful smile. He was dark-skinned, like Carl, and perfectly proportioned with piercing green eyes and a strong jawline. Marta smiled back at Carl and felt a huge weight lift from her mind.

The introductions continued. Marta could feel her energy reserves dwindling. She wished, in a way, that they hadn't gone to the trouble of throwing a party. It was a nice gesture and of course she would sacrifice her much-needed sleep for the occasion, but really she would rather have spent the night chatting with Holly, Tina and Rich over a round of hot chocolates.

It was only as she slipped away on the pretext of needing the toilet that she noticed a girl standing alone in the hallway in a chic fitted dress. She clearly wasn't in the mood for a party. Marta stopped dead in the doorway, watching as, slowly and serenely, Tash turned and stared at her.

'Marta,' she said quietly. 'Hi.'

Marta just stared back at her. She wasn't going to return Tash's greeting.

'I'm...' Tash took a deep breath and held it for a moment, as though mustering something within. 'I'm sorry.'

Marta waited. It would take more than a couple of words to restore their friendship – if indeed there was any friendship to restore.

'I guess it's been pretty tough for you, these last few months.' Tash wrung her hands, looking away as soon as Marta met her eye. 'I imagine it didn't help, being kicked out and blamed for... well, *Jack*.'

Marta studied Tash's expression, which was hard to read. Tash's facial muscles rarely moved when she talked – Marta had always assumed this was because movement might dislodge her makeup – but this evening there was an air of awkwardness about her that Marta had never seen before. She was gnawing so hard on her lip that Marta wondered whether it might bleed.

'God, I'm hopeless at this. Help me out, will you? Say something.'

Marta frowned. 'What do you want me to say?'

'I don't know!' Tash gave a desperate shrug, her puppy dog eyes roaming the room. 'Tell me you're fine and you forgive me and we can be friends again! Or something.'

'Why are you saying these things now?'

'Because I only just realised!' yelped Tash, looking truly unsettled. 'I only just found out about Jack! I thought it was *you* leading *him* on, not the other way round. But then I found out about Plum and Kat and… and the others…'

'Plum and Kat?' Marta stared. She needed to be sure she understood correctly.

'Yes! For months, apparently. God knows how many others there were… are…' Tash's face hardened. 'I hope they all get *syphilis*.'

'So… he was doing… doing the business with all the girls, at the same time?' asked Marta.

'Yes!' hissed Tash hatefully. 'Stupid bastard. He just couldn't help himself!'

Marta let out a deep breath, letting the implications of what Tash had just said sink in. All the time Marta had been "with" Jack, he had also been with Tash and Kat and Plum *and others*… She thought back to the time at Hurlingham when Charles had accidentally called her Kat, and then to the time Jack had warned her of his supposedly undeserved reputation as a ladies' man. Then another flashback surfaced: the image of Tash with her Jack lookalike in the casino at the Cambridge ball. It *was* Jack. He had a whole harem of women; it was a wonder he had strung them all along for as long as he had.

'Did they know about you?' asked Marta.

Tash rolled her eyes. 'Well, Plum did, obviously. *Bitch*. And to think she was the one who told me about *you*. I guess Kat would've known, too. Not that it would've bothered her. *You* didn't know, did you?'

Marta shook her head. 'I thought he was with me! I only find out about you when you call me, eating my head off.'

Tash's angst melted a little. 'Biting, not eating,' she said, smiling. 'Yeah, sorry about that.'

Marta watched Tash as she continued to gnaw at her fingernail. Her eyes looked a little red beneath the makeup. Marta moved a bit closer. In all honesty, she had got over Jack pretty quickly. Despite having convinced herself that they were a great couple and that Jack was exactly the sort of English gentleman she was after, she had realised pretty quickly that he was in fact a heartless, selfish – not to mention violent – young man with whom she had almost nothing in common. She felt nothing for Jack. He was a mere blip in her past, a foolish mistake. For Tash, though, he was more than that. He had been her boyfriend for years, or so she had thought. Hers was a fragile disposition to begin with, and this realisation would have hit her hard. Marta surprised herself by reaching out and giving Tash a little squeeze round the shoulders.

Tash sniffed, wiping a tear from her eye and taking care not to smudge her mascara.

'How did you find out?' asked Marta as they pulled apart.

Tash sighed, extracting a small mirror from her bag and checking the state of her face. She seemed sad now, no longer angry or upset. 'Holly, actually. She told me what happened with Kat in your office and I pieced it together. He fell apart as soon as I confronted him – that's when I found out about Plum. Stupid fool let it slip.'

Marta leaned against the bannister, still marvelling at Jack's nerve and feeling outraged on Tash's behalf. Poor Tash. She was not a strong person. Of all the girls Jack could have chosen to be the "real" girlfriend, it seemed particularly cruel to have picked Tash: cruel, but smart. Tash would always come back to him. Like a yoyo, she would go back to Jack no matter what he put her through – except this, thought Marta. This time he had gone too far.

'He's going out with Kat now, apparently,' said Tash, smiling a little in her 'up tights' way. 'They're well-suited, I'd say.'

Marta smiled, pushing herself off the bannisters and grabbing Tash's hand. 'Come on. Let's get a drink.'

Tash had just filled their glasses when she let out a dramatic gasp. 'Oh God – I nearly forgot!' She handed over Marta's drink and then bounded off down the hallway. She reappeared seconds later, brandishing a bulging plastic bag that had been taped up at the top. 'I had to take it into work before I came here,' she said, by way of explanation for the apparently impenetrable tape. 'The fashion offence would've got me sacked.'

Marta knew what it was, even before she had ripped open the plastic.

'Thank you!' she cried, as soon as the turquoise fabric was within her grasp. Her beautiful Malina Q jacket burst out of the packaging. 'I thought you might have burned it!'

'I should've,' replied Tash, looking disdainfully at the garment as Marta rubbed it fondly against her cheek.

'Agh!' cried Rich, noisily dropping a tray of hot sausages onto the worktop, nursing his burnt fingers.

'Don't be such a *girl*,' said Holly, appearing beside him and slipping a hand around his waist as he sucked on his fingers. It was such uncharacteristic behaviour on Holly's part that Marta couldn't help staring. She exchanged a sideways glance with Tash.

'Holly,' said Marta, when the shock had worn off. There was a question she needed to ask. 'What will you do now you left Anderton's?'

Holly smiled, her eyes flicking up at Rich's. 'Well... I've got some ideas.' She looked hard at Marta. 'Some ideas I need to run past *you*.'

Marta frowned.

'I'll explain when we're sober. Oh!' Holly leapt across the kitchen. 'These came for you.' She lifted the huge bouquet of flowers that was leaning against the window, their stems wedged in an old shampoo bottle. 'Yeah – sorry about the vase.' She grimaced.

Marta tore at the envelope and pulled out the card, which was a typically English affair with a tasteless watercolour of a dog on the front.

Dear Marta,

We were so sorry to hear about your father. You are in our thoughts every day. Everyone at Stratisvision sends their fondest regards and we look forward to seeing you when you are back.

Let us know when you think you'll be ready to return to work. I'd like to discuss the possibility of taking you on as a full-time employee.

Best,
Patricia and the team x

'Is from my company!' cried Marta. 'They want me to work for them!'

'Course they do. Why wouldn't they?' Holly rolled her eyes.

Marta stared at the card, letting all the images of the last few months crash through her mind: the job interviews, the patronising comments, the blank looks at the name of her university, the knock-backs, the gentle suggestions that she find other work... *Finally*, here was a reputable company in her chosen field that valued her. The management of Stratisvision could see her potential. She had her foot on the ladder, at last. The words on the card started to blur and she realised she was crying.

'What's up?' asked Rich.

Marta laughed through the tears. 'I don't know! I am happy, but crying!'

'Here,' Tash handed her a tissue. 'I think you're tired.'

Marta nodded. 'Maybe I go and lie down on your bed, Holly?'

Holly looked at her watch. 'Um, yeah. Sure.'

Marta stumbled out of the kitchen, hunting through blurry eyes for her broken suitcase and thinking about the events of the last forty-eight hours.

As Marta deliberated between opening the case in the hallway and lugging it up the stairs in its entirety, the doorbell rang. She peered through the frosted door panel, hoping it wasn't a neighbour coming to complain.

The man on the doorstep smiled at her from inside a scooter helmet. Marta watched as he pulled it off, feeling the tears inexplicably start to well up again.

'Dominik?'

He stood there, grinning. 'Well? Can I come in?'

Marta opened the door in a daze. She hadn't even realised Dominik was still in the country. After the brief, awkward phone call she had made from the hospital the day before, she had assumed their paths were not destined to cross again. She had assumed, after everything she had put him through, that Dominik would be on the next available flight to Krakow.

'You're still here,' was all she could think of to say as she wiped the tears from her cheeks.

'Well, you took my ticket home, didn't you?' His eyes twinkled.

'But...' Marta lingered in the hallway, not sure she wanted to lead Dominik into the party.

'You look knackered,' he said.

'Thanks.'

'No, I just—'

'Don't worry. I know I do. I was just about to go and lie down. But...' Marta couldn't concentrate. She needed to find out: *was he still here because of her? Was he staying? Had he abandoned his plans to go back?*

'I see your bed's been taken.' He nodded towards the lounge, where the breakdancing competition was starting to get quite competitive. 'I've got one you can use.'

Marta looked at him, remembering their night together and wondering whether he meant...

'For sleeping in, I mean,' he added. His hair was a mess, as usual. His hazel eyes glinted in the hallway light.

Marta grinned. 'I'll get my jacket.'

55

Marta turned her head on the pillow and smiled. Dominik was watching her.

'Morning,' she stammered, trying to remember the details of the night before. Her memory was hazy through tiredness. Had they...?

'Just about,' he said, glancing up at the clock in the tiny room. Sunlight was pouring through the flimsy curtains.

Marta squinted and realised, with horror, that it was nearly midday.

'Tata! I need to find out how he is!' she gasped, feeling around under the bedclothes to discover that she was still wearing her underwear, which gave her a clue. To the side of the bed was a crumpled pile of clothes and, beside it, her wallet and phone. Dominik had been a gentleman last night.

There were two new text messages.

Thought you were supposed to be tired?! Have fun. U missed a great party. Tina xxx

Tata much better today – laughing & joking & annoying the nurses. They're moving him to the main ward! Miss you. Ewa xxx

Marta let out a sigh of relief and sank back onto the bed. 'He's fine.'

Dominik smiled, his eyes flicking down to her waist before meeting her eye again.

Marta couldn't help smiling. She felt so happy all of a sudden. She was with Dominik. Tata was going to be fine. She had a job. Holly and Rich were going out. She and Tash had made up and Jack was finally out of her life for good. Everything was finally working out.

'Why did you decide to stay?' she asked, reaching out under the flimsy sheet and pulling him close.

Dominik's body tensed up. 'Let's not talk about that now.' He gently tugged at the strap of her bra.

Marta could feel herself relenting to his physical presence, melting at his touch, but there was a niggling doubt at the back of her mind.

'You are staying, aren't you?' she asked.

Dominik said nothing.

'You're not going back to Krakow, are you?' Marta could hear the panic in her voice.

Dominik rolled onto his back and stared up at the slanting ceiling.

Marta felt something plummet inside her.

'You are!' cried Marta, unable to control her voice.

Dominik shook his head, avoiding her eye. 'I don't want to, especially not now. But I made up my mind.'

'But that was–' *before I came back,* Marta wanted to say. Perhaps that wasn't reason enough. Perhaps she had an overinflated sense of her own importance.

'I know.' He rolled back to face her and brushed a strand of hair off her face. Marta felt like crying. He couldn't walk away. He *couldn't.*

'It's different now, isn't it?' she asked softly.

Dominik hesitated. 'The thing is… it's hard over here. For me. It's not how I imagined it. I know I laugh and joke about Barry's place, but… seriously, it was getting me down. That was the best I could do – handing out flyers in the street!'

340

'But you got a proper job—'

'Yeah, for about four weeks. I told you they went into liquidation, didn't I?'

Marta wasn't listening. 'There'll be other firms.'

'Other firms looking for a cheap scapegoat to blame for a management fuck-up? Yeah, great.'

Marta closed her eyes for a second. The outlook for a smart, qualified accountant couldn't be this bleak. 'Don't you think... I mean... don't you think we might have a chance? I feel as though we're finally starting to make it over here, to fit in, to—'

'No,' Dominik shook his head. 'No, *you're* starting to make it over here. You're fitting in. *I'm* not.'

Marta couldn't reply. She couldn't even look at him.

'It wasn't an easy decision to make,' he said softly, to the side of her face. 'But it's the right thing for me to do. I've got to go back.'

Marta fell silent. She pulled the sheet over her, feeling cold all of a sudden.

'I thought you were ambitious,' she challenged quietly, after a long pause.

'I was,' he replied. 'But I'm not Michael Marks. I'm an ordinary Pole, just like the other million. Nothing special. Nobody wants me here.'

'I do,' whispered Marta, so quietly that she wondered whether he had heard.

'I know.'

Marta stopped arguing. She reached out and touched his arm, feeling the curve of his bicep. He was leaving. These would be her last moments with him. She would have to get on with her life in England without Dominik.

It was possible. She could do it. She was strong, independent and resilient. She had a bunch of friends over here, a place to live and a good job. People liked her. Holly had hinted that she might even need to involve her in whatever it was she planned to do after leaving Anderton's. She had plenty to live for in England.

'You'll be fine here,' said Dominik, reaffirming her thoughts.

'You'll do well.'

Marta nodded silently.

'And Krakow's not far away, is it?'

Marta said nothing.

Dominik rolled on top of her and kissed her on the lips. 'You will visit, won't you?'

Marta ran her hand through his messy hair, reluctantly breaking into a smile. 'I'll think about it.'

56

'Remember, I don't pay you to be enterprising!' growled Holly, as Marta came back to replenish her supply of leaflets. 'In fact,' she went on, maintaining her angry look, 'I don't pay you at all!'

They both burst out laughing. Marta headed for the stack in the corner of the office, which was a cramped, boxlike room that was not dissimilar to Barry Roffey's; only it was cleaner and tidier.

'What d'you think?' asked Holly, tilting the computer screen as Marta passed.

The website looked great: simple, functional and professional – in perfect Polish as well as English. Marta rested her load on the desk and reached for the mouse.

'What shall I buy? Mmm, some *chleb*, I think, and *ziemniaki*… and *kapusta*. Does the checkout work? Can I order these now?'

'Yep,' Holly replied proudly. 'What's *kapusta*?'

'Cabbage.'

'Of course. Yeah, the only thing that doesn't work is the one-hour delivery slot. That'll improve though, as we get more users.'

Marta played around on the site, filling her basket with all sorts of produce she missed from back home: *ciasto, ciastko, barszcz czerwony*… it was easier than shopping back in Łomianki.

'I better go,' said Marta, straightening up and retrieving her load.

'Hey, Marta,' said Holly, as she opened the door.

'What?'

'I've been thinking.'

'I know. You always think, Holly. Think, think, think! Never stop thinking – even when you asleep!'

Holly smiled. 'Yeah, well this time I've had a particular thought that affects you.'

'Oh?'

'Well, I owe you for your help on polskisklep.'

Marta screwed up her nose. 'I owe you for giving me a place to stay and an agency that give me a job!'

'No, that was nothing. Really. I mean, you're here in your lunch hour, giving out leaflets... I want to repay the favour. I want you to have my bedroom in the flat.'

Marta stared, taking in the meaning of Holly's words. 'You moving out?'

Holly smiled, shaking her head. 'No, I'm not moving out.'

'Then...'

Holly looked sheepish. Slowly, Marta understood: Holly was moving into Richard's bedroom.

'But...' Holly looked at her. 'You wouldn't need to pay any more–'

'This is good news, Holly! Am so excited!'

'Yeah, I thought you would be. The furniture can stay, if you need–'

'Not about *that*!' cried Marta. 'Am excited about that but also am excited for *you*!'

Holly was blushing. 'Well, yeah. Anyway. So... thanks again. I'll see you later.'

'See you later!' Marta yelled as she leapt, two by two, down the rotten wooden staircase. She was still grinning as she started handing out her last wad of leaflets.

It was amazing how quickly polskisklep.com had come together. Three weeks of hard work and long hours on Holly's part and it was a working operation. Holly was used to that, Marta supposed. She had continued to lead an Anderton's lifestyle since leaving the firm – barely sleeping, working weekends and eating her lunch one-handed at her desk – but now she was doing it for a cause, not for some faceless corporate machine.

Polskisklep had been Holly's secret brainchild for months, it turned out. She had been working on an ecommerce project at work when it had occurred to her that all over London, Polish delicatessens and supermarkets were making good money from immigrants like Marta who wanted familiar food from back home. But nobody was doing it online.

Somehow, and Marta still hadn't worked out how, Holly had built a prototype website while she was still at Anderton's and tested the concept with a number of Hammersmith Poles before quitting her job and revealing her plans. With Marta's help, she had teamed up with some Polish suppliers who sent over weekly shipments; small for now, but enough to fill the refrigerated warehouse in Acton and keep the local delivery firm busy. It was a modest operation, but it would grow as more people discovered the website, which was why Marta was spending her lunch hours pounding the streets, armed with flyers.

Holly hadn't done it all by herself, of course. Ironically enough, after a week of scouring CVs for a potential business partner and finding no one who fitted the bill in both commercial and technical know-how, Holly had found the solution in her own flat, holding hands with Marta.

The solution – a qualified accountant and native Pole with a love of computers – was, at this point in time, leaping around outside Hammersmith tube station as Marta slammed the door shut behind her.

'*Cześć*,' she said, laughing as Dominik instinctively offered her a leaflet.

'Oh, it's you.' He retracted the leaflet and reached out to draw her closer.

'How's it going?' she asked, pulling away from an overzealous kiss. 'No straying out of your zone?'

'No.'

'No dumping?'

He grinned. 'No.'
'No funny business?'
'Not yet. Maybe later.'

Wish there was more?

There is!

You can find out more about Polly Courtney and her books on:

www.pollycourtney.com
www.twitter.com/PollyCourtney
www.facebook.com/PollyCourtneyBooks

If you enjoyed this book, please do leave an honest review on Amazon or anywhere else, as it helps to spread the word. Thanks!

Lightning Source UK Ltd.
Milton Keynes UK
UKOW02f1128100315

247607UK00004B/195/P